Red Clover

Florence Osmund

ISBN-13: 978-0-99151-850-0
ISBN-10: 0-99151-850-0
LCCN: 2014903283

DISCLAIMER

This is a work of fiction. Names, characters, places, and incidents are either the product of the author's imagination or are used fictitiously. Any resemblance to actual persons, living or dead, business establishments, events, or locales is entirely coincidental.

ACKNOWLEDGEMENTS

I wish to thank the following people for their assistance in creating this book.

Most of all, thank you to all my friends and family for your support and encouragement while I satisfy my impulse to write. Your continued faith in me is gratifying.

To my editor, Carrie Cantor, thank you for your insightful feedback. You have a gift for being critical and encouraging at the same time, and for that, I am greatly appreciative.

I wish to acknowledge graphic designer, Deborah Bradseth of Tugboat Design, for a compelling cover design, clever illustration at the end of the book, and meticulous print and e-book formatting.

A special thank you, Marge Bousson, for giving the manuscript that final once over. I admire your attention to detail and creative insight.

And thank you, John Konefes, for helping me with horticulture terminology and the "male perspective" required to write this book.

Red Clover

1 | Special Doesn't Cut It

Eight-year-old Lee Winekoop entered the front parlor to find his mother sitting in her favorite Louis XV chair reading an issue of *Town & Country*. An identical chair occupied the space immediately next to it for his father. Without knowing why, Lee had never liked those chairs, nor the room they were in. The parlor—with its twelve-foot ornate ceiling and stilted furniture—made him feel tiny, unimportant, and uncomfortable. But then he didn't feel very comfortable anywhere in the eighteen-room lakefront mansion in the wealthiest section of Evanston, Illinois.

Her black hair was pulled back into a perfectly coiffed bun at the nape of her neck, and the cultured pearl necklace Lee's father had given her years ago lay flat upon her flawless ivory skin. She did not bother to look up from her magazine.

"Where's Kate?"

He ignored her question as to his nanny's whereabouts and did not allow the queasy feeling in his stomach to stop him from asking the question that had been on his mind for a long time.

"Why are Nelson and Bennett so much older than me?"

His mother sighed and momentarily lifted her gaze from the magazine. "Older than *I*, dear."

Why does she care about grammar when I'm trying to figure out something this important?

"Older than I, then. Why is that?"

"I don't know what you mean, Lee."

His stomach began to churn. "Nelson was born in 1950 and Bennett just two years after that. Then it was another eight years until I was born. They're so close to each other, and then there's me. Why is that?"

She looked past him, as if searching for the answer. After a long pause, she said, "It just happened that way. Not all children are spaced evenly apart." She made a face he knew all too well when she didn't want to deal with something. "Where *is* that woman?"

"They have dark hair, and mine is light."

"That happens in families."

"And I have green eyes."

"Your father—"

"No, Mother. Father has hazel eyes." Lee's heart was pounding. A child interrupting an adult while talking was forbidden in his family. "Did you want me when I was born?"

His mother's pursed lips and stone-faced stare told him he might have gone too far with that one. He hoped she would answer the question but was afraid at the same time.

Her face softened. "Of course I wanted you."

"Do you know what my initials spell?"

"I don't know what you're talking about."

"Think about it, Mother. My name is Lee Oliver Winekoop. My initials spell L-O-W. Did you know that when you named me?"

She shifted her petite body in the chair and frowned. "What on earth has gotten into you? Maybe I need to make a special appointment with Dr. Jerry. Are you feeling all right?"

She was referring to Dr. Jerry Osgood, the psychologist Lee had been seeing for two years, to make him more like his brothers he thought. What his mother didn't know was how much he was already trying to be like them.

He almost laughed aloud at her question. When did he ever feel all right?

"Nelson's initials spell N-E-W."

"So?"

"And Bennett's are B-M-W. Mine spell out L-O-W. Why did you do that to me, Mother?"

"Lee, you're being overly sensitive. I'm sure...that is...I never gave any thought to what your initials would spell out when I named you. I wish you would stop being so querulous."

"Who was Nelson named after?" Lee knew the answer, but he wanted to hear her say it.

She shifted her gaze to something across the room and hesitated a moment before responding. "Uncle Nelson. Why do you ask?"

"Who was Bennett named after?"

She closed her eyes for a brief moment. "What difference does it make?"

"It was Grandfather, wasn't it?"

"Yes," she said. She appeared as if she was about to sneeze. Lee waited for that to happen, and when it didn't, he asked the question that interested him the most.

"So who was I named after?"

She stared into Lee's eyes for several seconds before answering. "No one in particular, dear, I just fancied the name." The wistful look on her face wasn't one Lee had ever seen before.

"So you took the time to name them after someone special in the family, but when it came time to name me, you just picked some old name? And Lee is a girl's name anyway."

"Now you're being impertinent, young man. Did it occur to you that perhaps someone... Sometimes a family name can be... Where is Kate?" she asked, her face twitching with frustration.

Lee ignored her sensitivity to his questions and continued with his mission to get to the bottom of what had been bothering him for months. He shifted his weight.

"Do you know what happened on the day Nelson was born?" he asked.

"Yes, it was unbearably hot. I was nearly overcome by heat on the way to the hospital, and then I had to endure two hours of exasperating labor."

She doesn't get it.

"Do you know what else happened?"

She dabbed her brow with the monogrammed lace handkerchief she carried in her sleeve. "No, but I'm sure you're about to tell me."

"There was a doctor right here in Chicago who did the first kidney transplant."

She took in a deep breath. "What does that have to do with anything?"

"And on the day Bennett was born, Mickey Mantle hit his first grand-slammer."

She crossed her arms across her chest. "That's nice, dear. What's a grand-slammer?"

"Guess what happened on the day I was born."

The little color she had in her face disappeared. "Please don't aggravate this occasion by making me guess, Lee. What difference do all these trivialities make?"

"On my birthday, *The Flintstones* was on television for the first time." He studied his mother's face for a reaction. "Don't you understand? That's the most important thing that happened on my birthday. That's all they could come up with for that day."

"That's all *who* could come up with?"

"Whoever puts together the list of important things that happen on each day. I checked it out at the library. It's all there in black and white."

"Lee, mothers have no control over what day their children are born. And I certainly did not have any knowledge of or influence over Mickey Mantle or *The Flankstones* or any other cultural phenomenon. What is your point?" Then she began to "shout," which for her meant speaking at a volume just above a whisper. "Kate! Where are you?"

A sudden whiff of her perfume made him feel faint. He backed away from her.

"It's *The Flintstones*, Mother. It's a silly cartoon show. It just seems kind of funny, that's all."

"Are you saying that if you were born one day sooner or one day later, it may have been advantageous for you in some way?"

"All I know is that if I had been born sooner, I wouldn't be so far behind."

"Behind what?"

"Nelson and Bennett."

"It's not a race, dear. And you shouldn't be comparing yourself to them—they are from...they're much...older and they'll..."

"And they'll what? Amount to something someday, but I won't?"

"Why would you say such a thing?"

"Father said it first, Mother."

"Lee, dear, you're special to us. You're not like Nelson or Bennett, and we don't expect you to be. And it's your own aspirations that will determine what you do in life."

He broke off eye contact with her and turned to walk away but then stopped and turned to face her again. "And then there's Uncle Nelson's birthday gifts. How do you explain *that*?" he asked before turning away from her.

"I'll call Dr. Jerry in the morning," she said to his back.

"If it makes you feel better, Mother," he mumbled.

Lee knew that Uncle Nelson had given Bennett ten thousand dollars' worth of blue-chip stocks on the day he was born, and to Nelson, his namesake, one hundred acres of land in Colorado. Lee had been given his uncle's coin collection. While Lee had never actually seen the coins—they had been placed in a bank safe-deposit box—and he didn't know how the three gifts compared in value, something told him he had gotten the short end of the stick.

Hands deeply implanted in his pockets, Lee shuffled back to his bedroom, shutting the door behind him and leaving all his unanswered questions to linger on the other side. Regardless of what "aspirations" were, special didn't cut it.

His bedroom was large, professionally decorated, and furnished with everything a boy could want. But even ten times as many things wouldn't have made Lee feel any better about himself. Despite his diligent preparation, this latest encounter with his mother had failed miserably, and he now realized he wasn't likely to ever get straight answers from her.

He wished his brothers were a better source for finding things out, but while they had all grown up in the same family—same house, same everything—they were clearly different, and not just in age. He wished he knew what they had done differently, how he had missed the boat.

Mulling over where to get the answers to his burning questions, Lee realized he had never been in either of his brother's bedrooms, and he was curious about what might be in there, what clues could be hiding inside. He opened his bedroom door a crack and poked his head through to see if the coast was clear. Nelson's bedroom was at the opposite end of the hall from his, toward the back of the house. Family members with bedrooms at the back of the house, overlooking Lake

Michigan, had the most status Lee noticed. Lee's room was at the very front of the house, same status as the guest room, one more thing that bugged him.

He turned the doorknob and entered Nelson's room. He had peeked in a few times before when his brother's door was open, but because he'd had no business being in that section of the hallway, he hadn't stopped to take much of it in.

Entering the room, he shut the door behind him. Nelson's room was much bigger than his own. The furniture was bigger, and there was more of it. There was a bathroom and walk-in closet too. Lee inhaled deeply. Even the smell of the room was different, but he couldn't put his finger on why.

Sitting down in Nelson's rolling desk chair, he felt lost. He opened the middle drawer and shuffled through the pens, paper clips, loose change. There was a ticket stub for *West Side Story* at Lincoln Center, which Nelson had recently attended with his brother and mother in New York, and a sappy Valentine's Day card from his girlfriend.

A Swiss Army knife caught his attention. He picked it up and pulled out one of the blades.

I wonder how old he was when he got this.

It looked old, and thinking Nelson wouldn't miss it, he slipped the knife into his pocket.

Lee sifted through the rest of the desk drawers and not finding anything of interest, proceeded to Nelson's dresser, where he found the same things he had in his own drawers—pretty much whatever the maid had put in there. He was beginning to think this was a waste of time, since Nelson had probably taken all the good stuff with him to college. While Lee didn't know exactly what he was looking for, he figured any token of his brother's past activities would give him a better understanding of him—a better understanding of how *he* should be.

He wandered into the closet, which was half the size of Lee's entire bedroom, where he found another dresser way in the back. He went through each of the drawers—old textbooks, a chess game, a transistor radio.

Then he hit the jackpot.

Magazines. A trove of them. With pictures of nearly naked ladies on the covers. He took one out of the drawer, and with barely enough light coming in from the small window behind the dresser, flipped through the pages to the centerfold. He stared at it for a long moment, not breathing in a single molecule of air. He had no idea ladies looked like that underneath their clothes. Sitting down on the floor, he flipped through the other pages. When he saw the two naked women together, really close together, he quickly closed the magazine and put it on the floor, face down.

Wanting to take full advantage of the scant light coming through the window, Lee had to move two gym bags, several tennis rackets, and a suitcase in order to crawl into the tight space behind the dresser. He pulled everything back in place, sat under the window, and opened the magazine to page one.

* * *

Lee woke up to the sound of sirens. After he got his bearings, he stood up and looked out the window into the darkness of the side yard. Standing on his tiptoes and craning his neck, he could see through the window to the street. Police cars with their lights blazing were everywhere!

Anxious to see what all the commotion was about, he quickly dug his way out of his hiding place and raced for the door. But when he heard an unfamiliar man's voice coming from the hallway, he stopped short of opening it.

"I know you said you looked up here, Mrs. Winekoop," the man yelled, "but a second sweep won't hurt. Kids have an uncanny way of fitting into the darndest places."

Lee's chest tightened, and suddenly his skin felt like it was on fire. When his stomach started lurching, he knew an anxiety attack was about to erupt. Frozen in place, he stood in the middle of Nelson's room, shaking, until someone opened the door.

Lee didn't know who was more surprised—he or the policeman. He was big and tall, the biggest man Lee had ever seen, and he didn't look very friendly.

"What the..." He turned around and shouted, "I found him. He's in here."

Within seconds, his mother appeared in the doorway. "Oh, my. Where on earth have you been?"

"I don't feel so good," Lee said in a weak voice.

His mother walked over to him and took his hand. "Let's get you lying down." She looked at the policeman. "Will you please excuse me? I'll just be a minute."

Lee's mother led him to his bedroom, turned down the comforter on his bed, and told him to crawl in—shoes, clothes, and all. "Just lie here quietly while I take care of...things."

He lay there, afraid to move, for what seemed like a long time, until both his mother and father came into his room.

His father's voice was low but his tone harsh. "Where on earth were you—"

"Please, Henry, let me handle this."

"Just keep in mind, Abigale, that a few minutes ago, we had five police cars in front of our house and the makings of a search party getting ready to—"

"I know. I was there." She sat on the edge of the bed and looked down at Lee. "Sweetheart, we couldn't find you anywhere. Where were you all this time?"

"What time is it?"

"It's almost eight o'clock. Where have you been? Were you in Nelson's room the whole time?"

Lee nodded.

Lee's father disappeared.

"We looked in there. Even under the bed, in the closet. Didn't you hear us?"

Lee shook his head. "I don't feel very good. I think I'm having an anxiety attack."

"Maybe you should rest then. I'll get—"

"This is what the little ingrate was up to," his father shrieked. He waved the magazine in the air. "Looking at smut! Eight goddamn years old, and he's looking at naked women! What the hell got into you, you sorry excuse for a—"

"Henry! Stop it. I said I'll handle this. It's—"

"It's my house! And the way this should be handled is with a good whooping. Sneaky little bas..."

Before his father could finish his sentence, his mother stood up, right in his face. "I said I will handle this, and I will. And it won't be by corporal punishment. Now, leave us alone, so I can talk privately with my son."

His father threw the magazine down and darted out the door.

"Where did you get the magazine, Lee?"

He didn't want to tattle on Nelson. "I just found it."

"You have to tell me the truth. You didn't just find it. Where did you get it?"

He didn't respond.

"From another boy?"

Lee remained silent.

"You're making this harder than it has to be." She paused. "If you don't tell me, I'm sure your father will get to the bottom of it. Now tell me where you got it."

"In Nelson's room."

"Don't lie to me. He would never have such a thing in his room."

"Okay. Don't believe me. I don't care. It wasn't what I was looking for in the first place. I just ran across it in a drawer. It was just there, so I looked at it. I think I must have fallen asleep 'cause when I woke up, I saw all the police cars out front."

"But we searched that room."

"There's a space in the closet, behind the brown dresser, by the window. I was back there."

"Good heavens. Do you have any idea how we worried when we couldn't find you?"

"No."

"We didn't know if you had run off, were kidnapped, or what."

"I'm sorry."

His mother heaved a sigh and turned toward the door. "Someone will be in to check on you a little later. Try to get some rest."

"Mother?"

"What is it?"

"Whose turn was it to watch me today?"

"Apparently there was a scheduling misunderstanding with Kate."

"Is she here now?"

"Kate is no longer with us. Your father took care of that."

Lee waited for the maid to check in on him before climbing out of bed and tiptoeing down the stairs to the second-floor landing. He positioned himself behind the tall potted plant where he knew he could hear what was going on in the front foyer without being seen. His parents' voices were low but audible.

"...and I'll say it again," his father was saying. "There's something wrong with that boy, and the sooner you take care of it, the better off we'll all be."

"And *I've* said it before, and *I'll* say it again," his mother responded. "It's not that easy. He hasn't been seeing Dr. Jerry for that long, and I think he's making headway. I just wish you'd be more—"

"The boy doesn't need some fancy shrink to see what's wrong with him. Send him off to Hampshire like I suggested a year ago. They specialize in kids like him. It's not that far from the New York apartment. You could stay there and be near him."

"First of all, it's more than two hundred miles from our apartment, and secondly, I am not sending him off to some boarding school. That's not the answer."

"Well, he doesn't fit in here, and if you'd like me to go into the reasons why, just let me know. And this last incident is just—"

"This may come as a shock to you, but that *Playboy* magazine came out of Nelson's room."

"I suppose he told you that. And, of course, you believed him."

"I believe him."

"Don't be so naive. He's lying, and that makes the whole situation worse. Now we can't trust him. Look, you're ultimately responsible for half of Evanston's police force on our doorstep looking for that kid. It's a good thing they don't charge for their services. Would you like me to calculate just how much that would cost?"

"You're all about money."

"You bet I am. And you can also bet our two sons will take after me."

Lee heard footsteps and got ready to flee.

"Do what you want. I don't care," his father said.

A door slammed.

Lee huddled behind the planter, ready to run to his room if he heard his mother coming up the stairs. Instead, he heard her crying.

He couldn't bear to hear her sobs and wanted to run to her and tell her everything would be all right. He forced back his own tears. He needed to be strong.

On the way back to his bedroom, Lee went to Nelson's room and slipped the Swiss Army knife into his brother's desk drawer. Back in his own bed, he replayed his parents' conversation in his head.

So many of the things his father had said disturbed him, but none had hurt as deeply as, "Do what you want. I don't care."

2 | Best in Class

Eventually, the drama resulting from the *Playboy* magazine incident waned, and things in the Winekoop residence returned to normal. Lee steered clear of his father, which wasn't hard to do, and refrained from asking his mother any more discomposed questions about his existence. Instead, he kept them safely bottled up inside and hoped when he got older he would understand why he was so different from his brothers, why his father seemed to hate him so...and what those naked girls in the magazine were doing.

In spite of what his mother kept telling him, by the time he turned ten, Lee had eavesdropped on his parents enough times to know his father really did expect him to be like his brothers, and if he could be more like them, maybe his father would like him better. But he hardly knew his brothers. Bennett was a junior in high school, and Nelson was in his first year at Harvard. Bennett was okay...sometimes. But Lee still didn't feel that comfortable talking to him. Nelson was so much older, he seemed more like an uncle than a brother, a distant uncle at that.

Due to their age differences, they had no common interests and usually came together only at the dinner table. Lee remembered that when he was younger, Bennett had played with him a few times but never for very long, usually getting pulled away to do something else. After Bennett left, Lee would go on playing as though he was still there, pretending Bennett liked him and wanted to be his older brother. Even at ten, Lee knew that wasn't right.

Visits with Dr. Jerry often focused on Lee's "self-esteem," but Lee didn't understand how he could possibly feel good about himself when he was such a disappointment to his parents. In Lee's mind, there was his family...and then there was him. He felt like he didn't have anyone, except for his mother, who would stick up for him when he needed it. And he almost always needed it when his father got involved, like on Lee's first day of school.

"The boy is not normal," Lee had overheard his father tell his mother on that day.

"That's not true, Henry. All his tests come back in the normal range," she responded.

"So much for the tests."

Lee understood that his brothers were at the top of the so-called normal range. If they were any indication of normal, Lee conceded he was likely close to the bottom of the range. Had he tested high enough in their entrance exam, Lee would be attending the same elite private grammar school as his brothers. Instead, his mother had enrolled him in a less prestigious private school, and his first day had been disastrous. The other students had teased him, and his teacher had called him Leonard all day.

"I've made arrangements to have him home-schooled by tutors," his mother had told his father that evening.

"Just because he had a bad first day doesn't mean you yank him out of school. What a waste of your money."

For reasons unknown to Lee, it was clear that any money spent on him came from his mother.

"Nelson and Bennett loved going to school at his age," his father had said.

"Don't you understand, Henry? It doesn't matter what happened to them. He's so traumatized about this, nothing we say about Nelson and Bennett will make any difference."

"You deal with it then. He's all yours."

Now, at ten, Lee had been exposed to fourteen tutors, some of whom had lasted just one semester. Unlike his brothers, he struggled to get passing grades. Unlike his brothers, he struggled with everything.

"I'm not sure what to do," Lee heard his mother say to his father one night when they thought he was asleep. "I consulted with Dr. Ballou last week when I was in New York."

"Who?"

"You remember him, the one we met at the Silversteins last month, the one who was on *Phil Donahue*."

"Yes, I do remember him. Everything he said was just vague enough to hold some truth. How much is this one going to cost you?"

"He told me he would be willing to review Lee's case but it would be difficult for him to form any opinions without seeing him. I think I'm going to spend this summer in the New York apartment with Lee and see what Dr. Ballou can do for him."

"Do what you want," his father grumbled. "At least that damn apartment will get some use."

One thing Lee and his father agreed upon—seeing yet another doctor was a giant waste of time. He dreaded having to hear more of the same stuff he had been hearing from Dr. Jerry for as long as he could remember. He argued against going, but at ten, he had little influence over...just about anything.

For the next four weeks, Lee met with Dr. Ballou for an hour and a half, twice a week. In between, Lee and his mother took long walks in Central Park, fed the pigeons, and went on extravagant shopping trips. Lee watched television whenever his mother felt the need for one of her frequent naps. *Jeopardy* was his favorite show, and whenever he answered a question right, he wondered if either of his older brothers would have been able to do so, or even his father. When he came across the soap opera *All My Children,* he got excited, thinking he might learn about how other families worked. Instead, he learned that some families were even more confusing than his own.

At the end of their sessions, the New York doctor recommended a female therapist in Chicago, who was supposed to be able to help Lee develop "a more positive perception" of himself and "relieve some of his social anxieties." He saw that doctor seventy-four times over eighteen months before his mother allowed him to stop.

The Chicago doctor was no different from any of the others Lee had seen over the years—not at all friendly. This confused him—each one had indicated they wanted him to be open with them, but how could he when they appeared so distant? Lee didn't trust most of them either, having overheard his father say once that it wasn't in their best interest to cure him in order to keep those checks coming in from his mother. As a result, Lee revealed very little to any of them.

When Lee turned fourteen, Bennett had just graduated first in his class at Yale and was about to enter law school. Nelson had an MBA from Harvard with two years at Barclays, well on his way to a lucrative career in investment banking. In addition to their high intellect, both brothers had matured into strong, physically fit young men. With narrow shoulders and skinny arms, Lee felt his body was yet another one of his hopeless shortcomings, at least compared to his brothers.

Lee had little to do that summer except agonize over what his parents had in mind for him for high school. The thought of having to attend a school after all the years of being home-schooled horrified him. While he struggled with getting passing grades from his tutors, at least he didn't have to deal with other children and teachers who weren't handpicked by his mother. Thankful his parents were too preoccupied with other things to pay much attention to him—his father with some big real estate deal, and his mother with the annual American Red Cross fundraiser—Lee waited for a decision to be made about his schooling.

When his mother informed him he would have to attend high school, he was devastated. He was now going to have to face what he feared most—the unknown.

On the morning of his first day, Lee awoke in a full-blown panic attack. He huddled in the corner of his room, trembling, his fists clenched, breathing erratically, until his mother came looking for him.

Paralyzed and barely able to speak, he managed to whisper, "Just leave me here for a while until it passes, Mother."

Dr. Jerry had told him to relax when he felt an attack coming on, practice the deep breathing exercises he had shown him, and imagine himself in a safe place. It helped.

"What about school?"

"I can't go. What if I get a panic attack there?"

"You'll take the paper bag out of your briefcase and slowly breathe into it, like Dr. Jerry demonstrated for you. Then you'll ask to be excused to go to the nurse's office."

"It feels like I'm going to die when I have one of these, Mother. It feels like someone is choking me. I'm cold, and then I'm hot. It's horrible. I don't want to go through it again, not two days in a row." He couldn't hold back the tears any longer. "You have no idea how scary it is. I'm not going to school."

"Lee, we've been over this numerous times. You have to go to school. It's not a choice for either of us. The law requires it."

"I don't see why I can't continue to be home-schooled."

"We'll discuss it further after dinner...when your father gets home."

When his father arrived, his parents talked behind closed doors. Thirty minutes later, they summoned him.

"Lee, we have agreed to allow you to continue being home-schooled," his mother said.

His father stood across the room, staring out the window while she talked, his stony profile telling Lee he wasn't happy with the decision.

"But here is the arrangement. We think you need social interaction with other children, so you must spend some time with children your own age doing something outside of your regular school work."

"Like what?"

His father was quick to respond. "Sports. Just pick a sport," he said, as if it was a no-brainer.

"You've got to be kidding. I throw like a girl. When I run, I usually end up twisting an ankle. I can't stand up on ice skates, and I'm deathly afraid of water. What do you expect me to do?"

"Anything, boy. Just pick *something*." His father's voice tightened.

"How about karate?" Lee said without thinking. The previous month, Lee had snuck out of the house on a Sunday afternoon when his parents weren't home and had gone to see *Enter the Dragon* with Bruce Lee, a movie his parents would not have allowed him to see due to his age.

His parents looked at him in disbelief.

"What's wrong with that?" Lee asked.

"What's right with it?" his father asked.

"It's a sport. It involves interaction with other children my own age. Isn't that what you want?"

"Karate is—"

"Henry, wait a minute. He does have a point, we must admit."

"Not karate."

"Why not?" she asked.

His father's twisted face said it all. To him, the only sports worth anything were traditional team sports, like football, basketball, baseball, and soccer. He walked away mumbling.

Lee signed up for karate classes with nine other twelve- to fourteen-year-olds. Neither of his parents attended his first lesson, for which Lee was grateful. When he came home, they asked him how it had gone.

"It was okay, I guess. We didn't really do anything but listen to Sensei Kim talk. Living in harmony. Spiritual awakening. You know...all that kind of stuff."

"Really. And what do you think about 'all that stuff,' as you so eloquently put it?" his father asked without looking up from his newspaper.

"I like it."

"That's just great," his father said.

He went to the class three times a week and enjoyed it. During down time, the other boys talked about cutting lawns and shoveling sidewalks to earn spending money, watching television shows like *Chico and the Man* and *Happy Days,* and playing Pac-Man in the arcade at the local roller rink. Lee was curious about the cassette-tape players they all said they had in their bedrooms where they listened to popular musicians Lee had never heard of, like Bob Dylan, Queen, and Steppenwolf. The only music allowed in his home was classical, played from stereo components housed in a floor-to-ceiling entertainment center his father had custom-built in his den.

After several weeks of classes, Lee overheard his mother talking on the phone with Sensei Kim.

"The best in the class? Really?"

For some reason, she never mentioned that phone call to Lee.

3 | "Don't Expect Him to Change"

In June of 1977, Lee unceremoniously received his high school diploma in the mail. By that time, he had earned his brown belt in karate, something that went unrecognized by his family. He relished the sport and discovered early on that it involved much more than learning how to kick and punch for the purpose of self-defense. Mental development was also an essential aspect to it, as well as unifying the mind, body, and spirit—concepts that he quickly grasped but terrified him at the same time.

One week after he received his diploma, his parents asked him to join them in the parlor. The setting made Lee nervous—they rarely asked him to join them in the parlor, and when they did, it always meant there would be a difficult conversation to come.

His parents were sipping their usual after-dinner port. His father didn't waste any time asking Lee what his plans were now that he had finished high school. It wasn't as though his father hadn't asked that question before, and Lee knew he now had to do something besides petition for more time. The painful look on his mother's face made him even more nervous.

"Believe it or not, I have a plan, Father." Lee had dreaded this conversation for months and wondered if he would be able to get through it without vomiting, passing out, or going into a full-blown panic attack. "Oakton Community College offers a variety of horticulture classes, and they also have a karate team."

Lee avoided eye contact with either parent as he held his breath waiting for their reaction. When he did look at them, his eyes darted back and forth between his mother's pursed lips and the enlarged vein in his father's neck. Seconds of silence felt like hours.

"What's wrong with the University of Wisconsin?" his father asked. "I told you I can get you in there." His father was a UW alumnus, member of the Bascom Hill Society, and major donor.

"I understand why you might want to consider community college as opposed to a regular college," his mother interjected. "Given the fact you've been home-schooled your entire life, attending a four-year college might be a bit overwhelming. And then of course, there are your grades. Will you consider transferring to a regular college after two years?"

"Let me get this straight. Are you telling us—"

"Henry, let Lee respond to my question first...please."

"I'm not thinking that far ahead, Mother."

"Figures," his father grumbled. "I don't understand why—"

His mother finished the sentence. "Why horticulture, dear?"

"I think it's an honorable field of study. Studying the soil, plant propagation and breeding, cultivation and environmental factors. The world needs people who understand this."

His father got up to leave.

"Where are you going, Henry?"

"Out for a walk."

"Don't worry about him, Mother," Lee said when he heard the front door close. "He has never believed in me or supported any of my decisions up to this point. Don't expect him to change now."

Lee left the parlor for the dining room and stood in the shadow of the massive antique breakfront, one of his several safe havens for eavesdropping on his parents. He had learned over the years that this was sometimes the only way to find out what they were thinking.

Twenty minutes later, his father returned.

"Did you have to walk out on him at this pivotal moment in his life, when he's talking to us about his future?"

"What future? Where can a sword-swinging, leg-kicking kid who has taken a few gardening classes from a community college go? What is that boy thinking?"

"Henry, don't you see it's a start? We know he's not like Bennett and Nelson, but Lee will succeed in life. It may take him a little longer than the others, but he will eventually get there."

"First of all, I never mentioned Nelson or Bennett."

"You didn't have to—I know what you're thinking. Can't you recognize the merit in his furthering his education when he's struggled his whole life with his schoolwork? Could you give him just a little credit for that?"

"I don't get it, Abbey. I will never get it. The boy has an IQ of 132, for god's sake," he mumbled under his breath.

When Lee was a sophomore in high school, his mother had asked Dr. Jerry to arrange for an IQ test. To everyone's surprise, he had tested very high.

"Don't forget what we were told, Henry, about children in the genius range."

"What hogwash are you referring to this time?"

"I don't understand why you're so hard on him when we know he has what often accompanies a high IQ—a difficult time with social relationships, frequent bouts of feeling inadequate, and an obsession with being different."

"Those are just excuses. Face it, Abbey, he *is* different. Just excuses."

* * *

Lee entered the community college in Des Plaines, about ten miles away, and continued to live at home. He joined the karate team the first semester. But while he managed to maintain decent grades in all of his classes, he still had made no friends after two months and feared he would always fail miserably when it came to relationships with his peers. One of the problems was that he avoided talking to people—afraid he would say the wrong thing, afraid of what they might think of him, afraid they would immediately see his flaws and judge him. And girls were the scariest.

One day during his second semester, after sitting through a long, monotonous biology class, Lee walked down the hall behind one of his classmates, Trevor. He was close enough to overhear him ask the pretty blonde by his side out on a date, obviously for the first time. The boy made it look easy, so normal. Lee remembered something Dr. Jerry had told him many years earlier: "To not try new things guarantees you'll never be able to do them."

The next day, as Lee strolled across the campus on his way to the library, he spotted a girl named Catherine Tynes a hundred feet or so in front of him. Catherine was in the same horticulture program, a year behind Lee but in many of the same classes. With honey-colored hair, sleepy brown eyes, and a nice figure, she may not have been the prettiest or hippest girl in school, but she was a good student.

"Hey Catherine," he called to her. "Wait up."

She turned around and smiled. "Hey, Lee. What's up?"

"Nothing much. That was some exam we had in botany yesterday. How do you think you did?"

"I'm pretty sure I aced it. And you?"

"I think I did okay."

They walked side-by-side for several minutes without saying anything.

"Would you like to go out with me sometime?" he blurted out, forgetting everything he had learned from observing Trevor the day before.

"Sure," she said without turning her head.

"Would you be free for dinner this Saturday?"

"Mm-hm."

One of the few things Lee did know about asking a girl out was not to assume too much. "Do you want me to pick you up, or would you prefer we meet somewhere?"

"You can pick me up."

They exchanged phone numbers, and once he had her address and they had agreed on a time, they parted ways.

Damn. That wasn't hard at all.

As he drove home from school the following Thursday, Lee started having second thoughts about his date with Catherine. It didn't feel right, and he was afraid the only reason he had asked her out was because he wanted to feel more normal, more like Trevor, more like just about every other young male on the face of the earth.

He pulled into a gas station to use the payphone. He hadn't told his parents or anyone else about the date and didn't want to take a chance of getting caught cancelling it from their home phone. After picking up and then putting down the receiver for the third time, he got into his car and drove off. Cancelling the date didn't seem right either, especially since it would have to involve making up a phony excuse. He resolved to go through with it.

On Saturday, Lee coated his stomach with Pepto-Bismol before he said goodbye to his mother, who believed him to be meeting with some other students for a study group, and drove to the nearest gas station to change into the clothes he had stashed in the trunk of his car earlier. As he was changing in the tight quarters of the bathroom stall, he worried that Catherine might think him dorky in a sports jacket and tie. Too late now—that's all he had with him.

Catherine lived in Des Plaines in a neighborhood comprised mostly of small bungalows on tiny lots. He located her address, loosened his tie a bit to look more casual, and walked to her front door.

Before he could ring the bell, Catherine flung open the door to greet him. She wore a short red skirt and what Lee thought may have been a t-shirt at one time—an outfit much less conservative than she typically wore to school. He was glad he had at least loosened his tie.

"You didn't say to dress up. Sorry."

"No problem," he told her. "You look nice. Ready to go?"

"Sure."

On the way to the restaurant, he asked her how long her family had lived in Des Plaines.

"They don't. Well, not anymore, anyway. My dad bought me that house after he divorced my mom. Guilt trip I think."

"Guilt trip?"

"Yeah, long story."

"So where do they live now?"

"My mother moved to Miami, as far away from him as she could get. He lives in downtown Chicago with the girl who used to be my best friend."

"Ouch. That must have been hard to accept."

"That's where the house story comes in. Do you mind if I turn on the radio?"

"No, go right ahead."

The radio had been tuned to WFMT, a classical music station. As soon as the music came on, she laughed.

"Tell me you don't listen to that."

"Well, actually, I do."

She twirled the tuner until she found a station to her liking. What emanated from the car's dashboard sounded more like noise than music.

"I love Def Leppard," she told him.

"Is that right? Look, I made reservations at Bluewater Grill, but if you'd like to go somewhere else..."

"No. That's fine. Sounds fancy."

"Good. We're here."

He opened the restaurant door for her and followed her inside, hoping he hadn't made a big mistake by not cancelling the date, but fearing he had.

Dinner conversation was difficult. Lee had come prepared with an arsenal of questions to keep the conversation flowing, but all he got from Catherine were one-word answers.

"So, did you grow up in Des Plaines?"

"Yes."

"Nice place to grow up?"

"So-so."

"Do you have any brothers or sisters?"

"No."

"What did you think about Whittiker's 'sermon' last week on the threatened seed diversity in third world countries? I thought at one point the man was going to break down in tears."

"He had some good points."

"He went a little overboard, don't you think?"

"Mmm...maybe."

"And Osborne talking about the Dutch scientists who added the firefly enzyme to tobacco plants and made them glow. Pretty amazing stuff."

"Mm-hm.

By the time the main course was served, Catherine had said very few words but managed to slurp down two alcohol-laced Long Island iced teas and was looking around for the waiter.

"Another iced tea?" he asked her.

"Is that okay?"

"I didn't think to ask you if you were twenty-one."

"Just turned." She twisted around in her chair in order to see behind her. "Waiter!"

Lee ate faster than he usually did, wanting the date to end as soon as possible. Catherine was clearly not his type, and he suspected she felt the same way about him. He drank two cups of coffee while she ate a generous portion of chocolate cake and polished off her third drink. Sixty-five minutes after they had walked in the front door, he paid the bill, and they left.

He didn't know what to say on the drive back. If it had gone well, he had been prepared to ask her if she wanted to see a movie the following weekend, but now that was out of the question. She broke the silence when they were a few blocks from her house.

"I had a nice time."

Lee figured she was just being polite. He followed suit. "Me too."

He pulled up in front of her house.

"Wanna come in?"

"Come in?" *I can't believe she wants to continue this.*

She reached over to touch the side of his face. "You know. For a nightcap." She leaned in for a kiss. Lee instinctively backed away.

"I think maybe you've had too much to drink, Catherine."

"So you're not coming in?" The pained look on her face caused him to panic. She looked as though she was about to cry.

Lee went for the door handle. "C'mon. I'll walk you to your door."

"Don't bother," she said through a whimper.

"I'm sorry. I'm not sure what to—"

"Go to hell," she muttered as she opened the car door.

Lee opened his door and walked around to her side of the car, but by then she was out of the car and halfway down her front walk, the middle finger of her right hand high in the air.

Lee stood beside his car staring at Catherine's front door for a long moment, dumbfounded by her behavior. He tried to make sense of what had just happened and how he could have handled it any differently. Was intimacy really expected after a first date? Was she hurt? Insulted? Was she drunk? Did she seduce all her dates like that, or was this the one time she had mustered enough courage to be the pursuer, only to have him dismiss her advances? He didn't know.

A woman wearing a bathrobe and a turban on her head emerged from the house next door. She stood on her porch with her arms crossed staring at him, compelling Lee to slip back into his car and drive off.

By the time he arrived home, Lee knew three things for sure: His first date had been a disaster. He would never again go on a date for the wrong reason. And before he asked a girl out again, he would get to know her.

"To not try new things guarantees you'll never be able to do them."

Well, I tried something new, Dr. Jerry. What does that guarantee?

The following Monday, he and Catherine arrived at exactly the same time to an ecology class and were forced to take the only two remaining vacant chairs, next to each other. At the end of class, before the teacher had even finished giving them their homework assignment, Catherine scooted out of the classroom. Lee never saw her after that.

He felt terrible about everything having to do with Catherine— their lousy date followed by his rebuff to her advances, the pain he saw in her face afterwards, the story about her guilt-ridden father buying her off, her mother's departure, and now her absence from classes. He felt guilty for the part he had played in all of it and wavered between calling her, in an effort to make amends, and letting it go. In the end, not wanting to risk making the situation worse, he let it go.

* * *

After two years of community college, Lee applied to Cornell University, and although his grades were mediocre at best and not all his community college credits were transferrable, he was accepted into their horticultural program. Lee suspected his karate skills had played a decisive role, as Cornell had one of the highest-ranking karate teams in the country, and Lee's solid skills made him a good candidate for the team. That, coupled with the school's declining enrollment for the previous two years, had definitely worked in his favor.

He moved into a private dorm room and quickly settled into a busy schedule of horticulture and karate classes. Lee had to admit it was a strange combination of interests and understood that no matter what direction he took with either of them, he would remain his father's biggest disappointment.

4 | FRIENDS OF DOROTHY

Lee's first year at Cornell flew by. Officially, because not all his credits transferred, he was enrolled as a sophomore, but by cramming in extra courses, he caught up to being a junior within two quarters. Why he did this, he wasn't sure—now he was that much closer to having to decide what he was going to do after college.

Lee managed to do reasonably well academically, and perhaps even more importantly, he was able to establish a rapport with some of his professors, especially those who were invested in medical research through the genetic modification of plants, which Lee found fascinating.

One professor who took an interest in Lee was Carl Engstrom. He taught genetics, and during one of their after-class discussions about how genetically modified organisms could potentially change the environment, he told Lee about an East Indian researcher named Phoolendu Radhakrishnananan. His groundbreaking work in the genetic modification of plants was controversial among other researchers, but that didn't seem to deter him from continuing his endeavors. Lee was so captivated by what the professor had to say about him and his research, he promptly called him at his University of Illinois research facility outside of Springfield.

Dr. Radhakrishnananan was generous with his time and talked at length about his cancer research projects, especially his most recent endeavors involving crown gall disease. Genetic modification related to medical cures was unchartered territory, making his research exciting but, as Lee's college professor had pointed out, debatable.

When the doctor heard that Lee lived in Evanston, he offered him an internship over the summer. While he was unable to pay Lee, he did offer him a place to stay in the back of the lab.

When Lee told his parents of his plan for the summer, he was not surprised at their reaction.

"Are you kidding?" his father asked. "You're going to spend the summer working for some Punjab for nothing, living in the back of his laboratory? Have you lost all your senses, boy?"

"Henry, you don't have to be—"

"There's nothing wrong with an internship...as long as you get paid for it, and you're not camping out in some remote area of southern Illinois. It's not practical, and it's not safe." He turned away and headed out of the room. "End of discussion."

"I'm over eighteen," Lee said to his mother once his father had left.

"I know. What do you plan to do?"

"I'm going to spend the summer with a brilliant research scientist from whom I expect to learn more about genetic modification in plants than I could ever learn at any college."

"You have my blessing, son."

A month later, Lee packed a bag and drove to Springfield, feeling nervous but very excited. Hoping to make a good impression on the doctor, Lee spent the four-hour drive rehearsing some opening lines. He also practiced pronouncing the doctor's unwieldy name.

The research facility included four greenhouses, two laboratories, and five acres of land, well outside of the city. The doctor stood in front of the larger of the two buildings as Lee drove up. The sweet smell of strawberries wafted through the air, making Lee think he was off to a very pleasant start.

"Hello, Dr. Radhakrishnananan," he said as he extended his hand. Slightly shorter than Lee, with thick, wavy black hair and a dark complexion, the man greeted Lee with a faint smile and a strong handshake.

"Call me Dr. Rad. Everyone does."

"Okay, Dr. Rad it is." Lee tried not to show his disappointment after four hours of practicing his name.

It turned out that Lee was one of two assistants. The other was a blond sophomore from the University of Illinois named Robin who immediately put Lee at ease with her sweet smile and easy-going manner. She was wearing an outfit he knew would horrify his mother—stonewashed jeans, a t-shirt with an advertisement on it, and high-top tennis shoes. They talked about Dr. Rad the first day.

"Twice today he told me to do something, and then questioned me about it later, as if he had never told me to do it," Lee told her.

"This is my second summer," she said. "Get used to it. He does that to me all the time. It's just one of his many quirks. Wait until you're here a month and he asks you what your name is. He still does that to me every once in a while." She laughed. "Just go along with it. It's easier."

"Has it been a good experience?" Lee asked.

"My dad is the dean of students at U of I, and he thinks Dr. Rad's a genius...a bit eccentric, but a genius. That's why I'm here. My dad says you can't get this kind of training anywhere else in this country."

And so Lee and Robin assisted Dr. Rad in his numerous vegetable, fruit, and red clover projects throughout the summer. They began work at sunup, stopped for a brief lunch, and worked until sundown. Their assignments varied. Some days they spent outdoors maintaining crops and occasionally field equipment. Other days they worked in the greenhouses harvesting seeds, tending to seedlings, assisting Dr. Rad with field experiments, and keeping the environment sterile. On lab days, they collected, recorded, and organized data.

Lee and Robin often went into town for dinner, after which Lee would return to his room in the lab and Robin to her parents' home nearby.

The research projects fascinated Lee, and while Dr. Rad was generous with his time in explaining things, Lee often couldn't understand some of it due to Dr. Rad's thick accent and rapid speech, and there were only so many times he felt he could ask him to repeat himself.

When Lee wasn't thinking about the work he was doing, he thought about Robin. She was the first girl he had ever known as more than just a casual acquaintance, and he thought he might be attracted to her. He suspected other boys his age would have fantasized about being in bed with someone as pretty as Robin, but when he forced himself to think about what it would feel like to be close to her, really close to her, it did nothing for him. At first, he rationalized that by telling himself she just wasn't his type. But that only triggered the question as to what was his type. *I have no type.*

One day when Dr. Rad was away at a lecture, Lee and Robin took a longer-than-normal lunch break. Eventually, he got up the nerve to ask her if she had a boyfriend.

"No, silly. I'm a homo," she replied.

What? He didn't know any homosexuals, nor had he ever heard anyone utter that word before. *Isn't that just grand. The first girl I think I may like is a homosexual...the second girl, if you count Catherine.*

"I'm sorry...I mean...no, I'm not sorry. I mean...I *am* sorry but not that you're a homosexual. Actually, I don't know why I'm sorry." He paused to catch his breath. "Can we start over?"

Robin took it in stride. "I'm the one who should apologize. I know it shocks people to hear me say that. I just don't hide it like some others do. I refuse to. If someone doesn't like me for who I am—a *homo*—then that's just too bad. I am who I am."

Lee liked her style and high level of self-confidence.

"Can I ask you something very personal?" he asked. "If you don't want to talk about it, just say so."

Robin nodded.

"How do you know you're a homosexual?" His stomach knotted up as he waited for her to answer.

"First of all, you can say *homo.* Or even *queer.* And *gay* is okay even for girls, but I hate the word *lesbian* for some reason. Anyway, I knew from when I was just a kid I was different from the other girls. I didn't know why. I just knew I was. Then in fifth grade, Bobby Wentworth kissed me. I didn't see it coming. I was so appalled, I ran into the bathroom and washed my mouth out with soap. Looking back at it, I would say that was probably the beginning."

She had known she was different from other girls. That sounded familiar.

"Do your parents know?"

"They do now."

"And they're okay with it?" He wished he hadn't said that. "I mean..."

"I know what you mean. It's okay. At first, they thought—like a lot of other people do—that I needed to get treated for it. It took time to convince them it was no longer considered a mental illness. Probably the worst few months of my life. But I have very loving parents. Eventually, they accepted it and me for who I am. My mother has even attended a few PFLAG meetings."

"PFLAG?"

"Parents and Friends of Lesbians and Gays. I think if my parents had their druthers, I wouldn't be this way. 'Course, if I had my druthers, I wouldn't be this way either."

"You don't have a choice?"

"Not the way I look at it."

"So do you have a...uh, a girlfriend?"

"No, not at the moment. Last year I dated someone for almost ten months until I discovered she was cheating on me...with a man of all things. So we broke up. God, I felt betrayed." She didn't say anything for a long moment. "I really loved her. I haven't dated anyone since." She paused. "Okay, so now you know way more about me than I do you. What's your story, Lee? Do you have a girlfriend?"

Since Robin had talked about herself so openly, Lee thought he should do the same, even though he didn't have that much to tell. Still, he worried about what she would think of him if he told her everything.

"No, I don't have a girlfriend. I've never had a girlfriend. In fact, I've only been on one date in my whole life, and that was a disaster."

"How come?"

Lee shook his head. "Long story."

"I would think girls would find you cute."

Lee blushed. "I don't know about that."

"Do you have any brothers and sisters?"

"I have two older brothers who are...well, normal."

"Like you're not?"

"That's a long story too."

"Well, you seem perfectly normal to me." She leaned over and kissed him on the cheek—his first kiss, and from a homosexual.

"Hey, why don't we go out one night. You can take me to a regular bar for a drink, and then I'll take you to one of my hangouts. It'll be fun!"

"I don't know..."

"C'mon. I haven't been out in weeks, and something tells me you need to get out more too. Just for a couple of drinks. Friday, after we finish up here."

"Well...okay."

After thinking it through, Lee decided his plan with Robin wasn't such a good idea, and over the course of the next two days, he practiced a few different ways to tell her he wasn't going to go through with it. But the more he thought about it, the more he found he wanted to support someone who had also suffered the consequences of being different. And what harm could there be in it?

On Friday, they wrapped up their work in the lab by six o'clock and drove in separate cars to Champaign. Not being familiar with the town, Lee relied on Robin to pick both bars. Their first stop was The Flyin' Frog, not too far from the U of I campus, on a busy street with many other bars. Hundreds of college students roamed the sidewalks and streets, laughing, talking, and obviously having a good time.

Inside the Flyin' Frog, twenty or so people Lee and Robin's age sat at the bar or at one of the tiny tables that surrounded the empty dance floor. He approached the bar and ordered two beers while Robin stood on the periphery. Beers in hand, he walked across the dance floor and handed one to Robin.

He glanced around the room. "Not very lively, is it?" he asked Robin.

"Pretty early. Most kids don't even come out on a Friday night until ten or so."

They drank their beers and watched two couples slow-dance to *In the Air Tonight* by Phil Collins.

A half hour later, it was time to move on.

Rosco's, one of Robin's frequent haunts, was in another section of town on a far less travelled street. Lee followed Robin to a parking lot behind the nightclub and then spent ten minutes trying to find a place to park.

"They draw quite a crowd, don't they?" he asked her after parking his car in the last row of the lot.

"You should see it for their late show—cars parked a half-mile up and down the streets in all directions."

"There's a show?"

"Just wait, my naive little hetero. You're about to be enlightened."

Lee opened the door, allowing a deafening blast of noise to escape from inside the bar. A man's voice seemed to come out of nowhere. "That'll be five dollars each," he said.

Lee looked around for whoever it was who asked him for the five dollars, but all he saw was a very unattractive girl with bright red hair wearing a blue boa around her neck. The poor girl had glopped so much makeup onto her face that it looked distorted.

Robin nudged him in the back. "Pay the lady, Lee."

"Pay who?"

Robin took the ten-dollar bill from his hand and handed it to the redhead. "C'mon. I'll buy the first round," she said to Lee.

Trying not to think too much about what he had just seen, Lee followed Robin through the crowd, nudging his way through scores of mostly young men, many of whom wore outlandish outfits. Lots of leather. Lots of feathers. And sometimes not much else. One man wore nothing but a leather jacket and a pair of very brief briefs.

They eventually reached the bar where three topless male bartenders were serving up drinks. Robin ordered two beers. As soon as two bar stools opened up, they sat down.

Lee turned around to see what was going on behind him. The crowded dance floor bustled with men making explicitly sexual dance moves. They didn't appear to be in couples, at least not for very long. Like moths to flames, they were constantly being drawn to other parts of the dance floor in search of a new partner.

Embarrassed, Lee looked away from the dancers only to spot two gold-colored cages hoisted ten feet above their heads, each holding a nearly naked male moving his body in an even more provocative way than those on the dance floor. The more Lee observed, the more foolish he felt being there.

"So...what do you think?" Robin asked.

He turned around to face her. "I think I'm way out of my element here, but now that I've said that aloud, I've felt out of my element my whole life, so I don't know why this shouldn't be any different."

Robin smiled. "Just think of it as a new kind of different."

Lee felt something rub up against his leg and turned to find a shirtless man about his age smiling at him.

"Hello," he said to the man.

"Hi there. You can call me LaRue. Actually, you can call me anything you want, honey." He held out his hand, palm down. Lee wasn't sure what to do with it, so he did nothing. The man frowned. "Don't tell me. You're not a friend of Dorothy's?"

"I beg your pardon."

Robin poked him in the back. "He's coming on to you, but he doesn't know if you're his type or not," she whispered.

"No, I don't think so," he replied to the man. He glanced down and saw he wasn't wearing anything but a pair of black briefs and a pink scarf tied around his waist.

"Too bad. You're cute."

"Nice meeting you," Lee said, now feeling completely uncomfortable.

He didn't know where to rest his eyes—the mirror behind the bar made it impossible to avoid looking at the bizarre characters who surrounded him. He focused on their faces, as that region of their bodies was the least shocking. He gave them credit for one thing—they knew how to have a good time.

Lee guzzled the last of his beer and turned to Robin. "I think I've seen enough. Are you almost finished?"

"You got it. Let's go."

They were halfway to the door when it burst open. The first policeman to enter held a megaphone to his mouth. "No one leave!" he shouted. "This is a raid!" A stream of policemen rushed in after him, causing complete pandemonium. The overlapping high-pitched screams from the patrons made it impossible to hear what the police were saying.

Lee turned around to seek out Robin, but she was nowhere to be seen. Several people headed toward the back of the bar, and Lee followed suit.

But before he got more than a few feet, a policeman grabbed his arm and said, "You're not going anywhere."

He pushed Lee into a corner with about twenty-five others and said, "If any of you move, you'll be tased."

Lee stood among the other detainees, petrified of what was going to happen next. Where was Robin? Had she gotten away?

They were escorted to one of several paddy wagons parked in front of the nightclub. Lee took a seat next to the guy at the bar who had hit on him.

"First bust?" he asked.

Lee nodded. "What are we being busted for?"

"Oh, they'll come up with something, you can be sure. They think if they harass us enough, we'll go away."

"You've been arrested before?"

"Many times, honey."

A policeman slammed the back door shut, and a minute later, the vehicle started moving.

"What happens now?" he asked LaRue.

"They'll put us all in a cell, and then book us one by one. We'll be out in a few hours."

LaRue turned out to be right. Squeezed into a holding cell, they were called out one by one for booking. Robin was not among them. Lee was one of the first pulled out. They searched him and then took down his name, address, date of birth, social security number, and place of employment. When he told them he was a student, they asked for the name of his school. After being photographed and fingerprinted, he was led back to the cell.

When everyone had been booked, they were each handed a Desk Appearance ticket that included a court date. The charge was public lewdness. They were told they could leave.

Lee followed the others outside, and not knowing what else to do, stood with them while they talked about how they were going to get back to their cars. The group headed down the street. Lee followed.

They walked several blocks until they came upon a drug store. One of the more conservatively dressed men went in and called for several taxis. It was a twenty-minute ride back to Rosco's, four people to a taxi.

Lee stewed the entire weekend over what happened, highly upset with Robin for abandoning him. He didn't have her home phone number, so he couldn't call her, but she could have called him at the lab.

When Robin arrived to work the next day, Lee was talking with Dr. Rad about their tasks for the morning. She joined them but avoided eye contact. They were assigned to pruning peach saplings in the main greenhouse, and as soon as Dr. Rad was out of earshot, he confronted her.

"Where the hell were you Friday night? Do you know what happened to me?"

"I heard. Look, I'm sorry. But when I saw that door burst open, I knew what was coming. My parents are understanding, but not that understanding. And my father being dean and everything...and I was there with a fake ID, so I would get whatever you got plus drinking as a minor. I had to book it out of there."

"Thanks a heap."

"I'm sorry. What did they get you with?"

"Public lewdness. And they asked me for the name of my school. Why would they need to know that?"

"What's your school's policy on students having an arrest record?"

"I have no idea. This may come as a surprise to you, but that subject has never come up for me before now."

"I don't blame you for being mad at me. I never should have taken you there."

"You got that right. And you could have called me over the weekend...you know, to see if I made it out okay. I would have called you, but I don't have your number."

She jotted down her number and handed it to him.

I don't need it now.

He thought he knew her. Now he wasn't so sure who she was—a friend who panicked and ran or just some self-absorbed girl who couldn't care less about what happened to him. He didn't know if he was supposed to forgive someone for doing something like that.

Lee and Robin were cordial to each other as they finished up their internship that summer. The charges against Lee were dropped, and Robin offered to compensate him for any expenses he had incurred due to the arrest. He declined the offer. They shook hands on their last day and wished each other well.

* * *

Back at Cornell, Lee was assigned to the same private dorm room he'd had the previous year. When he arrived, an envelope with his name on it was waiting for him, summoning him to the office of the dean of students.

Lee's stomach churned as he walked across campus to get there. Since the lewdness charges had been dropped, he didn't think that was why he was being summoned, but he couldn't think of any other reason.

Dean Larsen was an older man, with an expressionless face and imposing demeanor. His six-and-a-half-foot frame towered over Lee.

He led Lee into his office. "Sit down, son," he said to him.

The dean stared at Lee for several seconds and then looked down at the open file in front of him.

"Public lewdness." He crossed his arms over his protruding belly and peered at Lee over his reading glasses. "What do you have to say for yourself?"

"Those charges were dropped, sir."

"I didn't ask you that."

"A bar I was in was raided. Maybe there were people in there guilty of lewd behavior. I don't know. But I wasn't one of them. They just hauled us all to the station."

"You go to Rosco's often?"

"That was my first time."

"How was it for you?"

Lee felt his throat tighten. "I was clearly outside of my normal element, sir. A so-called friend invited me there as her guest. I had no idea what I was getting into. And I can assure you I was not involved in any lewd conduct. That's not me. Never has been nor will it ever be."

"But being there does demonstrate poor judgment at the very least. Wouldn't you agree?"

"Yes, I agree."

"Are you aware of the school's admission policy on applicants with arrest records?"

"No, but I can guess what it is."

"When was the last time you read our Student Code of Conduct manual?"

"I read it at the beginning of my first year here."

"I suggest you read it again."

"Yes, sir."

"I could recommend a suspension to the Disciplinary Committee, and given who's on that committee, I'd say your chances of being suspended are pretty good. You could get up to a year."

"But the charges were dropped."

"Doesn't matter." He looked down at the file. "Says here the case was dismissed after you were arrested." He leaned back in his chair. "Or I could recommend a year's probation. Of course, probation means exclusion from all extracurricular activities."

"Like attending football games and such?" Lee couldn't care less about football.

"Like you're off the karate team for the year."

What?

"Sir, once you're kicked off the team, you can't rejoin." He was one belt away from a ninth-degree black belt, the highest skill level attainable.

"Maybe you should have thought about that before you went into that fag bar."

Lee stared at him, not believing he had heard right.

"Is your so-called friend a Cornell student?"

"No, sir." As perturbed as he was with the way Robin had abandoned him at the nightclub in favor of her own self-interests, he wasn't going to say anything that would vilify her for being different.

"Were there any other Cornell students there with you?"

"Not with me."

"But they were there?"

"Not that I'm aware of. I was there for only—"

"Do you really think it's relevant how long you were there?"

"No, sir."

"I'm going to recommend probation. You'll hear from us in writing."

"With all due respect, sir, I don't—"

"Wanna go for suspension?"

"No, sir."

"Good day, Mr. Winekoop."

* * *

When Lee found it hard to concentrate on his studies in his third week of the new quarter, he knew it was more than just a matter of getting back into the swing of things after having had the summer off. And he was having other problems: constant nausea, lack of sleep, and a general feeling of inadequacy and helplessness—shades of his childhood he had thought were behind him. By week five of the ten-week quarter, he was failing most of his classes.

Following the student counselor's advice, he dropped two of his six classes, agreeing that it was too heavy a course load but knowing in his heart that wasn't the problem. After all, he had carried the same number of classes, in addition to karate, the previous year and had maintained a 3.0 GPA, a requirement to remain on the karate team.

He missed karate. On his way from his dorm room to class, Lee occasionally stopped by the exhibition room to watch his former teammates sparring. His longing to be back in it made him wonder if he would have provided the dean with Robin's name and school if he would have lessoned punishment. He thought about calling her to let her know that, but in the end, decided against it.

Karate had given him that smidgen of self-confidence—more than he had ever had before. It had allowed him to void all thoughts from his head during performances except for two things—responding to his opponent's moves and finding opportunities to make his own. That sort of mindfulness was such a welcome reprieve from his usual insecurities.

Now that was gone.

He considered dropping out of school. Maybe he was just fooling himself about being able to get a college degree. Maybe he was still caught in that trap of trying to meet someone else's expectations. The more he thought about it, the more sense it made to drop out. He had no plan for after he graduated, so what was the point? Why postpone the inevitable?

Lee stopped by the karate exhibition room one last time. Instead of the usual sparring going on, the room had been set up with hundreds of folding chairs and a dais. Students were streaming toward the building. He walked toward the front door to check it out.

"Who's speaking today?" he asked one of the students rushing into the building. He ignored Lee. He had to ask several others before getting an answer.

"Grandmaster Tatsuo Suzuki," someone shouted at him.

Lee was aware of him—anyone who studied Wado-Ryu was aware of him. One of the youngest men to achieve the highest rank attainable in Wado-Ryu, Susuki had gone on to form the first Wado Federation in England and had been instrumental in spreading Wado-Ryu throughout Europe. A scholar of the Zen doctrine, the man was highly revered in the karate community.

Tickets would be required, of that Lee was certain. Determined to get in, he hid out in the men's room until the nearest half-hour on the clock and then went through the now-closed double doors of the exhibition room. He stood in the back of the room and waited for the lecture to begin.

Suzuki's topic was the significance of fear. Fear arises out of helplessness, he explained, and when we feel helpless, our instinct is to run. But if you train yourself to transform all that valuable energy into a positive motivating force, it turns into self-confidence that allows you to face the fear. Suzuki defined anxiety as nothing more than drawn-out fear. Lee had never looked at it that way. Suzuki went on to say that anxiety arises from the mind's perception of stress as a danger to the body, causing the body to respond by going into panic mode—a lot of wasted energy.

Lee had heard ideas like these expressed before, but for some reason, they hadn't completely resonated with him until now.

An hour and a half later, on his way back to his dorm room, Lee stopped by the Office of Student Affairs to inquire about getting help.

With the benefit of a private tutor, Lee raised his GPA to 3.3 by the end of the second quarter, and that was after adding back the two classes he had dropped the previous quarter.

* * *

With graduation less than a year away, Lee knew he had to have a plan for what to do next, whether to continue with more schooling or something else, before he visited his parents during spring break. During the taxi ride home from O'Hare Airport, he practiced what he planned to tell them, ignoring the taxi driver's periodic curious looks in his rear-view mirror each time he tweaked his speech.

"It may be a long shot, but I've applied to Cornell's grad school," he told his parents after they had engaged in a suitable amount of small talk. "I can't get in with my current GPA, but if I can score at least in the ninety-fifth percentile on the GRE, they'll let me in on a conditional admission." Lee had always tested exceptionally well—it was class participation, written assignments, and class presentations that typically brought down his grades.

"More gardening?" his father asked, with more than a hint of sarcasm.

"Henry! If you would take the time to understand what horticulture is about...and stop being so ignorant."

It was just like his father to ignore the fact he was about to graduate from college, so his father's reaction didn't surprise him. What surprised him was his mother calling him ignorant.

"I do apologize," his father said in an arrogant tone. "Your mother is right. I have no right to criticize. Why don't you tell me about all the stimulating facets of horticulture so I am enlightened."

"Maybe some other time, Father."

* * *

Lee studied the entire summer, scored in the ninety-seventh percentile on the GRE, and was accepted into Cornell's graduate school's Department of Horticulture. Following in Dr. Rad's footsteps, he decided to concentrate on plant genetics.

The summer after his first year, he interned again for Dr. Rad. One day, as they were readying some slides in the lab, Lee asked the doctor if he knew much about the genetic modification of tobacco plants being done in Holland.

"It's fascinating work," he responded. "I'm envious of their freedoms."

"How so?"

"You see what I'm up against here. The research is expensive, and funding is a constant problem. The money the Dutch earmark for this kind of research is significantly more than they will ever make available here. In fact, I'm not sure how much longer I will be able to continue. I try to stay six months ahead of the game. It's the best I can do."

In the course of their work together, Lee picked Dr. Rad's brain as much as he could. He maintained copious notes from their discussions. Dr. Rad's most fascinating research involved the study of cancer in the plant kingdom. The doctor was sure that once they found a cure for crown gall disease in plants, they would be on the way to finding the cure for cancer in humans. For this research, Dr. Rad preferred to use red clover, a perennial herb particularly susceptible to crown gall.

Two other interns worked alongside Lee that summer—a foreign exchange student from Guatemala whose English was barely understandable, and a bookwormish young man who had even worse social skills than Lee. No one joked about Dr. Rad's absentmindedness. No one went to dinner with anyone else. They didn't even make chitchat with each other. Lee reverted to being socially withdrawn with constant feelings of restlessness and nervousness—feelings he had thought were behind him.

Lee thought about Robin often that summer. In spite of the ill will he still felt toward her, he couldn't get her out of his mind, and that bothered him. The fact that he had dreams about her confused him even more. When he had a dream about making love to her, he called his childhood psychologist, Dr. Jerry.

"Dr. Jerry, I realize you specialize in counseling children, but since we have such a long history together, I wonder if I could talk to you about something that's been bothering me."

"Of course, Lee. What's on your mind?"

Lee told the doctor about Robin and the disturbing thoughts and dreams he was having about her.

"Tell me about her good points."

"For starters, she accepted me for who I am from the beginning and continued to even after she got to know me."

"Anything else?"

"She didn't appear to have any expectations of me."

"Go on."

"I felt comfortable with her, and...I think I see where this is going."

Dr. Jerry laughed. "Tell me where it's going."

"Consciously, I'm confused with why I'm thinking about someone who I would never be with—she's a homosexual, has a wild side to her, and can be inconsiderate. But what I'm really drawn to are her good points."

"Not bad. Let me add a couple of things to that analysis. Sometimes we are drawn to relationships we can't have. Why? Because they're safe. Afraid of relationships? Then go for someone you can't have."

"Because then there's no chance of having to face that fear."

"Yes, and even if the unlikely relationship does take off, and it fails, there's a logical explanation for it."

"All tied up in a nice, neat little package."

"Mm-hm."

"Using avoidance to maintain the symptoms of anxiety."

"So you really were listening to me some of the time back then," he said, laughing.

"Some of it sunk in."

"As I recall, we talked a lot about your childhood fears. Most people stop identifying themselves as a child when they're faced with responsibilities that scared them as a child. Facing your fears—allowing them in, understanding them, learning from them—is a sign of maturity and helps you transform into an adult.

"Turning negatives into positives."

"Exactly. As for the dreams, there are many schools of thought on why we have them and what they mean. One theory is that the people, places, and things in your dreams are actually symbolic of something else, often an unresolved issue in your life."

"Like having meaningful relationships."

"Like that. And getting back to Robin, keep in mind the only reason you had a relationship with her was because you were both captive in the same space. In other words, you didn't choose to be in a relationship with her. Think about it— you found someone who accepted you for who you are without even trying. Now think about what could happen if you sought out a relationship on your own, with someone who possesses the qualities you value in a person, someone with similar interests, similar lifestyle."

"That's an interesting thought."

"I've helped you then?"

"Yes, you have." He paused for a moment. "Would you mind if we kept this conversation just between us? Please send your bill to me, not my parents."

"You're an adult now, Lee. Of course I will. Good luck, and do keep in touch."

He was glad he had made the call.

5 | Breaking Away

The closer Lee came to finishing grad school, knowing he had to face what to do next, the more anxious he became. He considered applying to the school's PhD program, but the obstacles were numerous. For starters, he couldn't come up with a clear statement of purpose. After stewing over it for several weeks, he finally admitted to himself the only reason he wanted to enter the program was that he didn't know what else to do.

Lee found himself obsessing over the successes of his brothers, something he had been told a thousand times not to do. Bennett, thirty-five, married and the father of three, was a named partner in a law firm that specialized in corporate and labor law but also provided legal advice to the underprivileged, many of them illegal immigrants. And if that wasn't enough, he worked with their mother on two or three major charitable events throughout the year.

Thirty-seven-year-old Nelson had married the daughter of a New York socialite, and they had twin boys. Nelson was sought after by all the major investment banking firms for his ability to structure mergers and acquisitions in short timeframes.

The national unemployment rate was the lowest it had been in seven years, and jobs were plentiful. Lee began considering the different opportunities for someone with a master's degree in horticulture. At the Cornell library, he scoured the want ads from big-city newspapers to see what they had to offer.

The Philadelphia zoo had an opening for a zoo horticulturist; a government office in San Francisco needed a director of grounds; and a nursery in San Diego was advertising for a greenhouse manager. But nothing appealed to him. Working in a zoo, while certainly a respectable position, would have garnered too much criticism from his family, and he wasn't sure he wanted to be around so many animals and the general public on a daily basis. The director of grounds position in San Francisco was at a girls' prep school—he couldn't imagine being one of a few males among hundreds of teenage girls. Managing a greenhouse seemed awfully boring.

Until he could find something more permanent, Lee checked in with Dr. Rad to see if he needed any help. The good news was Dr. Rad had received a grant that would carry him for another year. The bad news was he already had sufficient student help.

After his graduation, Lee told his parents he needed a break after all the schooling and asked permission to stay at their home in Lake Geneva for a few months while he sorted things out. His mother thought it would be precisely what he needed and immediately started arranging to transfer one of their cooks, Shaneta, to the lake house. His father thought he was stalling, and Lee really couldn't argue with that assessment.

Lee loaded up his ten-year-old Datsun 240Z with his clothes and a few personal items and headed for the lake house. He had received the car for his sixteenth birthday and refused to trade it in for anything newer even though his mother had offered to buy him a brand-new Porsche when he had graduated from college. The Datsun was Lee's most valuable possession. No one else had ever driven it. It was his and only his.

As he pulled up to the lake house, Lee was immediately reminded of the pretentiousness of the two-story plantation style home. He parked in front of the three-car attached garage and walked to the front door between the twenty-foot-high pillars that supported a decorative portico. While he had his own key, he rang the doorbell to let any of the servants who might be inside know he had arrived. The Evanston servants lived in the Winekoop home in third-floor living quarters, but the lake-house servants had to commute from wherever they lived.

Receiving no answer to the doorbell, Lee let himself inside. The substantial foyer spanned both stories, boasting a large crystal chandelier in its center that hung from a twelve-foot heavy-gauge anchor link chain.

Like the other two Winekoop residences, this one displayed excessively formal decor—ornate furniture, dramatic artwork, elegant draperies on all the windows—too much aesthetics and not enough function in Lee's opinion. On the first floor were a formal dining room, a large living room with a stone fireplace that took up one entire wall, an African Mahogany Crotch paneled study, two bathrooms, an oversized eat-in kitchen, and a sunroom. Upstairs were five bedrooms and three more bathrooms.

The one room Lee actually liked was the sunroom overlooking the expansive patio that gradually stepped down a couple hundred feet to the lake. He had to admit their landscaper had done an exemplary job of mixing the right combination of greenery, flowers, and seating. He loved the way the radiant orange zinnias and yellow Calibrachoa led down to the boardwalk, giving it a natural look and feel quite different from the interior of the house.

Of the five bedrooms on the second floor, Lee chose the one with a terrace overlooking the lake. The room was large by most people's standards, twenty-five-by-forty feet, with its own bathroom. The Winekoops didn't do anything on a small scale.

Before even unpacking, Lee curled up on one of the chaises on the terrace and mindlessly watched the rays of the full moon dance on the surface of the lake. Eventually, his mind wandered to memories of times when he was a scared child and the only people around were the hired help. Now he didn't even have that.

After an hour of feeling sorry for himself, Lee unpacked the few things he had brought with him, got undressed, and climbed into the elaborately carved four-poster bed, feeling a lot like a child pretending to be a grown-up. After a half-hour of mentally beating himself up for not being as mature as his brothers had been at his age, he fell asleep.

The next day, Lee ventured down to the kitchen to see what he could find to eat. The cook, Shaneta, wouldn't be arriving for a few days, so he was on his own. Never having had to prepare his own meals before, he didn't know what to expect to find.

The refrigerator contained a few things that had obviously been placed there by the staff for their own use. The freezer didn't prove to be any more promising. Sonya, the maid, arrived at the house as he was searching the cupboards and recommended a diner in town where he could get a good hearty breakfast, so he headed there.

The breakfast smells at Miss Sally's were intoxicating, and for a brief moment, Lee felt guilty savoring them. He remembered how when he was young, he would sneak into the kitchen to enjoy the aromas of whatever was being prepared by the cooks but then would inevitably get reprimanded by his mother, who didn't like him to be in the kitchen with "the help." As he studied the other patrons at the diner, a few looked back at him. He tried to imagine what they thought of him. Did they wonder why he was all alone, why he wasn't working or in school? Did anyone care?

After breakfast, not able to bring himself to go back to the big empty structure he now called home, Lee walked up and down Center Street. The business district seemed to appeal to women, with all the boutique-like shops and cute little restaurants. *Hannah and Her Sisters* was listed on the marquee of the local movie theater. Not much of a man's town, he thought.

He drove around the lake and down WI-67 into neighboring towns, stopping at a roadside stand in Sharon to pick up some fruit to tide him over until the cook arrived. He asked the gangly pimple-faced boy behind the stand what people there did for fun.

"Nothin'," he replied with a deadpan expression. "Unless you're rich, it's very boring 'round here."

Lee laughed. "So what do the rich people do for fun?"

"They sail around the lake in their fancy boats, go to country clubs, play golf, get laid. How the hell do I know?"

Well, that was helpful.

Four miles out of Rockton, after driving on a long stretch of road with nothing but open fields on either side, he spotted a roadside bar called the Deer Bottom Inn and Brewery and pulled into the small parking lot.

It was obvious as soon as he walked in how the establishment had gotten its name: mounted high on the wall in the smoke-filled room hung the posterior of a white-tailed deer. A dozen or so seats at the bar and as many small four-seater tables filled the dimly lit room. He sat down at one end of the bar. A slow country-western song resonated from a beat-up jukebox in the corner.

The bar was more crowded than he would have expected so early in the day. The two men on his left were discussing the Bears' last season. Lee knew they had been ranked number one in something or other but didn't know what. Their discussion soon switched to McClaskey's decision to sever all ties with the Honey Bear cheerleaders, which seemed to garner more of their attention than the team's performance. A couple on his right appeared to be arguing over her spending habits, something about no one needing thirty-five pairs of shoes.

Fearful someone would try to strike up a conversation with him, and he would have nothing to say, Lee considered leaving without ordering anything, but before he could decide, a bartender came over and asked him what he wanted to order. She was a tall buxom blonde, somewhere in her twenties, wearing neon-green tights and an oversized shirt with the top three buttons open, the type of girl men his age fantasized about.

Popping her gum, she asked, "What's your pleasure?"

His pleasure would have been a nice vintage port or a snifter of French cognac, but in a place called Deer Bottom Inn, he thought better of it.

"A beer, please."

She raised one eyebrow and threw her glance toward the chalkboard behind the bar that listed the varieties of beer they carried. "The first three are ones we brew ourselves."

"How about a Budweiser?" It was the only brand he had ever tried.

She poured a glass of beer from the tap and slid it down the bar a good ten feet. It stopped precisely in front of him. He thanked her with a nod and smile and then turned his attention to the menu she had placed in front of him. It was limited: wings, burgers, pizza, pulled-pork sandwiches, and French fries.

"The pizza is the best around. We make it fresh in the back," she said. It was hard not to notice the young woman's curves—the deep opening of her shirt left little to one's imagination. When he realized he was staring at her chest, he quickly looked away.

"No, thanks. Not really that hungry." Now not knowing where to look, Lee focused on the deer's rear end above the bar, while the pretty bartender dried a highball glass a few feet down the bar.

"Pretty clever, huh?" she said.

"Pardon me?"

"The deer ass."

"I guess. What's behind it?"

Her face broke into a wide grin. "You are."

He gave her a puzzled look.

She walked closer to him and glanced up at the mounted carcass. "Do you know how many people have come in here and asked that question? Think about it."

It took him several seconds. "Oh...I get it." He read the name badge pinned to her blouse. "What's CJ stand for?"

"CJ," she said through a smile. She had a nice smile.

Without any encouragement, CJ stopped by to chat with him in between customers. He learned that she lived with her two young sons in a rented house on a large piece of property in Durand just south of the Illinois-Wisconsin border. In the evening, while CJ tended bar, her sister watched her kids. CJ didn't mention where their father was, if there was one in the picture.

He tried to imagine himself with a girl like her, but it was hard to form an image in his head when he had so little to go by. He wondered how guys even knew if a girl would want to go on a date with them. *Where do you learn this stuff?* He figured it would have been a whole lot easier to have started learning about girls when he was twelve and was *expected* to be naive and awkward.

He finished his beer, put a ten-dollar bill on the bar, and got up to leave.

CJ glanced at the ten spot. "Change?"

"No, but thanks."

 "For what?"

"For talking to me."

While it may have been just an out-of-the-way small-town bar that catered to middle-class blue-collar locals, Lee left feeling a little better than he had when he'd first walked in.

6 | Uncle Nelson Is Dead

Having just left the pleasing modesty of Deer Bottom Inn, Lee didn't feel much like going back to the opulent lake house, but he had nowhere else to go. He pulled into the driveway, parked his car, and walked through the front door, sinking back into the hollow mood he'd been in when he'd left earlier that day.

Sitting in one of the imposing high-backed chairs in the front room, he studied the room's impersonal character—the baby grand piano in the corner, the bronze statues, the imported throw rug in the middle of the room with its indiscernible figures woven into it. He perused the three Baroque-style paintings signifying triumph, power, and control that his father no doubt had selected and which had probably cost more than most people made in a year. It was as if someone had been told to design a room that would make most people feel uncomfortable. Mission accomplished.

He climbed the stairs to the second floor. The atmosphere wasn't much different up there except for the one back bedroom that had been recently emptied for painting and carpeting. He hunkered down on the hard sub-flooring, drew up his knees, and buried his face in his arms, thinking about his brothers' perfect lives and wondering what was wrong with him.

* * *

A warm streak of sunlight created a bright path from the bedroom window to the hallway door, blinding Lee for a brief moment. His body ached after spending the night on the hard floor, and his stomach growled from not having eaten anything substantial since breakfast the day before. He sat there for a minute thinking about how stupid it had been to sleep on the floor when he was steps away from a number of soft beds in lavishly furnished bedrooms.

He found Shaneta, the cook who his mother had sent from their Evanston home, in the kitchen cooking breakfast—one more servant he didn't want to deal with but probably needed. Even though he had watched his family members deal with "the help" his entire life, he had never gotten the hang of it. Being terse with them seemed cold and condescending, but treating them in a friendly way didn't seem right either.

The sound of the phone ringing interrupted his thoughts. Sonya came in and announced his mother on the phone.

When he picked it up, he immediately detected the distress in her voice. Uncle Nelson had died of a massive heart attack. The funeral was in three days. While Lee had met his mother's favorite uncle only a few times when he was very young, he was well aware of her fondness for him and felt he had an obligation to be there for her.

Uncle Nelson had always been somewhat of an enigma to Lee. His mother had always talked about him as though he was a close relative, but the man never came to family get-togethers nor had the Winekoops ever gone to his home in Indiana. Lee didn't even know if he had a family—somehow he had never thought to ask. Lee's mother spoke of him as a generous and loving man, but Lee had no evidence of that other than the coin collection the man had given him when he was born.

While driving to Evanston the day before the funeral, Lee agonized over what to tell his parents about his future plans. Of course, he had no plans, and the closer he got to home, the closer he came to the realization that he wasn't going to be able to come up with one.

When he walked into the house, his parents were in the middle of an argument.

"I don't see why I have to go," his father said.

This seemed insensitive, even for him.

"For appearance's sake, Henry."

"You're asking too much this time. And for God's sake, you're acting like you're still—"

"Just one more time won't—"

When Lee entered the room, his mother turned to greet him. Her eyes were red and swollen.

"Mother, is everything all right?"

She reached out to him, pulling him into her arms so quickly and solidly, it stunned him. She hugged him for several seconds, something Lee didn't remember her ever having done before. Her perfume overwhelmed him, causing a momentary wave of nausea, "Level Four" as he had referred to it his whole life, precursor to a panic attack. He took in a deep breath and let it out slowly before she let go of him.

His father left the room without saying anything more.

"Are you okay, Mother?"

Her hunched shoulders made her appear much shorter than she actually was. She shook her head. "No, not really."

"I'm sorry for your loss." He didn't know what else to say.

"It's your loss too," she sobbed.

"Yes, of course," he said, not knowing why it was a loss for him. He hadn't known the man. "What's with Father?"

His mother didn't answer.

"Will he be going to the funeral?"

"He'll go," she whispered.

The next morning, two limos transported everyone to Uncle Nelson's hometown of Valparaiso, Indiana, for the funeral. Lee, his parents, and his two brothers rode in one car and his brothers' families in the other.

His mother was painfully quiet in the car, staring out the window for long periods, appearing to be in some other place. After a half hour of silence, she turned to Lee and asked, "So what have you decided to do now, Lee?"

Even though he was expecting the question, he was surprised at the timing of it. "I'm thinking about going on for my PhD." He had come up with that one right out of the air. He had no intention of doing that.

"In gardening?" his father asked.

Lee didn't respond.

"Horticulture, Henry."

"Right. Horticulture."

Lee was tempted to say *No, I thought I'd take up home economics this time and specialize in sewing.* "I could do some very important research with a PhD. Maybe make a difference."

"A difference in what? Flowers and vegetables?" his father snapped.

His brothers turned their gazes out their respective windows, not uttering a word.

Lee took a few seconds to compose himself before responding. "A difference in medical science. They are starting to do unbelievable things in genetic modification these days."

"And...so what?" Henry asked.

"So...if we can figure out a way to manipulate DNA molecules to produce modified plants, maybe we can do the same in animals and humans."

"I'll ask it again. So what? Where's the money in it?"

"We're here," his mother said, putting an end to the conversation.

Mourners streamed into the funeral home. Lee's father opened his door to exit the car.

"Wait," Lee's mother said.

"What?"

"We're not going in."

"Why?" his father asked. Lee could tell he was annoyed.

"I just can't."

"Abigale, we drove all this—"

"I know. But I just can't go in. Please. Let's go home."

"We're going in."

"No. We're not." Her voice was soft, but her statement was resolute.

Lee and his brothers looked at each other in disbelief.

"Shall I tell the other driver to turn around, Mother?" Bennett finally asked.

"Yes," his mother said.

No one uttered another word on the never-ending ride back to the Winekoop household. Once there, everyone went their separate ways.

Lee went into his bedroom. Propped up against the desk lamp was a sealed envelope with his name on it. Inside was a letter written on crème-colored stationery with the insignia nos printed in gold-embossed lettering at the top. He scanned to the bottom of the page—it had been signed "Nelson."

My Dear Lee,

For reasons you may never appreciate, I have asked your mother not to tell you about my health issues until after I'm gone. If you are reading this letter, that time must have arrived.

I didn't want you to hear about your inheritance from someone who was completely unfamiliar to you, so I am telling you about it in this letter. That said, I regret not having been closer to you. Someday you'll understand why.

My estate will be divided ten ways, and you are among the beneficiaries.

There is a piece of land in Harvard, Illinois I own, 684 acres to be exact, that I want you to have. Now, that may not seem like a lot to you right now, but I predict, after an appropriate length of time, you will know just what to do with it to make it worthy. And I want to help you with that, too, so I have put $500,000 in a trustee-managed account for you.

I have significant faith in you, Lee. I know you won't let down your mother, yourself, or me.

Sincerely,
Nelson

Lee curled up on the bed, and finding the letter's content too overwhelming to fully digest, he fell asleep, fully clothed.

7 | No Trespassing

Lee awoke the next morning temporarily immobilized by an intense headache. He lay in bed, occupying himself with mindless thoughts, until the headache gradually subsided.

He was even more bewildered by the content of Uncle Nelson's letter after sleeping on it. The most troubling aspect of it was the line, "I know you won't let down your mother, yourself, or me." Lee had spent his entire life letting people down. After rereading the letter and not understanding it any better, he shoved it into a pocket of his backpack.

The thought of going downstairs to his family made the situation even more unsettling. He had no idea whether his parents were aware of what the letter said. Lee took his time showering and getting dressed. Then he drew in a deep breath and prepared himself for the worst.

As he descended the stairs, he heard his mother say, "Stop. We don't know that for sure, Henry."

His parents and brothers, all sitting at the dining room table drinking coffee, stopped talking when he entered the room.

"It's about time," Henry said.

"Sorry. I must have overslept."

"So you read Uncle Nelson's letter?" Henry asked.

"Henry, give him a chance to get settled," his mother said. "What would you like for breakfast, dear?"

"I'm not very hungry, thank you." He glanced at his father.

"So?" Henry asked.

"He writes a nice letter."

"I mean what did you think of what he had to say?"

Now Lee was sorry he had been the last to come down. They probably all knew what each other had inherited.

Lee turned to his brothers. "I assume we got the same letter," he said as he nervously tapped his fingers together under the table. They shrugged. "So what did you two think?"

Nelson spoke first. "We always knew he was wealthy, but half a million each?"

Lee tried not to let his sigh of relief be heard. "Right. That's how I felt too."

He didn't know why his brothers were looking at him so strangely but figured it had something to do with the conversation that had transpired prior to his joining them. He felt left out—but that was nothing unusual.

Henry grunted. "Well, I can predict how you and Bennett will handle your inheritance," he said to Nelson, "but how about you, Lee? What will be—"

"Henry, can't you give him time to—"

Henry got up from his chair. "I'm going to the office," he said, leaving everyone else speechless.

"What is he so angry about?" Lee asked.

No one answered.

"Did I miss something this morning?"

"No, dear. You didn't miss anything," his mother responded. She looked tired, her face more pallid than usual. "Are you going back to Lake Geneva, Lee? Or will you be staying here for a while?"

He was convinced they all knew something he didn't, and suddenly he felt like an intruder in his own home. "I'm going back, Mother. I just need to gather my things."

"I wish you'd stay." She reached out and touched his arm. "I could use the company."

"Let him go, Mother," Nelson said with little emotion.

That was all Lee needed to hear. He got up from the table and faced his mother. "I'm going to be on my way now. I've got a lot of thinking to do. I'm very sorry about Uncle Nelson. I know you were very close to him. I'll call you in a few days."

No one else said a word.

Lee felt bad about not staying. His mother had never reached out to him like that, making him feel that much worse.

He wondered whether he would have learned how his brothers' inheritances were structured if he had stuck around longer, but the liklihood they may have received theirs in cash, while his had to be managed by a trustee, was probably better left uncertain. He was curious what they had gotten in addition to the money but figured maybe that too was better left unexplained.

He thought about the most puzzling aspects of the letter on his drive home.

"For reasons you may never appreciate, I have asked your mother not to tell you about my health issues until after I'm gone."

What reasons would I not appreciate? What does that even mean?

"I regret not having been closer to you, and someday you'll understand why."

Did he say the same thing to Nelson and Bennett in their letters?

"I predict that after an appropriate length of time, you will know just what to do with it to make it worthy."

An advanced degree in horticulture aside, what can I possibly do with 684 acres of land? Apparently, Uncle Nelson was able to predict I would know what to do with it to make it worthy. How does one make land worthy? And where is Harvey anyway? Or was it Harvard?

"I have put $500,000 in a trustee-managed account."

If that means what I think it means, a trustee will have control over how I use the money. Is the money somehow tied to making the land worthy?

"I know you won't let down your mother, yourself, or me."

How about letting Father down? Maybe Uncle Nelson knew I already had that one covered.

The more he thought about it, the more he surmised the man was rather brazen to be putting such pressure on someone he hardly knew.

* * *

The next morning, Lee received a call from his late uncle's attorney. The man advised him of the exact location of the property he had inherited and gave him contact information for Basil Stonebugger, the trustee assigned to his account.

As soon as Lee got off the phone, he got in his car and drove twenty miles to Harvard. On the outskirts of town, there was a sign that read:

Welcome to Harvard, Illinois
Milk Center of the World
Population 5,279

It soon became apparent where the town had gotten its moniker—there were dairy cows everywhere.

His uncle's attorney had told him it was a large piece of fenced land on the east side of town, easy to find because of the license-plate-sized signs displaying his uncle's initials, NOS, that were clipped all along the fence line.

He drove down Diggens Street toward the outskirts of town. When he saw his uncle's monogram, he slowed down, taking in the vastness of it. After continuing another mile until reaching Attenberg Road, he turned left and went another mile. He tried to imagine why his uncle had put so many signs around the property: there had to be at least a hundred of them. When he reached the end of the fence line, he pulled over and got out of his car. Unable to see the whole property from this vantage point, he hopped the fence and walked into the scruffy vegetation for a better look.

Twenty minutes later, when he had reached the highest point of the acreage, he realized the property was a mixture of wildflowers, prairie shrubs, grasses, and several small groves of trees. He stood there for several minutes, enjoying the cool breeze against his face, the sound of distant songbirds, and the satisfying feeling of standing on earth he actually owned. When he saw movement in the grass ten feet from him, he froze. And when he saw a black cat peeking from behind a low shrub, he laughed.

"Hey there, fella. What are you doing on my property?"

The cat ran off.

He scanned the property from one end to the other. "Now what the hell am I supposed to do with all this?" he said aloud.

Sighing deeply, he turned around to head back toward his car. About twenty-five feet in front of him stood a uniformed sheriff, his gun drawn, muscles bulging beneath his shirt.

"You're trespassing, son," the officer declared without removing his dark wraparound sunglasses.

Not exactly the Harvard, Illinois, greeting Lee had expected.

He put his hands in the air. "Actually, I'm not, Officer. You see, I—"

"Shut up. Kneel down, and put your hands behind your back."

He did as he was told. The officer cuffed him, then helped him to his feet and patted him down.

"I can explain why I'm here, Officer."

"You can explain it at the station." The officer guided him along the fence line back toward the road.

"What about my car?"

"It won't go anywhere."

Lee got into the back seat of the sheriff's car and kept silent on the ride to the station, his heart pounding high in his chest.

When they arrived at the station, Lee was escorted to a room no bigger than his Lake Geneva bedroom. The nameplate on the desk read Bernard DeRam. The sheriff removed the cuffs and asked Lee for his ID. Lee handed over his driver's license.

The sheriff stared at the document and took off his hat to reveal a military-style flat top haircut. "Winekoop," he said. "Now would you like to tell me what you were doing trespassing on that property? And don't lie to me. If there's one thing I hate, it's a liar."

"Nelson Sedgwick is, I mean *was,* my great uncle. He left me that property in his will."

DeRam stared at him with a skeptical eye. "The man who owns that property is not a Sedgwick. That's how much you know. His name is...never mind what his name is. Who do you take me for, boy, some kind of moron?"

Lee thought for a moment before responding, realizing he had better be careful what he said. "We can call my uncle's attorney. He'll vouch for me."

"*We* don't have to call anyone. *You* need to prove you have the right to be on the property. That's how it works around here. Do you have a deed?"

"I don't have it yet, but if you allow me to call my uncle's attorney, like I said, I am sure he will straighten things out."

The sheriff pointed to the phone. "Make your call."

Lee explained his situation to the attorney, then turned to DeRam and asked, "Would you like verbal or a faxed written verification that I am the legal owner of the property?"

"Gimme the phone," he grunted.

The sheriff took the phone and said nothing for several seconds. "How do I know you're even legit?" After a few more seconds, he said, "No, that won't be necessary. Goodbye."

He slid Lee's license across the desk. "You're free to go."

"What about my car?"

"What about it?"

"It's across town. How am I supposed to get there?"

"It's not that far. You can walk, can't you...you being a Winekoop and all?"

Lee held his breath for a moment, wishing he could knock the mile-high chip on the sheriff's shoulder right off.

"Thank you, Officer. I hope you enjoy the rest of your day." He turned toward the door and left the station. "Asshole," he said under his breath when he was ten steps outside of the building.

"What did you say?" Lee turned around to see DeRam in the doorway.

"I said I'm certainly going to enjoy the walk back to my car, Officer."

"You know, partner, it looks like you now own about twenty percent of this town, land-wise that is. I suggest you don't let that go to your head."

Lee smiled. "Wouldn't think of it." He gave the sheriff a sloppy salute before he turned toward the road.

It took him over an hour to find his car, having not paid attention to the location of the sheriff's station in relationship to where he had parked. When he finally reached the vehicle, he slammed his fist on the front fender, wincing in pain afterwards and getting angry with himself for hurting his hand.

Once in his Datsun, he headed straight for Deer Bottom Inn, thinking a cold beer was just what he needed. Not to mention a friendly face, like that of CJ, the sassy bartender.

But the bartender on duty was an older man...wearing no smile.

"What'll it be?"

"Budweiser."

He handed Lee the beer.

"CJ's not here today?" Lee asked.

"Not her shift."

So much for a friendly face.

Lee glanced at his watch. The bar closed at two. If CJ worked the second shift, that meant she probably didn't get to work until six or so. Disappointed, he finished his beer and went home to the lavish surroundings he hated more and more each day. As he drove up to the house, he pictured himself pitching a tent on his new property and living there instead, maybe next to the stream on the northwest corner.

Ha! I wonder what dear old Father would think of that.

"You'll know what to do with it to make it worthy," Uncle Nelson had written. A tent could be considered worthy...well, maybe not to everyone.

He headed for the study to find a dictionary.

Worthy, *adjective*
1. having adequate or great merit, character, or value.
2. of commendable excellence or merit; deserving.

Merit, *noun*
1. claim to respect and praise; excellence; worth.
2. something that deserves a reward or commendation; a commendable quality, act, etc.

Value, *noun*
1. relative worth, merit, or importance.
2. monetary or material worth, as in commerce or trade.

He ran out of words to look up, and he still didn't know how to interpret his uncle's message.

The phone interrupted his thoughts. Sonya entered the study to announce Mr. Basil Stonebugger as the caller. After a short conversation, Lee and Mr. Stonebugger had arranged to meet the following afternoon in Chicago. Lee looked forward to the meeting, hoping Stonebugger would be able to shed some light on what he was supposed to do with 684 acres of land.

Shaneta entered the study. "What would you like for dinner, Mista Lee?" she asked in her thick Jamaican accent. Shaneta, who looked to be in her fifties, had been with the family for more than ten years and knew what he did and didn't like to eat.

What he really wanted for dinner was one of Deer Bottom Inn's greasy cheeseburgers served to him by CJ, the only person in the world he could even remotely call a friend at this point.

"You know what I like, Shaneta. Just surprise me."

He didn't want to be there. He didn't want Shaneta to cook for him. He didn't want to run into the maid everywhere he went. He didn't want to see the groundskeeper mowing the lawn or trimming the damn bushes.

He decided to wait until after eight o'clock to head back to the inn. If he spent a few hours there, by the time he got home, it would be time to go to bed. A fitting plan.

As soon as he walked in, he glimpsed CJ behind the bar.

"What'll it be my friend? A Bud?" she asked before Lee had even sat down.

He nodded.

She had a toughness, yet also a softness, about her. "You got it."

He took the bar stool on the end between the wall and the flip-top opening on the bar that allowed the bartenders to go in and out, presumably the least desirable seat at the bar for most people. Lee liked it because it put a safe distance between him and the other customers.

CJ slid the glass ten feet down the bar, making Lee smile when it landed directly in front of him.

"I don't know how you do that every time."

"Years of practice," she said as she turned to wait on other customers.

A few minutes later, she came over to Lee and asked, "So what's new in Lake Geneva?" She said the name of the town as if it left a bitter taste in her mouth. He wondered if she wanted to talk to him because she enjoyed his company, or if the generous tip he had given the previous time had something to do with it.

"Actually, I spent most of today in Harvard. Do you know anything about that town?"

She seemed to tense up at that question. Half grimacing, half smiling, she said, "The only thing I know about that town, darlin', is their Milk Days."

"Their what?"

"Every summer they have this major celebration, because they're the milk capital of the world or something. At least that's what they claim. With a parade and a dairy queen and tractor pulls and—this will getcha—they have bed races."

"Bed races."

"I swear to you. I couldn't make that up," she said as she slipped clean wine glasses in the overhead racks. "They race beds, and they whitewash the streets...to look like milk, I guess. I took my kids there last year for the first time, and they had a ball, but the whole thing seemed kinda lame to me."

"Milk Days."

"Milk Days. Hey, do me a favor." She slid a quarter across the bar. "Play 'Livin' on a Prayer' for me, will ya?" She turned to wait on other customers.

When she returned twenty minutes later, she had a fresh glass of Bud in her hand. "On the house," she said and walked away.

He watched her banter with the other customers—animated, always smiling, and quick with the smart-aleck remarks. She talked in slang and enunciated her words poorly, but for some reason, he didn't find it displeasing coming from her. She had a figure that would beckon most men, but it was her uninhibited, easy-going style, and that zany sort of charm she had about her that Lee found most attractive. Or maybe it was her honest face or her no-nonsense approach to things. CJ was everything he wasn't. Maybe that was it.

She made her way back to him. "You know what I think?"

Lee shook his head.

She leaned in and whispered, "I think you're new at this."

"With what?"

"You know, sitting at a bar in the middle of Boring Town USA and throwin' back a few cold ones with the locals."

He laughed. "So what gave me away?"

"Oh, just about everything, I suppose." She smiled big and clapped her hands. "Hey everyone," she shouted above the other conversations going on in the room. "This here's Lee, and he's new in these parts. Let's make him feel like he's one of us!"

Suddenly, he didn't like CJ so much.

The room got quiet. He studied the other customers, all of whom were gaping at him with solemn faces. He forced his mouth into a weak smile and held on to it just long enough to let them know he had a sense of humor. They all returned his half-hearted smile. He raised his eyebrows. They all raised their eyebrows. He picked up his glass of beer and took a sip. Everyone in the bar did the same. Lee raised his shoulders and let out an audible sigh. So did everyone else.

"Okay, okay. You got me," he said through a more genuine smile.

In amazingly close unison, they all said, "Okay, okay. You got me."

CJ doubled over in hysterics behind the bar.

"You're immature, CJ," he said.

Everyone said, "You're immature, CJ."

"Okay, how do I get this to stop?"

Someone from the opposite end of the bar yelled, "Buy the bar a round!"

Lee didn't know if the man was serious or not. "I think you should all buy *me* one for going along with this silly-ass prank!" he shouted.

With that, everyone laughed and went about their business. Joke over.

CJ waltzed over to him, still laughing, "So do you feel more at home now?"

"Very funny."

"You know, you're not half bad lookin' when you smile."

"Mm-hm."

"I think deep down you enjoyed it." She gave him a friendly smile. "Admit it."

"You think you've got me all figured out, don't you?"

"Maybe." She poured him another beer. "My father used to call it a little south of center."

"South of center?"

"You know, when someone isn't quite in the so-called normal range." She paused a moment. "Know what else my father taught me?"

"What's that?"

She leaned in close to him and whispered, "It should never be your goal to be normal. It should be your goal to be whole." She backed away from him and stared at him for a few seconds. "Ya know what? I think from now on I'm going to call you Soc. S-O-C, for south of center. No, Socrates. Soc for short."

"Soc?"

"Yeah."

"You're too clever."

"I try." She picked up a glass, washed it under the faucet, and dried it while she talked. "So, Socrates, what did you do in Harvard today that took all day?"

"I own some property there. I was checking it out."

"Like it was going to go somewhere?"

"First time I ever saw it actually."

"What kind of property?"

"A few acres of undeveloped land is all."

"How many is a few?"

He hesitated. "Six hundred and eighty-four."

CJ's eyes got big. "That's a lotta honkin' acres."

Lee shrugged.

Someone called her away from their conversation. Being one of only two bartenders in a standing-room-only bar, she had her hands full. He finished his beer and headed toward the door.

"Hey, Socrates."

He turned around.

"Keep laughing."

He shot her a quick wave and left the bar.

Lee thought about CJ's parting remarks on the drive home. He had to admit, he had enjoyed the laugh, even if it was at his own expense. He had never been one to laugh much. He would have said laughing just didn't come naturally for him...until now.

He realized that this night in the bar might have been the first time he had actually socialized with a group of people without feeling uncomfortable. The laughing had energized him. He wouldn't have anticipated that.

"You're someone who isn't quite in the so-called normal range," she had said.

His parents had spent a lot of money to get that diagnosis, and she had picked it up after their second casual meeting.

"It should never be your goal to be normal. It should be your goal to be whole."

He had to admit he had spent his entire life trying to achieve normal. What he hadn't realized until that moment was that he had been focusing on all the wrong things.

It amused him that he had spent most of his twenty-six years in one psychologist's office or another, and yet the most valuable piece of advice he had ever received had just come from a brassy twenty-something-year-old bartender named CJ.

8 | EBENEZER SCROOGE

B asil Stonebugger was a tall thin man with a bushy head of jet-black hair, a hawk-like face, and unusually large hands. He sat exceptionally erect in a big leather chair behind a massive desk where he began his discussion with Lee by defining the players.

"Your Uncle Nelson is called the grantor or the donor of the trust," he said in a grating voice. "You are the sole beneficiary, and I am the trustee." His speech was slow and deliberate, as though he felt Lee might not be able to keep up with or understand what he was saying. "You cannot withdraw any money from the trust without going through me."

He appeared to be wearing one of those invisible *I'm the only important one in the room* hats, the kind Lee imagined school principals wore when a kid was called into the office for doing something wrong. And the chair Lee sat in, which was too big for his slight frame, made him feel like *he* was in the principal's office.

He acknowledged what Stonebugger was saying with an occasional nod.

"Here are the terms and conditions. There are three." He looked down at a document on his desk and read from it. "Number one: Only the Trustee and the Beneficiary shall be privy to the terms and conditions of this trust. If the Beneficiary shares this information with anyone else, whatever is remaining in the fund, combined with proceeds from the sale of the land, will be donated to a charity of the Trustee's choosing. Two: Only the Trustee has authority to approve withdrawals from the trust fund, and the Trustee will approve withdrawals only if the money is used for the sole purpose of improving the Harvard acreage. And three: The increased value of the land must be shared with at least one other person, no earlier than one year and no later than three years after possession. If it isn't, whatever is remaining in the fund combined with proceeds from the sale of the land will be donated to a charity of the Trustee's choosing."

Lee stared at Stonebugger for several seconds without speaking.

"Questions?"

Are you kidding me?

"Mr. Winekoop?"

"First of all, did you know my uncle?"

"I knew him."

"Well, I didn't know him very well. Can you tell me something about him?"

"I think our time would be better spent discussing his will."

So much for this guy being accommodating. "Do you know why all this has to be a secret? The terms of the inheritance, that is. Why can't I share it with anyone?"

"I'm not sure."

"So you didn't speak with him about this before he died?"

"I didn't know I was named Trustee until after he died."

"So the way I understand it, you'll be making the decisions as to whether I can withdraw money from the trust based on whether you believe what I'm going to do with it will increase the value of the land. Do I have that right?"

"Yes."

"How will you do that?"

"I beg your pardon."

"How will you make that determination? What if I feel it will benefit the land value, but you don't?" A vision of the tent dashed through his mind.

"I have the legal right to make that determination."

"Mm-hm. And what's the part again about my having to include someone else in the deal?"

"It means just what it says."

His not revealing any more than he had to was getting annoying and made Lee suspicious of Stonebugger's intentions. For example, maybe he secretly wanted Lee to violate the terms of the trust in order to get all that money freed up for his favorite charity.

Or maybe I'm jumping to an unfair conviction.

"Can you give me an example?"

Stonebugger sat in silence for several seconds. "Let's say you decide to build a facility on your property where people with disfiguring diseases could get treatment. That would increase the value of the land because now the land would include a building. And other people, the patients, would benefit from it."

"Disfiguring diseases?"

"You asked for an example."

"Yes, I did."

"Do you have any more questions?"

Trust document in hand, Lee left Stonebugger's office, got into his car, and drove back to Lake Geneva. It took him most of the drive home to decide who the man reminded him of—the actor who had played Ebenezer Scrooge in the Broadway show his mother had taken him to in New York when he was ten.

I need to get that image out of my head.

9 | "You Can't Stay Here"

Lee awoke the next morning tired after a restless night. Thoughts about his inheritance, his family, and his life in general throughout the previous eight hours had left him knowing three things for sure.

One, the sooner he was out of the Lake Geneva house and in a place of his own, the better. Two, he didn't have enough in his bank account to keep him going forever, so he had to come up with a way to make a living. Three, he needed a long-range plan that satisfied the conditions of the trust fund. And maybe there was a fourth: Stonebugger wasn't likely going to make this complicated venture any less confounding.

As soon as he finished the breakfast Shaneta had prepared for him, Lee drove to the Harvard property for what he hoped was inspiration. The last thing he expected to see was the sheriff's car going in reverse along his property line on the outside of his fence.

Lee stood near the road waiting for the sheriff to reach him. When he did, the sheriff rolled down his window.

"Can I help you, Sheriff?"

"No."

Lee's heart pounded. He knew what he wanted to say but wasn't sure if the words would come out. "What brings you onto my property?" he asked.

The toothpick lodged between the sheriff's back teeth caused his speech to be slow and tight. "Not on your property." He tipped his hat. "Have a nice day."

"Before you go, Sheriff, can I ask you something?"

"Make it quick. I have better things to do with my time."

"Where would I get a permit to build a house on this property?"

The sheriff stared at him as if he had grown another head. "A what?"

"A permit to build a house. I'm assuming I would need a permit."

"Yeah. You'd need one all right." He removed his hat and scratched his head. "You know, I don't rightly know. Not my job." He put his car in gear.

"One more thing, Sheriff."

The sheriff gave him a *what-now?* look.

"Have a nice day yourself."

The sheriff glared at him before saying, "You know, boy, you're lucky there's only so much I can get away with wearing this uniform. I wouldn't ever push me when I'm in my civvies if I were you."

As soon as the sheriff disappeared from site, Lee leaned over and vomited...directly on his left shoe.

His stomach in a state of flux, Lee contemplated going to the back of the property to check out the general area from which he had seen the sheriff emerge. Instead, he went back to his car, cleaned off his shoe, and sat for a few minutes trying to sort things out.

The sheriff's intimidating behavior puzzled him—he was obviously no match for someone who wore a badge and carried a gun, so why would he feel the need to threaten him? Should he back off? Forget about doing anything with the land? Forsake the inheritance and go back to Illinois? The sheriff's behavior could be a sign of worse things to come, so maybe it would be a prudent decision to just forget the whole thing and go back to Illinois. He'd have nothing to lose.

Lee knew he was in over his head when it came to meeting the conditions of the trust. "The increased value of the land must be shared with at least one other person, no earlier than one year and no later than three years after possession." Who was he trying to kid? He had no clue as to how to make that happen.

He recalled a quote from one of his karate instructors. "The higher you climb the mountain, the greater your chance of falling, but the only chance you have for reaching the top." Visions of his past pathetic struggles with even the simplist things flashed through his head. That wasn't how he wanted to continue to live. He had to move on.

Up until now, Lee hadn't given too much thought to building a house on the property, and he had surprised himself with the permit question. But would a house pass the Scrooge test? That was the big question. He didn't see why not. He *had* said that a building would improve the value of the land.

Lee was tempted to walk the whole property to find the spot that screamed "Build a house here!" Instead, he decided to do the appropriate due diligence at the Lake Geneva Public Library.

The library served Lee well, as he spent hours browsing reference books and then finally checking out one he thought provided good basic information on building a house, covering everything from home styles, architects, permits, builders, budgeting, contracts, and insurance. Once home, he pored over the book's contents, and by the end of the day felt he had learned enough to work with an architect to design a home that suited him and the land.

Lee fell asleep that night in a blissful state. But while he tried to remain optimistic about what he was about to endeavor, based on his previous life experiences, he expected the feeling would be short-lived.

The following morning, when Lee called Mr. Stonebugger, his secretary answered the phone and informed him the attorney was not in. Lee explained his plan to build a house on his property and asked her if she knew or could find out what procedures he needed to follow. She explained he would have to submit his request in writing and then if it passed Mr. Stonebugger's initial approval, they would let him know what else to submit, like architectural drawings.

What does he care what style house I build? Ebenezer is sure being a pain in the ass.

* * *

As soon as Lee picked up the phone and heard his mother's voice on the line, his heart began to race. He hadn't talked to her since Uncle Nelson's funeral. He didn't know what frame of mind she would be in, and he feared she would ask him what he was up to. And while he had a plan of sorts, he didn't know if he could tell her about it based on the language in the trust document. He wished he understood it better.

"Hello, Mother." He chose to lie in order to avoid a long conversation. "You caught me just as I was headed out the door."

"Your father has business in Milwaukee on Thursday, and I was thinking of having him drop me off in Lake Geneva so we could visit."

He wondered what "visit" meant in terms of content and duration but was afraid to ask. "What time on Thursday?"

"We would get an early start and arrive around ten, ten-thirty. Then your father will go on to his business and be home later that evening. We would head back home early Friday morning. How does that sound?"

Lee tried to do the math in his head as to how many hours that meant for their visit, during which time he would have no place to escape. "Sure, Mother. That would be fine."

After hanging up, Lee reviewed the terms and conditions of the trust, which now confused him even more. He wasn't sure if he could tell anyone he was thinking of building a house on the land. His parents coming to visit only compounded the situation.

Telling them he didn't have a plan wouldn't go over very well. He supposed he could concoct a phony plan just to appease them. But then he'd have to keep building on it, and he didn't know how long he could keep that up. Or he could always tell them the truth, and then when Stonebugger found out about it, he'd lose everything. Then he wouldn't have to deal with any of this anymore. He wished that thought would stop provoking him.

* * *

Despite not having gotten much sleep for several nights, Lee managed to feign reasonably good spirits when his parents arrived two days later, something he unfortunately had had a lot of practice doing when living with them. Luckily, his father left within ten minutes of arriving.

"Shaneta is making us some tea, Mother. Why don't you get settled in your bedroom and then join me in the sunroom?" His take-charge conduct, albeit small by other people's standards, stunned him.

"Make sure it's herbal, dear," his mother said.

"Of course, Mother." Everyone who had ever worked under the rule of Abigale Sedgwick Winekoop was well aware she would drink nothing but herbal tea.

Ten minutes later, she joined Lee in the sunroom. "So, Lee, how have you been?"

"I've been fine. And you?"

"Tell me what you have been doing with yourself these days."

"Oh, a little of this, little of that. Getting to know this area better to see if this is where I want to settle down."

"Settle down?"

"Mm-hm." *Here it comes.*

His mother had a habit of sitting so straight in her chair, Lee worried that one day her body might freeze in that position. Today was no exception. "And what are you planning to do to settle down?"

"I'm not sure. I was thinking of maybe building a house for myself."

"Well, it is true you can't stay here indefinitely."

The comment took him by surprise. It didn't sound offhanded—it sounded as if it may have been something she and his father had discussed.

"Yes, I know. There are a few towns just south of here, some in Wisconsin and some in Illinois, that seem nice. Are you familiar with any of the neighboring towns?"

"No, dear. I can't say I am." A watery smile crossed her face. "I think Uncle Nelson owned a parcel of land somewhere around here. I wonder what happened to it after he died. I don't recall seeing it in his will."

"No?"

"Maybe he sold it. He owned so much. I couldn't keep track of everything."

Lee hoped she didn't notice his chest heaving.

They sipped their tea in stony silence for several moments before she said, "And then what?"

"And then what, what?"

"Let's say you find a nice piece of property and build a house on it. Then what?"

"Please, Mother, wouldn't that alone be enough of an accomplishment to tide me over for a little while? You wouldn't want me to burn myself out, would you?" He flashed her a wide smile.

"I know you're being facetious, Lee, but you know if your—"

"If Father were here, I wouldn't have said that."

She pursed her lips. "You know I only want success for you, don't you?"

"Yes, I believe you do. But will you please keep in mind that what you and Father and Nelson and Bennett believe is the definition of success, I may not."

"What is that supposed to mean?"

He rose from his chair, walked over to the wall of windows, and then turned to face her. "I'm just saying not everyone defines success in terms of money." He couldn't read her facial expression—somewhere between disbelief and controlled horror. "Sometimes you can make a positive difference in this world without making any money at it. I would say that could also define success." He had no idea what prompted him say that.

"Could you ask Shaneta to bring some more hot water, dear?"

Lee left the room and returned fearful of how this conversation was going to end. His mother had moved from her chair overlooking the lake to a sofa facing the interior of the room.

"Come. Sit here by me, Lee."

He didn't like the sound of that.

"I understand what you're saying about success. I really do. But you have to understand money is the essential foundation you need to amount to anything in life. All the other things—being happy, feeling good about what you do, making a difference in this world—you can have that too. But first, you need to be successful where it counts. You do understand that, don't you?"

"No, Mother, I don't. We all have different values, different priorities."

"What you're not hearing me say is that the Winekoops and Sam...the Winekoops of course, all have the same values."

"Who's Sam?"

"Look, Lee, I am just trying to smooth the way for you when your father arrives later tonight. Be prepared to hear the conditions for you continuing to stay here."

"Conditions?"

"He'll tell you about them."

"I think I'd rather hear them from you. Who's Sam?"

"There is no Sam. I don't know what I was thinking." She got up to leave. "I'm going to lie down for a while. I thought we'd go to the club for lunch. Have Helen wake me at eleven-thirty, will you please?"

"Yes, of course, Mother."

"And I wouldn't share your thoughts about what defines success with your father," she said before disappearing up the staircase.

After they returned home from lunch at the local country club, Lee's mother went back to her bedroom and didn't come back down until dinner, which was not unusual for her. For the evening meal, Shaneta prepared poached salmon, one of his mother's favorite meals but not something that appealed to Lee. He suspected Shaneta understood whom she had to please to keep her job.

They were drinking port in the living room when his father arrived. As his father poured a glass for himself, Lee's mother inquired about his meeting.

"This is how a business deal should go down." He turned to Lee. "Listen to this, Lee. You might learn something."

Lee responded with a weak nod. *Like I have any choice?*

Henry sat in the largest chair in the room, crossed his legs, and puffed out his chest.

"I walked into this deal prepared to purchase three commercial downtown buildings in the heart of the city. I came out with four, and the fourth one didn't cost me a cent."

"How did you manage that, dear?"

"Homework, Abbey. I did my homework. I hired a couple of good bird dogs to sniff out the owner's other properties and found out this fourth building had mostly short-term leases, and he's losing money on them. I already own a neighboring building where we just signed a new ten-year lease with Wisconsin Energy. They're going to take four floors where there are currently twenty other tenants whose leases are all coming up. I'll give them some attractive incentives to get as many of them as I can to sign a long-term lease in the new building, and everybody wins."

"But how did you get it for nothing?" Abigale asked.

"Because I played hardball in the beginning and gave them the impression I could back out of the deal without much provocation."

His father went on and on relaying a story that only proved to Lee just how manipulative his father could be when it came to money.

Henry stared at Lee. "If only you had inherited some of your—"

"Henry."

"Yes, dear." Henry got up and headed toward the stairs. "I'm turning in. This was a good day."

Lee's mother waited for her husband to be out of earshot before saying to Lee, "You might want to sleep in tomorrow...give us a chance to slip out before he remembers the real reason for our stopping by."

Lee really liked it when it appeared his mother was on his side.

Lee waited for his parents to leave the next morning and then typed the letter to Stonebugger. He kept it brief, thinking it wise not to divulge too much information—"the smaller the target, the less chance of being shot down"—one of his father's favorite sayings.

He felt somewhat transformed as he drove to the post office. Not completely grown up—after all, he still internally referred to his trustee as "Scrooge," and he didn't support himself, another factor he suspected disqualified him from bona fide adulthood. But at least he didn't feel like he was merely drifting along through life waiting for the next thing to happen.

I think I'm finally in the driver's seat. Now all I have to do is learn how to drive.

* * *

Stonebugger called him one evening the following week with a list of questions, all asked in the same dreadful monotone he had used in their first meeting. Lee answered as best he could and was told he would hear back from him by letter. As soon as he got off the phone, he told Shaneta he wouldn't be home for dinner and headed for Deer Bottom Inn.

Lee chose the route to the inn that took him by his property. When he was a half-mile from its nearest border, he saw a car pulling an enclosed trailer move from the shoulder onto the road. He slowed down and then followed the car to the corner of Attenberg Road and Route 173 where they both stopped for the Stop sign. As the other car turned left, Lee glanced inside and saw that the driver looked a lot like Sheriff DeRam.

Lee considered turning left and following the car, but thinking he was probably being paranoid about the sheriff, he decided against it and turned right, toward Rockton.

The inn was crowded. He half-listened to the song blaring from the jukebox while he waited for CJ to notice him.

"Hey, Socrates. What's cookin'?"

The sound of her voice calmed him. He acknowledged her question with a nod and smile.

She put her hand on the Bud tap and gave him an *Is-this-what-you-want?* look.

Lee nodded and mouthed, "And a menu."

She handed him the beer and said, "You don't need the stinkin' menu. You're having pizza."

"CJ?"

"Soc?"

"I've never had pizza before."

She stared at him. "You're shittin' me."

"Nope. Never had it. I wouldn't even know how to order it."

"What planet are you from, Dexter?"

"That's a provocative question."

"Ha! I'd respond to that if I knew what it meant."

"It means stimulating...but it can also mean aggravating."

"That's what I hate about big words—they have more than one meaning. Now, had you said that question was interesting, everyone would know what you mean. Looks like I'm gonna have to teach you to be more real, Soc." She walked away to wait on another customer.

Twenty minutes later, CJ brought him another beer and a pizza...fully loaded. He wished the light was better in the bar so he could identify what was on it.

"Don't look at it like it's a damn science project. Just pick up a slice and bite into it!"

By the time CJ came back to check on him, he had devoured half of the pizza.

"So?"

"It's good."

"Tell me you've never had mac 'n cheese either."

Lee shook his head.

"You're warped."

"Probably."

"You got any brothers or sisters?"

"Two brothers."

"Are they like you?"

"In what way?"

"In any way."

Lee thought about that for a moment. "Probably just the pizza and mac 'n cheese thing. Other than that, we're quite different."

If she only knew.

Later that evening, as he was driving home, Lee mused about the big loose snowflakes that had begun to fall from the night sky. It was an early snow, even by Wisconsin standards, the kind of snow he would liked to have played in as a child but was never allowed, something he had accepted at the time but now didn't understand.

When he got home, Lee got out of the car, threw his head back, and opened his mouth to catch one flake after another on his tongue. Twenty-four hours earlier, he had believed he was almost grown-up. Premature thinking apparently. What had CJ said? The important thing was to be whole. As far as he was concerned, catching snowflakes in his mouth got him closer to that goal.

Someday, when the time was right, he would thank CJ for the wisdom she had imparted to him.

* * *

Stonebugger's letter came three days later. He said he would approve the $50,000 withdrawal from the trust fund for the sole purpose of building a small house on the property, subject to his prior approval of the architectural plans, builder's contract, budget, and schedule.

Stonebugger wasn't about to let anything fall through the cracks—probably a good thing, Lee thought. *'Cause I really don't know what I'm doing here.*

The snow that had begun falling the night before had stopped, and the sun was trying to peek out from behind low cloud cover. He decided to take a run out to the property while the early-winter weather still allowed it.

He reached the property mid-afternoon, and as he walked the mile and a half from the road to the stream in the northwest corner, he started a mental To Do list.

1. Remove NOS signs.
2. Install gate; create parking space inside.
3. Check personal bank account balance.

He gazed out over the acres of snow-covered terrain. *This is my property. My property. Not Mother and Father's. Not Bennett's or Nelson's. It's mine to do with as I please. Well...almost.*

It wasn't cold enough to freeze the shallow stream, the width of which had now been reduced to no more than fifteen feet due to the accumulation of snow on its banks. It had a nice bend to it. He pictured a small house on the outside of the deepest part of the bend. Nothing fancy. Exactly the opposite, in fact. He wondered if log cabins were allowed. Although Scrooge probably wouldn't approve of that.

Lee headed toward the dense population of trees and brush in the northeast corner of the property. He walked into the wooded area for about a hundred feet before the brush made it difficult to navigate. Just when he thought about turning back, he saw a clearing ahead and trudged on.

The clearing took up three to four acres. Beyond it were more trees. He walked through it toward the edge of the property. A glint of sunlight reflecting off something in the distance—perhaps the metal of the fence—caught his attention.

Once through fifty feet or so of brush, he reached the fence and discovered a gate wide enough for a car. He opened it and entered the neighboring property, which had apparently been cleared in preparation for the next season's crop. He surveyed the fence line down to the road until his eyes rested on his car, a mile or so away, the same path he had seen the sheriff drive down days earlier.

4. Put lock on gate.

Lee closed the gate and walked back through the clearing, glancing down at the ground that had been revealed in the snow by his footsteps. He reached down and pulled up a plant consisting of mostly just roots—a series of long, thin grayish strands of plant life. Illinois had a wide diversity of native grasses and herbaceous plants, and because of his education, Lee knew all of them and their root systems. But he didn't recognize this one. He swished away the snow in a bigger area and uncovered even rows of the same species—clearly planted by someone at some point, and based on the clean cuts on the stems just above the ground, recently removed by someone.

Lee's expertise wasn't in agricultural crops, so he figured it was some grain or vegetable to which he had never been exposed. Curious as to how much had been planted, he kicked at the snow until all four edges of the field were revealed—roughly an acre. He reexamined the roots he had pulled up and then stuck them in his back pocket.

5. Identify crop in northeast corner.

Instead of driving home, Lee headed west, to the inn. When he walked in, he heard a song by Heart, a band that was starting to grow on him, playing on the jukebox.

> *In a wood full of princes*
> *Freedom is a kiss*
> *But the prince hides his face*
> *From dreams in the mist*

"Hey, Soc, what's crackalackin'?"

"Not too much, CJ."

"Regular brewski?"

"Sure," he responded, feeling like one of the guys...until he almost missed catching the beer CJ slid down the bar.

"Nice save, goober."

Very funny.

Thirty minutes passed before CJ got back to him. "Another one?"

Lee responded with a nod.

When she returned with the beer, he asked, "Do you know anyone from Harvard?"

She stared at him for a few seconds. "Next question."

"Just asking."

"I know some people."

"By any chance, do you know Sheriff DeRam?"

CJ looked past him, at something far off...way far off.

"Sorry. I didn't mean to—"

She walked away before he could finish his sentence.

Lee slipped out of the bar without drinking the rest of his beer, wishing he hadn't asked her the question. The last thing he wanted to do was alienate his only friend.

* * *

It didn't take long for Lee to discover he didn't have much choice in architects if he was to stay local. In fact, the closest one who would even consider a small project like the one he had in mind was in Rockford, and he wasn't thrilled about coming all the way to Harvard to see the property. It was only after Lee said he would pay him for his travel time, gas, and any other expenses he incurred that he agreed to do it.

Dennis Freborg, President of Freborg and Sons Architects, met Lee on his property the following week. He brought with him his grown son, David; five-year-old grandson, Duane; and his German shepherd, Gunther.

Lee led them to the northwest corner of the property where he pictured building the house. "What do you think?" he asked Dennis.

"I like the location. It has high elevation, and there's the stream and all. It could be quite charming, but have you thought about water, your septic system, and utilities, not to mention a long driveway. One good snow, and you could be grounded for a while."

Lee hadn't thought about any of those things.

"Look, I can produce plans for any type of house you want, but you'll have to figure out all these other things before you decide where to build it."

"Can you recommend a good builder?"

"That I can do. Earl Lundberg is one of the best in the area. He's reasonable, and he takes on small projects. I've worked a few jobs with him."

They were heading back toward the road where the cars were parked when Gunther started running off toward the woods near where Lee had discovered the gate a few days earlier.

"Gunther!" Dennis shouted. The dog kept running.

"I'll get him," his son said. "C'mon Duane."

Little Duane thought it great fun chasing after the dog, laughing his way through the tall grasses and shrubs, many of which were as tall as he was. Lee and Dennis followed them, walking more slowly.

"I haven't seen Gunther run like that since he was on the force."

"The force?"

"Gunther was a K-9 on the Chicago police force for five years. I took him in when he was ready to retire."

"Really? What did he do there?"

"Search and rescue. Sniffing out bombs, dead bodies, drugs, accelerants, stuff like that."

"Pretty impressive."

When they reached the edge of the wooded area, David, Duane, and Gunther emerged from it, heading back toward them. David had Gunther by the collar.

"I've never seen him act like that," David said. "He went berserk. Like maybe his training kicked in."

"Gee, I hope there aren't any dead bodies back there, Lee."

Lee laughed. "I hope not!"

* * *

Lee met with the builder three days later to talk about the issues Dennis had raised. Lee liked him from the start, and after he answered all the questions Lee had gleaned from the book he had borrowed from the library, he felt Earl would be a good choice.

Lee asked him what he thought about building a log cabin.

Earl shook his head. "You'll have nothing but problems, believe me. I wouldn't recommend it. If you want something simple and different, how about an A-frame?"

"What's an A-frame?"

Earl held up both hands, fingertips together, wrists apart. "Steep roofline that comes down close to the ground, like the letter A. Some would say they're no longer in style, but I like building them. Not much living space, but what's there is cozy. Ask Dennis about them."

"Thanks, I will."

When Lee got home, he was just entering the house through the garage when he heard the phone ringing. He waited to hear either Shaneta or Sonya's voice but instead the phone continued to ring. When he reached the kitchen, he answered it.

"Winekoop residence."

"Lee?"

"Mother?"

"Why are you answering the phone?"

CJ's face appeared in his mind's eye. "'Cause I live here?"

"Where are Shaneta and Sonya?"

"I have no idea, Mother. I just walked in the door."

"Where were you?"

He didn't answer right away.

I'm twenty-six years old, almost twenty-seven, and I have to answer to her as to where I've been?

"I just got back from drinking all afternoon in town where I blew all my money in a poker game and then wound things up with a real nice hooker."

"Lee! What's gotten into you?"

"Sorry, Mother. That was just my attempt at a little humor. I was out, that's all."

"Why don't you call me back when you can be a little less offensive."

"I'm sorr—" Click. She had hung up.

11 | "Ditch the Rich Boy"

After considering several scenarios as to how he could pull off developing his land in complete secrecy, none of which seemed plausible, Lee decided he had to tell his parents about it. He called Stonebugger for guidance.

"Hello, Mr. Stone...bugger," he stumbled over his name, pulling him back to his awkward teenage years when talking to adults made him so nervous he couldn't always get the words out.

"Yes, Mr. Winekoop." His voice sounded even more stilted than usual.

Lee asked him if it was permissible to tell his family about the inheritance of the land.

"Did you check to see what the trust document says?"

I wouldn't have called you if I could decipher it myself, Scrooge.

"Yes, I did, but I would like your interpretation, if you don't mind."

Lee waited patiently while he listened to the sound of papers shuffling.

"Since the manner in which you acquired the land is not part and parcel to the terms and conditions of the trust, it would be permissible to tell others how you acquired it."

A simple "yes" was all I needed.

"And what about putting a house on it? Same thing?"

"Yes."

His next call was to his mother.

"Hello, Mother?"

"Lee?"

"Yes, it's me."

"It is I."

"It is I." He pictured CJ rolling her eyes. "There's something I need to get off my chest."

"Are you in a less sarcastic state of mind today, dear?"

"Yes, and I'm sorry about the other day. I don't know what got into me."

"I'm listening."

"After Uncle Nelson died, as you know, we all inherited a piece of his estate."

"Yes, of course."

"Well, I never divulged everything I inherited from him. I didn't know if Bennett's and Nelson's inheritances were similar to mine, so I just never said anything."

"What are you getting at, Lee?"

"Uncle Nelson left me some land not far from here, in Harvard, Illinois." He waited for her response. It took several seconds.

"How much land, dear?"

"It's 684 acres."

"I wondered what had happened to his promised land."

"His what land?"

"His promised land. That's how he referred to it, but he never did reveal its exact location or what he was going to do with it. But I do remember the acreage for some reason. When he died, and it wasn't mentioned in his will, I thought maybe he had sold it somewhere down the line."

"What about Bennett and Nelson?"

"What about them?"

"Did they get anything beside the money?"

"No, just the five hundred thousand. That's a large piece of land."

"Yes, I know." He paused. "I'll make good use of it."

"I hope so. Have you done any more thinking about what you want to do?"

"No, Mother. I've been thinking about the land."

"Mm-hm."

After they hung up, Lee wasn't sure how to interpret his mother's reaction to his telling her about the land. At the very least, he had expected her to comment on his receiving more from his uncle than his brothers had.

Lee went to the dictionary in the study and looked up "promised land."

A longed-for place where complete satisfaction and happiness will be achieved.

The definition was a little too lofty to fully comprehend, but it did seem to fit in with the letter, Lee thought, especially his uncle's statement about Lee's doing something worthy with it. It surprised him to think Uncle Nelson had put that much thought, any thought at all, into giving him a piece of property he called the promised land, when he didn't really know him. And why him and not his brothers?

He created a mental list of additional questions to ask Stonebugger.

* * *

Lee had never been inside a hardware store nor had he ever pushed a shopping cart. He felt lost strolling up and down the aisles, observing one foreign object after another, each aisle with a different unfamiliar look, feel, and smell.

After wandering the store for ten minutes, a salesman approached him and asked if he needed help finding anything.

"No, thanks." He picked up a foot-long tool that had a jaw-like thing with teeth at one end and weighed a ton. The man didn't go away. Lee turned the tool over to view the other side. The man still didn't go away. He wondered if perhaps his Ivy League-style button-down shirt, khaki pants, and loafers gave off an *I really do need help* message, and that was why the salesman didn't leave.

"Here's the situation," Lee said. "I have a couple miles of fence line with small signs attached every hundred feet or so. I'm not sure how to remove them."

The man glanced down at the tool Lee held in his hands. "Well, for starters, not by using a pipe wrench."

Lee put the tool back on the shelf.

"How are the signs attached?" the man asked.

"They have holes in each corner and a heavy metal thread has been twisted into them and attached to the fence."

"Chain-link fence?"

"Pardon me."

"Follow me." The man led the way to the next aisle to a display of sample fencing. "Does it look like this?"

"Yes." Chain-link. He would have to remember that.

"If you have a sign every hundred feet on two miles of fencing, that's going to take a while to remove them by hand. Why do you want them removed?"

"I just acquired the land, and I want to remove the previous owner's name."

"May I make a suggestion?"

"Sure."

"It would be a lot faster to paint over the name. Are the letters raised?"

"I'm not sure."

"If they're not raised, then the right color paint will cover the lettering so no one will be able to read it. And then you could always paint your own name on the signs if you want."

"I could do that?"

"Wouldn't be that hard. You could use a stencil."

Lee's expression must have screamed *I have no idea what you're talking about.*

"Follow me," the man said.

They reached the ready-made stencils located on the other side of the store. The man picked up one that read Private Property.

"You could have something like this made with your name or whatever it is you want painted on the signs. One swipe of a paintbrush and you've got yourself a new sign."

"Where would I go for that?"

"Let me ask you this. Do you like the idea of putting something new on the signs or would you rather remove them altogether?"

"I'm not sure." The idea of branding his property appealed to him, but replacing his uncle's initials with his, LOW, was out of the question, and the thought of painting *Winekoop* on all the signs seemed too...something.

"Know what I would do?"

Lee shook his head.

"I'd buy a pair of heavy-duty pliers, and then try removing the metal ties from one sign. See how long it takes and how it looks, and then do the math to estimate how long it would take to remove all of them. That could be your deciding factor. If you decide to leave them on, check to see if the letters are raised, in which case you can't do much with them except cover them up with a coat of paint. But if they're not, come back here, and by then I'll have a contact for you to get a stencil made. Make sense?"

"Yes."

They walked over to a display of pliers. The man picked up a large one and handed it to Lee. It was heavy and unwieldy. He was too embarrassed to ask the man how to use it.

"Is there anything else you need today?"

"I need a lock for a gate."

"What kind of gate?"

"The one on the chain-link fence."

He showed him a variety of locks two aisles down. Lee picked one he thought would fit.

"Will that do it then?"

"I think so."

The man reached out to shake his hand. "I'm Lenny, by the way. Lenny Vinik. Come back any time you need help."

Once in his car, Lee took a deep breath. He came from a family that hired others to do everything for them. What was he thinking? Even scarier, what would his parents and brothers think if they knew what he was attempting to do? More ridicule, no doubt.

Lee drove to his property and parked his car in the usual spot on the side of the road. Pliers in hand, he walked to a section of fence that was obstructed by a clump of high brush so as not to be seen by anyone passing by. If he was going to make a fool of himself, he wanted to do it in private.

The lettering on the signs was not raised—good start. The ends of the metal ties that pinned the sign to the fence had been twisted together several times after having been woven through the hole in each corner of the sign and then through a link in the fence. Someone must have spent a lot of time installing them. A lot of time.

He opened the pliers. Something clicked. He tried to close them, but they wouldn't close. "Okay, what did I just do?" he said out loud.

He fiddled with the pliers until they closed back again. "This is not going to go well," he muttered.

The sun was low in the sky. Lee glanced at his watch—4:33 p.m. He'd have to work fast before it was too dark to see what he was doing. He held the pliers open, grabbed the end of one of the ties, and tugged on it. His left hand slipped off the pliers, which fell to the ground with a heavy thump. He picked it up, planted his feet wide apart, and went in for another try at it.

After several more failed attempts, he glanced at his watch again—4:57. Twenty-four minutes, and he didn't have even one tie off. And he had cut the side of his hand on a rough spot on the fence. And his arm ached from the weight of the tool. And he knew he was not likely to ever get even one sign off the fence.

Giving up on the pliers project for the time being, he headed toward the back corner of the property to the gate.

Even in the scant light, Lee could see two sets of footprints in the snow ahead of him. As he got closer, he could see two sets of man-sized prints going in opposite directions but were likely made by the same person. He followed them through the large clearing—the same clearing where he had pulled up the mystery roots—to the gate. They continued on the other side of the gate and then stopped...right next to a set of tire tracks.

He closed the gate and affixed the lock he had bought.

* * *

CJ greeted him in her usual style. "If it isn't Socrates. Lookin' for a Bud?"

He nodded, smiled, took his favorite stool at the end of the bar, and waited for his mug to come sliding down the bar toward him. Instead, CJ walked it over to him.

"Com'ere. You've got grease or something on your face." She took a napkin and dabbed at his cheek, then examined his hand. "What the hell! Have you been in a fight?"

Lee laughed. "Yeah, with a pliers."

"Let me guess. The pliers won?"

"Something like that."

She walked away and came back with several Band-Aids. "Here. I don't want you getting any blood on my bar."

"Can I ask you a personal question?"

"Shoot."

"What is that you're wearing on your legs?"

"Get with it, Soc. They're leg-warmers."

Inside?

"CJ!" someone yelled from the other end of the bar. "Phone."

CJ walked away and picked up the phone, her back to Lee. After several seconds, she turned around, tore off her apron, and said to the other bartender, "Cover for me. Travis is in the Emergency Room." She ran out of the bar.

Lee followed her out into the parking lot and called to her to wait up.

"Can't talk now. My son broke his leg," she said, without looking back.

He caught up to her as she was standing next to her car, an old beat-up gold Camaro. "Let me drive you. You're too upset."

"No. I need my car." Her hand was shaking so badly, she struggled putting the key in the door lock.

"Let me drive you. We can take care of your car later."

She stared at him for a long moment before consenting. "Okay, let's go."

Lee guided her toward his Datsun. "What hospital?"

"Swedish American. I know how to get there."

Lee tried to calm her down on the fifteen-mile drive to the hospital. "How did it happen? Do you know?"

"Frankie said he fell out of a tree."

"Frankie?"

"My sister. She was watching them."

She had two sons. Travis was the younger one, only six. Wayne was nine. She explained Travis was the more rambunctious of the two, a child who would try most anything without any forethought. Wayne, though older, was less assertive, more predictable, and much easier to parent.

When they reached the entrance to the ER, CJ had her door open before Lee even brought the car to a complete stop. Lee parked his car and went inside to find CJ.

The ER was very crowded, and hospital staff were busily scurrying around. From what Lee could discern, there had been a serious car pile-up on Route 51—people were lined up on gurneys in the hallway outside of the treatment area. Lee had never been in an emergency room before, and the combined smells of rubbing alcohol and disinfectants made him feel lightheaded.

Soon he heard CJ's voice and followed it to one of the treatment bays.

"May I come in?"

CJ sat on the bed, one of her hands on a young boy's thigh and the other one pushing his tousled sandy-colored hair off his forehead. He had an *I-don't-know-what-all-the-fuss-is-about* look on his face.

Without taking her eyes off him, she responded, "Sure. Come on in."

A woman who appeared to be older than CJ stood in the corner with a child who Lee assumed to be CJ's other son, Wayne. The woman surveyed Lee with a skeptical eye.

"Everything okay?" he asked CJ.

"Yeah. He's okay." She turned toward Lee and introduced him—as Socrates—to her sons and her sister, Frankie.

He held out his hand. "Nice to meet you, Frankie."

She shook his hand. "It's Francine."

He didn't know quite how to read her. They didn't look much like sisters. CJ was tall, blond, and curvy. Her sister was shorter, brunette, and wore conservative loose-fitting clothing that hid her figure.

CJ's attention was on Travis. "It was a bad break, a compound fracture," she told him.

An hour and a half later, Travis was ready to be released. They all walked out of the hospital together, Travis on crutches, having mastered their use very quickly.

"How do you want to do this?" he asked CJ. "Do you want me to drive you and Travis home?"

"What about my car?"

"After you get him settled, I can drive you back to the bar so—"

"The restaurant," Francine corrected him.

"I mean restaurant, so you can pick up your car."

"Okay."

CJ and Travis sat in the back seat. Wayne rode with Francine. CJ gave Lee directions to her house.

She lived thirty minutes away on the outskirts of town where most of the houses sat on at least an acre of land zoned as farmland. Many of the homesteads included a barn or two, including CJ's. A long dirt driveway led to her house. CJ pointed to a section of yard that appeared to serve as a parking area. Francine pulled up beside him.

"C'mon in, Soc. Take a load off for a bit while I get things settled in," she told him.

The small clapboard house was in need of repair, with several missing shingles on the roof, broken downspouts, tattered screens, and sagging stairs leading to the porch. A variety of bikes and toys were strewn around the yard.

CJ led the way through a mudroom to the kitchen from which Lee could see the main living area. The house was small but neat and clean.

Once CJ got Travis settled in the living room, she, Francine, and Lee sat at the 1950s-style kitchen table on a variety of mismatched chairs.

"Want a brewski? I know I sure do." CJ went to the frig, pulled out two beers, and handed one to Lee. "Frankie doesn't drink."

Francine gave Lee a confused look. "So your name is Socrates? Really?"

CJ let out a loud guffaw.

"Not really. That's just CJ's nickname for me."

"I see."

"It's a long story," CJ added.

"I'm sure it is," said Francine. She turned to CJ. "Are you going back to work, hon?"

"I think he's fine. It's not like he hasn't been through this before. Will you be okay with him?"

"Sure. Go."

After they finished their beers, Lee led the way to his car and opened the door for her. "What's so funny?" he asked her when he caught her smirking.

"I am so not used to this."

"What?"

"A guy opening the door for me."

"No? I thought all men opened doors for ladies."

"Hey, who are you calling a lady?" Her laugh was loud and nervous.

Lee didn't know what to say, so he said nothing.

"It's just that I haven't been—"

"Hey, you don't have to explain anything to me," Lee responded before she could go any further.

"I know."

On the way back to Deer Bottom, he wanted to ask her about the boys' father, but didn't dare. There was no disputing they were brothers, but they didn't look much like CJ.

It occurred to him that, except for his mother, Catherine, and Robin a few times, he had never been in a car with a woman before. A surge of something rose up into his chest, soon followed by an all-too-familiar queasiness in his stomach.

CJ broke the awkward silence. "I appreciate you taking me to the hospital, Soc. I admit I was probably too upset to drive. My sons are my world, and when anything happens to them, well, I panic."

"Travis looked pretty comfortable on those crutches."

"This is his second broken leg. He's had two broken wrists and a concussion as well."

"Clumsy?"

"No. Fearless. He's a climber. Has been since birth. He'll climb anything if you don't watch him. Today, all it took was for Frankie to go into the house to the bathroom, and when she went back outside, he had managed to climb that big oak tree on the side of my house. I wish I could talk the landlord into trimming the lower branches for me, but..."

"I know someone who could do that for you." He had no idea where that came from.

"Really?"

"Sure, and he owes me a favor. I'm sure he'll do it for nothing." *I can't believe I just said that. Who do I know who can trim a tree?*

"Hey, that would be great. I suppose I'll have to—"

The sound of a blaring siren behind them interrupted her.

She turned around to look behind them. "Shit," she said under her breath.

Lee saw in his rearview mirror that a sheriff's car was closing in on him. "What did I do?" He slowed down and pulled over to the side of the road.

"I'm sorry, Soc. I really am."

He looked over at CJ. "Why are *you* sorry?"

Before she could answer, Sheriff DeRam appeared at his window, and before Lee could roll it all the way down, he shouted, "Get out!"

"What?"

"Do you need a translator, asshole? Get out of the car," DeRam barked, his chest puffed out proving he could probably bench-press more than Lee weighed.

Lee's chest tightened. As he got out of the car, he glanced down at the sheriff's gun in his side holster. The strap that held the gun in had been unfastened.

"What's the problem, Sheriff?" he asked.

"Shut up, and walk to my car."

Lee felt his heartbeat quicken and did as he was told.

"Get in the back seat, and stay there until I return."

DeRam slammed the car door and walked away, lingering for several seconds behind Lee's car before walking to the passenger door. Lee watched as CJ rolled down her window and spoke with the sheriff. Their exchange was highly animated.

After what felt like an eternity, the sheriff returned to his car and opened the back door for Lee.

"Get out."

Lee got out of the car and, for an instant, didn't know what to do. He opened his mouth to ask a question, but the sheriff interrupted him before he got a word out.

"You've got a broken tail light. Get it fixed. And while you're at it, why don't you keep right on goin' with your sorry preppy ass and get out of my town." With that, he got into his car and sped off, hurling up a surge of gravel in the car's wake.

Lee returned to his car to find CJ choking back tears. "What's wrong? What did he say to you?"

"Let's just go," she said through clenched teeth.

He had no experience dealing with someone else's emotions, let alone a girl's. Not knowing what else to do, Lee started the car and pulled onto the road. They drove for five long minutes before CJ broke the silence.

"He's such an asshole."

"I can't argue that point."

"He broke your tail light, you know."

"How do you know?"

"'Cause I heard it break while he was standing behind your car." She turned toward him. "Socrates, I don't know how to tell you this, but I think you had better start sleeping with one eye open."

"Why is that?"

"Because, my friend," she said with deliberation in her voice, "Bern is the father of my two children, and he is really pissed to see me with you."

Lee momentarily lost control of the car and let it veer toward the middle of the road for a brief moment. "He's what?"

"You heard me. I need to fill you in on a few things. Can we go somewhere to talk? Somewhere where he can't find us?"

The man has a gun.

"Like where?"

"Let's go somewhere over the state line, out of his jurisdiction...like Beloit. It's only a few minutes from here."

They didn't talk during the ten-minute ride to Beloit, Wisconsin. Once there, Lee parked his car behind a church, where it couldn't be seen from the road.

CJ took a deep breath. "Okay. Bern has had the hots for me for nine years, since I was sixteen. He was twenty-six at the time. I was pretty naive at sixteen, and having no parents to speak of, I was free to do pretty much as I pleased, so I hung out with him. Until my sister found out, that is. But by that time, we had already gone all the way, and well, nine months later, here's Wayne."

"You had Wayne at sixteen?"

"Well, I was seventeen by then. Anyway, my father was...well, we didn't know where he was, and my mother drank a lot, so Frankie helped me through the whole thing, and after Mom died, I moved in with Frankie, and she's helped me raise him."

That explained something about Francine's protective demeanor he had observed. Lee thought about having had the luxury of both parents, nannies, nursemaids, and tutors, and yet he still had a difficult time growing up. How on earth had she managed?

"That had to be hard to do," he said. "Where was DeRam? He didn't help you?"

"At the time, I thought we'd get married as soon as he found out I was pregnant. But, instead, the asshole booked it."

"Booked it?"

"Vanished. He left the sheriff's office for a while. I heard he was living in Wisconsin somewhere. Frankie convinced me I was better off without him."

Neither of them spoke for a long moment. Lee hoped she would continue with the story, especially about how Travis came to be. He couldn't imagine how DeRam could be Travis's father too, not after what CJ had just told him.

"Anyway, eventually I got the job at Deer Bottom and found this house to rent, and I thought I was getting my life back together when the jerk shows up at my door one night." She hesitated. "And he'd been drinking."

Her demeanor told Lee she especially didn't like talking about this part of her story.

"He told me all this stuff about how sorry he was for leaving me, that he still loved me and wanted to make a go of it. Be a real family. A whole lot of shit, that's all it was, but I saw through it and told him no."

"That must have taken some fortitude."

"Some what?"

"Guts."

"Yeah." She paused. "But it didn't work." She spoke the next sentence in slow, tight words. "Bern doesn't take no for an answer. He...forced himself on me."

"What?"

"I was so scared. Little Wayne was in bed upstairs, and all I could think of was he would hear the commotion and come downstairs and see us. Afterwards, I ended up kicking Bern...well, where it hurts, and he left."

"And then there was Travis?"

CJ bowed her head and responded with a nod.

Lee reached over and touched her arm.

"I didn't like that guy the minute I laid eyes on him, but now... What exactly did he say to you back there?"

"He heard Travis's name on the police radio and got to the hospital just in time to see us leave together."

"What did he say to you?"

"He went in to see Travis and—"

"What did he say to you?"

"He said if he ever catches me with you again..."

"What?"

"You'll get hurt."

"He can't make threats like that."

"Well, he just did."

"I caught him on my property, you know."

"You did?"

Lee told her about the time the sheriff cuffed him and brought him into the station.

"Like *you* were trespassing on *his* property?"

"Something like that."

"Asshole."

"Let me ask you something, CJ. Is it common knowledge that he's the father of your children?"

"I don't know. Obviously, Frankie knows, but other than her, I never told anyone. I've always just told people that their father isn't in the picture anymore. And he made it clear when I told him I was pregnant the first time that if I ever told anyone he was the father, I'd be sorry. But you know how gossip is."

"Is his name on their birth certificates?"

"On Wayne's, not on Travis's."

"Do they know?"

"No."

"What else did he say to you in my car?"

She stared out the side window.

"Tell me everything, CJ. I need to know everything."

"He said we belonged together, we could still make a good life together."

"And you said what?"

"I told him to go to hell."

"Anything else?"

CJ shook her head.

"What do you want to do?"

"Can you take me to work?"

"To get your car so you can go home, or are you going to finish your shift?"

"No, I'm going to go home. I'm too upset to work."

Lee took her back to the inn and watched as she walked to her car. When he saw her pluck a white piece of paper from underneath her windshield wiper, he got out of his car and approached her.

"What does it say?"

She handed it to him.

DITCH THE RICH BOY

She shot him a guarded smile. "You didn't tell me you were rich, Socrates."

Lee smiled back. "You didn't ask."

12 | "I Kid You Not"

ee tried to wrap his brain around CJ's story about DeRam. Things like that didn't happen in his family, or if they did, they weren't discussed. No one in his family talked as openly as CJ did on any subject, and the more he came to know CJ, the more he thought that might be why he liked her. But not in a romantic way, at least he didn't think so. Either way, he was now uncertain as to how much he should get to know her, for both his and her safety.

After dinner, when Lee went to the trunk of his car to remove the case of beer he had bought earlier, he discovered the shriveled plant he had uprooted from his property the previous month. Once inside, he retrieved a box of college textbooks from the back of his closet and pulled out a plant-identification guide that focused on root systems.

Nothing matched, but the deterioration of the specimen made it hard to tell. He wished Dr. Rad lived closer. He would know. He found it hard to believe his uncle had had anything to do with planting any kind of crop. But regardless of who had planted it, why would someone pick such a remote corner of the property?

* * *

With the end of the year fast approaching, Lee had to decide how he would spend Thanksgiving and Christmas. He was fairly sure he was expected to spend both holidays with his family in their Evanston home but felt this could be an opportune time to change those expectations. However, after careful consideration, and given the fact that he couldn't come up with a reasonable excuse for not doing so, Lee decided to go home for Thanksgiving—but not stay overnight. It meant being on the road a long time for such a short visit—an hour and a half each way, assuming the roads were clear—but Lee felt the compromise was worth it.

His mother made his decision about where he would spend Christmas easier when she told Lee the family would be spending the holiday in their New York apartment that year. He explained to her that he would have a difficult time getting away, being in the throes of planning the new house, an explanation she seemed to readily accept.

* * *

Eager to proceed with plans for his house, Lee met his architect at the property and told him that he and Earl had talked about an A-frame.

"I like designing them, and it looks like you have the perfect setting for one here, but some people, women in particular, don't like them."

"Why not?"

"There's usually just a ladder to the upstairs loft, which is normally the master bedroom. Women like stairs."

"Hmm. Well, that wouldn't bother me."

"Why don't you come back with me to my office, so we can talk about the scope of the project. Then I can price it out and draw up a contract."

After three weeks, Lee had enough of a plan for Stonebugger to sign off on, which he did. The fifteen-hundred-square-foot two-story A-frame house was to be situated in the northwest corner of the property, with a large loft master bedroom and bathroom on the second floor that had expansive windows facing southeast, giving Lee the broadest view of his land. A combination living room and dining room, two small bedrooms, a kitchen, and a bath would occupy the first floor.

The house would be built on a slight rise adjacent to the narrow stream that ran through that corner of the property. Tall pines provided a perfect backdrop, the blank canvas he needed for landscaping the rest of the area surrounding the structure.

* * *

Anxious to tell someone about his house plans, Lee drove to Deer Bottom Inn. But once in the parking lot, he had half a mind to turn the car around and return home without going in. He vacillated between being mindful of DeRam's stand and stay away from CJ and ignoring him. If he knew what CJ thought of him, it would help. If she thought of him as just some gawky misfit who didn't have anyone else to talk to, he would have no problem backing away. But if what they had was a burgeoning friendship, something he particularly valued, then why should he let some jerk get between them? Okay, so the jerk happened to be the father of her kids, but still...

He walked in and saw CJ behind the bar. Luckily, there was one stool open at the counter, and he plopped himself down on it.

"What's cookin', Soc?"

"Not much, CJ. Not much."

She flashed him one of her sideways smiles. "Then why do you have that shit-eatin' grin on your face?"

She had set the tone for the conversation, so he felt safe in proceeding. He reached out for the beer that was sliding down the bar toward him. "When you have a spare minute, I want to show you something."

CJ's spare minute didn't come until close to a half hour later. She wiped her hands on her apron and leaned up against the bar in front of him.

"So, whatcha got?"

Lee took out a reduced copy of the plans for the A-frame and watched her face as she flipped through the pages. "What do you think?"

"Yours?"

"It will be. I'm having it built on my property in Harvard."

"Pretty spiffy."

"Thanks."

"When do you start?"

"The contractor thinks he can start in June."

"No kidding."

"I kid you not." He had heard Johnny Carson say that on the *Tonight Show* once and surprised himself at being able to actually fit it into a conversation.

CJ shot him a smirk before she went to wait on other customers.

* * *

Every time Lee opened the trunk of his car, the scraggly roots he had pulled up from the corner of his property reminded him he wanted to get them identified. He decided to pay Dr. Rad a visit after seeing his family on Easter.

The closer Lee got to his parent's house on Easter morning, the more his stomach tensed up—like being seasick but without the sea. Everyone in his immediate family would be there for the noon meal, and at some point, he would have to tell them of his plans to build the A-frame. He practiced several possible speeches while he drove.

"Hi, everyone. Guess what. I'm building an A-frame house on the property Uncle Nelson left me. Isn't that just grand?"

"You know that property Uncle Nelson left me? Oh...you didn't know about that? Well, he left me a piece of property, and I decided to build a house on it."

"Hey, you elitists I call my family. I'm gonna do something I'm sure you would never do in a million years because you would think it's beneath you. And stupid. I'm going to build a fifteen-hundred-square-foot A-frame house on that land in Harvard, Illinois, that Uncle Nelson left me, in the middle of nowhere, and I'm going to live happily ever after in it. Now put that in your pipe and smoke it."

As he pulled into the driveway, the sheer sight of their three-story brick Georgian-style mansion caused bile to rise up into his stomach. Inside were thirteen rooms that had been furnished by the best decorators money could buy, each one holding painful memories no amount of money could extinguish.

A maid let him into the house. The first person he saw was his mother who was fiddling with an elaborate orchid arrangement in the front foyer.

"They should have been more generous with the orchids for this arrangement. Have you lost weight, dear? You look painfully thin," she asked Lee without looking up.

A flash of his father's image appeared and then disappeared behind her in the hallway. Before Lee could say as much as hello to him, he was gone.

"No, Mother. In fact I think I've gained a few pounds." *Thanks to beer and the wonderful junk food I've been getting at Deer Bottom.*

"Why don't you join the others in the front parlor. I'll be there in a minute."

He braced himself and entered the parlor. Nelson and his wife, Yvonne, were sitting on a French provincial sofa on one side of the enormous coffee table, with Bennett and his wife, Daphne, on the other. His father sat in one of the Queen Anne high-backed chairs. When his mother entered the room a minute later, she sat next to her husband. Lee suspected his brothers' collective five children were being kept somewhere out of sight by a nanny or two. Everyone sipped ice tea. He listened while his brothers talked about their wonderful, successful lives as their parents beamed with pride.

"It's just a small facility. They can accommodate a hundred cots," said Bennett about his newest project, a shelter on the south side of Chicago in one of the poorest Hispanic neighborhoods.

"Perhaps we could work together, Bennett," his mother chimed in. "As you know, I'm on the board of the Southside Food Depository. Why don't you call me on Monday, and we'll discuss it."

"It may go down in history as one of the most lucrative mergers in the pharmaceutical industry," said Nelson, talking about his latest project at work.

"And now we can buy that little summer cottage in Door County we've been eying," said Yvonne. Lee pictured the size of the "little" summer cottage to which she was referring—probably five times the size of his soon-to-be main residence.

"Did we tell you Odessa was selected to represent her class at the regional math competition in Springfield?"

Of course she was. She's a Winekoop.

After everyone had had a turn telling the others about their latest feats, all eyes turned to Lee, his father's stare the most intense.

"I suppose you're all wondering what I've been up to."

He decided to dive in...headfirst.

"I'm building a house in the town of Harvard, Illinois."

He waited for reaction...any reaction.

His mother broke the silence. "On Uncle Nelson's property?"

"Well, Mother, it's my property now...remember?"

"*Your* property?" his father asked, his tone just short of hostile.

"Uncle Nelson left it to me when he died."

Henry made a guttural sound. "I didn't know that."

"Neither did we," said Bennett. "How much property? And where in God's name is Harvard?"

"It's 684 acres, about twenty miles southwest of Lake Geneva."

"Never heard of it," Henry growled.

"Uncle Nelson referred to it as his 'promised land,'" his mother said.

"That's a joke."

"Henry! Please keep your comments to yourself."

Why would he change now, Mother?

"I don't know what Uncle Nelson had in mind for that property," his mother continued, "but I'm sure Lee will make the most of it. I think it's admirable you're building a house on it. And I can put you in touch with a highly qualified architect. I'll call him tomor—"

"I have an architect, Mother. He's local and knows the area."

"I see, and what about—"

"And I have a builder, too. Also a local."

"Oh. What kind of house are you going to build?"

"An A-frame."

"You're kidding."

"Henry..."

"I'm building a fifteen-hundred-square-foot three-bedroom A-frame house, nestled in a clump of tall pine trees next to a bubbling stream. In Harvard, Illinois. Milk center of the world. Population 5,279."

The silence hung in the air like morning fog.

And I've already been handcuffed once and dragged off my property by an arrogant sheriff who knocked up my new best friend...my only friend...not once, but twice, and—

His thoughts were interrupted by his father's abrupt exit from the room.

"Don't mind him, Lee. He just needs time to get used to the idea."

What idea is that, Mother? That now he's convinced there is no hope for his youngest son's success in life? You mean that idea?

Family conversation continued through their meal but was strained. His father's aloofness was disheartening and his mother's silence saddening. The children behaved exactly the way he and his brothers had behaved their whole lives at the dinner table—seen and not heard.

He was glad he had plans to visit Dr. Rad and availed himself of that excuse to leave right after he'd taken the last bite of dessert.

13 | RECLAIMING THE PASSION

During the four-hour drive down Route 55 to Dr. Rad's research facility, Lee reminisced about his intern days—the orchards, the experimental gardens, the vibrant red clover field he and Robin enjoyed working in the most. They were good memories. He supposed he was taking a chance Dr. Rad would be there, but since he lived on the premises and didn't celebrate Easter in his religion, he was fairly confident he would find him there, probably working if he knew him like he thought he did. He exited the highway and drove five miles to the long gravel road that led to the facility.

Lee parked his car, and not seeing any sign of life, wandered around the property behind the lab buildings to where several experimental gardens had been planted. What he saw shocked him. The massive grid of once meticulously maintained orchards and gardens was now overgrown with prairie grass, weeds, and saplings. Bittersweet vines strangled the trunks of the apple and cherry trees.

Dr. Rad's pickup truck, an old rusted-out Ford, sat in the middle of one of the orchards, its hood propped open and weeds growing through the engine compartment.

Lee walked to the largest of the four greenhouses. Most of its windows were broken. Peering inside, he saw nothing but dead plants.

Dr. Rad had devoted his life to those projects. Whatever had caused him to let it all go to ruin had to have been serious.

Lee wiped off some of the thick dirt on the back window of the main lab building where Dr. Rad had often spent the night. The twin bed, small kitchen table, and two chairs that he remembered so well were still there. He walked around to the front of the building and tried to open the door, but it was locked.

Lee's next thought was to get in touch with Robin to see if she knew anything. Luckily, he had kept her phone number in his wallet all these years. He drove to the nearest gas station and called her.

"You know, I think about you every once in a while, Lee. How are things going?"

They engaged in a bit of chitchat before Lee got to the subject at hand. He explained the state of affairs at Dr. Rad's research facility and asked her if she had any idea what had happened. She told him that the doctor lost funding for his work and had to leave the university. She had heard he was living with a relative in

Peoria, and said she would ask her father if he had any additional information. She promised to call Lee back if she found out anything more.

Images of the destroyed research facility nagged at Lee during his drive home. He regretted not having kept in touch with his former mentor. All that research down the drain...unless maybe he was able to get someone else to fund his work. He could only hope so.

* * *

Lee awoke with a start. The clock said three a.m. Wiping the beads of perspiration off his brow, he reflected on the dream he'd just had about Dr. Rad. The doctor had been much older—bent over, grey haired, and walking with a cane. A broken man. Not a typical dream for Lee, whose nightmares usually involved him walking down a dark alley with an axe in his hand or trying to locate a bathroom only to find the edge of a cliff instead.

Not able to fall back asleep, Lee went down to the kitchen, opened a bottle of Bud, and sat in the sunroom. The wide beam of the full moon reflected on the calm water like a spotlight. And that's when it hit him—how he could satisfy the third condition of Uncle Nelson's trust. He knew exactly what his next conversation with Dr. Rad would encompass. Now he just had to find him.

* * *

Several days later, Robin called Lee with an address in Peoria for Dr. Rad, but no phone number. The very next day, Lee set off on another four-hour excursion.

After driving past numerous cornfields and the Caterpillar world headquarters, he finally reached the heart of Peoria. He pulled into a parking lot to study the street map he had brought with him. He headed to Dr. Rad's house on Monarch Street and found himself in what was obviously a poorer section of town—mostly older clapboard homes in various stages of disrepair. Dr. Rad's street was empty except for a young woman pushing a baby carriage.

Lee climbed the few crumbled steps that led to the small front stoop of Dr. Rad's residence and pressed the doorbell.

A middle-aged Indian woman answered the door.

"May I help you?" she asked. Her accent was as thick as Dr. Rad's.

"I'm Lee Winekoop, a friend of Dr. Rad's. I understand he's living here, and I would like to visit with him."

"Hello, Mr. Winekoop. I'm Adishree. I'll tell my brother you're here," she said as she ushered him in. She left him standing in the small foyer, inhaling the distinct aroma of curry. When she returned, she led him into a small living room whose windows were covered by heavy drapes, making it difficult for him to see.

"Lee. Come in." The voice startled him. Dr. Rad was sitting in a dark corner of the room. A plaid blanket covered his lap. "It's good to see you. Sit down." He smiled with his mouth, but his eyes appeared sad.

Dr. Rad had aged considerably in the five years since Lee had last seen him. He was thinner and frail looking. The veins in his hands bulged like they were about to burst.

"How are you, Dr. Rad?"

Lee hoped his sad face did not reflect what was in his heart.

"I'm all right, Lee." He turned toward his sister and asked her to bring them some tea. The doctor looked back at Lee. "How did you find me?"

"Someone from the university gave me your address. I hope that was okay."

"They still send me materials—materials I don't need or want."

"What happened?"

"We didn't get funding renewed from our primary grantor, whose interests seem to be more in the area of technology these days. I couldn't find anyone else to sponsor me." He smiled. "This may come as a surprise to you, but I'm considered somewhat of a kook in most research circles." His voice went up an octave when he said the word *kook*.

Lee forced a smile. "What about all your research?"

Dr. Rad shrugged.

"When did this happen?"

"It seems like an eternity ago, but I suppose it was just about eighteen months."

"I went to your lab looking for you."

Adishree entered the room with a tray, poured tea for the two men, and then disappeared.

"Dr. Rad, if someone were to sponsor you again, could you pick up where you left off?"

"No one will sponsor me. My ideas are too farfetched. And I have a difficult time presenting them." He slumped even further down in his chair. "Sometimes, even I think they're unrealistic."

Lee hoped the determined, albeit eccentric, scientist he had worked with several years earlier was still somewhere in there. "Let's say someone *was* willing to sponsor you. What would you say to that?"

"Having the rug pulled out from under me was devastating. I'm too old to go through that again."

Lee leaned forward. "Let me tell you a little something about myself. I grew up with family members very different from me—every one of them. They all thought *I* was a kook. They still do. My parents and two brothers are some of the most successful people you'll ever meet. And me? Well, I spent my childhood in more psychologists' offices than I care to remember. I was told I wouldn't amount to anything because I wasn't like them."

Lee stared past Dr. Rad for a moment, steadying himself for what he was about to do.

"I know I'll eventually find out where I belong in life." He took his time getting the right words out. "And I would give anything to have a dream, a goal, a passion like yours. You can't give up on that."

Dr. Rad said nothing for a long minute, and when he did, his speech was slow and succinct. "It takes a lot of money, my young man, and land. I no longer have access to the university property. I appreciate your enthusiasm, Lee, but my research days are gone."

"I have the land. I have almost seven hundred acres of land. And I have some money." He suppressed a proud smile. "Look, I don't have all the answers, and maybe this won't work at all, but I sure would like to pursue it. But it won't work if you consider yourself defeated." He paused. "What do you say?"

"So you are a kook too. Go ahead. I'm listening."

* * *

Lee took the next several days building a case for allowing Dr. Rad to resume his research on Lee's land, the challenge being to convince Stonebugger the endeavor would improve the property. Otherwise, he wouldn't be able to use trust fund money for it, and he didn't have anywhere near enough money in his bank account to sponsor him that way. To help him make his case, he first looked up the word *improve* in the dictionary.

Improve, *verb*
to make (land) more useful, profitable, or valuable

Useful, *adjective*
1. able to be used advantageously, beneficially, or for several purposes
2. helpful or serviceable

Profitable, *adjective*
yielding profit, remunerative, beneficial, or useful

Valuable, *adjective*
1. having qualities worthy of respect, admiration, or esteem
2. of considerable use, service, or importance

Lee believed all the definitions supported the idea of using the land to sponsor research that could result in finding a cure or prevention for cancer. But he knew Stonebugger wouldn't be so easily convinced. When he thought he had all the ammunition he needed, he made an appointment to see him.

When the day arrived, Lee sat in Stonebugger's waiting room, sweating, tapping his fingers on the arm of the chair until the receptionist gave him a dirty look. He wished he had practiced his speech on someone else before coming.

"What is on your mind today, Mr. Winekoop?" he asked when they were both seated in his office.

His voice cracked like that of an adolescent boy when he began to speak. "I'm here to talk about a proposal for improving a portion of my land."

"This is something separate from the house?"

"Yes."

Stonebugger's expressionless stare made him shiver.

"Go on."

"There's a brilliant research scientist who has spent the last several years at the University of Illinois studying genetic modification in foods. He recently lost his funding, and I think it would be a huge improvement to my land to allow him to continue with his research."

"Just how is that?"

"This research is valuable."

"Apparently the U of I didn't think so."

"There just weren't enough funds to go around. It had nothing to do with the quality of his research."

"If it was as valuable as you say, they would have found the funds, or someone else would have picked him up."

"Let me explain the nature of—"

"Let me explain something to *you*, Mr. Winekoop. I am beholden to your uncle's will, and my interpretation of what he meant by improving the property was something like the house you're building, or maybe raising a crop, or like the medical facility I talked about earlier with you. I don't believe the notion of having a scientist—one who couldn't make it with the University of Illinois—conducting plant experiments is what he had in mind."

"But—"

Stonebugger got up from his chair, giving Lee no choice but to leave.

As he drove away thinking about their conversation, Lee became increasingly angry. Ebenezer hadn't even give him the chance to talk about crown gall disease and Dr. Rad's theory that if you could find a cure for this disease in plants, you could potentially find a cure for cancer in humans, Lee's strongest argument for the validity of the research. And now he had to tell Dr. Rad he had failed after getting him excited about returning to his cherished work.

Later, Lee went over to the inn for a late dinner. After his meeting with Stonebugger, he looked forward to seeing a friendly face. When he sat down at the bar, he saw CJ several yards away with her back to him. When she turned toward him, the bruise on the side of her face was noticeable even in the dimly lit room.

She walked toward him, her expression as serious as he had ever seen it.

"What on earth happened to you?"

"Nothing. I'm just clumsy." She proceeded to pour him a beer. Lee waited for her to make eye contact, and when she didn't he reached out to touch her arm, but she turned and scooted away before he could get her attention.

CJ continued to avoid him. When he signaled for her to come get his food order, she said something to the other bartender, who then went over to take Lee's order.

He left the inn as soon as he had finished his dinner, without ever speaking to CJ, and sat in his car in the parking lot for two hours until the bar closed. When CJ eventually came out and headed toward her car, he got out and approached her.

"CJ, I need to talk to you," he said, walking up behind her.

She didn't turn around to face him. "Not tonight."

He continued to follow her. "CJ, please stop and talk to me."

"No!" She unlocked her car door and proceeded to climb in.

"Is everything all right, CJ?" a deep male voice behind Lee shouted.

CJ waved to the inn's other bartender standing just outside the front door, started her car, and drove away, leaving Lee standing alone in the middle of the parking lot.

"You'd best be going," the bartender said to Lee.

Lee turned around and acknowledged him with a nod before he headed toward his car, wondering what that had been about.

For the next few days, Lee thought of nothing else beyond his two challenges: how to get a second crack at convincing Stonebugger to let him support Dr. Rad's research and how to affirm CJ's general well-being without making her feel like he was interfering in her life. CJ wasn't actually a close friend—he didn't even have her phone number—and he ran the risk of alienating her if he meddled in her personal affairs.

Both issues mattered to him, and Lee wasn't sure which one would affect him more if it didn't have a favorable outcome.

14 | "You Need to Leave"

Lee called Stonebugger's office and left a voice-mail message requesting a meeting. Two days later, when his second voice-mail message went unanswered, Lee called a third time. This time his secretary answered. She apologized for not getting back to him, but Mr. Stonebugger had taken a leave of absence, and she was having difficulty following up with everyone in a timely manner.

"I have business with him, and it's important," Lee told her. "What can I do?"

She suggested he write a letter stating his business and send it to her and she would talk to him about it.

Frustrated with the impending delay in dealing with Stonebugger, Lee rambled into the sunroom and plopped down on the chair nearest the windows. The reflection of the trees on the lake had a calming effect and reminded Lee of the trees on his property where he planned to build the house.

What would cause someone to take a leave of absence? Illness probably. But based on what the secretary had said, Stonebugger was well enough to work from home. Maybe it was a family member. Whatever the case, with Ebenezer's attention to his work now compromised, Lee figured he needed more ammunition than ever to fire at him, and the most promising source was Dr. Rad.

The long drive to Peoria gave Lee time to think about how he could construct a new letter to Stonebugger with his plan. He would have to be judicious in the way he crafted it, as this second chance would likely be his last.

He found Dr. Rad slumped in the same chair he had been sitting in during the last visit, with the same blanket draped over his lap and wearing the same broken facial expression. This surprised Lee, as he had left Dr. Rad in good spirits just weeks earlier.

"It's good to see you again, Dr. Rad," he said.

Dr. Rad responded with a nod.

"I need to pick your brain on something."

"I'm afraid there may not be much to pick from, son," he said weakly.

"Please bear with me. This is important."

Dr. Rad nodded.

"Tell me all you know about the parallelism between cancer in plants and humans."

The doctor shook his head and viewed Lee with lifeless eyes.

"What's wrong?"

"Tell me where you are going with this."

"The last time I was here, you gave me the go-ahead to try to help you get back on track with your research. I think, if I'm very smart about it, I can do just that. But I need your help." He paused. "Please don't give up on this."

"For whose benefit are you doing this, Lee?"

"Mine. I couldn't care less about you," he said through a smile.

Dr. Rad's suppressed smile revealed he understood the sarcasm in Lee's remark. "Okay. I'll give you the big picture, and if you want, you can go through my journals and pick up the smaller details."

"That's just what I wanted to hear."

Lee spent the next three hours listening to Dr. Rad talk about plant cancer, specifically crown gall disease. He told Lee of two Johns Hopkins University School of Medicine consultants who had recently completed research that involved using the plant alkaloid camptothecin to interfere with cancerous tumors in monkeys. Dr. Rad was excited about their findings and thought their groundbreaking research could potentially augment his own.

"I have to ask you, Dr. Rad, why didn't you pursue working with them?"

"I tried, but at that time, the university was already focusing on other research, and I didn't have the financial support I needed."

When they finished talking, Lee stayed for a lunch prepared by Dr. Rad's sister, and then went into the spare bedroom where all the doctor's research books, journals, and notes were stored. He turned down the invitation to join them for dinner and instead worked long into the evening. Between what he had gathered that day and the copious notes he had taken when he had interned with Dr. Rad, he believed he had everything he needed.

"I ran across your notes on Henrietta Ray," he said to Dr. Rad afterwards. "Can you tell me what the connection is between what she's doing at Texas A&M and your research?"

"She's using red clover to try to convert some of the leaf cell chemicals in order to prevent protein from breaking down, so the cattle or sheep or whatever animals graze on it get more protein in their systems. She wanted to know more about some of my extraction techniques."

"Your notes ended rather abruptly. What happened?"

"I'm not sure. She stopped communicating for some reason."

Lee prepared to leave. The expression on Dr. Rad's face, and the brusque wave he gave Lee on his way out, told Lee the good doctor might still not be completely on board with him, but he wasn't going to let that deter him. He was on a mission.

The next day, he contacted his former Cornell biochemistry professor and told him of Dr. Rad's research and the potential link to the recent research performed at Johns Hopkins University. The professor told Lee he had met one of the Hopkins researchers at a conference in Washington the previous month and was intrigued with the idea of getting him and Dr. Rad together. He offered to contact him.

Next, Lee called Robin and asked her if she could help him get letters of recommendation from the University of Illinois regarding Dr. Rad's research. She was certain she could, given that her father was still the dean of students there and had connections.

The next call he made was the most difficult, but it had the potential of having the greatest impact on Dr. Rad's work.

"Hello, Father?"

"Yes."

"How are you?"

"I'm fine."

"I have a favor to ask of you."

"Go ahead."

"I'm told the University of Wisconsin has plans to build a medical research facility outside of Lake Geneva. They're not publicly disclosing this, but I have reason to believe they may be using unprecedented plant genetic modification techniques in their research at this new facility."

"What's that got to do with me?"

"I'm getting to that. Do you remember Dr. Rad, the U of I researcher I worked under as an intern in between semesters at Cornell?"

"Vaguely."

"Well, he has done phenomenal work in this area, and I would like to put the right people at UW in touch with him. I was hoping that with your contacts, you could help me with that."

Silence.

"Are you still there?"

"Yes, I'm here."

"So can you help me with this?"

"Send me something I can work with. Keep it short...and intelligent. Anything else?"

"No, Father. That was it. Goodbye."

* * *

It didn't take long for Lee's former Cornell professor to tell him the Hopkins researcher was interested in Dr. Rad's work and would meet with him. A few days later, Lee received a glowing letter of recommendation for Dr. Rad from the chair of the Department of Biological Sciences at the University of Illinois.

After hearing nothing back from his father two weeks after he had personally delivered the synopsis of Dr. Rad's genetic modification work to him, he asked his mother about it.

"He's been very busy lately."

"He has no intention of making the call, does he?"

"I'm sure he'll get to it as soon as he can, Lee."

"It means a lot to me."

"I know, dear."

Surrendering to the expectation that his father wouldn't come through, Lee drafted a three-page letter to Stonebugger that he believed contained the right balance of science and persuasion. He drove to the nearest mailbox and said a silent prayer as he dropped it in. Then he drove to his property where the contractor had broken ground for his house the day before.

The sight of an excavator, bulldozer, and front-end loader made him beam. If it hadn't been for his research on what it took to build a house, he would have had no idea what these things were or what they were used for. He walked to the edge of the massive hole that would be the basement and foundation for the house.

Later, he went to the inn for "a cold one." He was disappointed CJ was not behind the bar.

"Where's CJ tonight?" he asked the bartender.

"Called in sick."

He downed his beer and left.

Lee headed west toward Durand where CJ lived, although he didn't know what he would do once he got there. When he reached her house, which was only partially visible from the road, he pulled onto the shoulder and sat for a few moments. He wished he had her phone number, as a phone call would have been far less intrusive than a knock on her door. The more he thought about knocking, the more he thought that was a bad idea. Sighing, he put the car in drive and pulled up a couple of feet to turn around and head home.

He shot one last glance toward her house and saw the tail end of a sheriff's patrol car in her driveway. Lee knew McHenry County had more than one sheriff's car in its fleet, but odds were this one belonged to the father of CJ's children. His mind raced through the possible scenarios of why DeRam would be there. Perhaps CJ had called in sick in order to spend time with him—a discouraging thought, but he had to consider the possibility. His next thought was even more disturbing: what if she was in trouble and needed help?

Lee instinctively got out of the car and started walking up the driveway toward the house.

"No! I said no!"

CJ's voice was unmistakable.

Lee ran to the door and tried to open it. It was locked. He backed up to get a running start and slammed his body against it. The door gave way, and he flew into CJ's living room, landing on his shoulder not ten feet from her and DeRam, whose trousers were partially down. The half-naked sheriff had CJ pressed up against the sofa. The fear on her face incited Lee to act.

Words he had heard his karate masters speak through the years raced through his head.

Keep a calm mind and your emotions under control.
Use words first before you strike.

"What the fuck are you doing here?" De Ram shouted.

Lee stood tall. "Get off her," he said in a calm voice.

"Mind your own goddamn business!" DeRam's upper body twisted as he reached over CJ toward his utility belt that lay on the sofa cushion next to them and grabbed his gun.

Using a move he hadn't practiced since his last karate class, Lee deftly kicked the gun out of his hand and sent it flying into the hallway.

The look of surprise on DeRam's red face quickly turned into a menacing scowl. "What the fuck?"

Clumsily pulling up his pants, he stood and faced Lee.

"Get in the other room," Lee said to CJ, without taking his eyes off DeRam. She did as he said.

"You fucking bastard. Who the hell do you think you are busting in here like that?" He glanced over to where his gun had landed.

"You need to leave."

"You know who you're talking to, prick head? You've just busted into someone else's home and damaged her property in the process. I ought to arrest you."

Lee maintained his composure. "You need to leave."

DeRam took a step closer, showing Lee his clenched fist, as he used the other hand to hold up his pants. "You're going to be taught a lesson, rich boy."

"I wouldn't try that if I were you."

DeRam lunged at him.

Lee ducked out of his way.

"Now you're really pissing me off, you son-of-a-bitch."

Though fighting the urge to explode, Lee managed to remain calm, exactly as he had been taught in karate class.

DeRam lunged repeatedly, and each time Lee ducked out of his way. Then DeRam bent over, pulled out a knife from underneath his pant leg, and lifted it as though to strike. Lee heard a gasp from CJ, who was now peering around the corner from the hallway.

Lee kicked the knife from DeRam's hand, inflicting a strong reverse foot punch to his forehead. He executed the blow in such a way as to stun DeRam and avoid causing a serious injury. Lee then initiated a side-thrust kick to his ribs that caused the sheriff to collapse to the floor. CJ ran into the room to retrieve both the gun and the knife and then quickly ran out again.

The sheriff lay face-up, pants halfway down, his eyes shut and teeth clamped tight in a grimace. He rubbed his right side.

"CJ!" Lee cried out. "Can you bring a blanket or something to cover him up?"

CJ entered the room with a tablecloth. She threw it over him and asked, "Is he okay?"

Lee nodded and walked over to the sofa to remove the set of handcuffs from the sheriff's utility belt.

"What do you think you're doing?"

"Just for our protection until we figure out what to do with you."

"Go to hell." The sheriff attempted to sit up, but instead winced in pain and lay back down again.

Lee attached one end of the handcuffs to DeRam's left wrist, forced his arm through the leg of the radiator, and attached the other end of the cuffs to his right wrist, making it impossible for him to do anything but stay lying on his back latched to the radiator.

"What should we do?" CJ whispered.

"Let's go in the other room." Once out of earshot from the sheriff, Lee asked, "Are you all right?"

"Yeah."

"You sound terrible."

"I have a cold or the flu or something."

"Where are your kids?"

"With Frankie. She's watching them at her house so they don't catch it. So what are we going to do with him? Should we call an ambulance?"

"We could, but he'll be all right. He may have a headache for a couple of days, and his ribs may be sore for a while, but he'll be fine."

"What happens when we let him up?"

"Did he hurt you?"

CJ turned her head.

"Look at me. Did he hurt you?"

"He was forcing himself on me when you came flying in. Those are some kick-ass moves you have!"

"And the bruise on your face from last week? I can still see it."

"He caught me at my car after work one night, and when I ducked to avoid him trying to kiss me, I hit my face on the edge of the car door. Bastard."

"How did he get in today?"

"He said he wanted to talk."

"And you let him in?"

"He looked sincere, and I thought I could handle him, so..."

Lee stared at her.

"I know. I know. I shouldn't have let him in."

"Do you want to press charges against him?"

"Like what?"

"Attempted rape. Assault. I don't know all the possible charges."

DeRam mumbled something from the other room.

"We can call the police, or the sheriff's department. Who has jurisdiction here?" Lee asked.

"The sheriff...but even though Bern is from another district, they all know each other, and..."

"And what?"

"They all stick up for each other, turn a blind eye to certain things."

"So why don't we let the good sheriff decide what we do?"

"You're kidding, right?"

DeRam let out another guttural noise and shouted, "Get me the fuck out of these cuffs!"

Lee led the way back to the living room and stood over him. "Not so fast, DeRam. We need to make a decision here, and you get the deciding vote."

"Shut the fuck up, and get me out of these."

"Be patient, Sheriff." He paused long enough to make the sheriff grimace. "Now, we could call for an ambulance to make sure you're all right. Of course, they would ask all sorts of questions, and I, being a witness to an attempted rape, would answer their questions with utmost candor. Then again, we could call law enforcement and make formal charges against you. Let's see, attempted rape on her, assault on me with a deadly weapon. Have I left anything out?"

"You asshole."

"Didn't your parents teach you it isn't nice to call people names?"

"Shut the fuck up."

"What's your vote, Sheriff?"

"Look, CJ and I were just getting into a romantic moment when you broke down the door," DeRam said, his tone contrite. He glared at CJ. "When she told me she didn't want to go any further, I was going to back off. You just came in right before I had a chance to do that. Now take these cuffs off me. I'll leave, and we can all forget this ever happened."

"Excuse us for a minute, will you, Sheriff?"

Lee led CJ to the kitchen and whispered, "We have him in a sticky position, and he knows it. What do you want to do?"

"I want to let him go and forget it ever happened, like he said, but what about tomorrow...or next week...or next month? I'm afraid of what he'll try to pull."

"It's not too late to call an ambulance. That would show we care about his well-being, but it would also open up an investigation."

"I don't know."

Lee gave her a moment to think it through.

"I wish he would just go away."

"I know. I do too." He touched her shoulder. "C'mon. I have a plan." He led her back to the living room and stood over DeRam, his slight body looming over the cowering sheriff.

"We're going to let you go, DeRam. But I suggest you go from here straight to the public library and read up on black belt karate. You may find it interesting."

"Just unlock these fucking cuffs."

"Where's the key, Sheriff?"

"In my back pocket, Winecrap."

"Roll over."

The sheriff grunted.

"Roll over, or I'll do it for you."

When DeRam didn't move, Lee took his foot and rolled him over enough to expose his back pocket. He pulled the tablecloth over him to cover his bare butt and reached into one of his back pockets. He touched something soft inside and pulled it out.

"What's this?" Lee held up what looked like a hand-rolled cigarette.

No response.

Lee showed it to CJ. Her grin said it all.

Lee stooped down to reach into the other pocket, retrieved the key, and unlocked the cuffs.

Once free, the sheriff scrambled to adjust his pants, and after getting up off the floor, grabbed his gun, knife, and handcuffs, all of which CJ had placed on the dining room table. He bolted out the front door, mumbling something inaudible on the way.

Lee and CJ stared at each other for several seconds, and when CJ looked as if she was going to cry, Lee hugged her for a brief moment before sitting down with her on the sofa.

"Look...he forgot his belt," she said.

"I'll take care of it. Are you all right?" he asked her.

"Yeah."

"I'll get someone over here to fix your door."

"Will you stay with me until that's done?"

"Of course."

"The phone's in the kitchen. Hey, what are you going to do with the joint?" she asked.

"Nothing for now."

Lee called his contractor and asked him if he would send someone over right away to fix the door and then asked if he could recommend someone to install a security system on the house and trim the tree in the back, the one Travis had climbed.

CJ had her head in her hands when Lee returned to the living room.

"What's wrong?"

"I hate him!" She raised her head up to look at Lee. "And the worst part is he's so unpredictable, and there...I wish we could put a fence around where I live and work to keep him out. I just want to be free of him. Is that asking so much?"

He wanted to console her, put his arms around her, let her know things would be all right, but he knew he couldn't promise that.

"No. It's not asking so much."

On his way out, Lee stopped his car at the end of CJ's driveway, got out, and prominently hung the sheriff's bulky utility belt on a low branch of a box-elder maple tree where the sheriff, and anyone else driving by, could easily see it.

15 | Bittersweet Victory

Two weeks after Lee had sent the letter to Stonebugger, he received a call from his secretary.

"Your request has been approved," she said.

Did I hear correctly?

"Is there anything he and I need to discuss then?"

"No. I'll put his response to your letter in the mail today."

There was sadness in her voice. "Is everything all right?"

"Mr. Stonebugger lost his sister yesterday...to cancer."

The news surprised him. "I'm sorry to hear that. Had she been ill long?"

"I'm not sure. Mr. Stonebugger is a very private man. All I know is he's been taking care of her for the past two months."

"How is he doing?"

"Not well." Her voice cracked. "Apparently they were very close."

"I'm sorry to hear that too. If there's anything I can do to help..."

"He did ask that you keep him apprised of the progress of your friend's work, the cancer research."

"Of course, I will."

"He said he couldn't think of a more righteous way to increase the value of your land." She paused. "Mr. Winekoop, behind Mr. Stonebugger's gruff exterior is a man with a lot of compassion. He has a big heart." Her voice drifted off to where Lee could barely hear her.

"If I send a letter of condolence to his office, will you see to it he gets it?"

"Yes, of course."

It was a bittersweet victory.

* * *

Lee was halfway out the door on his way to tell Dr. Rad the good news when the phone rang. It was Dennis Freborg telling him the town had denied him the permit to build his house.

"But they already dug the hole. Are you aware of that?"

"You don't need a permit to dig a hole. Because the plans were so straightforward, and I've designed so many other homes in Harvard, and Earl has built just as many, we took a chance getting started early, knowing we wouldn't have any problem getting a permit."

"Why was it denied then?"

"Are you sitting down?"

"No, but I can be."

"Apparently, there is an old building code still on the books that requires each newly built home to be able to accommodate at least one horse-and-buggy in a building separate from the house that is of a certain size and construction."

"What?"

"I knew there had to be some mistake, so I called the building department and talked to the person who issues permits. She cited the code for me. I asked her how many homes had been built in Harvard during the last fifty years and how many of them were required to build a stable for a horse-and-buggy. She said, and I quote, 'I'm just doing what I've been told. If you have an issue with this, you'll have to take it up at the next open city council meeting.'"

"Good grief. When is that?"

"Next one is in two weeks."

"This is bogus."

"Oh, it's bogus all right. How do you want me to proceed?"

"Do we have any choice if we want to go ahead with the house?"

"Not that I can see."

"Then let's attend the next city council meeting."

* * *

It was hard for Lee to resist the temptation to exceed the speed limit on his way to Dr. Rad's house. Windows down and a George Michael song blaring on the radio, he put the house permit issue out of his mind for the moment and thought back a few years to when he had interned for Dr. Rad. He reveled in the thought of being involved in his research again.

He found Dr. Rad sitting on a rocking chair in the far corner of his small, cluttered back porch, staring into space.

"Dr. Rad?"

The doctor gave Lee a faint smile. "I was just thinking about you, Lee."

"That's good, because I've been thinking of you, too. I have some wonderful news."

"Hmm?"

Lee told him what he was able to offer: a lab and greenhouses designed to his specifications and fifty acres of land for his research. Then he told him about the Johns Hopkins researcher interested in meeting with him to discuss cancer research. It took Dr. Rad several seconds to respond.

"I don't know how to tell you this, but while I appreciate what you're trying to do for me, I don't know if I can go through it again. And for that reason, I have to—"

"What? You've got to be kidding me!"

"I wish I were."

The heaviness in Lee's chest made it difficult to get the words out. Dr. Rad's talent, his past research, his beliefs, his passion—he couldn't bear to think of it all going to waste. "You can't give up now."

"It's not like I haven't given this significant thought, Lee. It was one thing to be financially supported by big companies and the university, but for you to support me, an individual, a friend, what if I fail? I would never forgive myself."

"Fail at what? When is medical research a failure? 'It doesn't matter if you prove it right or prove it wrong, the value is in the proof.' *You* taught me that."

"Perhaps being away from it for so long has eroded some of my self-confidence."

"Well, you can't let that happen. That's all there is to it."

"Lee, I don't know what to say to you. I have spent practically my whole life dedicated to plant research, clawing my way to finding a cure for, or better yet, a prevention for cancer. More people criticized my work than praised it, but that didn't stop me. But when the rug was pulled out from beneath me in December of '86, I felt that was the end, not only to my research, but to my life in a way." He looked past Lee and paused for a moment. "Tell me something, why do *you* believe in me?"

Lee stared into Dr. Rad's eyes, beyond their surface. "Because you believed in yourself."

Lee took a few minutes to think of the right words.

"I had a nanny once who used to say, 'All you need in life are two things: curiosity and confidence.' Back then, I didn't understand it—I was too focused on what I thought was expected of me by others to understand self-confidence. Then I met you. I watched you work. I witnessed the outcome of your thought processes. I felt your passion. Sure, I saw how frustrated you got with the roadblocks you faced, but that didn't stop you, and that's when I realized you were what that saying was all about. And I wanted to be just like you.

"Dr. Rad, you can't give up—there's too much at stake here. And I'm asking you... No, I'm begging you not to give up on me."

Dr. Rad clasped his hands together and slowly raised them to his lips.

"When do we start?" he asked.

16 | "What Do You Want from Me?"

Lee and Dennis arrived a few minutes before the open forum portion of the city council meeting was supposed to begin. They waited in the hallway until the doors to the meeting room opened. The woman who opened the door seemed surprised to see them standing there.

"May I help you?" she asked them.

Dennis explained the reason for their appearance.

"We were told no open-forum agenda items had been submitted, so I'm afraid we've adjourned."

"I completed the necessary forms and submitted them two weeks ago," Dennis told her.

"Well, I'm not sure what happened then. Anyway, everyone is gone now."

Lee could feel the blood rising up his neck into his face. "Look, I'm trying to build a—"

Dennis grabbed his arm. "It's not her problem, Lee. Let's go." He waited until they were safely inside his car before he continued. "I don't know why, but there's some ridiculous game-playing going on here."

"I may know who's at the root of it."

"Who?"

Lee told him about DeRam.

"Really? Look, I'll do whatever I need to do to get your permit, but I'm going to have to start charging you extra for my time."

"That's certainly fair. Do whatever it is you need to do."

Three days later, Dennis called Lee to tell him he had called the Building Department, and the same woman he had spoken with earlier informed him that the permit was sitting on her desk—no horse-and-buggy structure required—and she was wondering why it was taking so long for someone to pick it up.

* * *

At eight a.m., two days after the permit had been secured, Lundberg's construction crew began getting ready to pour the foundation for Lee's house. But by noon, a city inspector had shut them down.

Lee was livid when Earl told him what happened. "Tell me I didn't hear you right, Earl. That's preposterous."

Earl had explained there was another old law on the books in Harvard that stated no licensed contractor could subcontract work from any person or company that charged more than the price fixed by the local craft societies. The law referenced an 1836 price book for thirty-one categories of construction work. The inspector had cited them for twelve violations.

"They're going out of their way to either cause you unnecessary delays or stop you from developing this property altogether," he told Lee.

"So what do we do now?"

"Well, the inspector admitted the price book was outdated and they didn't have a current one, so he said as long as I produce two more estimates for each trade to show my good faith in providing you with the most economical services, he would give us the go-ahead."

"How long will that take?"

"Luckily, I have at least one and in some cases two other estimates, so I'm a little ahead of the game. The problem is that I don't know where to find a third estimate for some things, like putting in sewer lines. There are only two outfits within fifty miles of here who do that."

"Do we have any recourse?"

"Not that I can see. They shut us down. If you ignore them and proceed anyway, you'll get fined, and my guess is they'll make those fines especially high for you. Or who knows, you could end up in jail."

"I want to proceed."

It took Earl three weeks to secure the required estimates, ten days to arrange for a meeting with the county inspector, and another week to free up his crew to pick up where they had left off.

By mid-May, Lee's house had been roughed in, and fifty acres of land had been cleared for building three greenhouses and a main lab for Dr. Rad. Lee's spirits were high—until he received a call from his mother, who told him the entire family intended to spend Memorial Day weekend in Lake Geneva...with him.

As unnerving as it was to be spending an entire weekend with his family, something unsettled Lee even more, and that was his concern for CJ following the incident with DeRam. He was at a loss for what to do next, if anything. He had talked to her on several occasions at the bar, and she had said she hadn't heard from DeRam since then, but Lee wasn't sure he believed her. After carefully considering the consequences of potentially butting too far into her business, he asked if he could come over to her house before she left for work the next day, and she said okay.

When CJ opened her door for Lee, he greeted her with a handful of wildflowers.

"Nice daisies," she said. "What's the occasion?"

"I found them alongside the road and thought you might like them...but they're not daisies."

CJ led him into the kitchen where she quickly reached for a vase. "So what are they?"

"Heath asters."

"Really. So tell me about heath asters, Socrates."

"*Aster ericoides.* Bees, butterflies, and wild turkeys love them."

"Oh, really? I'll have to remember that the next time I invite a wild turkey over."

"They grow well on dolomite prairie land, and we've got a lot of that in these parts."

"No shit. What's dolomite?"

"It's a calcium magnesium carbonate sediment a few feet below the surface. Very rich in nutrients."

"You're a regular *repository* of information." She laughed. "That was today's word on my Harvard Business School word-of-the-day calendar."

He gave her a puzzled look.

"One of the bar bums gave it to me for Christmas last year...probably as a joke. I didn't think I'd ever have an opportunity to use any of the words. Ha! Then I met you."

"Thank you...I think." They settled in at the kitchen table, the vase of flowers in front of them.

"Nice touch," he said referring to the cookie jar. A giant blue cartoon character riding a tricycle and blowing a trumpet was on the side of it.

"Thanks. He's a Smurf by the way. Got it with green stamps."

He gave her a blank stare.

"I'll explain some other time."

He wondered if green stamps had anything to do with social welfare, like food stamps. Up until now, he hadn't given much thought to how CJ had managed to raise two kids on a bartender's salary.

"So how are you? Really."

"I'm okay."

"You haven't heard from DeRam since that day?"

"I told you I haven't."

"I know, but we were in a crowded bar then. I wanted to make sure."

She looked at the flowers for a moment and then at him. "Can I ask you a question?"

"Sure."

"Why are you here?"

The question caught him off guard. "Because...I wanted to make sure DeRam has left you alone."

"No, I mean why are you really here?" She crossed her arms over her chest. "Why do you give a rat's ass about how I am? Who are you, anyway? What do you want from me?"

The pressure in his chest caused him to wince. "I don't want anything from you. I care about you. I like you."

"Why?"

"Because I'm human, and you're a nice person?"

"You know what I mean."

"No. I'm afraid I don't."

"People who show an interest in you want something. That's just human nature. So what do *you* want?"

"That's not true. I don't want anything from you."

"Liar."

He wondered how this visit could have gone any more wrong. While he may not have fully understood his intentions when it came to her, they were certainly not underhanded.

"I can't care about you without wanting something from you?"

She leaned back in her chair until its front legs lifted off the floor. "Think about it, Soc. As a kid, you pay attention to your mother because you need food, shelter, love. As a teen, you pay attention to your teachers because your father told you if you failed in school, there would be hell to pay. And then you pay attention to a man because you need..."

He suspected she was speaking from a distant past, reminding Lee things that happened years ago could grab you by the throat at any time. "You need what?"

Her mood changed. "Nothing. I don't need shit from anyone. You're getting off the subject."

"Am I?"

She got up. "Look, don't think for a minute I don't appreciate what you did to that asshole for me. I do. But...maybe you better go."

He remained seated. "I don't want to leave on a sour note."

"Looks like you're not going to get what you want then."

Lee stood up. "You're right. I do want something from you."

"Knew it."

"Do you have any plans for the weekend?"

"What?"

"Can we sit down?"

"No."

"May I sit down?"

"Suit yourself."

"My entire family is coming to my house for the weekend, all eleven of them. That's eleven against one—hardly an equal match."

CJ rolled her eyes and then sat back down. "Explain yourself."

"Look, I fit in with the rest of my family about as well as...well, I *don't* fit in is what I'm trying to say. That's the truth of it. I can't be, nor do I want to be, like them. Oh, there was a time there wasn't anything I wanted more than to be just like my brothers, but I stopped thinking like that when..."

She relaxed her posture some. "So you were like a fish tryin' to ride a bicycle?"

Lee laughed. "Well, yes, something like that."

"The peels of laughter emulate from within, while he stands on the outside forever looking in."

Lee reeled back in his chair, and after he'd recovered from the power of the words she'd uttered, he asked, "Where did *that* come from?"

"It's the first line of a poem I know."

"A poem."

"Some English guy wrote it. I don't remember his name. I found it in a book of poems in the library one time when I was in one of my weird moods, read it over and over again, and for some bizarre reason remembered it after all these years."

"What's the rest of it?"

"Not now. I'd hate to dazzle you with all the culture I possess in one shot. You were saying?"

"I was saying, I had to break away from my family in order to find myself, because I couldn't live in their elite world...and survive, let alone be happy, so..."

"So here you are. In your parents' house, trying to be yourself, but you don't know quite who that is yet, and they're all coming up for a nice long visit, and you'd rather be anywhere else but there. How am I doin'?"

"You're doing great. Look, I'm telling you things I've never told anyone before...except for my shrinks, of course."

"Okay, but what's all this got to do with me?"

"I thought I'd plan a barbecue for Saturday, and I would be eternally grateful if you and the boys would attend."

"You gotta be shittin' me. If you're saying *you* don't fit in, just how am *I* going to fit in?"

Lee shrugged. "You don't have to. Just show up, talk to them like you do at the bar with other perfect strangers, which you seem to do effortlessly, enjoy the food, and then go home. There'll be other kids there. We'll have things for them to do and..."

"So just how will you introduce me?"

Lee got up from his chair and made a sweeping arm gesture toward her. "May I present my good friend, CJ, to all of you royal—"

"Pains in the asses?"

"Very funny. Actually, they're usually very well behaved in social settings. Hey, I have an idea. Maybe I'll invite a few other people from here and try to outnumber them. Ha! This could be fun."

"Look, I'm sorry I misjudged you. Someday I'll have to tell you my whole story, and then you'll understand my trust issues. You can count me in, but only if there are other normal people there."

"Bring your sister, too. The more the merrier."

"Soc?"

"Yeah?"

"As far as Bern goes, I carry this with me at all times now." She reached in her pocket and pulled out a green and white metal canister not much bigger than a roll of Lifesavers.

"What's that?"

"Mace."

"Is that legal?"

"I don't know, and I don't care."

Lee didn't have much time to plan the barbecue. His guest list included CJ, her two sons, and Francine; Dr. Rad and his sister; the architect, Dennis Freborg, and his son, David; the builder, Earl Lundberg; and the hardware-store owner, Lenny Vinik, and his wife. He hadn't originally thought of inviting Lenny, but they had become pretty friendly in the course of Lee's many visits to his store to purchase whatever tool or gadget Bob Vila had just used on the latest episode of *This Old House*. It was fun and interesting learning about different tools, and he snickered at the notion his family was missing out by hiring everything done for them.

Lee felt good about the guest list. The playing field would be even—eleven Winekoops and eleven of his own guests.

Shaneta appeared to be overwhelmed at the idea of having to cook for a crowd that big by herself and asked for help. When Lee told her he wanted to make it a traditional barbecue with hot dogs, hamburgers, and potato salad, her eyes grew wide.

"You're not serious, Mista Lee."

"I'm totally serious."

She put her hands on her hips. "I have been your parents' cook for over ten years, and I can assure you they have never eaten a hot dog or a hamburger." She shook her head. "If Mrs. Winekoop was plannin' this, we'd be havin' roasted squab or grilled shrimp, maybe yellow tomatoes stuffed with wild mushrooms, and—"

"Well, she's not planning it, and we're having hot dogs and hamburgers."

"Oh, mi God. I can't wait to see this." She smiled. "Can I make deviled eggs too?"

"Of course."

"And watermelon?"

"Sure. And how about red, white, and blue cupcakes for dessert?"

Shaneta threw up her hands. "Wait 'til I tell Helen."

"And none of that lavender lemonade stuff. I want pure, unadulterated fresh-squeezed lemonade."

Shaneta clapped her hands together. "You got it."

"And soda and beer."

"How 'bout some chips and dip just to round things off?"

"Perfect."

* * *

The Winekoop procession of Mercedes and BMW cars arrived Saturday morning at eleven o'clock...in precise pecking order. His parents pulled in first. Nelson followed, with his wife, Yvonne, and their twin ten-year-old boys, Vincent and Virgil. Bringing up the rear were Bennett with his wife, Daphne, and their three children, eleven-year-old Odessa, eight-year-old Anna, and nine-year-old Bennett, Jr.

Lee watched them parade through the front door like a noon-time fashion show at one of New York's finest department stores—all dressed in Ralph Lauren, Burberry, and Calvin Klein, even the kids.

Upon seeing Lee greet her at the door sporting a new pair of jeans, plaid shirt, and tennis shoes—quite a change from his previous preppy style—his mother let out a gasp that echoed throughout the foyer. Shaneta's stifled titter emanating from the kitchen confirmed he had probably horrified his mother with his attire.

Lee's father and brothers returned to their cars to fetch the luggage. The children were escorted by one of the housekeepers to...somewhere. Lee led his mother and two sisters-in-law to the sunroom, the invisible being-in-charge feeling in his chest causing him to stand a little bit straighter as he walked.

"So how have you been, Lee? You move up here, and we never hear from you anymore," his mother asked in that all-too-familiar condescending tone of hers.

"I've been well, Mother. Everything is fine here."

"How is construction progressing?"

"Good. The house has been roughed in," he explained. "I'll take everyone to see it tomorrow if you want."

The men carried the suitcases upstairs, and when they returned, they all spent the next hour immersed in small talk. Shaneta interrupted them a couple of times to ask Lee about various details of the meal. After her third interruption, Lee's mother asked, "Why does she keep asking you questions, Lee? When did she start needing help planning a meal?"

"Actually, I planned the meal for this afternoon, and while we're on the subject, I've invited some friends to join us as well." He studied their faces, waiting for their reaction.

"What friends?" his father asked.

"What? I can't have friends?"

"What Henry meant was—"

Lee leaned forward in his chair. "I've met some nice people since I moved here, and they're coming to the barbecue this afternoon." He eyed his mother, then his father. "That is okay, isn't it?"

Silence.

"The cost is coming out of my own bank account, so..."

"That's not the point, Lee," his mother said.

"Then, what is the point?"

"We just weren't expecting other guests, that's all." She squirmed in her chair. "Of course, it's all right." She watched Henry stare out the window at something—something way out over the lake. "When will they be here, dear?"

"I told everyone noon."

She glanced at her watch. "Well, you'd better get changed then."

"This is what I'm wearing."

Everyone's eyes were on Lee.

"Lee, you can't be serious. You look like a...like a..."

"A bum," Henry blurted out.

Lee stood up. "Excuse me. I'm going to see how Shaneta is doing."

Shaneta gave him a comforting smile when he entered the kitchen. "How's it goin', Mista Lee?"

Lee put his arm around her shoulders. "Shaneta?"

"Yes, sir."

"Will you please call me Lee from now on, and drop the 'sir' business?"

Shaneta glared at him. "In front of Mista and Mrs. Winekoop too?"

"Especially in front of them."

"Yes, sir."

Lee reentered the sunroom and addressed his family members. "If you want to go outside now, you may. We have everything set up, and my other guests should be arriving shortly."

No one moved.

Lee turned away from them. "Whenever you're ready then," he mumbled under his breath.

Lenny and his wife were the first to arrive. Lenny had on the same bib overalls he wore in his store, but instead of a frayed-around-the-collar shirt, he had on a neatly pressed dress shirt. Lee showed them the Styrofoam coolers of beer and soda and pointed out the snack table that held a variety of chips, dips, vegetables, and fruit.

Lee introduced builder, Earl Lundberg, the next to arrive, to the Viniks and then walked toward the side of the house where he saw CJ and her clan approaching. He waved them over.

"C'mon in. We don't bite," he shouted.

"You gotta be kidding me, Soc," CJ whispered as she took in everything.

"This is your house?"

"Well, my parents' house."

"Are they here?" she whispered.

"They're inside. Hopefully, they'll come out soon."

Architect Dennis Freborg and his son, David, arrived next. Lee showed them around and then went over to where CJ stood with her sister.

"Having a good time?" he asked Francine.

"Yep."

They focused their attention across the lawn to where Lee had arranged for a local company called Parties by Patty to entertain the children. CJ's sons were getting their faces painted.

"My boys seem to be having fun. Why aren't your nieces and nephews over there?"

"Too messy for them, I would imagine."

"What's going to happen when the water balloon fights start?"

Lee saw that two of the party staff were using a hose to fill balloons with water.

"Well, we're not planning on fights, but there will be a balloon toss game. They probably won't be allowed to do that either."

"Poor things."

Shaneta approached Lee. "Are we ready to start cookin', Lee?"

"Sure."

"Who's that?" CJ asked.

Lee followed her gaze. "That's Dr. Rad and his sister, Adishree." Dr. Rad wore a suit coat and tie. Adishree wore a brown and gold sari.

"No kidding." CJ reached into her purse and pulled out a camera. "I couldn't resist bringing this. I hope you don't mind."

"Shoot away."

Lee walked over to greet Dr. Rad and Adishree. "I'm so glad you could make it. Let me introduce you to everyone."

As soon as the smell of hamburgers and hot dogs began to waft through the air, CJ's sons came running. They stood in front of the massive outdoor grill, paper plates in hands. Six-year-old Travis's shorts were twisted, and the Ninja Turtle that had been painted on the side of his face was now smeared and unrecognizable. Nine-year-old Wayne, sporting a long green snake that wrapped around his forehead and down his cheek and neck, had grass stains on his shorts and both knees.

"C'mere, you little flea turd," Wayne said to his younger brother. "How can you even walk in these?" He straightened out Travis's shorts. "Can't take you anywhere."

Lee's family emerged from the house onto the patio overlooking the back yard and the rest of Lee's guests. From his vantage point, Lee could see they were talking among themselves, even though their eyes were all fixated straight ahead and their lips barely moving. He could only imagine what they were saying to each other.

Dozens of hot dogs and hamburgers had been cooked and were ready for the taking on one end of a long banquet table that had been decorated with a red, white, and blue plastic tablecloth. The rest of the food—baked beans, deviled eggs, potato salad, and cole slaw—lay in neat rows down the length of table. At the other end were the desserts—thick watermelon slices, festive cupcakes, and dozens of Shaneta's homemade cookies.

Lee saw his mother look at his father, who shrugged his shoulders and then glanced over at Nelson, who turned his attention to his wife, Yvonne. Yvonne looked at her sister-in-law and so on. When the Winekoops had run out of family members to look at, they left the patio and made their way to the end of the food table, picked up paper plates, and followed Lee's other guests who were filling their plates with food. Lee watched his mother appraise the paper plate in front of her like she had never seen one before, as may actually have been the case.

Lee had arranged for everyone to sit around a second long narrow table near the picnic buffet. By the time the Winekoops arrived at the table, the only seats available were scattered among Lee's other guests. Lee watched the look of horror sweep across his mother's face. He nodded at her, and she sat down in the nearest open place, between CJ and Adishree.

For the first twenty minutes, Lee was the only Winekoop who engaged in conversation with the others.

"I'm so glad the rain held off. What a great day."

"Isn't the lake beautiful with all the sailboats and cabin cruisers trolling by?"

"How 'bout those Brewers—three wins in a row!"

The Winekoops kept silent, elbows in so as not to make physical contact with anyone, every once in a while glancing up at one of their own as though wanting to be saved from the awfulness of the situation.

CJ, who had taken several pictures after everyone had been seated, returned to her seat, and in her usual carefree style said to Abigale, "So, Lee's mother, how's it goin'?"

The collective Winekoop gasp hung in the air for several seconds.

From that moment on, conversation between his family and his friends, all of them initiated by his friends, commenced, and Lee just sat back and took in as much as possible.

Dr. Rad to Daphne, Bennett's wife: "So how are you related to my good friend Lee?"

Daphne leaned away from him. "I'm married to his brother." She turned to put her arm around her daughter's shoulders, seemingly to protect her from Dr. Rad.

CJ's sister, Francine, to Henry: "You have a very nice house. So what do you do, Mr. Winekoop?"

"I beg your pardon."

"What do you do?" Francine asked with deliberate slowness.

"I'm an investor." He glanced at his wife, who was staring at Adishree as though she was from some other planet.

"What do you invest in?"

Henry cleared his throat.

"I'm sorry. I didn't get that."

"Real estate mostly." He turned to address Travis, who sat on his other side and had been staring intently at him since they'd both sat down. "Is there something wrong, young man?"

"You've got long nose hairs."

"Good grief."

Francine to Lee's brother, Bennett: "I'll try you, then. What do you do?"

"I'm an attorney?"

"That's interesting. Where?"

"Chicago."

"What kind of law?"

"Corporate law, but..."

"Yes?"

Bennett paused. "But I spend a lot of my time doing pro bono work."

"Pro whato?"

"Pro bono. Helping those who can't afford legal representation."

"Do you ever help illegal migrant workers?"

"All the time."

"Are you any good?"

Bennett shot her a sidelong glance. "Of course I'm good."

"I see. You know former Senator Sam Wheland?"

Bennett's attention quickly heightened. "I know his work on immigration reform. Why do you ask?"

"Because I'm his part-time home nurse."

"Are you serious?"

Francine gave him a look that answered his question.

"I've been trying to get an appointment with him for months. I didn't know he was sick."

"He still has lots of good days. I can try to make that happen, the meeting that is. But you better not be kidding about being good. I've got a reputation to maintain. Let me have one of your business cards."

Nelson to Lee: "What on earth were you thinking, bringing us together with these people? Have you gone mad?" he whispered.

"These people are my friends," he whispered back. "Decent, law-abiding, morally upright everyday people."

"Right."

Lee noticed that his mother appeared to be on the verge of fainting. CJ's son, Wayne, who was sitting across from her, innocently asked, "You're not going to barf, are you?"

"Good heavens."

Dennis Freborg to Nelson's wife, Yvonne: "Nice affair."

"Pardon me?"

He raised his voice. "I said this is a nice affair."

"Yes, of course," she mumbled.

"Nice affair," he repeated.

Lenny to Bennett: "So I hear you're a lawyer."

"Yes, I am."

"I knew a lawyer once. Dumber than a box of rocks. Oh, I suspect he had a lot of schooling. Otherwise he couldn't be a lawyer." He paused to scratch his head. "Yeah, the cheese musta slipped off *that* cracker. I wonder whatever happened to him."

CJ to Bennett's daughter, Odessa: "That's some dress you're wearing. But how are you going to manage in the potato-sack races later?"

"The what?"

"The potato-sack races."

Bennett's wife, Daphne, to Odessa: "Never mind, dear. That would be for the other children."

CJ to Daphne: "Oh, you're wrong there. The adults play too. Barrel of laughs."

Dennis's son, David, to Nelson's son, Virgil: "So do you play any sports?"

"Squash."

"I said, do you play any sports?"

"Squash," he said louder.

Travis to his brother, Wayne: "Have you ever seen anything like this?" he whispered.

"Nope," he said under his breath. "Did you get a load of the twin hosers?"

"Makes me wanna barf."

Bennett's daughter, Anna, touched Adishree's sari. "This is very pretty," she said.

"*Shukriya, mera Baalika.*"

"Mom!"

One of the party planners dressed in a clown suit shouted, "Are all you party animals ready for a round of balloon toss?"

CJ's sons were the first to leave the table and follow the clown. The rest of

Lee's friends weren't far behind, including Dr. Rad and Adishree.

"Well, don't just sit there like bumps on a log. C'mon and join the others," Lee told his family. He got up, leaving eleven open-mouthed Winekoops sitting at the table.

"Mother, may we play?" asked one of Nelson and Yvonne's twin boys.

"No."

"Why?"

"Because you'll get wet," said Yvonne.

"So?"

"Nelson, I think it's time we take the children into the house, don't you?"

"But Mother..."

"Mind your mother, Virgil."

"May I have a piece of watermelon first?"

"No."

"Why?"

"It's too messy. It'll leave stains."

"But Mother..."

"Come along, boys."

Bennett and Daphne also got up to leave. Bennett Jr. asked, "Mother, I would like to stay out here and watch."

"No, we're going in now."

"Daphne," Bennett interjected, "what would it hurt if we just watched?"

She rolled her eyes. "Have it your way."

Lee's mother got up from her chair, picked up her paper plate, which still contained the same amount of food as it had when she'd first sat down, and said, "Imagine serving someone on this thing." She and Henry walked toward the house.

That left six couples tossing water-filled balloons back and forth, each taking a step back with each round. CJ's sons won, and the clown awarded them each a cheap little trinket, which they accepted with wide smiles.

The same couples joined in the potato-sack race. Dr. Rad and Adishree had to drop out when her sari kept tripping them up. Dennis and his son, David, won.

Francine and Lee, whose shirts were soaked with water from the balloon toss, walked back to the table where Bennett, his wife, and their three children remained seated.

"You guys are missing all the fun, you know," Francine said.

"We're quite fine here," said Bennett.

"You know, I said I would try to put you in touch with Senator Wheland, but I think I may just have to renege on that little promise."

Bennett appeared surprised but didn't say anything. "I'll do it only if you join me in a water-balloon toss."

Lee looked on with anticipation.

"You have got to be kidding me."

"Do I look like I'm kidding?"

Bennett, still stone-faced, said, "No, you don't."

"What I'm thinking is that I could pair up with you, Bennett. Daphne could pair up with Bennett, Jr., and then the two girls." She took Bennett by the arm. "C'mon, Mr. Pro Bono. Let's see what you've got."

Bennett's three giggling children ran ahead. Daphne trailed several steps behind her husband, looking more than just a little perturbed.

The clown had a bullhorn in his hand. "Okay, one and all. Come gather here for the main event of the day!"

CJ grabbed Lee's arm and dragged him over to the balloon-toss area. The four couples lined up, three feet apart from each other, while everyone else gathered around to watch. Lee glanced toward the house and waved at the rest of his family. They didn't wave back. Shaneta, who watched from the kitchen window, had a camera held up to her face.

Francine, Bennett, Jr., Odessa, and Lee held the water-laden balloons.

"Is everybody ready?" the clown shouted.

"You bet," said Bennett, Jr.

"Bennett, if you throw that thing too hard, you'll have severe consequences to pay," Daphne said to her son.

"It's a game, Mother. Chill out."

Daphne pursed her lips. "Where did you learn such language?"

"On the count of three, toss your balloons. One...two...three."

Bennett caught his with ease. Daphne somehow managed to catch hers despite her long, perfectly manicured nails. Anna fumbled with hers for several shaky seconds but then recovered.

Lee threw his balloon to CJ with extreme care. She gave him a *you-can-be-nice-if-you-want* smirk.

The onlookers cheered.

"Okay, boys and girls, take one giant step back." He waited for everyone to follow his instructions. "You in the yellow sweater so neatly placed around your shoulders, I said a *giant* step."

Daphne scowled and then stepped back in line with the others.

"One...two...three...throw!"

Bennett tossed his balloon two feet to the right of Francine, who made an impressive dive to the ground and managed to catch it.

"Hey, Bennett, where did you learn how to throw—in an all-girls school?"

Bennett, Jr., doubled over laughing at Francine's remark at the exact moment Daphne threw her balloon to him, hitting him squarely on the top of his head.

"Oh, no! Your sweater." She approached her son, arms outstretched.

Bennett, Jr., stood up. "Mother, it's a sweater." He pulled it off over his head and held it out in front of him. "It'll dry. Don't be such a—"

"Bennett," his father said. "Watch your words."

"You guys just don't get it, do you?" Bennett Jr. said as he stomped off toward the house, but not before grabbing a piece of watermelon. Daphne cautiously backed away from the line of balloon-throwers and then followed her son toward the house.

Anna squealed and threw her balloon to her sister, Odessa, who caught it with ease.

Winding up like a baseball pitcher, CJ threw her balloon at Lee, overhand...hard.

"What?" Lee shouted as he reached up for the balloon. His fingers pierced the balloon, causing the water to splash down on his head. "Where did *you* learn to throw? At spring training?"

"Okay. One more step back, my friends," the clown yelled.

Francine had a devilish look on her face.

"Get him, Francine!" Anna shouted.

"Anna!" Bennett responded. "I'm your father. You're supposed to be on my side."

Anna giggled.

Francine took precise aim and threw the balloon at Bennett's face where, despite his dodging maneuver, it landed with a splat.

"Yea!" Anna squealed, as Bennett wiped the water off his face.

"It's up to you, laughing girl," the clown said. "You need to catch this one to win the game."

Odessa took her time before she gently tossed the balloon to her sister. Anna planted her feet wide apart and held out her hands. The balloon sailed through the air and into her arms. "I got it! I got it!" she screeched.

While everyone applauded the girls' victory, Anna snuck up behind her father and threw her balloon at the back of his head. Bennett stood still, stone-faced, until the laughter died down.

"Very funny, Anna," he said as he approached her, picking up a full balloon from the table on his way.

"Don't do it, Father."

"What did you say, darling?"

Anna squealed and ran from Bennett who raced across the lawn after her.

"You can't get me, Father. You throw like a girl, remember?" she yelled through her giggles.

"Come back here, you little imp," Bennett shouted as he chased his daughter.

"Hey, Bennett!" Francine shouted. "I would have put you in touch with the good Senator anyway...just so you know."

Bennett's stride didn't falter as he held up a fist and shook it in the air at Francine.

Lee glanced up at the sunroom windows where the rest of his family stood watching.

CJ put her arm around Lee. "This was one kick-ass barbecue, Soc. Nice goin'. But I bet you're in deep shit with your parents. Am I right?"

"Who cares. It was fun."

"We've gotta jam. Francine has a nursing gig in an hour." She kissed him on the cheek. "Thanks for inviting us." She turned away from him and started to walk away but then swirled back around to add, "Hey, Socrates. Looks like the tables have finally turned!"

Dr. Rad had had one too many beers. "Thank you, my son, for imbibing us. Let me know when I can see that fermile, that fervile, land of yours."

Adishree took him by the arm. "Do you mean fertile, my brother?"

"Fertile. That's what I said."

Lenny shook Lee's hand. "We had a great time, Lee. Wish I could have promoted my store to your family, but I figured that would be about as senseless as nailin' a screen door on a submarine. No disrespect intended."

Architect Dennis Freborg shook Lee's hand. "Can't remember when I've laughed so much. Makes me glad I'm just a simple man with simple needs. Thanks, Lee. It was a real eye-opener...and I mean that in a good way."

"See you 'round, Lee. We're gonna start with the flooring on Tuesday," Lundberg said with a salute. "Nice party."

After the last guest had left, Lee surveyed the back yard—balloon remnants everywhere, skid marks on the once-pristine lawn, paper plates and napkins carelessly placed wherever the occasional breeze off the lake had taken them. In spite of what was likely waiting for him inside, he was pleased about the party, and for a blissful, fleeting moment, his mind went to a place where his family was proud of him, proud he had become his own person.

The walk into the house was arduous, and Lee made it last as long as possible, taking one long stride after another through the grass. Glancing up at the empty sunroom windows, he wondered from which room his family was conspiring against him.

When he entered the house, he found that all of the adult Winekoops had changed clothes and were seated in the living room, while the children were in the foyer, huddled together like a flock of sheep. All their suitcases had been moved from the second floor bedrooms and were lined up all the way from the living room to the front foyer.

"Leaving so soon?" he asked no one in particular.

"Sit down, Lee," his father said.

Not about to give in to his old ways by responding like a well-trained soldier, he sat on the arm of one of the overstuffed chairs, dangling one leg over the side.

"Sit in the chair properly, Lee." His mother appeared disgusted. "Show some respect."

He slid into the seat of the chair, feeling like a scolded six-year-old.

Henry continued. "I have to say we are all very disappointed in you, Lee. This charade was uncalled for and shows us you are no closer to maturity than you were a year ago. If I had my—"

"Henry, stop!" his mother interjected.

His father's words came as no surprise to Lee, but they still stung. "I don't know exactly what you're referring to, Father, but if it has anything to do with my other guests, I suggest you put it—"

"Who do you think you are, talking to me like that? I have half a mind to—"

"Henry!"

"Who do I think I am? I am me, Father. Lee Oliver Winekoop. Someone you have never known...and obviously still don't know. I'm not like you. I'm not like anyone in this room. I'm me. I'm an individual with my own needs, my own values, my own likes and dislikes that make me unique. I am my own person, not the embodiment of your expectations."

His words poured out of his mouth as if being manipulated by some outside source.

"I'm not going to live your dream, and the sooner you understand that, the better. And you want to know something else? I'm proud of myself. In fact. I couldn't be any more proud of myself for—"

"Lee, what Henry was trying to—"

"Stop, Mother. Stop trying to smooth things over by rewording what he said. You've done that my whole life, and I always saw through it. Let him say what he means. I may not like what he has to say, but I respect his right to say it." He could feel the sweat dripping down the back of his neck. "Let him say what a loser he thinks I am. Let him say he thought all along I would never amount to anything. Let him say what he thinks."

The silence was daunting.

Bennett walked over to Lee, put his hand on his shoulder, and whispered, "You best stop, Lee." His wife followed him toward the children in the foyer.

Nelson squirmed in his chair. His wife, Yvonne, stared at the wall.

"I see your bags are packed too," Lee said to Nelson. "Feel free to leave any time." Lee watched Nelson and his wife leave the room to join Bennett and his family, who now had their suitcases in hand and were exiting through the front door.

"I guess seeing my new house is out of the question now," he said to his mother.

"Some other time, dear." She turned to her husband. "Henry? Are we ready to go?"

She got up from her chair. "I'm sorry things didn't go well, sweetheart," she said to Lee.

Lee watched his parents walk out the front door, all the tension in the room drifting out after them.

It may not have gone well for you, Mother, but for me, things went splendidly!

18 | "He's Not Who You Think"

The ice-cold "brewski" Lee pulled from the refrigerator consoled him. He draped his lanky body out on the sunroom sofa, shoes and all.

Shaneta interrupted his thoughts about the day's events. "So how are we feelin', Mista...I mean Lee?"

Lee sat up and patted the sofa seat next to him. "Sit down with me, Shaneta."

She gave him a puzzled look.

"C'mon. I think you know by now I'm fairly harmless."

Shaneta eased onto the sofa. "Oh, I know that, but I've never..."

"I know. But things are different with me."

"With all due respect, Lee, you're not the one who signs mi paycheck."

He laughed. "Good point. But I assure you whatever we talk about stays between you and me." He held out his hand. "Deal?"

Shaneta hesitated, but finally shook on it. "Deal," she agreed. "So let me ask you, how do you think your party went?"

"For me, it couldn't have been any better. Thank you for all your help." He gazed out the window where the clean-up crew was bringing the backyard back to its normal state. "And as for my guests, well, I think they had a good time, too."

"And your family?"

"Not so good. What do you think?"

Shaneta's smile said it all. "Oh, mi God. When Mrs. Winekoop had no choice but to sit between CJ and...what is Dr. Rad's sister's name again?"

"Adishree."

"And Adishree...well, I guess she couldn't have gotten any paler."

"Did you get some good pictures?"

"Some real good ones."

"You must show them to me when they're developed. Maybe we'll make an album. CJ was taking pictures too. We'll call it Lee's 1987 Memorial Day Emancipation album."

"You know, Lee, I feel a little emancipated too."

"How do you mean?"

"You know, always havin' to act like...well, their servant, like I'm not a human bein' first. Always havin' to mind mi p's and q's, worried if I open mi mouth I might say the wrong thing." She reached out and touched Lee's hand.

"You're not like that, and I do appreciate that, but then again..."

"Then again, what?" He waited for a response but got none. "Well, I'm glad you realize I'm not like them. But did you see Bennett and his kids doing the water-balloon toss?"

"I sure did, and I got pictures to prove it!" The smile left her face. "How do you think they got that way, Lee?"

"Out of touch with reality you mean?"

"Somethin' like that."

"Well, Shaneta, that *is* their reality. My mother, she grew up in that same kind of family—wealthy, everything done for her, not much exposure to how regular people live—so that explains it for her. But my father, well, I don't quite get that myself. His father was a Chicago policeman who had to moonlight just to keep his family fed and clothed. I don't know. I was never very close to him."

"Yes, I know."

"Shaneta, this conversation we're having right now, you and me—you could combine all the conversations I've had with my parents over the years and they wouldn't amount to this one in terms of honesty."

Shaneta's expression turned serious. Lee got the feeling she was uncomfortable all of a sudden.

"What's wrong?"

"Nothin'." She got up.

"Where are you going?"

"I've got work to do, Mista Lee.

"Shaneta, something's wrong. Is it something I said?"

"No, sir."

"Please sit back down. Please?"

Shaneta sat.

"Something is bothering you. I can tell. Do you want talk about it?"

"No."

"You might feel better."

She shook her head. "No, I won't." She got up again to leave, and this time Lee let her go. Ten minutes later, she returned.

"I have no business tellin' you this."

"Telling me what?"

"I know better than to butt into someone else's business."

"Shaneta, you can tell me anything."

"I could get fired over tellin' you this."

"Shaneta, what is it?"

"I'm only tellin' you this because...well, I'm thinkin' if I were in your boots, I would want to know. But I need this job, and..."

"I will not repeat what you're about to tell me. I promise."

"Cross your heart and hope to die?"

"What?"

"Nothin'. It's just an expression." She sat down and smoothed out the crisp white apron she always wore. "After Mista and Mrs. Winekoop came in the house, right before the water balloons...well, I overheard them talkin'. I wasn't eavesdroppin' or anything. I never do that. But, you know, when you've got things to do...well... I shouldn't be tellin' you this."

"Look, if it's going to make you uncomfortable, you shouldn't tell me."

Shaneta stared at him for several seconds. "No, I would want to know. Lee, your father threatened to have you disowned."

"Disowned?"

"There's more. Oh, my. This should be comin' from your parents, Mista Lee." Tears welled up in her eyes. "May the lawd take mi life if I'm doin' the wrong thing."

The bile rose up into Lee's throat.

"Lee, your father...he's not who you think he is."

"What are you talking about?"

"He's not your real father." She clasped her hand over her mouth. "Now I've said it."

"Not my real father?"

"No."

"So who is he?"

"I shouldn't be the one tellin' you this."

"Shaneta, if you say that one more time..."

"I know, but it's so true."

"Are you going to continue?"

"Lee, your real father...your real father was your Uncle Nelson."

19 | DISOWNED

Had he understood her correctly? Even if he had been able to speak after hearing Shaneta utter those few earthshaking words, he wouldn't have known what to say.

He tried to form a mental image of his uncle, but all he could remember was that he had been tall, not fat or thin, and maybe had a receding hairline.

"I'm sorry, Lee, to be the one to tell you this. It's just that—"

"And my mother?"

Shaneta shook her head. "From what I heard, she was someone who he had...well, relations with, someone who left you on your father's doorstep, so to speak."

"What? Who would do that?"

"I shouldn't say."

"Shaneta, you've told me this much. What could be any worse?"

"Mista Winekoop refers to her as 'his whore.'"

"Who's whore?"

"Uncle Nelson's."

"Are you sure you know what you're talking about? This is preposterous."

"You can't be a devoted servant to people and not know their business. Believe me, I know everything. Every thing."

This must be a dream. I want to wake up. Now.

"Okay, so how did I end up with..." All of a sudden, he didn't know what to call his parents. "Them."

"That was your mother's doing. She wanted you to have a good home, a decent upbringing."

"Uncle Nelson. I never knew him."

"I know. I'm sure that was deliberate on everyone's part."

"Everyone's? Do my brothers know?"

Shaneta acknowledged what he feared with a slight nod.

"What?"

"Lee, please don't hate me for tellin' you this."

"*Everyone* knows?" He tried to remember what she had said last. Something about hating her. "Hate you? No, I don't hate you." He took a deep breath.

Shaneta appeared as though she might burst at any moment. He reached out for her hand.

"Look, if this is all true, it appears you are the first person in my life who has ever been honest with me. How could I possibly hate you?" He rose up and stood in front of her. "Come here."

They hugged for a long moment, and when they separated, he said, "No, I don't hate you. You, my dear Shaneta, may very well be my savior."

"If they ever find out I told you, well..."

"Shaneta, if they ever find out, and they certainly won't hear it from me, you don't have to worry about a thing. I'll have your back. And that goes both ways. You're never to tell anyone you told me."

She took a couple of steps back. "Well, as mi son would say, 'Never trouble trouble until trouble troubles you.'"

"I'll take that to mean you agree."

After Shaneta left for the day, Lee poured himself a glass of Scotch, went outside to the back patio, and reclined in one of the chaise lounges. The first gulp of alcohol hit the back of his throat hard and roared through his chest like thunder before settling in his stomach.

His life now began to make sense: The secrecy of the terms of his inheritance and the fact that Uncle Nelson had left more to him than to his brothers. His brothers. They weren't really his brothers after all. His sisters-in-law and their children...did they all know?

Shaneta knew, so all the other staff must know as well.

Was I the only one who didn't know?

And his mother—his real mother, the person his father referred to as "Uncle Nelson's whore"—had she been a prostitute? Or was that merely his word for someone who'd had a child out of wedlock? Having sex with someone outside of marriage was the most contemptuous of sins in his father's eyes.

No wonder he had no use for me. I was the product of someone's immorality.

Learning from an outsider about what was arguably the most fundamental aspect of his identity was in some ways more unsettling than the news itself. And even more humiliating was that by this time, he really should have figured it out for himself.

What did "disowned" mean? Certainly out of their will, at the very least. And probably out of their house before long. And their lives. He made a mental note to call Earl on Monday to get an estimated finish date on his house. At least he had that to his name.

A cardinal began to sing a tune from high up in a nearby willow tree, a song that started out sad, but by the time the bird finished the melody, sounded quite cheerful. As Lee contemplated the potential loss of his family, he thought of how he envied the bird's ability to nonchalantly change his tune and then just fly away.

Hours later, having spent a restless night in bed reliving Shaneta's revelation,

Lee stared at the alarm clock until the numbers came into focus—four a.m. What a day. One minute he had been tossing a water-filled balloon to his best friend, CJ, having more fun than he'd ever had in his life, and the next minute he was being told by the family cook, of all people, that his parents weren't his real parents and were talking about disowning him. Even the many seasoned psychologists he'd seen in his short life would have been taken aback with this one.

What disturbed him most was the betrayal by everyone in his family—his so-called parents, his real father, and while he had never had much of a relationship with them, even his brothers. But then, maybe his brothers hadn't felt any obligation to tell him. After all, he was nothing but some poor bastard their mother had apparently felt compelled to take in.

He pictured Henry throwing a fit when his wife wanted to bring a third child into their family. They already had two perfect sons, a ten-year-old and a twelve-year-old. An ideal household. Shangri-la.

He thought about Uncle Nelson, his real father. Who was he? How dare he disregard his own son? His mother talked about him as though he was a close, loving family member, yet he had never come to any family functions. She had talked about him as though she was in constant contact with him, yet Lee couldn't remember them doing things together or even talking on the phone. He wondered if they had ever talked about him or if that had been considered taboo.

Uncle Nelson's last name was Sedgwick, indicating he was his mother's father's brother. Lee's grandparents had died before Lee was born, so he wasn't able to make any connection that way.

And his real mother? Who was she? Who would give up her own baby? Where was she?

Lee stared out the window over the water, as though the answers to his questions existed somewhere beneath the gentle waves. Were they so ashamed that this atrocity had happened in their perfect little family that they'd continue to hide the truth...even after the man was dead?

He laughed aloud. *No wonder I always thought I was different, out-of-place, unwelcome in the family. It was true!*

Lee wondered how he could possibly face these people now, unless it was to confront them with their secret. He pictured himself venting his newfound anger at them—it would serve them right—and then never speaking to them again. Maybe they wouldn't even care.

His thoughts drifted back to his father, his real father, his deceased father. There was obviously a story about how Lee came to be. Would he ever get to hear it? And if so, who would be the one to tell it to him?

Regardless of his father's absence in his life, he suddenly thought he should be mournful over the man's death. He tried to conjure up some emotion, but felt nothing.

Lee watched the sun begin its daily ascent over the lake.

I might have other family members out there somewhere.

The burden of that uncertainty compelled him to put that thought aside for the time being.

He walked to the window and stared at the reflection of the sunrise on the water, the feelings of hurt, anger, and confusion colliding inside his head.

Still, there was an inexplicable feeling of relief deep in his chest, like a fistful of balloons had just been released into the sky.

20 | JUST WHO'S NORMAL?

Bennett called Lee several days after the barbecue to thank him for introducing him to Francine, who had come through with her promise to put him in touch with Senator Wheland. He was thrilled to have succeeded in scheduling a meeting with Wheland to discuss possible collaboration on a couple of projects involving immigration reform.

"Glad I could help. And I'm glad you had such a good time at the barbecue too." It was different talking with him knowing he had no familial ties with him.

"I'm sure you meant well."

"Meant well?"

"You know what I mean."

"No, I don't. I meant well? Is that what you were thinking when you were chasing your daughter around the yard with a water balloon?"

Bennett didn't respond.

A wave of emotion swept over him, one he hadn't experienced before, one that spurred him to say what had been irking him ever since the barbecue. "What's with you, anyway? You were like a different person when you forgot for the moment you were a Winekoop."

"You're being impertinent."

"You sound like Mother."

"It's unfortunate more of her didn't rub off on *you*."

Lee could feel the warmth creeping up his neck. "You are so damn pretentious, just like the rest of them."

"And you are out of line."

"Maybe I am. But do tell me, exactly why did you all leave in such a huff that day?"

"That would seem evident."

"Enlighten me."

"We're obviously not used to eating off paper plates and fraternizing with..."

"With whom? Someone like Francine, who put you in touch with someone you couldn't get in to see on your own? Someone like that?"

Bennett offered no response.

"You're too much, you know that? You know what your problem is? You think more about what others think of you than what you think of yourself."

"That comment is indicative of your selfishness."

"Are you kidding me? Why don't you ditch those highfalutin words you spit out like a robot and say what you mean? What are you afraid of anyway?"

"You don't know what you're talking about."

"Don't I?"

"You, my friend, have no respect for our family, but then..."

"But then, what?" Lee waited for him to say *But you're not really part of this family anyway.*

"Look, my intent for this phone call was to properly thank you for something. But I can see by your boorish behavior, you are incapable of graciously receiving it.

"Now you sound like Father."

"Goodbye, Lee."

He hadn't intended to pick a fight with Bennett. Between his two brothers, he always felt Bennett was the more tolerant one. Knowing his real identity was making Lee feel boldly assertive, and he didn't know if he should embrace that or try to repress it.

In any case, it felt good.

* * *

Lee buried himself as much as he could in the process of building his new house, keeping in close communication with the builder and general contractor. Between daily visits to the property and frequent visits to Deer Bottom Inn, he managed to keep his mind off his family—his real one and the one he had erroneously called family for the first twenty-seven years of his life. Since the barbecue, he'd heard nothing from any of his family members other than Bennett, and in the aftermath of that conversation, he wasn't so sure they'd ever be speaking again.

Working with Dr. Rad on planning the greenhouses and labs now made him uneasy, which was especially ironic since he had been the one who had preached to Dr. Rad about how much would be lost if he didn't continue his work. It was one thing to develop the land when he thought he had inherited it from an uncle he barely knew, an uncle who inexplicably had imposed some peculiar restrictions on him. But the matter took on new meaning now that he knew it had come from his father. Now the peculiar restrictions stirred up an intense desire in him to know what they were all about.

Two weeks after his conversation with Bennett, he stopped at the inn for dinner and was happy to find CJ behind the bar.

"Hey, Soc, what's happenin'?"

"Just picked out some interesting prairie stone for my fireplace."

"Cool. Gonna invite us over to toast some marshmallows when it's done?"

"You know, that's a great idea. I'll have to throw a housewarming party."

"Most definitely. Your family included. Wouldn't be any frickin' fun without them."

"Very funny."

"We've got sloppy joes today. Can we fix you one?"

Lee gave her a blank stare.

"Get real. You've never had one, right?" Lee remained silent. "I don't believe this. I'm going to order one for you." She turned away from him. "Dag, you were born into *some* family."

Lee chuckled under his breath, wondering how long it would take him to tell her his real family story.

* * *

Ten weeks went by without any communication from anyone in his family, not even his mother, and Lee struggled with whether or not to call her. In spite of his pact with Shaneta, he wondered if maybe they knew he knew and that was why no one had called him. He didn't know if that was a good or bad thing. While he felt remorseful about the family disconnect, especially with his mother, he was afraid of how their relationship would change once everything was out in the open.

When Lee's builder gave him an August 18 completion date for the house, he panicked. Three weeks wasn't much time to get ready to move in. During his next visit to the inn, he asked CJ if she would help him shop for furniture and appliances.

"Soc, I am so lame when it comes to that sort of thing. I don't think you would want my help. But Francine, now she's another story. I think she must have been an interior decorator in a past life. I'll bet she'd help you with it. I'll ask her."

Francine insisted on visiting the house before going on their expedition. She came armed with a clipboard and sketched each room—showing its exact dimensions and indicating the location of every window and door—something Lee never would have thought of doing. She suggested they shop at Porters of Racine, Wisconsin's oldest and finest furniture store. Lee took advantage of the opportunity on the sixty-mile drive to get to know her better.

"So you're a nurse. Where did you go to school?"

"Truman College."

"In Chicago?"

"Mm-hm. I have an RN degree but would love to get my master's someday."

"What's holding you back?"

"Money mostly, but also time. I work part-time at Rockford Memorial, do volunteer work for the Cancer Research Institute, occasionally take on home nursing jobs, and of course, watch over Travis and Wayne while CJ is working. It keeps me hopping."

"How long would it take you to get your master's?"

"Two years if I could go full-time. Three or four if part-time, depending on how much time I could put into it."

"Tell me more about the Cancer Research Institute."

"Wonderful organization. They've been around since 1891. Their main focus is immunology and immunotherapy. Last year, Dr. Tonegawa won the Nobel Prize in Medicine for his discovery of the genetic principle for the generation of antibody diversity."

"I'm not going to pretend I understand what that means."

"I know. I don't fully understand it either. That's why I want to go back for my master's."

"Do they ever conduct cancer research on plants?"

"Not that I'm aware of. Right now they're working on a huge project involving the cloning of CTLA-4."

"And that is?"

"Cytotoxic T lymphocyte."

"Okay."

"It's a protein receptor, and understanding it means better understanding cancer and the immune system."

"Very interesting. What do you do for them?"

"Fundraising, mostly. Whatever I can do from home."

"So have you ever been married?"

"No, not me. I have too many other things I want to accomplish first. Marriage would just get in the way."

"May I ask how old you are, Francine?"

"Twenty-seven, a year and a half older than CJ."

"I still can't believe CJ is twenty-five with a nine-year-old son."

"She'll be twenty-six in November. That louse."

"Who?"

"DeRam. CJ told me she told you everything."

"Yes, she did. He's dangerous."

"The kidnapping was the worst."

"The what?"

"Oops. She told me she told you everything."

"She never told me about a kidnapping."

"I have a big mouth."

"Are you going to tell me about it?"

"I suppose I have to now. As soon as Bern heard CJ was pregnant, the first time, he skedaddled out of town, but when Wayne was five months old, he returned. I think at that point, CJ may have thought there could still be a chance they could be together. She rationalized his behavior by saying he left town because he just got scared.”

“I get the feeling it took a while for her to see what trouble he was.”

“Lee, there are times now I don’t think she totally gets it, but that’s another story. Anyway, one day he comes over to our house while I’m at work. CJ is hanging clothes out on the line with little Wayne in his buggy. The phone rings, and she asks him if he’d keep an eye on the baby for a minute. When she comes out, he’s gone and so is Wayne.”

“You have got to be kidding me.”

“I wish I was.”

“So what happened?”

“She panicked. Said she was afraid to call the police because of who he was. She didn’t have a car to go look for them. She was on her way to the neighbor’s house to get help when he pulled in the driveway.”

“Unbelievable.”

“He opens the car door, and there’s Wayne lying on the front seat, his little head right next to the butt of Bern’s rifle. And that bastard has the nerve to say, ‘We went for a little ride. Did you miss us?’“

“I’m speechless. What a jerk. How did CJ react?”

“She told him if he ever pulled a stunt like that again, she would have him arrested for kidnapping. He just laughed.”

“That is beyond outrageous. I’ve had a few run-ins with him myself. What is his problem, anyway?”

“I think the whole problem is that he has an obsession with her, and he uses scare tactics in an effort to get her back. I don’t think he loves her. I don’t think he even really wants her back, and I’m sure he doesn’t want a relationship with those two boys. I think he just can’t accept rejection.”

“That’s troubling on so many levels.”

“We all know he’s dangerous, a loose cannon, and he carries a gun. I am scared for her every day, mace or no mace. Thank you, by the way, for arranging for that security system in her house. At least she has that now. And I can’t believe your incredible timing, finding him at her house that day. I don’t know what would have happened if you hadn’t burst through that door.”

“I know.”

“So where did you learn karate?”

Lee explained his passion for it despite his family members’ view of it as sheer foolishness. “The dynamics of my family are fairly inexplicable.”

“Well, I got a good glimpse of them on Memorial Day. They’re...different. But I have to say I think your brother Bennett started to come around.” She laughed. “A little time away from the rest of them, and he could be close to being like one of us.”

Us? Holy shit, does she think I’m normal?

21 | "You're Under Arrest"

Lee did a final walk-through of the house with Earl to create a punch list of items that needed attention. Afterwards, Lee plopped himself down in the middle of the living room floor to take it all in. He felt happy and excited, but at the same time scared. But most of all he felt satisfied—a feeling he wanted to bottle up and put on his new mantle.

Later that day, he felt compelled to let his parents, or whoever they were, know he was moving out of their lake house. After long internal deliberations with himself about what he was going to say, he called his mother.

"As soon as I'm settled, I would love for everyone to come for a visit," he told her through gritted teeth. While extending an invitation to someone who had betrayed him his whole life was agonizingly painful, he knew it was the right thing to do.

"We'll see, Lee. Henry is still, shall we say, disturbed by your behavior Memorial Day weekend. He needs time to—"

Her words sucked any politeness he had right out of him. "I understand. Well, I must be going. I'll call you with my new phone number as soon as it's installed. Goodbye..." He stopped short of calling her Mother. "Well, goodbye then."

As soon as he hung up, he regretted ending the phone conversation so abruptly, but when she practically defended his father's contempt for him, all he could think of was getting away from them as soon as possible.

He went to the kitchen to say goodbye to Shaneta. First, he gave her a big hug, and when he let go, she had tears in her eyes. "I'm going to miss you," he told her.

"I'm goin' to miss you, too, Lee."

"When are you going back to Evanston?"

"I'm not," she said as she clutched a dishtowel close to her chest.

"You're not?"

"Mrs. Winekoop said they don't need a second cook there, and when they come here, they plan to eat at the club."

He was fairly sure he hadn't heard her correctly. Her thick accent made it hard to understand her at times, and the added emotion in her voice now made it even harder. "What did you say?"

Shaneta didn't respond.

"Does this have to do with Memorial Day weekend?"

She shook her head. "I don't know. When you moved in and they sent me up here, I thought maybe I was on my way out. Mrs. Winekoop was findin' things wrong with mi work lately."

"I have a good mind to tell her—"

"Don't, Lee. It will only make matters worse."

"Where will you go?"

"She told me I can stay workin' here until I find somethin' else. As long as I'm gone by Labor Day when they have their big fall soiree. They're bein' very generous, Lee. A good severance check and everythin'."

The current job market wouldn't be kind to someone Shaneta's age, and being a black woman with a thick accent made her even less marketable.

"Shaneta, when I said back in May I'd have your back, I meant it. If you can't find something in the next...Labor Day? That's in less than three weeks."

"I know."

"Look, you won't be able to—"

"I can go to Detroit and live with mi sister."

"Your sister?"

"It will be fine."

"Your sister, the one you said has one boyfriend after another coming to live with her?"

"She'll calm down...one of these days."

"Is that what you want?"

"Until I find somethin' else."

"No, I won't hear of it. Look, they're starting to build the greenhouses for Dr. Rad, and—"

"Dr. Rad?"

Oh, shit. Can I say that? Too late now. I already did.

"Yes, I am partnering with him on his research. He's going to manage fifty acres of my land, live here, do his research here."

He tried to recall the exact language of the terms of his inheritance. All he remembered was he couldn't divulge them to anyone.

"What I was about to say, is you can stay with me. I have two extra bedrooms on the first floor, and then..."

"Then what? All I would be doin' is postponin' the inevitable."

"You can stay with me until we figure something out. In fact, I insist on it. And let's face it, we're kind of kindred souls at this point. Don't you think?"

"Oh, no. What will your family think?"

"Do we care?"

Shaneta's smile revealed her response.

"I guess the fair thing for me to do would be to let you see it first, before you move in. Why don't you come with me now. I just have to load all my things in the car, and that won't take but a few minutes."

"I can't just leave like that. I have..."

"You have what?"

Shaneta shrugged. "Well, nothin' I guess. I'll meet you in the car. One more thing, Lee."

"Yes?"

"Dr. Rad."

"What about him?"

She hesitated. "Nothin'."

* * *

It took Lee little time to settle into his new house, which quickly came to feel more like a home than any place he had ever lived. The furniture Francine had helped him pick out suited him—it was masculine, but not too masculine, and cozy and fit well with the A-frame style of the house.

Shaneta settled into her new room with surprising ease. He took her shopping to pick out sheets, towels, curtains, and a bedspread—a gesture Shaneta considered magnanimous. She chose the room in the northeast corner of the house, the one with a sliding door that opened onto a private rear deck and offered a clear view of the rest of the property.

Of course, she insisted on doing all the cooking and cleaning and told him if he said no, she was going to do it anyway.

"Just give me some notice when you're not goin' to be here for dinner," she told him. "So I don't cook for nothin'."

"I wasn't very good about that before, was I?"

She pursed her lips. "But I was bein' paid, so I couldn't say anythin'."

"We'll start over. Deal?"

"So can I throw in some good down-home Jamaican food for you from time to time?"

"You bet. Say, let's invite CJ and her clan over for a housewarming party. Some other people too. All Jamaican food. Will you help me with it?" He paused. "And then join us?"

"When?"

"How about Labor Day weekend?"

"Be careful, my friend, I could get used to this."

* * *

"Toss me a cold one, will ya, CJ?" There were more people than usual at the inn. "So what's going on? It's a madhouse in here," he said to her.

"There's a going-away party for some McHenry County sheriff going on."

"McHenry County?"

"Mm-hm."

"Is DeRam here?"

"Yeah, he's here."

"Has he said anything to you?"

"Nope."

"Good. Let's hope it stays that way."

"I gotta go. They're running me ragged."

"Stop back when you have a minute, okay?"

She gave him an affirmative head jerk and disappeared to the other end of the bar.

It didn't take DeRam long to spot Lee. He approached him with his usual cop-like swagger even though he wasn't wearing his uniform. Lee didn't get up off his bar stool.

"So what keeps you comin' back here, Winecrap?"

"The name is Winekoop."

He laughed. "Yeah, I know."

DeRam's disgusting smile made Lee want to slap it right off his face.

"It's a free country...at least the last time I looked."

"You're messin' around where you shouldn't be, karate boy."

Lee shrugged. "I haven't broken any laws. And you?"

DeRam lowered his voice. "Just make sure you know what business is yours to mind and what belongs to someone else, ya hear?"

"I'm sorry. Did you say something? It's so loud in—"

The sheriff leaned in and whispered near Lee's ear, "You heard me, smart ass." His cheap cologne caused Lee to stifle a cough.

Lee watched him walk back to his group. Whatever DeRam said to the others caused two of them to slap him on his back. Lee cringed at the thought DeRam was bragging about bullying him.

After the party was over and the crowd at the bar had thinned out, CJ made her way over to Lee.

"Everything okay?" she asked.

"Yep."

"What did he say to you?"

"Nothing. Just some bullshit."

"Why, Socrates, I've never heard you swear before."

"He does that to me. Listen. I'm all moved in to my new place, and so is Shaneta, but that's another story. We're going to—"

"Get outta here. You and Shaneta?"

"Not that way, you ditz."

"Ditz? Did you just call me a ditz?"

"Sorry. I got carried away."

"Well, keep it up. It suits you."

"Anyway, we're going to throw a little housewarming party on Labor Day weekend, and I'd love it if you, Francine, and the boys could come."

"Most definitely. Can we bring something?"

"Just yourselves. And just so you know, Shaneta is cooking a boatload of authentic Jamaican food."

"A theme party, then. None of us has ever had Jamaican food." She shot him a sidelong grin. "So what will your family eat?"

"They won't be there. They always have a big Labor Day affair at the lake house on that weekend."

"You're not going?"

"Apparently I wasn't invited."

"Whoa."

"Long story."

* * *

Lee stopped by Earl Lundberg's office the next day to ask him about building a small guesthouse on the property. Earl told him that he could probably start construction in November, and it would take about the same amount of time as the first house, maybe less if he didn't go A-frame. They talked a bit about the costs, and then Lee said he would be back in touch with Earl about it.

His next stop was Rockford Coin and Stamp to get an appraisal on the coin collection he had inherited from "Uncle Nelson," which was still in a safe deposit box in Chicago. He had seen it only once a few years back, at which time he had jotted down descriptions of some of the more interesting-looking coins.

Lee described what he thought he had to the owner of the store, who said he would be more than happy to appraise them, but due to the potentially high value of the collection, only if they met on neutral territory with a third party present. Lee called the Winekoop family attorney in Chicago and arranged for the three of them to meet at the bank the following week for the appraisal.

When Lee got home, he called Stonebugger's secretary and asked her if she would ask Stonebugger if he had any issue with him constructing buildings on the property using his own funds, not from the trust fund. She said she'd get back to him.

The next week, Lee drove seventy miles to the First Chicago Bank, where the coin collection had been residing for the past twenty-seven years, to meet with the attorney and the Rockford coin expert. When the three had settled themselves at a large table in a private room, the appraiser tenderly opened the oversized lockbox containing Lee's inheritance. He inspected each coin through a magnifying lens attached to his glasses, stuck a label with a number on each, and created a written inventory that included the coin's shape, color, denomination, date, size, and inscription. He did this with amazing speed, picking up a coin with his left hand and hand-writing the information with his right, sometimes picking up the next coin before he had finished writing about the previous one.

When all was said and done, the inventory included 253 coins. The appraiser told them off the top of his head, it wouldn't surprise him if Lee had a quarter of a million dollars worth of coins.

He went on to explain that he would provide Lee with estimates of market value and replacement value for each coin, as well as recent auction prices if available. He said he had no doubt that all the coins were authentic, but if Lee required certificates of authenticity, there would be an extra cost. When Lee asked him if he would consider buying some of the coins himself, he said that he would indeed and could give Lee a better price than a wholesaler.

Lee basked in the satisfaction he was feeling from being in control of his own actions. Determined to keep the ambiguity of his family situation from interfering with his newfound gratification, he vowed, at least for now, to avoid any communication with them.

Two weeks later, the coin appraisal arrived in a large box—one sheet for each coin. In his cover letter, the proprietor provided a tally of $315,900 for the whole lot, the most valuable coin being a 1943 bronze wheat penny with an estimated market value of $55,000. He also included a list of the coins he wished to buy from Lee and what he was willing to pay for them. His offer totaled $75,000.

"Thank you, father," he said to the heavens. "You just paid for my guesthouse...and then some."

* * *

In the days preceding Labor Day, Lee woke up every morning to the intoxicating aromas of Shaneta's jerk-spiced chicken, ackee and saltfish, pilau, stewed peas, coco bread, banana fritters, and plantation tarts, as she prepared for the housewarming party.

On Labor Day morning, Lee dressed in a tie-dyed t-shirt Shaneta had made for him, khaki-colored linen pants, and a Panama hat. He went outside, and greeted by a warm sunny day, watched Shaneta decorate the patio with lanterns, bamboo torches, and red, yellow, and green streamers. She then placed bowls of bananas, mangos, and pineapples out on tables set with brightly colored paper tablecloths. The floral centerpiece, with a paper toucan nestled among the petals, was her finishing touch. To make his own contribution to the ambiance, Lee brought out a tape player and a recording of Jamaican folk music that he'd picked up at a local record store.

CJ, Francine, Wayne, and Travis arrived at noon, all sporting tropical shirts. One by one, gifts in hand, the other guests arrived, all the same people who had come to his Memorial Day barbecue, minus the Winekoops.

Once everyone had toured the new house, they all went out to the patio table where Shaneta had placed a half-hollowed-out coconut by each place setting, complete with a paper umbrella and hibiscus flower. Lee poured Jamaican punch into each one, spiked for those who wished to imbibe. The amount of food on the table would have easily fed twice the number of guests. Lee sat back and enjoyed the cheerful conversations while they passed the dishes around the table— conversations that differed considerably from the ones he'd overheard on Memorial Day...delightfully normal conversations.

At the end of the meal, Lee stood up and tapped a spoon on his water glass to get everyone's attention. He thanked Shaneta for her contribution to the party and invited his guests to partake in a lively limbo contest. Afterwards, he said the girls could have their nails painted by an artist who would soon arrive and that there would be dessert and a gift-opening ceremony after that.

Just as the limbo contest was about to begin, Lee saw his brother Bennett emerge from the side of the house. Lee hadn't spoken with him since their awkward run-in on the phone. His brother wasn't smiling, and Lee's first thought was that something had happened to their mother.

"Is everything okay?" he asked him.

"Yes, of course. I'm sorry. It looks like I picked a bad time to come see your new house," Bennett said.

What's he up to?

"No problem. You've met everyone here." Lee gave him a puzzled look. "I would have thought you'd be at the lake house today for their big Labor Day party...with your family."

"Can we talk in private for a minute? I won't take you from your guests for long. I promise."

"Okay." Lee excused himself and led Bennett into the house.

Bennett didn't waste any time getting to the purpose of his visit. "I'll make this short. I've done a lot of thinking since we last spoke, and I have to tell you, well...I have to tell you that you were right. You were absolutely right."

"About?"

"Me. I'm not connected with myself. I never *have* been. You said it perfectly that day on the phone—I've been more interested in what others think about me than I am in what I think about myself. It took me a while to come to that realization...even after you flung it in my face like you did."

"I'm sorry about that," Lee said.

"Don't be. I'm certainly not." He reached out for Lee's hand. "Peace?"

They shook hands.

"Of course."

They had never shaken hands before. Hadn't ever touched each other before. Lee studied Bennett's face. He hadn't realized until now just how handsome a man he was—strong jaw line, dark wavy hair, warm green eyes, and one of those smiles that made you feel at ease.

"And that speech you gave Mother and Father after the picnic, when you told them you were your own person, not someone molded by their expectations...bravo. They needed to hear that. We all needed to hear that."

"I was scared to death saying what I did."

"You had courage to say what you did."

"Thanks for saying that. Means a lot to me."

"You mean a lot to me, and I really mean that."

"So why aren't you at Mother's party?"

"I was. I feigned a headache so I could come over here."

"And your family?"

He hesitated before speaking. "Daphne left me. And she took the children with her."

"What?"

"She went back to Colorado to live with her parents."

"What about you? What about your kids?"

"I have an attorney. We're trying to work things out."

Lee put his hand on Bennett's shoulder. "I'm sorry, man. That really stinks."

"Tell me about it."

"I didn't know you two were, well, having trouble."

"I didn't realize myself our marriage was in such trouble until I came home from work one day, and she and the kids were gone."

"You've got to be kidding. No warning? No note?"

"Oh, there was a note all right. From her attorney."

"Jesus. So she's divorcing you?"

"Well, the letter was cleverly written. They're suggesting no action will be taken for at least six months while we make an effort to work things out, but I think that's just for show because when someone files under irreconcilable differences, the courts ask you what you've done to try to resolve the differences. They want to be able to say she spent six months trying to save the marriage."

"Seems like such a ruse."

"It is. Look, I'm going to leave now. You've got other guests. I just had to clear the air with you before any more time passed."

"Why don't you stay? We can talk more after everyone leaves."

"No, I'll get going. I'll call you later this week." He turned and headed for the door. After opening it, he turned back around. "Lee?"

"Yes."

"Thanks for the wake-up call." He left without waiting for a response.

Lee went back out to the yard where the limbo contest was in full swing. CJ's boys, who had an unfair advantage being much closer to the ground than the men, were clearly going to be the winners.

Lee finished watching the game and then chatted with the men while the women had their nails painted with fanciful Jamaican designs. When that had been completed, he gathered everyone around him while he opened the presents.

He grabbed CJ's gift first. It was a teenage mutant ninja turtle cookie jar that her boys had picked out.

From Francine, a cookbook, *The Joy of Cooking*. "I figured you didn't know how to do much in the kitchen."

From Earl Lundberg, his builder, a home fire extinguisher. "Looks like this goes right along with *The Joy of Cooking*, he said and then laughed loudly at his own joke.

From architect Dennis Freborg, a brass horseshoe, which Lee learned signified good luck in a new home.

From hardware store owner, Lenny Vinik, a starter toolbox. "I'll explain what each one does later."

From Dr. Rad and Adishree, three welcome mats—one for each door. "Thank you for making me feel so welcome, my friend."

From Shaneta: A "Kiss the Cook" apron. "I may want to borrow this from time to time," she teased.

As Lee was about to lift his glass of Jamaican punch to toast everyone, he heard the bark of a vaguely familiar voice.

"Lee Oliver Winekoop...you're under arrest."

When Lee looked up, he saw Bernard DeRam in his sheriff's uniform accompanied by another officer.

"What?"

"You heard me." DeRam walked over to Lee, holding up a pair of handcuffs.

"What for?"

"Illegal harvesting and possession of marijuana. Turn around."

Arrested for growing marijuana in front of all of his friends. It made no sense. Lee struggled in the back seat of DeRam's patrol car to find a position in which the handcuffs didn't cut into his wrists. Convinced it was one of the sheriff's sick scare tactics, Lee felt confident the ordeal would soon be over. But what if DeRam was capable of fabricating enough evidence to convince a judge or jury he was guilty? Then what? He'd be a convicted felon? He'd go to jail! And then what? He'd have a criminal record? The whole thing was overwhelming.

"You're not going to get away with this, DeRam."

DeRam and his partner kept silent on the ride to their office. Once inside, they escorted Lee to a separate room in the back where there were three holding cells. DeRam removed the cuffs and gave Lee a gentle shove into one of the cells.

"You don't have any weapons on you, do you?"

"No."

DeRam closed the cell door.

"I get to make one phone call, right?"

"In due time," DeRam said and left the room.

Lee could hear the two men talking but couldn't make out what they were saying. Ten minutes passed. He was eager to call Bennett, who was a lawyer and was likely to be home by now. He would have to use his one phone call to call home and ask Shaneta to find Bennett's home phone number in his address book and tell him what happened.

Thirty more minutes passed. The longer Lee sat on the hard surface of the metal cot, the more outraged he became. Even when he was able to straighten everything out and have the charges dropped, he feared there would always be doubt in his friends' minds as to whether he was guilty on some level.

Ninety minutes after he entered the cell, the hallway door opened. DeRam entered the room followed by Bennett.

"You can have twenty minutes. Then I'll be back," DeRam said before he let Bennett into Lee's cell.

The two brothers shook hands and sat down on the narrow cot. "How did you know I was here?" Lee asked.

"I'll fill you in later. I've just spent fifteen minutes with the sheriff, and I'm not getting any straight answers. Have you been officially arrested?"

"He said I was under arrest."

"I know. Shaneta told me that part. But did anyone read you your rights?"

"No."

"Take your fingerprints?"

"No."

"Mug shot?"

"No."

Bennett lowered his voice to a whisper. "I asked him for a copy of the arrest warrant, and he stalled. Something is fishy."

"Bennett, what they're charging me with is—"

"Stop. I don't want to talk about it in here. Let's wait it out. You okay?"

Lee nodded. "Thanks for coming."

DeRam returned and said, "Your arraignment has been set for nine o'clock tomorrow morning."

"I'll put up the bail money," Bennett told DeRam.

"Won't know that amount until we see the judge tomorrow."

"I want a copy of the arrest warrant."

"You'll have it before you leave. Do you need more time with my prisoner?"

Lee wanted to punch him.

"Yes."

DeRam left.

"What does this mean?" Lee asked his brother.

"I'm afraid it means a night in jail."

"What?"

"I don't know how things work in this jurisdiction, but it looks like bail has to be set by a judge, and today is a holiday. No judges."

"He can't get away with this," Lee whispered. "This is all—"

"It's not going to do any good getting all riled up about it now. My advice to you is to play it cool. I'll meet you in court in the morning with someone from my firm who has criminal defense experience, which I don't, and we'll get to the bottom of this. I promise."

"I can't believe this is happening."

"Can I bring you anything?"

"No." He looked around the cell. "What am I supposed to do in here in the meantime?"

"Think about what you've done wrong and repent?"

"Was that supposed to be funny?"

"Yes."

"Well, it wasn't."

Bennett clapped his hand over Lee's, bringing a stop to Lee's absentminded finger tapping. "I'm going to get you through this, Lee."

"I know."

* * *

Lee looked at his watch for about the tenth time since he'd been escorted to the courtroom—8:55 a.m. The hearing was to begin in five minutes, and Bennett had not yet arrived. Lee had no experience with judges, courtrooms, lawyers, or legal proceedings of any kind. The knot in his stomach tightened. Was this Bennett's idea of a cruel joke?

At twenty-five past nine, the judge entered the courtroom.

"Everyone please rise."

Lee was afraid his knees weren't going to support him. While he was still standing, Bennett slipped in beside him and cupped his elbow, providing some comfort.

You okay?" Bennett asked.

The judge asked them to be seated.

"Where were you?" Lee whispered.

"Getting you off."

"Case number 478-A has been dismissed. Mr. Winekoop, you are free to go."

Lee looked at Bennett. "We can go?"

Bennett stood up. "Thank you, your honor."

"Court dismissed."

Bennett bent down and whispered to Lee, "Don't say anything until we're in my car. C'mon. Let's go."

They exited the courtroom and entered the foyer.

The voice that called out to them from behind was unmistakably DeRam's. "You won't be so lucky next time, karate boy."

Lee turned around to face him, but all he saw was his back walking toward the side door. For a fleeting moment, he wanted to sneak up behind him and give him a few well-deserved kicks. But Bennett grabbed his arm and led him out the front door.

Once in Bennett's car, they sat in silence for several seconds.

"What just happened in there?" Lee asked.

Bennett turned toward him. "Bernard DeRam is an asshole."

"You'll get no argument from me on that."

"Let's go. I'll explain what happened on the way."

"You had me scared shitless when you didn't show up by nine o'clock."

"Sorry about that, but my partner and I were in the judge's chambers by eight-thirty. It took longer than we expected."

"You were?"

"Jerry, my partner, called the clerk's office yesterday and asked her enough questions to raise suspicion that the charges may have been fabricated."

Lee studied his brother's profile. "But you never asked me if I did anything wrong?"

Bennett took his eyes off the road for a brief moment to look at Lee. "Please."

That touched him.

"Anyway, his questions prompted the clerk to schedule a pre-hearing meeting in the judge's chambers. This is where it gets good. DeRam's paperwork was full of holes. The arrest warrant didn't even have a judge's signature on it. Even I caught that one. By the time the judge was finished with him for conducting such shoddy police work, DeRam was stumbling over his words like a babbling fool. I almost felt sorry for him."

"So what happens now?"

"Nothing. The charges were never officially filed, so it won't be recorded as an arrest. I have a copy of the release, and it states you were brought in for questioning. That's all. It will have no effect on your record."

"Thank goodness."

"By the way..."

"What?"

"DeRam brought up a previous arrest on your record. Now, I'm sure he must have made it up, but—"

"He didn't make it up."

"Public lewdness?"

"The short version of that story is that I was in the wrong place at the wrong time. And no, I wasn't guilty of any lewd behavior, believe me. The charges were dropped."

"After you were arrested, right?"

"Yes."

"So now you have an arrest record."

"Yes."

"When this is all over, I'll help you get that expunged."

"I can never repay you."

"Don't worry about it. How was jail?"

"Which time?"

Bennett chuckled. "My brother, the jailbird. *This* time."

"I don't think they could have found a thinner pad for the cot if they'd tried. Hey, you didn't tell me how you got to the jail so quickly."

"After I left your place, I got about halfway home and pictured the empty house I would be setting foot in. So I turned around, hoping by the time I got back to your house, your guests would have gone and we could pick up our conversation where we left off. When I got there, I was greeted by a rather hysterical Shaneta. Now I have a hard time understanding that woman when she's calm, so I had *no* idea what she was saying to me in her excited state. Luckily, CJ and Francine were still there. They told me what happened, and I immediately drove to the sheriff's office."

"Good timing."

"Why does DeRam have it in for you?"

Lee explained everything to him.

"He may not be so stupid the next time. You sure you want stay here?"

"Stay where?"

"In Harvard. I know you just built a house and all, but why not consider moving back to Evanston, away from this guy."

"No way." He thought about the magnitude of Bennett's suggestion. "Look, I've allowed others to control what I do my whole life. I'm done with that."

"And I admire you for that, but I still worry about you out here, no neighbors within shouting distance, and that gun-toting jerk on the loose. Who knows what he's capable of doing?"

"I appreciate your concern, but if I start running from things, it will be like taking a giant step backward, and that's not the direction I'm headed."

Once at home, Lee and Bennett sat in Lee's living room while Shaneta busied herself in the kitchen making them breakfast.

"It's gotta be rough having your family ripped out from under you like that," Lee said.

"Those kids mean everything to me. And you know what the sad thing is? I didn't realize just how much they meant to me until they were gone."

"One of my many therapists had a sign hanging in her office that said, 'Appreciate what you have before it becomes what you had.' Whenever I looked at it, I thought what a strange saying to have in a psychologist's office. After all, most people are there because they need to change something they have."

"Maybe it should read, 'Appreciate what you love' instead of 'what you have.'" He stared past Lee for a few seconds. "My priorities have been so screwed up. A typical day for me meant leaving for work before the kids got up and getting home after they'd gone to bed. I've missed a big chunk of their growing up. Instead of being so immersed in motions, briefs, and judgments, I should have been helping my children with their homework, doing fun things with them, and...helping Daphne set boundaries. Do you know, I couldn't even tell you who their best friends are, or their favorite food, or what they watch on television. It's downright shameful."

"You're pretty good at beating yourself up."

"Someone has to do it." He smiled. "Besides you."

"Something tells me you're never going to let me forget that."

"You got that right, little brother."

Little brother? So does he not know?

"So what about Daphne?"

"What about her?"

"Do you miss her?"

Bennett didn't answer for a long moment. "No, I don't. I realize now we're too very different people. Up until recently, I would have said we had the same interests, the same values and goals. But not now. No, I don't miss her, but I do miss being with someone, and I miss those kids. And just when..." His voice trailed off.

"When what?"

"Your barbecue..." His voice cracked. "I can't tell you, man, how much fun we had in that stupid balloon-toss game. We'd never done anything like that before. It was just plain *fun.*"

"What did Daphne think of it?"

"Oh, my God. She threw a fit after we got home. Called me a 'barbarian.' Said I embarrassed her. Said the children would need therapy to get over the spectacle we made of ourselves. And then every day after that, she withdrew further and further away from me, until it was just plain uncomfortable being around her."

"And then she left."

"And then she left. With the kids. That's another thing she yelled at me about. Calling them *kids.* 'They're our children, Bennett. Not some disgusting barnyard animal.' And then you gave me the 'You're such a phony' lecture, and I started to really think about how my life has been molded by Mother and Father, and that very little of me has had the chance to surface."

"I know."

"Yes, I know you know. You had it harder than any of—"

"No, Bennett. I *know.*"

Bennett stared at him for several seconds. "You know what?"

"I know who I am."

"Yes, and I'm very happy for you man, you've been able to—"

"Listen to me. I know who I *really* am. I know who my real father and mother are...well, at least my father."

"No shit!"

23 | LINKED BY BLOOD

"Look, man," Bennett said after nearly an hour of discussion about their complicated family dynamics, "I never liked the idea of keeping you in the dark, but you know how it is with Mother and Father."

"Of course, I do. And I don't blame you for going along with it, believe me."

"So you're okay with it?"

"With what?"

"Uncle Nelson being your father and well, your real mother, uh..."

"What exactly do you know about her?"

"Not much. One time, Father referred to her as his whore—Uncle Nelson's, that is—but I don't know the whole story. I was only eight or nine at the time, but I do remember it happening. Mother had just returned from spending the summer in New York. It wasn't long after that that you were brought into the house. We were told we had a new little brother, and we knew not to ask questions."

"So for a time you thought I was your full-blooded brother. At what point did you realize I wasn't?"

"We overheard Father one day. Let's say everyone in the household overheard him. And then Mother told us we could never talk about it."

"Do you know if Uncle Nelson had a family, a wife, any other children?"

"I'm pretty sure he was married, but if he had other children, no one ever talked about them."

"I could have half-brothers and -sisters out there. What did he do for a living anyway? All I ever heard was he owned a printing company, he was involved in some of the same charities as Mother, and he traveled a lot. By any chance, do you know the name of the printing company?"

"No, I don't. I do know it was in Indiana, outside of Gary, I think. All I remember is Mother used to say his biggest clients owned newspapers, and I remember that because she used to hit them up occasionally for contributions to her charities. You could ask her."

"I don't want to broach the subject of Uncle Nelson with her until I'm ready to open the entire can of worms."

"So it wasn't Mother who told you?"

"No."

"Who was it then?"

"I figured out some things for myself." It didn't feel good lying to Bennett, not after the terrific candid discussion they had just had, but he couldn't betray Shaneta.

"So when *are* you going to let on to Mother and Father that you know?"

"When the time is right. But not now. I have too many other things to worry about. Can we keep this between the two us for the time being?"

"You got it. And Lee?"

"Yeah."

"I'm glad we talked."

"Me, too, Bennett. Me, too."

* * *

Each of Lee's guests called that afternoon to check that he was okay. He explained the incident as an unfortunate miscarriage of justice.

He was more open with CJ when she called.

"Hey, Soc. Are you still talking to me?"

"Of course. Why?"

"Because if it wasn't for me, none of this would have happened."

"Don't even think of it that way."

"He's such a son-of-a-bitch! I could just kill him. I'm so sorry, Soc."

Lee told her he was fine and tried to distract her by filling in the details of how DeRam had screwed up and how Bennett had saved his ass.

"What are you going to do now?" she asked.

"I'm more concerned about you."

"I'll be fine."

"Look, this man is desperate, dangerous, and unpredictable. That's a bad combination."

"I can handle myself."

"CJ."

"What?"

"You're in denial."

"It helps me cope."

"It won't keep you safe."

"Yes, sir."

"CJ."

"I'll be careful. I promise."

"You better."

"Bye…jailbird."

* * *

The plans for Lee's guesthouse were finished at the same time construction for Dr. Rad's lab and greenhouses was completed. Lee picked up Dr. Rad in a ten-foot rented U-Haul truck, big enough for a few pieces of furniture and all the doctor's worldly possessions. Per Dr. Rad's request, his living space had been designed to be small and simple, just one room and a bathroom situated in the back of the lab.

Fifty acres of land had been carved out in one quadrant of the property for Dr. Rad's operation. Surrounded on three sides by groves of mature trees, the lab and three greenhouses sat near the center of the quadrant, leaving roughly fifteen acres in the front and another fifteen in the back left open for his plantings. It was a substantially larger area than he had ever had before for his research.

After he helped Dr. Rad get settled in, Lee returned home, only to find Shaneta standing in the doorway, obviously agitated.

"Mista Lee, Miss CJ called. She asked if you could come over. She sounded vexed."

"Vexed?"

"How do you say...upset."

"Did she say what was wrong?"

"No. She just asked you to come."

Lee turned around. "Call her back. Tell her I'm on my way."

All he thought about on the way to CJ's was what he would do to DeRam if he had hurt her in any way.

He pulled into CJ's long driveway. CJ met him on her front porch, her eyes red and puffy.

"What's wrong?"

CJ led him to the corner of the porch to two Adirondack chairs. "It's Bern," she said in a voice barely above a whisper.

Blood rose up Lee's neck. "What did he do?" he asked through gritted teeth.

"He called Wayne. Well, no, he didn't call him, he called me, but it wasn't him on the phone. It was some little boy asking for Wayne. The kid said he went to school with him, so naturally I handed the phone to Wayne. Then Bern got on and proceeded to tell him he was his father," she said through muffled cries.

"Good grief. What was Wayne's reaction?"

"All I heard him say was, 'You're not my father,' and he handed the phone back to me. I took the phone, prepared to give him a piece of mind, but all I heard was a dial tone. Then Wayne ran into his room and slammed the door. He won't come out."

"Have you talked to him at all?"

"Just through the door. I tried to open it, but he's blocked it with something, probably his dresser." She swiped the tears from her cheeks. "I wanted to explain things, but I was so upset, I just couldn't seem to get the right words out." She blinked back more tears. "I know this has nothing to do with you, and I know it's not fair to even ask you for help, but..."

Lee took her hands in his. "Where's Travis?"

"In the bedroom with Wayne. They share it."

"Let's think this through logically."

"That's why I called you. You think logically. I don't always."

"Do you have in your mind the words you intended to use when the time was right to tell them about their father?"

"I thought I did, but now I'm not so sure. And they need to hear it together, but Travis is only six. He'll be seven next month. That's too young."

"Sounds like Mr. Wonderful hasn't left you much of a choice. I'll see if I can push their door open. Are you ready?"

"As ready as I'll ever be."

Lee pushed the boys' bedroom door open enough to poke in his head. It looked nothing like his bedroom when he was their age—unmade beds, clothes and a variety of toys strewn about, and several posters crudely affixed to the walls with Scotch tape, the most prominent one promoting a film called *RoboCop*.

"Hi, boys."

Wayne turned around. "What are you doing here?"

"Your mother wants to talk with you, both of you. Can she come in?"

"No. We don't want to talk to her. She lied to us, and we don't wanna hear no more lies."

Lee turned around to look at CJ who mouthed, "I had told them their father lived far away."

He pushed the door open a few more inches and squeezed farther into their room. "Can I tell you something?"

"Do we have a choice?" Wayne asked.

"May I come in?"

Receiving no answer, Lee pushed the door open the rest of the way and let himself in.

"Can I push the dresser back where it belongs for you?"

"Nothing is stopping you, far as I can tell," Wayne said under his breath.

Lee moved the dresser to its rightful place next to the door. "You guys are pretty strong for your size."

"Mom says we're wiry," Travis said with a lisp, evidence of his missing two front teeth.

Lee sat down on one of the twin beds. "Come over here, guys. Let me tell you a story."

Wayne rolled his eyes and then sat down on the far edge of the bed. Travis did the same.

"The two of you and me...we're a lot the same."

"Yeah, right."

"Mm-hm. Here I am, twenty-seven years old, and do you know what I just found out?" Lee whispered.

Travis was wide-eyed. "What? Tell us."

"I just found out the man I called Dad all these years...well, he isn't really my dad after all."

"Dag," Wayne uttered with quiet empathy.

"And my mother?" Lee added.

"Not your real mother either?" Travis asked.

Lee shook his head.

"For real?"

"For real."

Wayne's demeanor changed. "You're not telling us this just to make us feel better, are you?"

It was hard not to laugh at the innocence of his question.

"Wayne, I would never lie to you. You have my word."

"Mom says if you lie, it'll come back to bite you," Travis chimed in. "Whatever that means."

"Your mom is right. You should never lie, but here's the thing. Sometimes parents don't tell you the truth because they think you're not ready to hear it yet."

"Yeah? You're twenty-seven. How old do you have to be to hear some things?" Wayne asked.

"Now that's a good point. My case is a little different. My parents kept the truth from me because..."

The young boys sat in silence, waiting for him to finish the sentence.

"Well, maybe that's for another time. The point is maybe parents don't always use the best judgment. Sometimes they make mistakes. But in your case, I can assure you your mom thought she was doing the right thing to wait until you were a little older to tell you about—"

"Who? The scumbag?" Wayne interjected.

"Yeah, the scumbag?" Travis parroted.

"Can we call in your mother now? This is a conversation she wants to have with you."

"Go ahead," Wayne said, rolling his eyes.

"Will you stay here too?" asked Travis.

CJ appeared in the doorway. "Yeah, can you please stay, Soc?" she asked.

They spent the next hour talking about families, relationships, and the fact that Travis had lost his pet bullfrog in the living room earlier that day and couldn't find it. At the end of the discussion, CJ asked the boys if they would look for the frog while she talked to Lee on the front porch.

"Thank you, Lee. You made this *so* much easier."

"What are you going to do now?"

"About what?"

"About DeRam."

"He *is* their father. What *can* I do?"

Lee thought about Bennett and how much he cherished his children.

"Now this may be a crazy idea, but do you think he would listen to reason?" he asked her. "What if the three of us sat down and talked things through like rational people? And established some reasonable ground rules, for example."

"First of all, he's not one to follow rules. Secondly, he's not a rational person…never was. Third, he isn't interested in establishing a relationship with his sons, ground rules and everything. And fourth, you're the *last* person he'd listen to."

"He's *never* been rational?"

"Never. And resistance only makes him worse. That's why I let him in this last time. If I had resisted, that would have just made him twice as determined. Bern is someone who won't stop until he gets what he wants."

"And he wants two things. You. And me out of the picture."

"Exactly. And believe me, if I thought it would make a difference, I would tell him there's nothing going on between us, but it won't. I know him. You're a threat because you're another man."

It was the first time either of them had made any reference to their relationship. He put her exact words in the back of his mind for the moment. "And what we want is *him* out of the picture."

"Lots of luck. He's a malignant, vengeful person, and there's nothing anyone can do about it."

"I'm not willing to accept you can't do anything about it, not yet anyway. Are you okay for now?"

"Yeah."

"So what are you going to do when he comes over the next time?"

"Keep the doors locked. I won't let him in."

"But you just said that will make him even more determined."

"I don't know what else to do."

"I think you need to know what you can do legally. If I find the right lawyer for you, will you do that?"

"I can't afford a lawyer. I can barely afford to live."

"Don't worry about that for now. You can pay me back."

"You're a good friend, Soc."

Lee smiled. "Just remember that when I ask you for something."

"Saw that comin'."

"Seriously, I'm glad I was able to help with the boys, but I have to tell you, my stomach was doing crazy flip-flops the whole time I was in there. You know I have no experience in this."

"Yes, you do."

"What do you mean?"

"I heard you tell my boys about your parents."

"Oh, that."

"So when did they finally tell you?"

"They didn't. Someone else did, very recently. They don't know I know."

"Holy crap! Are you kidding me?"

"My brother Bennett knows I know. He came back to my house after I was released from jail, and we talked." Lee felt grateful all over again for that conversation.

CJ smiled. "Like I said, looks like the tables have finally turned."

"You said that to me before. What do you mean?"

"It's the last stanza of that poem I like."

> One day he can only hope and tables will turn.
> Until that day arrives
> and his loneliness evaporates he will remain
> the one who stands
> on the outside always looking in.

* * *

When Lee got home, he found a dead raccoon lying on his back porch. A string was tied around its neck, and attached to the string was a note on an index card.

SOMETIMES A GUNSHOT WORKS BETTER THAN A KICK

During the next few days, Lee thought about his conversation with CJ's sons. If someone had told him a year ago he would be having that kind of conversation with two little boys, he would have called them crazy. Now, he thought it to be completely reasonable. The phone interrupted his thoughts.

He had never heard Dr. Rad sound so excited. He told Lee the Johns Hopkins consultants just left after having visited his facilities. They seemed quite impressed with his work and asked if they could include him in a research grant they were seeking from the government. In addition, he told Lee, he had been contacted by a professor in the Department of Plant Pathology at Penn State asking him if he would be interested in co-writing a paper on crown gall disease. Her focus had been on grapes, and she felt his research on other plant types would enhance the paper and reach a wider audience.

Lee couldn't have been more pleased. It meant that not only was Dr. Rad expanding beyond what he had originally planned to do on Lee's property, but it appeared he was gaining respect from others in the research community.

He wished he felt as certain about Shaneta's future and was beginning to wonder if she had any long-range plans at all. She appeared to be comfortable living in his spare bedroom, maybe a little too comfortable. While he felt he owed her for having the courage to tell him about his parents, and he may have contributed to her losing her job, he hadn't intended for her living with him to be a permanent arrangement.

Lee decided to broach the subject with her one evening after dinner when they were enjoying a glass of wine on the front deck. The sun had begun its daily journey down the western sky behind the Red Sunset maple trees that lined his driveway, authenticating their name and giving credence to the fact that Lee was where he needed to be.

"They're going to break ground on the guesthouse next week," he said to Shaneta.

"Ahead of schedule then."

"Almost a month. It could be completed by the end of the year."

"That's nice. Will it be another A-frame?"

"No. It's going to be a small three-bedroom cottage. Dennis created plans for one that fits nicely into the landscape but still blends in with mine."

"Will we be able to see it from here?"

Lee got up from his chair and walked over to the far end of the deck. He looked toward the back of his property to the intended site for the guesthouse, approximately a quarter mile from where he stood. "Probably." He paused to gather his thoughts. "We haven't talked about your plans, Shaneta. What do you want to do?"

"Well, Lee, I had hoped to be outta your hair before Dr. Rad moved in, but he moved in faster than I thought, and here I still am. I registered with an employment agency, but they weren't hopeful. Sonya said she might know of a family in Lake Geneva lookin' for a cook, but she hasn't called me back yet, so..."

"Well, I want you to know you are welcome to stay here as long as it takes. And when the guesthouse is finished, if you're still here, you can move in there. But I have to ask you, why did you want to be moved out before Dr. Rad moved in?"

She twisted her face as though she had just bitten into a sour grape. "He's a strange man. Do you know what he said to me the other day?"

"No, what?"

"It was right after he moved in, and I thought I would be nice and bring him a cup of coffee, so I—"

"You walked to his lab?"

"Yes, of course. How else do you think I would get there?"

"Shaneta, it's almost a mile between here and the lab."

"You're tellin' *me* that?"

Lee shook his head. "Anyway, what happened?"

"I put the coffee in a thermos to keep it nice and hot, and when I knocked, he said through the door, 'I'm single, Miss Shaneta, for good reason, but you can still leave the coffee.'"

"What?"

"That's what I said. And then he said something 'bout loco bread. That man is a little loco himself if he thinks I walked all that way 'cause I was interested in him. I just had extra coffee, and rather than throw it out..."

"Well, I'm not sure that was what he meant. Remember he comes from a country with completely different customs."

"And so do I. And did you catch how he looked at me at the housewarming party?"

"No, I can't say I did."

"Well, he did."

"I really don't think—"

She got up. "Anyway, I hope I answered your questions. I'm goin' to turn in now."

* * *

Even with all that was going on with his property improvements, Lee found himself constantly thinking about CJ. Following DeRam's inopportune confession to Wayne, CJ had accepted Lee's offer to meet with an attorney in Rockford to discuss DeRam's paternity rights. While DeRam hadn't made any parental demands, at least CJ was now informed of his rights in case he did.

Lee and CJ had become close friends, but he still struggled with how much he should be involved in her life. She had called him for help this last time, but with CJ, it had to be on her terms, so he knew he had to be cautious.

He felt completely inept when it came to relationships, with men *and* women. He recalled CJ's comment about there being nothing going on between them. It took that comment to confirm for him that was indeed the case, because he honestly didn't know. He made a mental note to have this discussion with Bennett the next time they had a brother-to-brother talk, which he hoped would become a regular occurrence.

* * *

A couple of days following his puzzling discussion with Shaneta about Dr. Rad, Lee was sitting on the front deck drinking a cup of coffee, when he saw Dr. Rad walking down the dirt road from his lab, thermos bottle in hand, clothes rumpled, with little beads of sweat glistening on his brow. As he neared Lee, he held the thermos out in front of him.

"Here, I wouldn't want her to think I was going to keep this." Expressionless, he set the thermos down on the deck floor. "Tell her the coffee wasn't half-bad, but I prefer tea," he mumbled.

Without another word, he turned and started back down the road.

"Hey, wait a minute, Dr. Rad. Can I give you a lift back?"

Dr. Rad shook his head and kept on walking, throwing up his hands every few feet as if having a lively conversation with himself.

Shaneta came out of the house. "What did he want?"

Lee held up the thermos.

"A likely excuse to come see me."

Lee had spoken to a variety of psychologists over the years about his difficulties developing relationships. Now, sitting on the other side of the therapist's desk, he realized understanding them wasn't any less of a challenge.

* * *

Three weeks after Dr. Rad had moved in, he presented Lee with a fifteen-page handwritten proposal on what he needed to restart his research, complete with crude aerial drawings for the various growing fields. In the back of the greenhouses, he proposed two three-acre, two two-acre, and five one-acre fields, each one for a separate fruit or vegetable. The entire front fifteen acres was designated for red clover. After leafing through the proposal, Lee turned to the last page where Dr. Rad estimated the start-up cost. If Stonebugger didn't approve it through the trust account, he would have to sell off a few more coins in order to fund it, something he was prepared to do.

Figuring interest from Johns Hopkins and Penn State was enough ratification for him, Lee accepted his proposal and asked Dr. Rad if there was anything he could do to help him at this time.

"You can help by getting Miss Shaneta some sort of transportation to and from my lab."

"What? Why?"

"She's complaining about the long walk. You know how she is...complains about everything."

"The long walk for what?"

"She insists on bringing me things—coffee, sweets, and occasionally leftovers from dinner."

"Really."

"I don't ask for it, I assure you..." His face flushed. "She just..."

"She just what?"

"I'll be going now," he said halfway across the room. "Thank you, my good friend. Thank you. Thank you. Thank you."

Coffee, sweets, and dinner? Lee had thought Shaneta couldn't stand Dr. Rad. And he had assumed the feeling was mutual.

Forget it. I'd need a degree in psychology to figure this out.

The opportunity to consider transportation for Shaneta to get around the property came the following week.

"Mista Lee, if I was able to get mi hands on a car, could you teach me how to drive?"

"I didn't realize you didn't know how to drive."

"Never learned. Didn't need to in Jamaica, and I always relied on others to drive me around here. But now...well, now I think if I'm goin' to start bein' more independent, I need to know how to drive."

Lee waited for the next sunny day to give Shaneta her first driving lesson in his Datsun. It didn't go well.

First, Shaneta wanted to jump in behind the wheel and start driving before having received any preliminary instructions. Then, as Lee painstakingly walked her through what all the levers, pedals, and knobs were, she seemed more interested in turning on the radio. When he finally allowed her to sit behind the wheel, instead of using the gear shift to put it in drive, she pulled down so hard on the windshield wiper lever, he thought it was going to break off.

After Lee went through the drill for the third time, Shaneta threw the car in Drive and stepped on the gas...hard.

"Stop! Put your foot on the brake!" he yelled at her.

"I'm drivin', Mista Lee. Look at me, I'm drivin'."

"Brake! Put your foot on the brake! The one on the left!" He reached for the wheel, but Shaneta had a tight grip on it. "Let me steer! Take your foot off the gas!"

By the time Shaneta found the wherewithal to take her foot off the gas, they were twenty feet into the knee-high grasses that lined the driveway. Then she stomped on the brake so hard, it caused Lee to fly into the dashboard and hit his head on the windshield.

"Put the gear in Park," he croaked.

"Would that be P then?"

"Yes, that would be P."

Shaneta got out of the car and proceeded to walk toward the house. "It's obvious you're not the right person to teach me how to drive," she said loud enough for him to hear.

You got that right.

The subject of teaching Shaneta how to drive never resurfaced, and her now-daily walks to Dr. Rad's lab made Lee feel guilty. Because Dr. Rad had told him he appreciated the meals and other things she brought him, he wanted to accommodate her in some way. Thinking there had to be a solution to her transportation issue that didn't involve driving a one-and-a-half-ton potentially lethal weapon, he made a visit to his family's golf club in Lake Geneva and purchased a golf cart whose top speed was fifteen miles per hour. The driving lesson on this vehicle proceeded significantly better. Key in ignition. Turn key. Two pedals. Two gears. Done.

* * *

"Looks awfully barren right now," Shaneta said. "I miss the pretty wild onions."

It was a balmy day in mid-October, and she and Lee were drinking their morning coffee on the front deck. Preparation for the red clover fields had begun a few weeks earlier—the land had been cleared and tilled.

"Just wait. Come late spring, the red clover will be blooming with so much color it will take your breath away."

After hundreds of trays of the clover seeds had been soaked in liquid nitrogen fertilizer, Lee had hired a commercial farmer out of Rockford to plant them with an industrial-size seed drill.

Lee stood up and gestured toward the field. "Fifteen acres of solid red blossoms, two feet tall or so, no two alike. Individually, they're not much to look at, but in a field this big, they'll form a continuous blanket of blooms, and in the morning when they're wet with dew, the sun will glisten off of them like nothing you've ever seen before. And when there's a gentle breeze, they'll all sway in synchrony, creating silent ripples across the field. Their smell is so sweet, Shaneta...sweet, like honey."

"Mmm...sounds beautiful, peaceful."

"It is. You'll see."

They sat in silence for a few minutes, sipping their coffee.

"Look…over there…peeking through the tall grasses," Shaneta said, pointing to a spot across the road. "I see that cat almost every day, but he won't come any closer than that."

"I saw that same cat the first time I set foot on this property. Must be a stray."

"Black cat. Bad luck."

Lee smiled. "Nope. Not this one."

"You know, I asked Raddie if he would carve out a tiny area for mi own little plot of clover. I don't need much."

Lee focused on Shaneta's profile for a long moment before she turned her head.

"What?" she asked.

"Raddie?"

"It's just a little nickname. What can I say, it just slipped out one day when we were...well, this is no business of yours, young man."

Lee kept his eyes on her while she rambled on.

"Stop lookin' at me."

"And just what are you going to use the clover for?"

"You don't know 'bout red clover? Hmmm. You use it for many things. You can dry the flowers for tea, put fresh ones in oil and use it to soften your skin, or use them in a salad. I have even dropped blossoms in the ice cube trays to brighten up drinks. You can put it in soup, and for coughin'? Well, there's nothin' like a little red clover tincture. I swear, for someone with such a high IQ, you don't know much, neither you nor Dr. Rad."

"Raddie."

"Shut up 'bout that man...please."

* * *

As soon as the back fifteen acres had been cleared, Dr. Rad told Lee the soil was unusually high in nitrogen, which he hadn't expected.

"So what do you think would cause just this one section to be like that?" Lee asked him.

"There's also lignite in the soil. I didn't expect to find that either."

"Lignite...as in coal?"

"Yes."

"What is lignite typically used for?"

"It's not very efficient to burn as fuel, and I'm not sure what plant life would even thrive in carbon- and ash-laden soil."

Lee thought back to when he had first set foot in that section of his property and found the strange thin grayish root strands.

"Wait a minute. There was something planted there at one time." He described the roots to Dr. Rad.

"Do you still have it?"

"Probably still in the trunk of my car, but..."

"Let's have a look."

Lee led the way to his car, which was parked in front of the lab next to the golf cart. He looked at the cart and then at Dr. Rad.

"Don't ask," Dr. Rad said.

"I won't."

Lee opened his trunk and pulled out the shriveled-up tangle of brittle roots.

Dr. Rad took it in his hands, fondled it, sniffed it.

"You know what this is?" he asked Lee.

"No. Do you?"

"It's ganja."

25 | ALONE

So someone had been cultivating marijuana on the property before Lee had inherited it. That explained the strangely placed gate in the northeast corner—an access point for working the field. It appeared to Lee that someone had taken full advantage of the property's having been untended, and the evidence pointed to DeRam as that someone.

It explained why DeRam had dragged him into his office the first day Lee had visited the property—he hadn't wanted Lee to discover the plants. When DeRam realized Lee was the new owner and was going to develop the property, he must have removed the plants, which explained the fresh cut marks on their stems and the time he saw that car and trailer leave his property. Maybe it had been DeRam. Maybe it had been DeRam hauling away all the evidence. It also explained Dennis Freborg's dog, the former K-9 member on the Chicago police force, going berserk in that section of the property.

Then DeRam tried to pin the crop on Lee in an effort to land Lee in jail. If he had succeeded with that, Lee would be out of the picture, and he could pursue CJ without his interference, and who knows, maybe plant another crop of marijuana. And then the plot had thickened when DeRam still felt threatened by Lee's involvement with CJ, so he had dragged her son into it by telling him he was his father, thinking that would strengthen his relationship with CJ and force Lee out of the picture. And the joint Lee found in DeRam's back pocket further supporting his suspicions.

It all made sense...almost. There was still the issue of the tire tracks he'd found shortly after discovering the harvested plants. If DeRam had acted alone, there would be no reason for him to return to the field after it had been cut down. So either he had an accomplice and was checking on his work, or maybe the arrogant sheriff had come back to admire his own work.

Lee had never considered himself a vengeful person, but the more he stewed over DeRam's conduct, the more tempting the thought of revenge became.

* * *

"I don't think they know you know," Bennett said as they were downing some beers in Lee's living room. "And for that reason, I don't think they feel any differently about you than they did before. My guess is that they expect you for Thanksgiving."

Lee hadn't spoken to any of his family members for almost two months, except for Bennett, who now came to visit him regularly, prompting the two brothers to become close.

"I don't think I want to be there." Lee was getting comfortable with the fact that he wasn't biologically related to any of them.

"And maybe I don't blame you, but I think it's pretty much expected."

"You know I invited everyone to come see my new house, and Mother declined."

"I know."

"So I think I'll decline for Thanksgiving as well. What's good for—"

"Think about it—you could go and suffer through the visit, or you could not go, in which case you'd piss off Dad and hurt Mother."

"Well, when you put it that way..."

"Take the high road, Lee. That's my advice for what it's worth."

Lee weighed his words for a moment. He didn't remember ever having been capable of taking the high road before.

"I guess I should. Will Daphne and the children be there?"

"The children will. Per court order, I get them every other major holiday. Daphne is going to fly out here with them and stay at a friend's while they spend Thanksgiving with me."

"That's got to be rough."

"Tell me about it. I can only imagine what nonsense about me she's been instilling in their brains."

"You know what...I will be there, but just for you...and your kids."

"Thanks, little brother."

Lee appreciated the familial implication, ambiguous as it was.

* * *

Lee decided he would spend Thanksgiving night at his parents' house, and if the conditions were right, he would confront them the following day about his real ancestry. It was time. He called his mother and told her of his intention to stay overnight.

"Well, dear, that may not be the best idea. You see...well, there may be others here. Yes, I think Bennett and the children may be staying overnight, and then there's—"

"That's fine then," he said, not wanting to hear the rest of the excuses. "I'll just be there for Thanksgiving then."

"Um... we thought maybe you had other plans... like with your new friends up there."

What?

"What are you saying? That you'd rather I didn't come at all?"

"Lee, dear, your father hasn't quite gotten over…I think it's just a matter of time though, and when—"

"Mother, I *know*." He couldn't stop himself from blurting it out.

"What, dear?"

"I know. I know all about Uncle Nelson. I know he's my real father."

She gasped.

Lee waited several seconds for her to say something, and when she didn't, he asked, "Are you there?"

She still didn't respond.

"Mother, say something."

"Who told you?"

He didn't feel good about lying. "No one had to tell me. I figured it out on my own."

"How long have you known?"

"It doesn't matter. I should have been told this a long time ago."

"I know, dear. I know. But you realize why we couldn't tell you, don't you?"

"Not really."

"His name would have been ruined, his reputation. And our name as well. Henry had businesses to protect. And I had my charities and—"

"Hold on a minute. So it didn't matter what all this did to me, just so it didn't affect any of you? And what are you talking about anyway? Why would you and Father have anything to lose? And why did you take me in in the first place if you were so worried about yourselves?" He realized he had gone too far, but he couldn't help reacting to her incredibly insensitive comment.

"You're my child. I couldn't have given you up."

He couldn't breathe. What was she saying? That she had relations with her own uncle? He knew he couldn't have heard right.

"Lee?"

"I didn't know that part of it."

"What part of it?"

"That you're my real mother."

"Well, whom did you think was your real mother?"

"Just someone Uncle Nelson had an affair with."

Silence.

"Mother?"

"Lee, Uncle Nelson is not really my uncle."

"What? Who is he, then?"

Her sigh included a sob. "His real name is Nelson Sambourg, not Sedgewick."

A chill went down his back. "I have to sit down, Mother. This is way more confusing than I originally thought. So you're telling me you had an affair with this man, got pregnant, had me... Wait a minute. How did you explain the pregnancy?"

"I stayed in the New York apartment that summer. Henry didn't know I was pregnant. No one did."

"What? Mother, this is making no sense."

"It's a rather complicated story."

"Well, how about giving me the short version. Start with how he found out."

"I assume you mean Henry. He came to New York on a surprise visit."

"And found you there...pregnant."

"Something like that."

"I don't get it. What was your plan?"

"I had made arrangements to put you up for adoption. No one would have known."

He closed his eyes for a brief moment, allowing that stunning blow to sink in.

"So why didn't you?"

She didn't respond right away. "When I saw your face for the first time, I knew...I couldn't do it."

"And Father?"

"He was furious with me, of course. But in the end, he had to go along with it. He had his reputation at stake."

"And you told him who the father was?"

"Yes, but not at first. That took strength I didn't have when—"

"Good grief, Mother. How could you—"

"Lee, I think I need to lie down. Will you ever forgive me?"

"I don't know. I need time to digest all this."

All of a sudden, the notion of not being welcomed home for Thanksgiving seemed rather trivial.

What am I supposed to do with this? Am I now the only one who knows the whole truth besides my parents? Besides Mother and her husband?

He didn't know how to refer to them even in his private thoughts. And while it was difficult for Lee to accept his mother violating what he had always thought was a strict moral code, how dare his father refer to his mother as a whore.

I will never again refer to that man as my father.

* * *

It took Lee several days before he found the courage to continue the conversation with his mother. He took a generous swig of Pepto-Bismol before picking up the phone.

"Mother, we need to talk further. I think I deserve to know everything."

"I know, dear, and I agree. Henry will be out of town on Thursday and Friday of this week. He's leaving at six on Thursday morning. Can you come here?"

"I'll be there well after he leaves on Thursday. Please let me know if his plans change. I do *not* want to run into him."

"I'll see you then. And Lee, I haven't told anyone of our previous conversation."

"I haven't either."

"Good. Let's keep it that way for now."

I know you'll have no trouble keeping it secret—you're a champion in that arena.

* * *

The sixty-mile drive to Evanston seemed to take much longer than usual, but it gave Lee ample time to formulate all the disconcerting questions that had been occupying his thoughts day and night for the past five days.

His mother greeted him at the front door and hugged him, leaving him feeling as though he was seeing her, feeling her touch, and smelling her perfume for the first time.

He led the way to the dining room where he hoped having a table between them would make the discussion they were about to have more valid...or something.

She called for tea.

"Where do you want me to start?"

"At the beginning, Mother. Please start at the beginning."

She clasped her hands and rested them on the table in front of her. She looked at him with soulful eyes for a long moment before she spoke.

"The beginning seems so long ago," she said through a sigh.

Her demeanor was surprisingly placid. He wondered if she was on medication of some kind.

"I met Nelson Sambourg at a City of Hope fundraiser in 1951. Nelson, my Nelson, was just a toddler."

"That's one of my questions, Mother. Why was Nelson named after him?"

"The fact your brother's name is Nelson is purely coincidental. He wasn't named for anyone in particular."

"But you told me, and I remember this distinctly, he was named after Uncle Nelson."

"I know." She stared past him. "I don't know." Her voice trailed off. "I suppose saying he was named after my uncle helped to reinforce the lies we were telling people about you."

"Go on."

"I hadn't bonded very well with Nelson after he was born, and I was very depressed. I think they have a name for it today, but back then, I didn't know what I was going through. I was extremely unhappy. And Henry...well, he wasn't very supportive. You know how he is."

"Yes, I do."

"Anyway, Nelson was so nice to me, such a good listener, so attentive—all the things Henry wasn't—and..."

"One thing led to another, and you had an affair with him."

"I did." She paused for a moment. "I did, and it was wrong. And I knew it was wrong. But I was lonely. I was so lonely, and Henry...well, I didn't feel emotionally connected to him at all, and I needed...as a woman, I needed that. It sounds like an excuse, I know. Please believe me when I say I know what I did was wrong, but..."

"I know. Go on, Mother."

"Then Bennett was born, and—"

"Bennett?"

"Yes. And when—"

"Mother, who is Bennett's father?"

"Henry."

"Mother?"

"And when Bennett was born, I thought..."

"Mother, you've come this far. Tell me the truth. Is Uncle Nelson Bennett's father as well?"

She looked down for several seconds and then looked up through watery eyes. "I believe in my heart of hearts that he's Henry's child, but if I'm being completely truthful about it, I can't be sure."

The thought of Bennett being his full brother took hold of Lee. He waffled for a moment between pressing the issue and letting it go. While it appeared she didn't want to know for sure, it seemed too vital to discard.

"What about DNA testing?"

"That's not accurate. I've looked into it."

"They're making strides in that area, Mother. And there are always blood tests..."

"May we go on?"

"Of course."

"Your two brothers look alike, so..."

He had to agree. Unlike Lee, they both resembled their mother. Neither had inherited any of Henry's features. "I know. Please continue. So Bennett was born..."

"And after that...well, Nelson and I decided to stop seeing each other. We remained out of touch for a year or so. Until...I ran into him at another charity event, and then...we both felt in our hearts we wanted to pick up where we had left off."

"So you and Henry weren't getting along this whole time?" Referring to him as "Henry" felt awkward, but "Father" was out of the question at this point.

"It's difficult to explain our relationship...even now. Perhaps some would call it a marriage of convenience. He needed a wife on his arm at all his noted events and someone to come home to, and I needed to uphold my family tradition in the charity world. We're good at supporting each other that way. But as far as a healthy, happy marriage...no, we've never had that."

"But you stayed together."

"Yes. For all those reasons, and, of course, for you children." She stared past him for a few seconds. "Anyway, it was January 1960, and Senator Kennedy had just announced his candidacy for president. He was coming to Chicago, and Nelson had a meeting with him. Nelson was very involved in the Congress for Cultural Freedom back then, and that's what they talked about."

"Really? The anti-communism group?"

"Yes."

"There was a scandal about them at one time being funded by the CIA I think."

"Allegations were made. Kennedy wanted to support and influence their cause without anyone knowing about it. Nelson was his intermediary."

"How did the two of them meet?"

"Nelson offered his family's printing business for many of their publications. Apparently Kennedy found him through that connection."

"Sounds intriguing. I wish I had been able to talk to him about it."

"I know, dear. He was so enamored by Jack Kennedy, but he couldn't talk about him, as he had to keep their relationship confidential, even with me. Anyway, that day, I stayed in Nelson's hotel room while the two of them met in a private room somewhere else in the hotel. When he returned to the room, he was so excited, and I was, too. Well, you were conceived that night."

Lee's heart pounded high in his chest. She made it sound so...so right. So legitimate somehow.

"We were so caught up in the moment, we weren't careful."

She stopped talking. As she rose up from her chair, he could see the tears welling up in her eyes. "I need to lie down," she whispered.

Lee got up from his chair.

"Are you okay, Mother?"

"I'm okay," she said when she was halfway to the stairs leading to the second floor bedrooms.

Lee was left alone to mull over all that he had just learned—his parent's disingenuous marriage, his mother's desperate need for emotional support, and Nelson's clandestine relationship with JFK. It was a lot to contemplate, but of all the crucial details his mother had just revealed, the one that struck him most was the fact that he had been conceived the same day his father had met with a future president of the United States.

How different his life would have been, he thought, had he grown up in a household with his mother and Nelson as a father. He fanticized about what it would have been like to have two loving parents growing up, no siblings to rival, and a father he could talk to, look up to, and respect. He pictured his mother very different in the presence of Nelson. He pictured her much softer, warmer, with a comforting smile instead of the stilted one she typically wore. He imagined her being expressive, lighthearted, and fun. He envisioned her being a good listener and helping him grow into adulthood, encouraging him in areas that he found of interest, and supporting his efforts. He pictured her not afraid.

Lee walked into the front parlor and took a long hard look at it. Of all the rooms in the house, this one bothered him the most. All the rooms were opulent, but this one rivaled ones in the Palace of Versailles with its extraordinary coved ceiling, hand-painted silk wall covering, massive carved marble fireplace, antique grand piano with intricately inlaid tortoiseshell and mother of pearl, matching gold gilt settees, and twelve-foot tall ornately carved secretare. He walked to the middle of the room and stepped onto the Sickle-Leaf Persian throw rug he had never stepped on before, perhaps no one had ever stepped on before. Like everything else in the room, touching it made him feel especially uneasy.

Whenever he had been summoned to the front parlor during his childhood, he knew he was about to be told something important. It was like entering into a den of uncertainty—he never knew what to expect. His parents always sat in their matching Louis XV chairs during these discussions. And afterward, regardless if it had been good or bad news, he always felt the same sick feeling in his stomach. Lee cringed as a wave of queasiness came over him, and while these chairs looked far less intimidating than when he was a child, he realized the terrorizing affect they had on him had remained.

Lee went to the kitchen for a glass of water and then retreated to the dining room to wait for his mother. When she reemerged, she had a glass of sherry in her hand.

"How are you feeling, Mother? Can we pick up where we left off?"

"Yes. I asked Bryah to have dinner ready by seven. Let's go in the front parlor. Would you like something to—"

"Mother, can we go somewhere else please?"

His mother shot him a bewildered look. "Of course, dear. How about the sunroom?"

The sunroom looked out on a half-acre of impeccably manicured lawn, sculpted hedges, and mature oak trees. Beyond the property was the edge of a high ridge overlooking Lake Michigan. The view gave Lee a reassuring sense of a world out there beyond the Winekoop family.

"Yes, that would be nice," he responded.

"Before I pick up where I left off, are *you* all right? I am telling you things that, well, may be shocking to you, and..."

"I'm okay. I don't think there's anything you could say at this point that would be too much for me to handle. Please continue. What happened when you realized you were pregnant, presumably soon after that hotel encounter?"

"So, I knew it wasn't Henry's, and of course he would know it couldn't have been his because...we weren't...well, we didn't..."

"I get it, Mother. Go on."

"I went into a real panic. It was out of the question to disgrace my family, and while you could get a legal abortion in some states, it wasn't something I could ever do. So, in my mind, the only solution was...a secret adoption."

"Mother."

"Yes, Lee."

"Thank you for not having an abortion."

She reached over and touched his hand. "I know." She wiped a lone tear from her cheek. "I didn't start showing until I was almost six months' pregnant, and that's when I planned a trip to our New York apartment. Henry didn't think anything of it since, as you know, I went there often without him. And by that time, we could be apart for long periods of time and think nothing of it. And Nelson and Bennett were at Camp Laurel for the summer, so..."

Lee knew Camp Laurel to be an exclusive summer camp in Maine his brothers had attended as children.

"But this time was different," she explained.

"How so?"

"I learned later he suspected I was having an affair. So he showed up in New York, unannounced, thinking he would catch me there with someone. But what he found instead was a very pregnant wife."

"I can't even imagine what his reaction was."

"It was bad, but in a peculiar way I felt he had come to rescue me."

"Rescue you."

"In a peculiar way."

"You said you didn't tell him whose baby it was right away."

"At first, he didn't seem interested in whose child it was — that it was someone else's child was enough. But after a while, he demanded to know, and he had the right to know, so I told him."

"Did he know him?"

"Yes. He had met Nelson and his wife several times at various events."

"His wife?"

"Yes, Nelson was also married."

His mother's facial expression said it all, and for a few seconds, he thought she was going to faint. When the color returned to her face, he didn't have the heart to explore Nelson's family life any further.

"So tell me more about Henry's reaction. How bad was it?"

"There was a lot of ranting and raving. It took him several hours to calm down, and when he did, he left the apartment. Didn't say a word. He just left."

"Making things even worse."

"Yes. At least when he was ranting and raving, I knew where he was and what was going through his mind."

"Did Uncle Nelson...Nelson...know you were pregnant?"

"Yes."

"And that you planned to give me up for adoption?"

"He wasn't in favor of that, not at first."

"What did he want you to do?"

"He couldn't come up with any other viable option, so eventually he went along with it. So Henry flew back to Chicago, and I stayed in New York until you were born. I had already made arrangements with the adoption agency, but as soon as I saw your face, well, I knew I couldn't go through with it. I called Henry and asked him to come to New York so we could talk."

"That had to be hard."

"I knew what I was up against, but I was determined to do the right thing. I'm not sure where I got the courage to ask him to accept you as his own son."

"He never did, you know."

"I know." She struggled to keep back the tears. "I'm sorry, Lee. I thought I was doing what was in your best interest."

"I understand."

No, I don't.

"Henry didn't show up until right after you were born, and when I was ready to be released, he said to me—I'll never forget his words—he said, 'I promised I would marry you for better or for worse, and I meant it.'"

"I think now that *I* need a break."

"Dinner will be ready in an hour."

Lee went to his old bedroom, kicked off his shoes, and lay down on his bed, face up, staring at the ceiling. If he concentrated real hard, he could make out a man's face camouflaged in the obscure swirls of the textured ceiling paint. He had a kind face—engaging eyes and just a curl of a smile. He looked away, and when he looked back, he couldn't find him again.

Bryah, the cook, made poached red snapper for dinner, one of Lee's favorite dishes. He and his mother ate in silence—like always—but this time for a different reason.

Later, after dinner, the conversation resumed, once his mother had had a couple of glasses of sherry. Lee joined her in a glass this time.

"So how did you come up with my name?"

"I always liked that name. Actually, I wanted to give Bennett that name, but Henry didn't like it."

Good one, Mother. Add one more thing to exacerbate Henry's contempt for me.

"And Oliver?"

"That's Nelson's middle name."

"And *he* didn't have a problem with that?"

"Who, Henry?"

"Yes." Deciding what to call him was getting increasingly difficult.

"I never told him."

"Never told him?"

"To this day, I don't think he knows your middle name."

"That's incredible."

"On many levels."

"So we get home, and how do you explain me to everyone?"

"We told people, including your brothers, that while I was in New York, I discovered I was pregnant, and instead of making the trip back here, I stayed in New York to have the baby."

"But at some point, everyone knows Nelson is my real father, everyone but me, of course. How did that happen?"

"When you were still a toddler, and the boys were in their early teens, Henry had one too many martinis one day and flew into one of his rages. By the time he was done yelling, everyone within a mile radius knew Nelson was your real father. It was so awful. I had to do quick damage control and tell your brothers and the help that Henry didn't mean anything he had said, and none of it was ever to be repeated."

Her words pulled at something inside his head. He closed his eyes, and an incident when he was very young flashed through his mind. He was hiding behind his mother's favorite front parlor chair. His father was in the room doing a lot of yelling. He knew his mother was there, but he didn't recollect her saying anything. He remembered his nanny grabbing him and taking him away.

"Lee?"

"Mm-hm."

"Are you okay?"

"Yes, Mother. I'm okay." He took a moment to compose himself. "So then everyone knew."

"Yes, but in spite of the incident, I believed we could go back to being the way we were, and..."

"And continue with the lies instead of—"

"Yes. Continue with the lies."

Feeling nauseous, Lee excused himself to use the bathroom. He leaned over the sink for a minute, and when nothing came up, he sat on the toilet lid, leaned back against the tank, and stared at the Cézanne nude his parents had purchased the last time they'd been vacationing in Europe. He didn't like the painting—too many dull drab colors for his taste. He figured Cézanne had painted it early in his career during his so-called "dark" period. Lee closed his eyes, longing to be out of his "dark" period. He stopped tapping his fingers on the side of the toilet as soon as he realized he was doing it. He wanted so to break that habit.

Lee thought back to how his tapping ritual had changed over the years—always a __ that couldn't be seen by others. His first recollection was when he was eight or nine. At that time, he tapped the index finger of his left hand on his left thumb. He later changed to his right hand. As a teen, he tapped a toe on the inside of his shoe.

He closed his eyes again and went through a series of mind-clearing and deep-breathing exercises he had learned from one of his doctors, until he felt like he was floating. Then he thought about how he wanted to feel and repeated that word over and over again until he felt relaxed. The word was "strong."

Feeling more in control, Lee returned to the sunroom, anxious for more of his questions to get answered.

"When did everyone start calling Nelson Sambourg Uncle Nelson? How did that come about?"

"Nelson wanted to be in the picture from the onset, and what better way to do that than as a long-lost family member."

"Really?"

"Yes. He felt responsible for you and worried that Henry, well, he…"

"Might not treat me like his other sons?"

"No, not that. Well, maybe it was that."

"And he went along with it? Inventing an uncle?"

"If you're referring to Henry, I didn't give him much of a choice."

"But Uncle Nelson rarely came over and never on holidays or birthdays or anything."

"He did when you were small. You probably don't remember it. But when Henry flew into that rage, well, Nelson's visits had to stop."

"You haven't really told me much about him." After the words escaped his lips, Lee realized he wasn't actually sure he was ready to hear what the man was like. But he pressed on. "What did he do for a living? What were his outside interests?"

"Nelson had many interests—his father's printing company and various real estate holdings. He had a significant amount of money tied up in the stock market that he managed himself. He was well-liked and respected and had a huge network of friends and acquaintances. He was involved in many things, but—"

"Is the printing company around here?'

"It's in Indiana. He inherited it when his father died. That's all I know."

"You don't know the name of it?"

"It may have been...Arietta. Or something like that. The name had a musical connotation, I remember. His father loved the symphony. So did he."

"So you and he were involved in some of the same charities?"

"Several. He was a very generous man. His father had left him a huge estate, and his philosophy was what he didn't earn himself, he should share."

"That's an interesting philosophy. What about his personal interests? What did he like to do for fun or relaxation?"

"I really don't know. When it came to his personal life, his life at home, he didn't share it with me, and quite frankly, I didn't want to know. The small world we had together was all I needed." She hung her head for a moment, and when she raised it back up, her expression was apologetic. "I'm not proud of any of this. Do you understand that?"

"Yes, Mother. I understand. Is there anything more?"

"I think I've told you everything."

"I have questions."

"Tomorrow then?"

"Yes, of course. When will he be home?"

"His plane gets in at six-thirty."

"I'll be gone well before then."

"Lee?"

"Yes."

"You remind me of him."

"In what way?"

"In many ways." She paused. "You have his eyes. Sometimes I have a hard time looking at you." Her voice cracked. "I'm sorry. You don't deserve that."

After he finished his sherry, Lee climbed the stairs to the second floor, but for some reason, he couldn't bear the thought of sleeping in his old bed. Instead, he fell asleep fully clothed in the overstuffed chair in the corner of his room, his state of mind before drifting off to sleep a sense of relief. No more lies.

The next morning they ate breakfast in the sunroom, something he hadn't remembered ever doing during all the years he had lived there. Apparently his mother had caught on to his apprehension for that room.

"So tell me what your thoughts are, Lee."

He stared at her, unsure what to say.

"I've unloaded so much on you. Tell me what you're thinking."

"I don't think you're a terrible person, if that's what you're fearing," he finally said.

She fixed her gaze on something outside the window. "Perhaps I did fear that."

"He didn't give you something you needed, something we all need, and you went elsewhere for it. Quite frankly, Mother, I don't blame you."

"Please tell me you won't leave me."

"Why would you think that?"

"I know you just said you didn't blame me for what I did, but let's face it..."

"I'm not going anywhere, Mother.

"He's not a bad person, Lee."

"Who?"

"Henry."

"He's treated me poorly my whole life, so unfortunately that's all I have for perspective."

"And he's not as strong a man as you and others may think."

"You're not going to tell me about how bad he had it as a child, are you? Because compared to how I—"

"He didn't have it very good."

"Then it's surprising he didn't go out of his way to make sure I didn't suffer the way he did."

"That's not fair, Lee. You don't know him."

"You can't lecture me on what's fair." He struggled to maintain his composure. "The man never even took the time to get to know me. Or did his so-called terrible childhood prevent him from doing that too."

She paused a long moment before speaking. "Lee, Henry grew up with his father's brother living in their house. Turner suffered from severe schizophrenia, and after it was evident he couldn't make it on his own and Henry's parents couldn't find the right place for him, they took him in. His behavior was bizarre. They hid him in their attic."

He had never heard this before. "Because they were afraid or embarrassed of him?"

"Both, I suspect. From an early age, Henry was forced to bring him meals and empty his bedpan."

Granted, that was bad.

"And that wasn't the worst of it. Turner repeatedly told Henry there were government spies everywhere watching them, and when the time was right, they were going to break into their home and do terrible things to them. He told him they had already taken out all his organs and replaced them with ones that contained maggots or something, and the next time they found him, they were going to replace his brain. Henry was young and believed him. He grew up scared, so scared he was afraid to leave the house, make friends, or even play in the backyard."

"Why didn't he tell his parents what was going on?"

"Because Turner warned Henry if he ever told anyone, he'd be next."

"How long did it go on like that?"

"His uncle committed suicide when Henry was a teenager, and Henry was the one who found him. Afterwards, he told his father all the crazy things Turner had said to him. But his father accused him of making it up, told him he was just making excuses for why he had no friends and did poorly in school. His father would call him names and say things to him that made him feel worthless, like a failure. I think that's what drove him to become the success he is today."

"To prove his father wrong?"

"Something like that."

"Why didn't you ever tell us this before? All you told us was his father bullied him."

"Until now, I didn't think you had to know the whole truth."

"And now?"

"I think it's important you understand him better, his past behavior toward you."

"I'm not following you."

"I think at some level you reminded him of the scared little boy he used to be, a little boy faced with big fears he had to keep a secret, fears he vowed as an adult to never have to face again."

"In which case he knew what I was going through and should have helped me."

"Be grateful he didn't try to help you. You see, Lee, he never did face those fears." She looked away from him and slowly rose to her feet. "And he's paying dearly for it now."

* * *

While his mother took a break from their discussion by lying down for a while, Lee carefully weighed her disturbing recount of his father's childhood. He tried to make sense of it, but he couldn't get past how anyone could take out his anger, or whatever it was he was feeling, on an innocent child, one suffering from similar inhibitions.

"He grew up scared," his mother had said.

Well, so did I. And you, Henry, were the major cause of that fear.

Lee didn't know whether to feel more sorry for Henry or for himself. Or was his mother the one who deserved the most sympathy? After all, she'd had to endure both of them for all these years.

He slid open one of the sliding glass doors to the patio, letting in a blast of cold November air, filling his lungs with its iciness before shutting the door. He turned around to find his mother had returned from her nap.

"Would now be a good time for me to ask questions...about things we haven't covered?" he asked her.

She feigned a smile. "Of course."

"Explain the birthday gifts Uncle Nelson gave us. If I have the timeline right, he wasn't even in the picture when Nelson was born."

"He wanted to give you something right after you were born, but he couldn't do that for you and not the others, so he gave Nelson and Bennett something at the same time, and we just let on they had received theirs when they were born. He gave you the coin collection his own father had given him when he was born, one he had added to all his life."

"What other lies are there?"

She looked past Lee. "I suppose there have been hundreds of lies over the years. Hundreds..." Her voice trailed off.

"Did he travel much?"

"Extensively."

Lee's mind kept wandering back to his father's printing company.

"How was he able to travel when he had a printing company to run?"

"He had a hand in running the company, but he had people to take care of the day-to-day things. I think the only reason he hung on to it was because it was his father's passion, not his."

"So what was *his* passion?"

She hesitated before answering. "That's an interesting question. I had never thought about that before now. I think it might have been the association he founded, I believe that's what it's called, whose members are people who do research out of various universities."

"Not the Association for Institutional Research?"

"Yes, I think that's it."

"I've heard of them. In fact, I think Dr. Rad may have received a grant from— Wait a minute. Is there a connection here?"

Abigale nodded.

"Uncle Nelson had something to do with my working under Dr. Rad?"

"All he did was make sure you were aware of his work through one of your college professors. He left the rest up to you."

"So he was aware of what I was doing?"

"He was aware of everything about you...your whole life."

"But we had no contact."

"I told him everything."

"How? How often did you see him?"

"I didn't see him often, maybe a few times a year. When we got together, it was usually in New York. He owned an apartment building near Central Park where we spent most of our time in one of the units that he kept for himself."

"So the affair continued. Until when, Mother?"

"Until he died."

That surprised him. Up until now, he had envisioned his mother's affair as past history. He thought back to her frequent trips to New York. It all made sense now.

"Was he with you in New York when you were expecting me?"

"Not too often. I didn't want him coming to our apartment, and I didn't go out much, as I was trying to hide the pregnancy."

"Please go on."

"We weren't physically together often…but he was always in my heart. We wrote each other letters. And for me, the essence of our relationship came from those letters more than anything else." She smiled faintly. "The ones he wrote were so personal, so passionate. I didn't feel so alone when I knew he was thinking about me like that."

"Did you keep them?"

"No. We each had a post office box to receive the letters, and after reading each one, as much as it pained me, I would destroy it. He did the same."

"What about after he died? How did that change things? Between you and…"

"Henry?"

Lee nodded.

"It didn't. We never talked about it."

"You never talked about it? How could you not talk about it?"

"By that time, maybe everything that could have been said had been said."

"Speaking of Uncle… I mean *Nelson*'s death, you made a big deal out of going to his funeral, but when we got there, you wouldn't go in. Why was that?"

"I had to go. We all had to go. And I thought we could just blend in with the crowd of people I knew would be there. But as soon as we drove up to the church and I saw his wife, Margaret, greeting people at the door, I couldn't bring myself to go in. I couldn't face her."

"Did you two know each other?"

"We had met a few times over the years at various charity events."

"Did she know about you and her husband?"

"Nelson didn't think so, but I wasn't so sure. I often thought that was why she decided to greet people outside of the church at his funeral—to keep me from coming in." She paused for a moment. "And I wouldn't have blamed her."

"Do I have any half-brothers or half-sisters?"

"Margaret couldn't have children."

"Aunts or uncles?"

"He never mentioned any other relatives."

"Here's another thing I don't understand. Why did he go along with all this?"

"Why did who go along with all of what?"

"Damn it! I don't know what to call him anymore. Henry. Anyway, you talked about his reputation, but I don't understand why anyone would think any less of him if he left you, knowing you cheated on him and had someone else's child. How would that have affected *his* reputation?"

"Henry relies on me for...well, for a number of things. He may not admit it, but he does. And I don't think many other women would put up with his...with his shortcomings, shall we say. And I rely on him too. Maybe we were made for each other in some respects."

"I realize relationships are never perfect, but when you think about yours, well, I'm still surprised you stayed together."

"It's amazing what you hold on to when you feel alone."

Isn't that the truth.

"What now? At what point do we drop this whole charade and start telling the truth, Mother?"

She didn't speak for several seconds. "I'm going to tell Henry about our talk when he gets home. It's time."

Lee woke up the next morning just before dawn and lay in his bed for hours, mulling over the conversations he'd had with his mother over the past two days, still in awe of the enormity of the situation. There was so much to absorb.

He felt surprisingly placid for someone who had just received such a massive dose of important facts about his family—facts most people would have learned gradually over a long period of time. But instead of feeling overwhelmed by all of it, he felt relieved.

Lee felt relieved the minute he told his mother he knew Nelson was his father—like a heavy burden had been lifted off him. The more they talked, the less resentment he felt toward her, and the more he wanted to get to know her and develop a new relationship with her.

He closed his eyes and began to understand how the stress of keeping a secret can far outweigh the consequences of revealing it, and that a clear sense of reality is worth its weight in gold. It was a momentous realization—one he knew would stay with him the rest of his life.

Finally hauling himself out of bed, he took an extra long hot shower and shifted his thoughts to DeRam and the threat he posed for CJ and her sons. Convinced he could make use of his certainty that the sheriff had been cultivating marijuana on his property, Lee phoned Bennett to get his take on it. But before he initiated that conversation with his brother, he told him about his mother…their mother.

"Are you kidding me? All this time we thought… Well, now it does make more sense as to why she brought you into the family. Jeez, it feels so unsettling to know this went on in our family."

"Imagine how I feel."

"Good grief! What's wrong with me? No, I can't even imagine how you feel. Holy shit. You've got to be going through… But you don't sound angry or anything."

"Oh, I've been there, believe me. But I try to focus on the upside of knowing the truth and having this now being out in the open, and that's what I think is helping me get through it."

"Does Father know you know yet?"

"He may by now. Mother was going to tell him."

Lee filled Bennett in on most of the other things their mother had told him.

"I can't tell you how badly I feel that you had to go through this, Lee. You didn't deserve any of it."

"Thanks, Bennett."

"And you know what else? I feel honored to have you as a brother." His voice cracked. "I mean that."

"You don't know how much that means to me."

Lee changed the subject before he completely lost control over his emotions and filled Bennett in on his suspicions about DeRam.

"So, this guy, this small-town sheriff, trespasses on your land, grows marijuana, and then tries to pin it on you with that ridiculous arrest?" Bennett asked.

"I can't prove anything, but I know that's what he did."

"What a piece of work. So what do you think he did with all the pot he cut out of the field after you caught him there?"

"I have no idea."

"How much do you think was there?"

"Again, no idea, but at least an acre."

"An acre? Are you kidding? That's a hell of a lot of pot!"

"What if someone were to get caught with that much pot?"

"A hundred plants or more is considered a Class 4 felony. That's hard prison time and a fine."

"How much?"

"In Illinois, up to three years and ten thousand dollars I think."

"No kidding."

"What are you thinking, Lee? You're not going to get involved in this...anymore than you already have, are you?"

"He's a constant threat to CJ, and look what he did to me. If he's in possession of that much illegal substance, shouldn't he be prosecuted?"

"I think you're asking for trouble."

"I think I have a civil obligation."

"And how do you think you could pull that off? Who would you tell?"

"I could turn him in to whoever he reports to."

"My dear brother, what about the 'blue code of silence'?"

"What's that?"

"There's a long-standing tradition among law enforcement officers to protect each other. You won't find anyone on the force who will take you seriously."

"Well, that's not fair. So what happens to corrupt cops?"

"Nothing. That's my point. Don't go there, Lee. If you stir things up, he could do worse things to you than he's already done."

"I despise the man."

"You have my advice. Stay away from that. May I change the subject?"

"Sure."

"I've been in contact with Senator Wheland, thanks to Francine, as you know."

"Mm-hm."

"Well, when he was at the top of his game, he was on one of President Carter's committees studying the law on immigrants and refugees, and their findings influenced a major law that was passed last year. It turns out he and I share the same beliefs on the law's shortcomings, and he's agreed to work with me on drafting a bill that addresses them. I don't know how to thank Francine—this wouldn't have happened without her help. Do you have any suggestions?"

"You can thank her in person on Thursday if you want. She'll be here for Shaneta's Thanksgiving dinner—Jamaican style."

Bennett explained that with his children in town, he wanted to spend every minute with them and wouldn't be able to make it.

After they hung up, Lee poured himself a glass of sherry and thought about the unparalleled joy of having a brother.

* * *

Lee had invited only five guests for Thanksgiving dinner—Dr. Rad, CJ and her boys, and Francine. Shaneta outdid herself with her preparations, which took days. The menu included corn soup, coco bread, jerk chicken, curried shrimp, baked plantains, sweet potato pudding, peas and rice, and rum cake for dessert.

Halfway through dinner, Francine, who seemed to be enjoying the food, asked Shaneta where she had found the unusual spices for the dishes.

"Not around here. We have to go to Milwaukee for them."

"Milwaukee?" Lee exclaimed.

"Yes, you have heard of it, I presume."

"Very funny. How do you get there?"

"You don't want to know."

Dr. Rad stared at his plate.

"Dr. Rad?"

"Mm-hm," he mumbled.

Good grief, he's taking her grocery shopping...seventy miles away, in Milwaukee?

The sound of someone knocking interrupted his thoughts. When he opened the front door, he was surprised and happy to see his brother.

"Bennett! Glad you could come. Come on in, man."

"Don't say anything, okay? Daphne pulled a fast one and picked up the children after they were at Mother and Father's for just a couple of hours. I got pissed off and left."

"No problem. We just started eating. Come on in and join us."

It was the first time Lee had seen Bennett since his mother had told him she wasn't completely sure about his paternity. He studied Bennett's face—he had dark hair and green eyes like their mother, as did his brother, Nelson.

After dinner, Wayne and Travis asked if they could go out on the golf cart, so Lee took CJ and the two boys out for a ride, leaving the others at the house. When they returned a half hour later, Lee found Bennett and Francine deep in conversation.

"Where are Dr. Rad and Shaneta?" he asked them.

"We don't know. After we all helped clear the table, they disappeared."

Lee surveyed the area. "Inside? How many places could they go?" He walked into the kitchen just as Dr. Rad and Shaneta were emerging through the back door.

"Everything all right?" he asked them.

Dr. Rad mumbled something and left for the living room.

Lee gave Shaneta a puzzled look.

"Don't look at me that way."

"Is everything okay?"

"Yes, of course," she said as she walked through the kitchen and toward her bedroom.

Lee joined the others, sans Dr. Rad.

"Where's Dr. Rad?"

"He said something none of us understood and left," CJ explained. "What's between those two anyway, Soc?"

"I have no idea, and I don't want to know. If he were alive today, not even the real Socrates could figure that one out."

"I think we had better be going," CJ said. "It's past the boys' bedtime."

Lee watched as everyone got into their respective cars, except for Bennett who went over to Francine's car. The two of them had a brief conversation before he got into his own vehicle and drove off.

Lee spent the next two hours doing the dishes, while Shaneta stayed holed up in her bedroom. When he was done, he poured himself a Scotch and relaxed with the previous day's local paper. Halfway through the paper, his thoughts drifted to his next project—a project he considered to be a major component of his life plan. Becoming whole, as CJ called it. Uncertain this idea was the right one, he had decided to keep the details of it to himself, his architect, and builder for the time being.

Turning his attention back to the newspaper, a short article buried in the middle of page eight soon caught his attention. Twenty-eight-year-old Randal Grossman of Harvard, Illinois, had been arrested and held overnight in the

McHenry County Sheriff's Office for burglary, assault on an officer, bribery, and resisting arrest. Grossman had posted bail and was released. Arraignment had been set for Friday. Arresting officer, Bernard DeRam, was not available for comment. Lee tore the article out of the paper and put it in his wallet.

* * *

The Deer Bottom Inn was extra busy the next night. CJ looked harried as she greeted him. When she was free, Lee motioned for her to come over to him.

"Do you happen to know a local named Randal Grossman?"

"Sure. Everybody does."

"Why? Does he have a reputation?"

"Francine went to school with him. Comes from a poor family, lots of kids, always in trouble. Has a long rap sheet. Everyone calls him Bulldog. And he *hates* Bern."

"Why is that?"

"Bulldog tried to date Bern's sister once when they were all just teenagers, and Bern beat the crap out of him. And, of course, it was Bern who arrested him most of the time over the years."

Lee told her about his latest arrest. "Does this sound like him, or do you think he's been falsely arrested, like what happened to me?"

"Knowing Bulldog, it could be true. He's been in trouble his whole life."

"Does he ever come in here?"

"Yeah. There's a bunch of regulars who play pool on Saturday night, and he's one of 'em. Why are you so interested in *him*?"

"Just curious, really. What's he like? Has he ever caused any trouble in here?"

"Just the normal rowdiness. He's not a bad guy when he's not getting into trouble. Hell, he can't be all bad. He trains seeing-eye dogs on the side."

* * *

As he contemplated his brother's advice about staying out of DeRam's business, Lee went through a mental exercise he'd learned from one of his therapists called "turning tables" when you're at odds with somebody. There was no question DeRam would go after *him* if the circumstances were reversed. Why? Because DeRam was the type of person who would take any action needed to prevent potential threats against himself. *Get them before they get me.* His therapist had told him that if you can rationalize what the other person would do without compromising your own principles, then you should consider doing it yourself. As absurd as it sounded to emulate someone he despised, he decided maybe it could work in this situation.

* * *

The parking lot was full when Lee arrived at the inn, so he had to park on the side of the road behind a half dozen other cars. Up until then, he had avoided late Saturday nights at the inn, as they tended to be crowded, but on this night, to get the right opportunity to talk to Bulldog, he figured he had to be there right at closing time.

The veil of cigarette smoke was so thick, Lee had to stop momentarily inside the door to allow his eyes to adjust. The jukebox, which had been turned way up, blasted out a song by Metallica, one of CJ's favorite bands.

Lee inched his way to the bar, and when CJ noticed him, she brought him a beer.

"What are you doing here this late?" she shouted.

"Just bummin'."

She shot him a doubtful look. "Hmmm. Forget to shave today?"

He shrugged and smiled.

"Nice threads." She raised an eyebrow.

She'd noticed the black leather bomber jacket he had bought for the occasion.

"Can't talk. Too busy," she said.

Lee nodded and made his way toward the back room where there was a pool table, a couple of foosball machines, and a dartboard. He was vaguely familiar with foosball—he had seen some of his fellow college students play it in the student lounge. And while he certainly understood the concept of pool and darts, he had never played either one. He positioned himself within viewing distance of the two foosball games underway, his back to the pool table, and sipped his beer.

Lee stared blankly at the foosball players. The two closest to him were twenty-something-year-old males. The other pair appeared to be boyfriend and girlfriend. He fixed his gaze on them, but his ears were tuned in to the conversation that was going on behind him at the pool table. As soon as he heard the name Bulldog, he shifted his position in order to see the pool players.

When Lee was certain he knew which one was Bulldog, he finished his beer and went outside. It was one-thirty, a half-hour from closing time.

Fiddling with a pack of cigarettes in his pocket, he waited nervously in the shadows of the building, hoping the jacket, two-day beard, and cigarettes would make him seem a little rough around the edges and thus more credible to someone like Bulldog. But he had never smoked before, and now he wished he had practiced beforehand.

When closing time arrived, Lee lit up the cigarette and took a long drag. He coughed hard and became lightheaded, fearing he might pass out. When he recovered several minutes later, people were streaming out of the bar and heading for their cars. Bulldog was one of the last ones to emerge. A little shorter than Lee and much stockier, the man walked with a decided limp, something Lee hadn't noticed in the bar.

Lee took in a deep breath and then shouted, "Hey, Bulldog!"

The man turned toward Lee.

"Gotta minute?" Lee asked.

"That depends who's askin'."

Lee walked toward him, the half-burned cigarette dangling from his two fingers. "I hear you train seeing-eye dogs," he said.

"So?"

"How does one go about getting one? I know someone in need." He raised the cigarette up to his mouth, pretending to take a puff.

"Midwest Guiding Eyes. They have a facility in Poplar Grove." He turned toward the street and started walking. Lee walked beside him. "What did you say your name was?"

"Lee. And there's something we may have in common."

"Yeah, what?"

"Sheriff Bernard DeRam. Got an opinion of him?"

Bulldog stopped and looked directly at Lee. "Calling that lying piece of shit a degenerate would be an insult to low-lifes everywhere."

"Like I said, we may have something in common."

27 | FUELING THE FIRE

Lee sat at his kitchen table, drinking a cup of coffee, enjoying his solitude now that Shaneta had moved into the guesthouse. His meeting with Bulldog had been nothing short of enlightening. It turned out that Lee, CJ, and Bulldog weren't the only ones with an axe to grind with the good sheriff. Throw DeRam's brother, his sister-in-law, and his sister-in-law's sister into the mix, and there would be enough players for a friendly game of volleyball…or a decent-sized lynch mob.

He had given Bulldog sufficient information to fuel the fire, and now all he could do was sit back and wait. In the meantime, he contemplated his new project. Lee's trust account, having met all its conditions, had been officially closed, allowing him to jump into things without prior approval—something Lee now appreciated more than before.

The new venture was expected to take up close to three hundred acres—five acres for the main building, greenhouses, and storage structures, and the rest sectioned off for evergreens, fruit trees, ornamentals, and shade trees. He hoped the mild weather would hold out until they broke ground—once they had the foundations poured, they could work through the winter, and then he could achieve the desired June Grand Opening date.

Creativity and unconventional thinking would be required to bring the project to fruition. Lee decided to seek advice from the most unconventional thinker he knew: Dr. Rad.

"I'm trying to combine retail sales, wholesale, and services into one business model," he explained to Dr. Rad one evening in his lab. "I have developed a model for each of these segments individually, but when I try to integrate them, I run into trouble. I've spent hours researching this, and I can't find anyone in the industry who has done this."

"If no one has done it in your industry, stop looking there. Look elsewhere."

"Like where?"

"Other industries."

"But they have different product lines, processes, operational costs, and marketing channels. How can they help me?"

"You'll apply what you can to whatever it is you need, and you'll make up the rest. And if what you make up doesn't quite work, you'll try something else."

"You make it sound so simple."

He laughed. "The concept *is* simple. Doing it is quite another thing. I've spent my life in research integrating just a little bit of my own intelligence with what others have already accomplished. They say ninety percent of innovation has already been discovered by someone else. You need to be innovative."

"It makes sense in theory. I'll have to think about what other industries combine business segments in ways similar to what I'm trying to do."

"It's not obvious to you?"

"What do you mean?"

"Deer Bottom Inn and Brewery."

"What?"

"Think about it. They brew their own beer and sell it to other establishments—that's wholesale. They sell it to individual customers like you—that's retail. And they provide services inside the bar. Isn't that what you're trying to do?"

"I don't know. Seems farfetched to me."

"You asked me for advice. That's my advice."

Lee thought about Dr. Rad's suggestion on his way home. It seemed crazy to him and potentially a waste of time, but he respected the doctor's wisdom and figured he didn't have anything to lose. He called CJ when he got home for the name and number of the inn's owner.

A few days later, Lee was reading the morning paper when he was interrupted by someone pounding on his front door. He opened it to find Shaneta agitated and out of breath.

"I just came back from Raddie's...big machines...end of your property...on Attenberg Road. Call the police!" she shrieked.

"Calm down, Shaneta. It's okay. I know all about it."

"What?"

"They're supposed to be here."

"And what are they doin'?"

Lee didn't respond.

"Okay, mi friend, why are you not telling me?"

"Telling you what?"

"Mista Lee, don't play games with me. You know how my curiosity is. I have to know everything. Every thing."

"Well, you're just going to have to be patient with me. You'll know in due time."

"That's not fair. I'll explode if I don't know."

"If you do explode, Shaneta, don't do it on my front porch. It'll make a mess."

She shot him a menacing look.

Feeling a little playful, he asked her, "Speaking of secrets, what were you doing just now at Raddie's place?"

"Nothing."

"Your face looks a little flushed. Everything okay?"

"I have to go." She turned toward the golf cart, which she had parked in Lee's driveway. "He's helpless. That man is helpless. I don't know how he exists from day to day." Her voice trailed off as she neared the cart.

Lee waved to her as she scooted down the driveway and out onto the road to the guesthouse before he jumped into his own car and drove to the far southeast corner of his property.

When he got to the locale, Lee found several pieces of earth-moving equipment clearing and leveling the land. The acrid odor of disturbed dirt smelled sweet. Without getting out of his car, Lee waved to the foreman.

"If this weather keeps up, they'll be able to pour the foundation next month," the man shouted.

"That's great! The sooner the better." Lee smiled and drove home. "Thank you, Father," he whispered to the heavens, hoping Nelson Sambourg would have approved of how forty-five of his coins were being spent, especially since his mother had told him he and his father before him had grown the collection, not cashed any of it in.

As he headed west down Attenberg Road, he saw Shaneta driving the golf cart down the dirt road as fast as it would go, toward Dr. Rad's place, bouncing up and down in the seat, her sweater and scarf streaming out behind her. He watched her disappear into the grove of trees that blocked his view of the lab.

Lee drove twenty-five miles to the Rockford Public Library where he spent the rest of the day in the business-book section. He needed to learn as much as he could about marketing, advertising, merchandising, and small-business management for the unfamiliar arena he was about to enter.

* * *

The first Christmas Eve in his new house shifted some of Lee's attention away from business development to preparations for a Christmas Eve gathering for their "makeshift family," as Shaneta called them—Dr. Rad, CJ and her sons, Francine, and Bennett. They decorated the house in traditional American and Jamaican holiday style, complete with a fifteen-foot northern white pine tree Lee had cut down from a small grove at the back of his property. They placed the tree in the living room, in front of the two-story bay of windows.

By the time everyone arrived, Lee's home was fragrant with a mixture of pine needles and potpourri. After enjoying a savory feast prepared by Shaneta, they all exchanged presents and listened to her tell stories of her childhood Christmases in Jamaica.

The guests started leaving close to nine o'clock. Bennett lingered behind, and when everyone had left, told Lee the latest news about his marriage.

"She's filed for divorce."

"You knew that was coming."

"Yes. I knew, but being served with the papers made it real."

"And the kids?"

"The *children*," he corrected him, "will be living with her, and I'll have visitation rights."

"At least she's not denying you that."

"Let her try."

"Are you two at least able to be civil to each other?"

"I am, but she's too bitter right now. Hopefully, that will change with time."

"What's she got to be bitter about?"

"She claims I didn't turn out to be the man she thought I was, that somehow I falsely presented myself to get her to marry me."

"That's ridiculous."

"You know Daphne's family."

"Not really."

"Her father is a big oil tycoon, and her mother hobnobs with the Kennedys. She's used to living high and being seen with important people, and she thought she was getting that with me."

"She did get that, didn't she?"

"In the beginning...until I started to see the light and realized I was really someone other than just a Winekoop."

"Speaking of them, what do you know about what's going on at the house?"

"With Mother and Father?"

"Yes."

"I don't know what's going on, but it seems there's an awful lot of tension there lately."

"I haven't talked to her since she said she was going to tell him that I know everything. Maybe that conversation took place."

"Well, that would do it," Bennett said.

* * *

It wasn't like Mother to not return phone calls. Lee had left three messages for her over ten days and was becoming worried enough to consider driving out to Evanston to check on her.

Finally, she called him back.

"I know you've been calling, but I didn't want to call you while Henry was still here. He's out of town on business now, so..."

"Is everything okay?"

"Yes, everything is okay."

"It doesn't sound like it."

"I'm just tired."

"Tired physically or emotionally?"

"A little of both, I suspect."

"How was Christmas?"

She sighed. "It was tolerable, I suppose."

"What do you mean?"

"I told Henry about our conversations."

"And?"

"And he reacted the way I expected."

"Not well?"

"No, dear."

"What did he say?" Despite the pain of it, Lee wanted to know.

"It doesn't matter, Lee."

"It matters to me."

His mother didn't speak.

"I know this is hard on you too. Believe me, I do. But keep in mind I grew up under that man's rejection and lived under a veil of lies from everyone who knew that I was another man's son. And if you don't think that had an adverse effect on me, and to a degree still does, you're mistaken. I deserve to at least be told the truth now, the whole truth, don't you think?" He had never spoken to his mother in that tone before.

His mother remained silent.

"Are you there, Mother?"

"Yes, I'm here." Her voice was softer than usual, her tone conciliatory. "And you are right on both counts. Yes, this is hard on me. And you deserve to know the whole truth. But now I'm tired and need to—"

"Please don't do this to me. Whenever you don't want to talk about something, you need to lie down. Pull up a chair, take a deep breath, and talk to me." He waited several seconds. "What did Henry say when you told him I knew?"

"He said..." She fell silent.

"Mother, if I was standing in front of you, I'd want to shake you right now. Just tell me."

"He said he's glad the whole...thing is over and..."

"Tell me the word he used. He didn't say *thing,* did he?" He waited for her to respond, and when she didn't, he said, "I can come over there, and we can finish this discussion in person."

"He called it a farce."

"What else did he say?"

"He took you out of his will, but I—"

"What else?"

"He questioned some of your skills."

"Mother."

"What?"

"What did he call me?"

"A loser. There, now I've said it. Are you happy?"

What Lee heard next was a sob and the sound of her hanging up the phone. He called her right back.

The cook answered the phone.

"Winekoop residence."

"Bryah, this is Lee. Put Mother back on, would you please?"

"She's gone to her room, Mister Lee."

"Please go get her, and tell her if she doesn't come to the phone, I'm going to drive out there."

"Yes, sir."

Lee waited several minutes, and when his mother got on the phone, he could barely hear her.

"I'm not a very strong person, Lee. I thought you knew that."

"Don't fool yourself, Mother. I suspect you're a lot stronger than you think. That's my opinion, anyway. Look, I'm sorry I pushed you so hard, but at this point in my life, I have to know the truth, no matter how heinous it is. I need that in order to move on. Otherwise, it's like carrying around a live hand-grenade in my back pocket. Pull the pin for me, Mother. Let me panic over it for a few seconds, and then I'll throw it as far as I can so as not to be threatened by it anymore."

"I'm not sure I like your choice of metaphors, but I do understand what you're saying. But what you need to understand about Henry is—"

"No, I don't have to understand anything when it comes to him." He struggled to keep his voice soft and calm. "All he cares about is himself. And what bothers me the most is he has no sympathy for me, the innocent victim in all this. He's nothing but a callous, self-absorbed human being, and I doubt he'll ever change. Honestly, I don't know how you can stay with him."

"Well, that could change."

"How's that?"

"Bringing this all out in the open has been a turning point in our lives."

"How so?"

"It was one thing when we were pretending about...well, about you. Now that we don't have to do that anymore, well, our relationship isn't the same. In some ways, I think the lies were what held our marriage together."

"Do you hear what you just said?"

"Yes, and now that I've said it out loud, I must admit it sounds rather absurd."

"So what are you going to do now?"

"I don't know, son." Her voice was barely audible. "I'm just waiting to see what happens."

"Mother, may I impart some wisdom I acquired during the past few years?"

Her sigh could be heard over the phone. "Yes, of course."

"If you keep letting things happen to you, you'll always be channeling someone else's course. Believe me, when I figured that out, I was a much stronger person, a much happier person. I'll take it one step further—I became my own person." He hadn't thought about it in those terms before, and he didn't know which made him more proud—the fact he had become his own person or the realization of what had given rise to it.

"That's easier, dear, when you're young. But look at me. I—"

"That's just an excuse." He paused, unsure how far to take this argument, given how much he had already said. "Let me ask you something. What are you most afraid of?"

"What do you mean?"

"I mean, you've spent your whole life with him trying to keep things on an even keel instead of living your own life. You've lived that way for so long, you don't know how things could be any different. Why have you done that? What are you afraid of?"

She hesitated. "That he'll leave me, I suppose."

"So?"

"And I need him."

"For what?" He didn't let her respond. "All I'm saying is you create your own happiness by the choices you make. If you rely completely on others, you'll never have it, at least not in the true sense of happiness."

"I'm sure you're right, dear." She stayed silent for several seconds. "Maybe I'll have Charles drive me to the lake house for a few days. If I do, could we spend some time together?"

"Of course, Mother. I'd like that."

* * *

Lee arrived at CJ's New Year's Day party at four o'clock, followed by Shaneta and Dr. Rad and then Francine and Bennett. The women worked in the kitchen while the men chatted in the living room. CJ's sons spent much of the time in their bedroom watching *Ferris Bueller's Day Off* on the video-cassette recorder Lee had bought them for Christmas.

Lee, Bennett, and Dr. Rad were discussing the new multifaceted business model Lee had created based on insight he had gained from the owner of Deer Bottom Inn, when the phone rang. Lee heard CJ answer it.

"What? You're kidding," she said. "When? No way. How long do you think?" She emerged from the kitchen, her face flushed.

She talked fast, in a hushed voice. "They arrested Bern last night. Caught him with over a hundred pounds of pot *and* stolen guns in his basement. Hauled his ass off in handcuffs. The feds, not the local police. Don't say anything to the boys. Not yet."

Travis and Wayne emerged from their bedroom.

"Boys, go wash up. We'll be eating soon."

"We just did."

"Go do it again."

CJ ran toward the kitchen and came back with a bottle of champagne. "I was going to serve this after dinner to toast in the new year, but I feel like doing it now." She poured everyone a glass.

All eyes were on Lee, who worked hard to appear as surprised as everyone else.

The boys entered the living room holding up their hands to show their mother they were clean. "How come everybody stops talking whenever we come into the room?" Wayne asked.

"Dinner's ready, boys. Go sit down at the table," CJ told them.

Dinner included roast turkey, garlic mashed potatoes, seasoned green beans, and hot buttered biscuits. Nothing fancy—just plain old down-home cooking, something Lee had never experienced until his first visit to the local diner, Miss Sally's, but had subsequently come to love. The adults kept the conversation focused on the food, but Lee knew it was CJ's announcement that was on everyone's mind.

After dinner, CJ assigned clean-up chores to her sons and then joined the others in the living room.

Francine spoke first. "Who called?" she asked in a whisper.

"Dick, at Deer Bottom. He overheard some of the off-duty cops talking about it in the bar this afternoon, so he didn't have many details. They said it was the biggest pot bust in the history of McHenry County."

"I wonder how they got on to him. And why the feds?" Francine asked.

CJ shrugged and turned to Bennett. "Do you know why the feds would be involved?"

"Could have something to do with him transporting it over state lines," he responded.

"CJ, you look like you're over the moon about this. But how do you really feel when you think about it?" Francine asked. "After all, he is—"

"We're done, Mom," Travis said.

"Good job, boys. It's almost eight o'clock, and you have school tomorrow. Time for bed."

"Tomorrow's Saturday, Mom."

"Never mind. You still need the rest."

"But, Mom…"

Their discussion resumed once the boys were out of earshot.

"I *am* over the moon," CJ said. "I hope he's locked up for a long, long time—father or no father."

"How long could he get, Bennett?" Lee asked.

"If the feds were involved, it's a big deal. A Class 4 felony under federal law? We're probably talking several years at least."

"I feel like I can breathe again," CJ said.

"Any chance he'll get off? He *is* a sheriff," Lee asked Bennett.

"I doubt it. They can get away with a lot locally, but not with the feds involved."

CJ smiled. "Serves him right. He deserves what he gets. More champagne, anyone?" she asked.

Lee was the last to leave. CJ followed him out onto the porch. "Hey," she said with her arms wrapped around herself against the cold evening air. "So did you have anything to do with it?"

"With what?"

"You know what."

"Goodnight, CJ. Thanks for dinner, and happy new year!"

* * *

Lee called CJ the following day. "How are you feeling, now that it's had time to sink in?" He knew deep down he had done the right thing, but he needed reassurance just the same.

"I slept better last night than I've slept in years. Does that answer your question?"

"What about the boys? Have you said anything to them?"

"I had to. I didn't want them to hear it from some kid in school, so I told them this morning."

"How did you explain it to them?"

"I told them he did something illegal and may have to spend some time in jail for it."

"How did they react?"

"They pretty much just accepted it. Wayne gave me a kiss on the cheek afterwards, and Travis wanted to know what was for lunch."

"How are *you*?"

"I'm happy. Look, he did the crime, so now he must pay. It has nothing to do with me. I just get to reap the benefit of being able to go to sleep each night with both eyes shut."

"CJ?"

"What."

"I'm happy for you."

"Thanks, Soc. Thanks for whatever you had to do with it, 'cause I know you did. And so does Frankie."

"Why? What did she say?"

"Nothing. Just on her way out last night with Bennett, she said—"

"Ha. You say that like they came together."

"They did."

"What?"

"You didn't know?"

"Know what?"

"That they came together."

"What?"

"Do we have a bad connection or something?"

"No, I heard you. Bennett and Francine came to your house yesterday together? As in what?"

"As in he got in his car. He drove to her house. He knocked on the—"

"Don't be a smart ass."

"Okay. All I know is he and Frankie have been talking, on the phone mostly, about whatever they have in common with Sam Wheland and other stuff, I guess. And then he asked her if she wanted him to pick her up for my dinner party. And she said, 'Sure.'"

"Hmm. He never mentioned it to me. I feel a little left out."

"You shouldn't. There's really nothing to it."

After they hung up, Lee called Bennett on the pretext of asking him how the roads had been when he drove home from CJ's the previous night.

"I didn't know you and Francine had come together," he said after their small talk.

"Mm-hm."

"You sly dog. You didn't tell me you two had something going on."

"There's nothing going on. All I did was offer to drive her to CJ's."

"So how did that just happen?"

"It just did, that's all. Look, she a great gal. The whole Senator Wheland thing was such a godsend to my cause. There's nothing more to it."

"For now."

"I'm still legally married, remember. I have to keep my nose clean. But if I'm honest about it..."

"Go on."

"I'm not going to lie. I've thought about what it would be like to be with someone again." He paused. "Someone genuine...like Francine."

"You deserve that."

"I'm not so sure of that. When I think back to my marriage, I think I may have been more wedded to my law firm than to Daphne. That wasn't fair."

"You're not thinking of reconciling with her, are you?"

"No. I guess I'm just feeling a little guilty about things."

Lee learned the divorce was moving ahead and that Bennett and his wife would have to appear in court at the end of the month. He was giving her more than half of everything they owned and would be paying alimony and child support.

"And the kids?"

"I talk to them as often as I can, but she intercepts their calls most of the time. I'll be glad when they're old enough to make their own calls. Hopefully, she will not have turned them against me by then."

"They're smart kids."

"I know, but if they hear from her how I am 'the bad guy' enough times, pretty soon it becomes a matter of fact.

They moved on to discuss DeRam's arrest. When Bennett insisted on knowing what Lee knew about it, Lee tried to maintain that he was as surprised as everyone else.

"Right, little brother."

"Okay, so I had a little something to do with it."

"Spill it."

"There's this guy in town who hates DeRam as much as I do. His nickname is Bulldog, if that gives you any indication about this guy's character. Anyway, he's been in his share of trouble over the years, has a record, but he's not a totally bad guy. So I find out DeRam recently arrested him for a burglary he didn't commit along with a bunch of other trumped-up charges, and this guy had no money for a decent lawyer and was looking at jail time for something he didn't do. So I helped him out."

"You paid for his lawyer?"

"I did."

"So this punk tells you he was arrested for something he didn't do. And you believed him?"

"Yes, I did."

"Why? You said he has a record."

"Because the burglary was at a Milwaukee gun store owned by one of DeRam's brothers, and the guy said he would bet any amount of money DeRam was somehow involved in it and was trying to pin it on him. Maybe even an inside job to get insurance money. It wouldn't be that farfetched."

"The same thing DeRam tried to pull on you."

"Right. It's his MO."

"But you still didn't know for sure, so you were taking a big risk getting involved. But go on."

"I know I didn't think it all the way through at the time. Looking back, I think I probably attached more importance to seeing DeRam suffer what he justly deserved than to any risk I was taking. Anyway, I put a little bug in Bulldog's ear that if police were to search DeRam's house for the stolen guns, they might also find a rather large stash of pot."

"So what was the probable cause for searching DeRam's house? No judge is going to issue a warrant on a hunch or an unsubstantiated suspicion."

"Well, it turns out DeRam's sister-in-law, the wife of the gun store owner, hates him. Thinks he's a bad influence on her husband and won't even let him around her kids. And Bulldog knew this because he's dating her sister, Roberta."

"Ah, the plot thickens."

"Something like that. Did I mention that this guy Bulldog walks with a limp?"

"No."

"He held up a gas station one time. Got caught running from the scene of the crime by DeRam...who shot him in the back of his knee."

"Ouch! That had to smart."

"I guess. Anyway, when Roberta heard about Bulldog's most recent arrest, she told her sister she wanted revenge against DeRam. So now we have two scrappy sisters *and* a reckless ex-con all wanting DeRam out of the picture, and I had the opportunity to help them make that happen."

"Now you're scaring me. Tell me you didn't do anything illegal."

"Of course not. *I* didn't, anyway. I'm not so sure about Roberta."

"Go on."

"So Bulldog gets Roberta to come on to DeRam at the Deer Bottom Inn one night after DeRam has had a few beers. She tells him she broke up with Bulldog—a lie, of course—is feeling pretty lonely, and starts flirting with him. He buys her drinks. One thing leads to another, and she goes home with him. Once she's in his house, she lays it on even thicker and gets him to drink more. Then when he's just short of passing out, she tells him she's been afraid to be alone in her apartment these days because Bulldog wasn't happy about their breakup. She tells him she's so scared of him, she's thinking about getting a gun.

"Well, DeRam is all over that. Apparently, he puffs out his chest and tells her he can take care of that for her, but she can't tell anyone where she got the gun. She tells him it has to be a small gun because, 'I'm just petrified of guns.' Roberta knew, of course, that many of the guns stolen from her brother-in-law's shop were 9mm revolvers."

"And here I thought this kind of thing only happened in the movies."

"From what I hear, Roberta is quite a character. I'd like to meet her one day. Anyway, DeRam disappears down his basement stairs and comes back with a nice little compact Beretta. She waits until he passes out on the sofa and then leaves. When she shows the gun to DeRam's brother, he verifies it's one of the stolen guns and gets livid that his own brother had something to do with the burglary. He goes to the Milwaukee police, who turn the case over to the feds."

"So there's your probable cause for the search warrant."

"And when they search his basement for the rest of the stolen weapons, voila! They find over a hundred pounds of marijuana."

"And DeRam gets arrested, thanks to you."

"All I did was come up with a few *what ifs* for three rather spirited individuals, shall we say. They came up with the plan and carried out the deed all on their own."

"Nice work, man."

"Thank you."

K nowing so little about his real father was beginning to gnaw at Lee. Here he was developing hundreds of acres of land to meet the man's criteria without having any idea what life experiences or thought processes had led to them, and now he didn't feel confident he was doing the right thing. Sure, Stonebugger had given him the go-ahead, but that may have been only because he was too overcome with grief over his sister's death to argue.

Determined to know more about Nelson Sambourg before he took his latest project any further, Lee went to the library and perused the names of printing companies listed in the Gary, Indiana Yellow Pages. There were fourteen companies. Arietta, the name his mother had thrown out, was not among them. She had said she thought the name of the company was musical. None of the names appeared musical to him, but he wrote down the addresses and phone numbers of all fourteen anyway.

When he got home, he called all of them and asked to speak to Nelson Sambourg. Not one of the people who answered knew anyone by that name.

Lee next got out a map of Indiana, wrote down the names of the four smaller towns surrounding Gary, and then called the library to see if they had Yellow Pages for these smaller towns. They did not.

Not to be deterred, Lee drove two and a half hours to Clarke Junction, Indiana, the first town on his list, and found a phone booth. He flipped through the Yellow Pages only to find there were no printing companies listed. There was none in Ivanhoe either. Black Oak listed one company, Sorenson's Printing. When Lee called the number, a recording told him it had been disconnected.

He stopped at a diner for lunch before heading out to Aetna, the last town on his list. Prepared to find nothing, he finished his sandwich and thought about the disheartening drive home he was likely to have.

The roadside sign indicated less than three thousand people lived in Aetna. He drove through the modest town looking for a gas station but found none until he was about five miles out of town. He pulled in, but the only phone book in their phone booth was the one for Gary, which he had previously examined. He went into the gas station.

"Do you know anything about Aetna?" he asked the young clerk behind the counter.

"Not much. What do ya wanna know?"

"I'm looking for a phone book for that town."

"Not sure if they have one. I think they're really part of Gary."

"Thanks."

Lee was almost to the door when the clerk called him back.

"They do have a library. You might wanna check there."

"Do you know where it's located?"

"Town ain't very big. Can't be too hard to find."

"Thanks."

He drove back to Aetna in search of the library, thinking this was probably a big waste of time, and when he found it—a tiny little shack of a building at the end of a residential street—he was sure of it. He went in and asked the woman behind the desk if they had a phone book for Aetna.

"Not a current one. We're annexed to Gary now, so we're included in theirs."

"If you have an older one, I'd like to see it."

She disappeared for several minutes and returned with a very thin book dated 1968, almost twenty years old. She handed it to him.

"Thanks. I'll bring it right back."

Lee took a seat at one of the two small tables in the center of the room. There were no Yellow Pages, so he had to scan each column of names in the entire book. And there it was, halfway down the second column of page one. Allegro Printing. Allegro was a familiar musical term meaning rapid tempo.

He stared at the name for a moment and then smiled when he realized he was experiencing what must be an "allegro" heartbeat.

"Can you tell me where I can find the nearest public phone?"

"Is it a local call?"

"Yes."

She glanced at the phone on her desk. "You can use this one if you want."

He hesitated. "It's kind of personal."

"Gas station is your best bet then. Closest one is in Gary."

Lee thanked the librarian and headed back to the gas station in Gary, excited about his find.

"May I speak to Nelson Sambourg, please?"

"Mr. Sambourg is no longer here. May I put you through to someone else who can help you?"

Bingo. "Perhaps. May I ask who the new owner is?"

"The company is currently in probate."

"May I speak with the current person in charge then?"

"If you tell me what you're looking for, perhaps I can direct you to the right person."

Lee hadn't thought through this scenario and had to think of something quickly. "I may be interested in purchasing the company."

"Then you'll want to speak with the executor of Mr. Sambourg's estate."

Wrong question. "Okay," Lee said, knowing full well who that was. "Can you give me his name and number?"

"His name is Basil Stonebugger." She gave him the number.

"Thank you."

"You're welcome."

Lee had originally thought he could make a connection with whomever was in charge, and pretending to be Nelson's nephew, ask if he could have one last look around the plant for old time's sake. He had concocted a long tale in his mind about how his uncle had brought him to the plant on weekends when he was a small boy and let him sit in his big desk chair pretending he was the boss and his uncle worked for him. No chance of doing that now.

He looked at the address he had jotted down at the library—800 North Lake Street. He remembered crossing over that street to get to Gary.

Lee retraced his route to Lake Street. When he found it, he took a chance and turned to the right. It didn't take him long to find the address.

The three-story brick building sat in the middle of a long stretch of road surrounded by other industrial buildings. He pulled into a parking lot across the street and parked his car facing the building. High above the front door, the company's name, faded and almost illegible, had been painted in white on the dark brick façade. He contemplated trying to pull off his original ruse by telling the receptionist he was Nelson's nephew, thinking she would have no reason to believe he was the one who had called earlier. What did he have to lose?

He rang the doorbell and was buzzed in. The reception area was just large enough for a small desk, four guest chairs, a side table, a plastic ficus tree, and a water cooler.

"May I help you?" the receptionist asked. With her grey hair piled up in a mound on top of her head and silver-rimmed glasses balancing on the end of her nose, she reminded Lee of the old woman who lived in the shoe from his favorite boyhood nursery rhyme. Her nameplate read Henrietta Davis.

"Hi. I have what may be a strange request."

"Yes?"

He told her the touching story of how Nelson, his favorite uncle, had brought him here when he was just a youngster.

Miss Davis listened attentively.

"I'm sorry for your loss, and I must admit, that was a moving story, but I'm afraid I can't let you have access inside."

"Why not? What would be the harm?"

"This company is in probate. I have strict orders from the executor of Mr. Sambourg's estate as to who can come and go, and you're not on that list."

"Who *is* on that list?"

"Employees, lawyers, tax people, and then of course there are prospective buyers. Except for employees, no one is admitted without an appointment."

"May I ask how many employees work here?"

"Now? Not that many. Each additional week this place stays in limbo, the more people leave. It's a shame I tell you."

"How long have you been here?"

"Twenty-three years."

"So you must have known my uncle well."

"I met him a few times over the years. He typically didn't come in during normal business hours. Someone else ran the place. Look, I've probably said too much already. It's only a matter of time before I get the boot. And look at me. I'm fifty-nine years old. Where am I going to find another job? I have a sick husband at home who can't work, and I'm carrying the load. So I would appreciate it if you'd leave before I get in trouble."

"Okay. I'm sorry. I didn't mean to bother you."

Lee sat in his car and mindlessly stared at the Allegro sign for several minutes before driving off. Feeling defeated and sorry for himself, he went back and forth between feeling compassion for his mother and resenting her all over again for everything—for having the affair, for telling lie after lie throughout his life, for sharing so little about his father with him. But then he thought of Henry, and he couldn't help but feel sympathy for her.

He started beating himself up for wasting an entire day on a wild goose chase and decided not to tell anyone about it. He had been foolish to think he could gain entry to his father's printing company with that pathetic story he had concocted. He had handled the whole thing like an ignorant kid instead of a mature adult.

When Lee reached the sign welcoming him into Illinois, he was on the verge of tears and decided he'd better pull into a rest stop to collect himself. He parked away from the other vehicles to think things through. He questioned the importance of getting to know more about the man who had fathered him. After all, that was all in the past. Maybe he should be concentrating more on the future.

Then Lee thought about DeRam, his nemesis, the man he hated, the man he had helped throw in jail...the man who always got what he wanted. He wondered what he would do in Lee's situation.

The sun was low in the sky by the time he got back to Allegro Printing—and only a thin ribbon of orange was visible in Lee's rearview mirror. He parked in the far corner of the parking lot, away from the twenty or so other cars that were clustered near the building by what appeared to be the loading dock. Next to the wide overhead door were several steps leading up to a regular-sized door.

The overhead door opened a few minutes after six, and several men in dark blue uniforms exited the building and sat on the edge of the platform, their legs dangling in front of the rubber bumper that protected the dock when trucks backed in. Some of them smoked, while others opened up lunch boxes. Lee wondered if any of them had known his father, and if so, would they be willing to talk to him.

While he contemplated trying to start up a conversation with them, a truck from a laundry service pulled into the lot and backed into the far bay of the loading dock, away from the workers. The driver got out, waved to the men, and proceeded to unload his truck. One of the workers got up and disappeared into the darkness of the plant. When he returned, he was carrying bags of what Lee assumed were soiled uniforms, which he threw in the back of the truck. In less than ten minutes, the laundry truck had come and gone.

Lee watched while the men finished eating and one by one left the dock. A few lingered behind to have one more cigarette. By six-thirty, the dock was empty, the overhead door closed.

Based on the number of cars in the parking lot, Lee figured only half of the workers had come out on the dock for their break. He waited fifteen minutes for the other half to appear, and when they didn't, he got out of his car and walked nonchalantly toward the building.

Light was visible underneath the door. He climbed the steps and peeked in the small window to see a short hallway and three closed doors. The one closest to him was marked Dock Superintendent. The other two were unmarked. He tried the door. It wasn't locked.

With his heart pounding high in his chest, Lee opened the door. He hesitated a brief moment before letting himself in. The thought of getting caught crossed his mind but didn't dissuade him from continuing inside. He walked to the first door on his left and put his ear up against it. Hearing nothing, he carefully opened it. Even in the dim light, he could see it was the inside of the loading dock. He closed the door and approached the second one.

As soon as he opened the second door, he could hear the distant clapping sound of what he assumed were the printing presses. Complete darkness inside prevented him from seeing what was in front of him. He felt along the wall on either side of the door for a light switch, and finding none, groped his way around the room until he discovered another door and a light switch. He flicked it on.

He was standing in a storage room filled with boxes and office equipment. Peering out the door into a wide hallway, he saw two elevator doors. To his left, he knew, was the loading dock. To his right was a closed door with a sign on it that read PRIVATE.

Unflinching, Lee opened the door and peeked in. Scant light from the streetlamp streaming through the large front window allowed him to see the reception area he had been in earlier that day. He stepped inside, waited a moment to listen for noises, and when hearing none, started snooping.

He sat down behind the desk and opened a drawer. Inside was a piece of paper containing a typewritten list of names, the first of which was Basil Stonebugger. At the top of the list were the words "Permission to Enter." He didn't recognize any of the other names. The other drawers in the desk didn't reveal anything of interest.

Lee sat at the desk staring at the ficus tree long enough to realize there was a door behind it. He moved the tree, opened the door, and peered in.

The room smelled of stale cigar smoke, and it took Lee a moment to adjust to it before entering the shadowy room. He opened the wide vertical blinds that covered the large storefront-like window, allowing in light from the streetlamp.

The first thing that caught his eye was the brass nameplate that had been prominently placed on the expansive desk—NELSON O. SAMBOURG, PRESIDENT.

Lee sat down behind the desk and closed his eyes so he could fully experience the feeling of sitting in his father's worn leather chair. A chill rippled through his body, causing a sensation in his chest so strong he felt on the verge of fainting. After he composed himself, he turned the chair around to inspect the four photographs on the credenza behind him.

On the far left was a photo of a fortyish man shaking hands with John F. Kennedy. He picked up the photo. He realized the man was probably his father, but he didn't look anything like what Lee had imagined. The man was half a foot taller than the president, handsome, with a full head of hair. He looked more like an actor than an owner of a printing company. Their attire, the width of their ties in particular, gave away the age of the photo.

Lee tried to picture his mother with this handsome man. It wasn't hard to do.

Next was a more recent photo of him, approximately age sixty, with his arm around a woman Lee assumed to be his wife.

The third photo was of a young man and woman posing in front of a 1920's roadster. A small boy and girl sat on the running board.

The remaining photo was of a young girl, possibly a teenager, sitting on a bed surrounded by stuffed animals. Written on the bottom was LORETTA, MARCH 10, 1941.

Lee remembered his mother telling him his father was sixty-six when he died, so that would have made him around twenty-one when the photo of the teenage girl was taken. He couldn't make any connection. His mother also told him she wasn't aware of Nelson having had any other family. So who was Loretta?

He studied the photograph of the two adults and two children, then slipped the photo out of its frame. On the back of the photo someone had scrawled in pencil MOM, DAD, LORETTA, AND ME 1926 OR '27.

Lee digested the inscription for a minute. It appeared Nelson might have had a sister, or if not a sister perhaps some other close female relative. Then again, perhaps Loretta was just a neighborhood girl who happened to be playing with him that day.

A loud thud overhead interrupted his thoughts. He held his breath for a few minutes, waiting. When all was quiet again, except for the distant hum of the machinery, he proceeded with his search.

What he saw when he opened the top left drawer of the desk startled him. Placed in the same type of frame as the other photographs was an image of his mother. Lee recognized it as one of her older publicity photos she used to provide to the society pages when they wrote about her various charity events. He stared at it, and when he realized how much Bennett took after her, he shivered. He slipped the photo out of the frame. On the back, in her handwriting were the words LOVE ALWAYS, ABBEY.

In the bottom of the drawer, he found a stack of envelopes, each bearing Nelson's handwritten name and a Chicago post office box address. There was no return address on any of the letters. He opened the one on top. It started out "My Dearest Nelson" and ended with "Love, Abbey." He didn't have it in his heart to read what was in between.

The rest of the file drawers in the desk revealed little, so Lee moved on to the four-drawer file cabinet. The top two drawers appeared to be the typical kinds of business-related files one would find in a company president's office.

The third drawer contained many files related to the Congress for Cultural Freedom. He scanned the file folder labels—Conferences, Contributions, Correspondence, Publications. He flipped though each folder and found nothing out of the ordinary.

The bottom drawer contained files related to AIR, the Association for Institutional Research. He removed the first file folder labeled BOARD MEMBERS. At the top of the list was Basil Stonebugger's name, with the title vice president of grants.

The second folder contained a list of donors. The name Abigale Sedgwick Winekoop appeared many times throughout the list, the latest entry for her being the previous year.

Another folder, a very thick one, contained newspaper clippings, copies of articles, and sheets torn from magazines, all having to do with one topic—psoriasis.

Finding nothing of interest in the remaining folders, Lee took a break and sat back in his father's chair to survey the room. A college diploma from Northwestern University hung on one side of the door. On the other side was a hounds-and-fox painting. A bookshelf with a few reference books and artifacts had been positioned on one wall next to another door.

He opened the door to reveal a bathroom.

From the bookshelf, he picked up a carved wooden elephant with the inscription MADE IN INDIA. He wished he knew if his father had been to India or if someone had just given it to him.

Some of the reference books pertained to printing and others to medicine, making Lee even more curious about him. His mother had never mentioned any ties to medicine.

Something changed outside the room. Lee could no longer hear the reverberation of running machinery overhead. He sat still while the sound of closing doors echoed from the back of the building. He could feel the vibration of what he thought might be the overhead door on the loading dock being raised. Two minutes later, he looked out the window to see a line of cars exiting the parking lot. It was nine o'clock. The second shift must have just ended, an hour earlier than he had anticipated.

Lee waited several minutes before making his way to the back of the building. When he saw only his own car in the parking lot, he walked through the storage room and headed back toward his father's office.

The elevator doors caught his attention. Feeling adventurous, he pushed the button to go up. The powerful sound of the elevator caused him to jump. When the elevator door opened, Lee stepped inside and pushed the 2 button.

When the elevator door opened again, Lee was taken aback by the pungent smell of chemicals. The room was enormous. The two rows of machinery flanking either side of a twenty-foot aisle were at least twice as tall as he was. He walked the length of the machines and tried to envision pages of newspaper flowing through each section of the press. A wrought-iron stairway took him to the third floor where there were a dozen or so smaller pieces of equipment.

When he'd finished his tour, he went back to the first floor, glad he had taken time to see the operation, even if it wasn't running at the time.

As Lee passed through the storage room, he pulled off the plastic cover of an old Xerox copier, similar to the kind he had used in the Cornell library years earlier, the kind that broke down after just about every use. He hit the On button, and the display lit up. To his relief, it did not malfunction while he made copies of the four photographs, the AIR board member list, and his father's college diploma.

He left through the back exit with his photocopies, the wooden elephant, his father's nameplate, and his mother's letters, making sure the door was securely closed behind him so no other unauthorized person would have the opportunity to do what he had just done.

S taring at the carved wooden elephant and the brass nameplate now proudly displayed on his new fireplace mantle, alongside the photocopy of the picture of his father shaking hands with JFK, Lee felt he knew his father a little better. But not enough to be completely satisfied. He continued to ask his mother questions, and she continued to be conspicuously unresponsive, either because the only aspect of him she knew had taken place in the bedroom, or because it was just too painful to talk about him.

He wanted to know more. He needed to know more, and he figured Stonebugger might be his only hope. He regretted not having pursued a meeting with him sooner. Lee had just received a letter informing him that Stonebugger had retired. Hopeful he would still be willing to meet with him, Lee called Stonebugger's office and explained to his secretary the personal nature of his request.

The next day, the secretary called to tell him that Mr. Stonebugger was amenable but only if Lee's mother was made aware of the nature of the discussion. Lee agreed, and a meeting was arranged to take place in Stonebugger's office the following Sunday.

When he called his mother to tell her, she sighed and said, "I've told you everything, Lee."

"With all due respect, Mother, you've told me very little. And you admitted yourself your relationship with him was narrowly focused. I want to know more."

"I admit I didn't live in his real world—our relationship was cultivated completely outside of that. What I'm trying to say is I don't know what you're going to find, and I don't want you to be disappointed."

He didn't believe her. He suspected the real reason she didn't want him to learn more about the man was so she could preserve the Utopian image she had of him.

"From my perspective, the truth is better than ignorance, even if it's hard to take."

She didn't speak for a long moment. "This is important to you, isn't it?"

"Very important."

"Then I hope you find what you're looking for."

After Lee hung up, he gazed out the front window at his acreage. A mild winter had given way to spring, allowing the stems in the massive fields of red clover to push their way above the soil like a platoon of billowy soldiers. The structures for his current project had been completed before the first heavy snowfall, allowing Lee and the contractors to concentrate on the interiors. With the grand opening scheduled for June 21, the project was right on schedule.

After driving to Chicago, Lee parked his car near Stonebugger's office and gave himself a few minutes to calm his nerves. He had no idea what to expect from the meeting.

It was evident from Stonebugger's face that he still bore the pain of his sister's death, and now Lee felt guilty for initiating the meeting.

"I'm very sorry for your loss, Mr. Stonebugger."

"Thank you. Have a seat, and please call me Basil." His voice was soft, almost wistful.

"Yes, of course." Lee sat down across from him. "First of all, I appreciate your agreeing to meet with me. I want you to know I wouldn't have bothered you about this if it wasn't so important to me."

"I understand. Believe me, I do."

"I know Nelson Sambourg was my father."

Stonebugger nodded.

"And I know you had a long-standing relationship with him."

"Yes, I did."

"Can you tell me about him?"

He studied Lee's face for a few seconds before speaking. "We grew up in the same town, Valparaiso, Indiana. We lived two blocks from each other."

"So you went to school together?"

"We were best friends all through school."

"And college?"

"He went to Northwestern. I went to Purdue."

"What was he like? What were his interests? And most importantly, did he have any family?"

Basil didn't respond right away. Instead, he got up and stared out the window at the empty city street below. Stonebugger's office was in the heart of Chicago's Loop district, which was typically deserted on weekends. "I loved him like a brother. We did everything together as kids. Played sports, went fishing, double dated, got into trouble. His family? His parents were good people. His father built that printing company from nothing. Amassed a fortune from nothing. Very smart man."

"Did he have brothers and sisters?"

Basil didn't speak for several seconds. "He had a sister. She died."

Lee waited for him to say more.

Finally, Basil turned around. "Her name was Loretta. Beautiful girl." Lee thought about the little girl in the photograph from his father's office.

Basil sat back down. He folded his hands and rested them on his desk. "She took her own life."

Lee hadn't expected to hear that. "How tragic."

"They were close...like Gladys and me."

"How old was she?"

"Nineteen."

"Can you tell me what happened?"

Basil took his time answering. He leaned back in his chair and closed his eyes for a few seconds. "You deserve to know. You *should* know who your father was and what he was all about."

The expression on Stonebugger's face told Lee he was pained by the memories.

"Loretta was what most people would call a perfect child—well-mannered, smart, caring, a real pleasure to be around. Nelson doted on her, protected her when she needed it, even when she tormented him the way little sisters can do. I know. I had two younger sisters to contend with myself. When she was about thirteen, it happened. And it happened fast."

"What's that?"

"She developed a severe case of psoriasis, and it was on her face. Are you familiar with the disease?" Lee shook his head. "It's such a cruel disease when it attacks visible parts of the body. Thick, red, scaly patches of skin cells form raised plaques of skin, as they're called. They didn't pose a serious health risk, I don't think, and the physical discomfort was tolerable. It was the teasing, the cruel names she was called, and rejection from her classmates and even adults that caused her demise."

"That's why she took her own life?"

Basil nodded.

Lee tried to imagine what the girl must have gone through. "How did my father take it?"

"Not well. He was a few years older than she and in his senior year at Northwestern. He came home for the funeral and didn't go back to school. Couldn't go back. At least not then. It wasn't until years later he took the few courses he had left to finish his degree."

"And his parents. That had to be so hard on them."

"Yes, they took it hard. His mother died a few years later from congestive heart failure, and his father died shortly after that."

"Leaving Nelson with no family."

"Exactly. I shouldn't say this, but the man was so lonely and distraught from losing his family, I think he married the first woman who came along."

"That would have been Margaret?"

"Mm-hm."

"And they had no children."

"That's correct. Another emotional letdown for him."

"Do you know if she knew about me?"

"Nelson believed, or wanted to believe, she wasn't aware of his affair with your mother, but I think she did. Whether she knew about you or not, I don't know."

Lee had hoped for a more definitive answer.

"I understand he inherited the printing business when his father died."

"He did. But he didn't have much interest in it. He didn't have much interest in much of anything back then. He let others manage the business while he did other things, trying to find happiness, I guess. There was a lot of drinking and gambling going on in his circle of friends." He shook his head. "He looked like hell most of the time. Margaret threatened to leave him. When I found out about the affair he was having with your mother..." He paused. "Sorry."

"It's okay to talk about it. My mother has been very open with me."

"That's when I stepped in and had a heart-to-heart talk with him."

"And what happened?"

"He calmed down some. And then I asked him one day what he was so angry about all the time. He broke down and said it was Loretta's senseless death. We talked for hours about it that day…something we should have done years before. At the end of our talk, he swore he would do something about it, even though he didn't know what."

"Is this story going to lead to his founding the Association for Institutional Research?"

"You've been doing some investigative work."

Lee smiled. "Some."

"Well, you are absolutely right. He was one of the founding fathers, and they asked me if I would oversee the administrative aspect of issuing grants. The first grant we issued was to two Northwestern Medical School professors interested in finding the early diagnosis and treatment of acromegaly, another disfiguring condition, one that results in abnormally large tissues in the hands and feet. It took your father several years before he found anyone to conduct research on psoriasis, and by that time, he was completely immersed in the AIR and its work. He was devoted to medical research of all kinds, but especially disfiguring diseases."

"That's why you said something about building a treatment facility for people with disfiguring diseases as an example of a way for me to increase the value of the land."

"That's actually what he had planned for it."

Lee let that sink in for a moment and wondered why Stonebugger hadn't told him that from the beginning. "Mother said he had referred to it as 'the promised land.'"

"He talked about it for years, but for some reason, nothing ever came of it."

"So he wanted me to carry out what he didn't."

"I'm assuming that was his intent."

"Why didn't he come right out and say that in his will?"

"I think it was because he knew you well enough through your mother to know for you to succeed in life, you had to figure things out for yourself." He paused. "Unlike your brothers who were handed things on a platter and were able to run with it. I don't mean any disrespect toward them. That's just how it was, or so he told me."

"Yes, that was pretty much how it was. I'm surprised to hear he knew me that well. To tell you the truth, I'm surprised to hear my mother knew me that well."

Basil laughed. "When you're a parent yourself, you'll understand. Yes, he knew all about you. Your underutilized intellect, your struggle to fit in, your fears. Your mother told him everything."

"If he knew how much I was struggling, I wonder why he didn't come clean and rescue me."

"My guess is if he had any regrets in life, that would have been it. He agonized over it. Believe me when I tell you that." Basil let out a long sigh.

"I'm thinking back to our first couple of meetings. You were pretty hard on me."

"Now here comes my regret. But first, understand I had just lost my life-long friend, a friend I loved, admired, and believed in. I had watched him struggle for years over the death of his sister and then his parents. I witnessed all his bad decisions and then listened to numerous plans to do something in his sister's memory that never came to fruition. And then when he bought that land and told me his plan for it, I thought he was on to something, and I was so happy for him. A stronger Nelson had emerged. So when I discovered you were the beneficiary and read the terms and conditions he put in his will as to how you were to use the land...well, now I thought I was going to have to witness his dream falling apart, and I was resentful."

"You had no faith in me."

"It wasn't that, Lee. I thought he was making it too restrictive...for anyone, let alone someone who was struggling to find himself."

"But you finally came around."

"I would argue it was you who came around. I think the old coot knew exactly what he was doing. What if he hadn't put those restrictions on you, or what if there had been no restrictions at all? Would we be sitting here having this discussion?"

"Probably not."

"Is this helpful? Do you think you know him a little better now?"

"Yes, I do. I have a different perspective now. Thank you."

"You're welcome. Now, please bring me up-to-date on what you're doing."

Lee told him about the progress on the research facility. When he mentioned Dr. Rad's name, Basil gave him a puzzled look.

"Dr. Rad? Short for a much longer name, right?"

"Yes."

"The University of Illinois. I can't believe I didn't make the connection earlier."

"Mother told me Nelson was indirectly responsible for putting us together."

"I never met the man, but I was involved in awarding him a small grant several years ago. Nelson met him. Thought he was eccentric but a brilliant researcher. Nelson's real interest, though, was in his work with red clover."

"How is that?"

"Nelson had been talking with the University of Maryland Medical Center about their research in treating skin inflammations, such as psoriasis. It was through them he met Dr. Rad."

"What's the connection with red clover?"

"UM was one of the first institutions to use red clover in medical research."

A sharp rap on the front door startled Lee as he sat in his living room drinking his third cup of coffee, listening to music, waiting for the rain to stop so he could check out the glass that had been installed in the greenhouses the day before.

Shaneta stood on his doorstep, soaking wet, her shoes caked with mud. She clutched a soggy sack of...something.

"This isn't workin'."

Lee looked her up and down. "What isn't working?"

"Look out there," she said, pointing to the dirt road leading to Dr. Rad's lab.

"I don't see anything."

"Exactly. That's because it sank in the mud."

"What sank in the mud?"

"The golf cart. What else do you think I would be talkin' 'bout?"

"Shaneta, why did you take the golf cart out on a dirt road in this rain? Couldn't you have guessed that would happen?"

Shaneta gave him a look that defied any answer.

"Would you like to come in and clean yourself up?"

"No. I would like a ride to Raddie's. He's waitin' for me."

"Looking like that?"

"He doesn't care what I look like. He's hungry."

"Well, if you ask me—"

"No one is askin' you...with all due respect."

"I'm only saying—"

"Can you just give me a ride...please?"

Lee spread a tarp on the floor of his car and made a mental note to consider buying a pickup truck so he wouldn't have to get his car dirty when things like this happened. He drove Shaneta to Dr. Rad's lab, the long way around, on paved roads.

"That kitchen of his isn't much to cook in," she said on the way.

"You've been cooking there for him?" That seemed to explain why she hadn't cooked anything for Lee since moving into the guesthouse.

"Why else would I be carryin' 'round a bag of raw food?"

He had no answer.

"It would be nice for him to have a better kitchen... and maybe a place for me to sleep."

"A place to sleep?" The guesthouse was a half-mile down the dirt road from Dr. Rad's lab.

"And a covered walkway so I could walk to his place when it rains. My fanny can't take much more of that cart."

"Are you asking me to build another house...for you?"

"Nothin' too fancy."

"So you want to live with him?"

"Are you kiddin' me? With that man? Are you outta your mind?"

The paved road ended, and Lee was forced to take a chance driving on the temporary dirt road the construction crew had created.

"Okay, let me get this straight. You want a bigger kitchen to cook in for Dr. Rad and yourself, and you want a separate place to sleep, close to him but not too close, and you don't want to have to be in the rain when you go serve him his meals...or whatever."

"That's pretty much it."

"So an extension to his living quarters with a very long hallway."

"Perfect."

"And what does he think about this?"

"How do I know?"

"Don't you think this should be something you talk about...together?"

"You can't talk to that man."

"Would you like me to mediate?"

"You can use whatever big word you want as long as you make it happen...okay?"

Lee glanced over at the resolute woman beside him. "Okay, I'll talk to him."

* * *

Lee left Rockford Coin and Stamp with a check for $10,000, just enough to pay for the addition to Dr. Rad's lab for Shaneta—a bedroom, a good-sized kitchen, and a bathroom. He hoped the twenty-five-foot tunnel connecting the two residences would prove long enough for the two of them to coexist in a relatively peaceful manner, but not too long that he had to withstand Shaneta's complaints about the long walk she had to suffer in order to bring him his meals.

Shaneta and Dr. Rad's relationship was nothing short of puzzling. They came from entirely different cultures, had widely different educational backgrounds, practiced different religions, and had grown up in different social classes, but none of these issues appeared to impede their relationship. Perhaps most odd was that even though they were both unattached adults, with seemingly nothing to hide, neither of them would admit they were in a relationship, affirmation for Lee that when it came to relationships, some things were beyond explanation.

* * *

It was the usual small Monday-night crowd at Deer Bottom. Without even asking him, CJ brought Lee a beer and the special for the night—bratwurst and fries.

"It's on the house," she said.

"What's the occasion?"

"The Bernmeister got five years."

"Really?"

"In Marion."

"Federal prison."

"Yep." She held up her glass of club soda and clanked it against his beer mug. "The bum deserves every minute of it."

"How are the boys?"

"They seemed okay with it. Wayne said, 'Maybe he'll be different when he gets out with all that time he has to think about things.' Pretty astute for a ten-year-old, I would say."

"Sure is."

"Are you coming to Francine's for Easter?"

"With bells on."

"Bennett's coming."

"I know. He told me."

"So will Shaneta and Raddie be there?"

"As far as I know. They pretty much do their own thing these days."

"When will the tunnel project be finished?"

"I'm hoping by the middle of June."

"How's your secret project coming along?"

"I want to talk to you about that...but not here. Could I come over tomorrow morning?"

"Long as it's after ten."

He finished his beer. "I'll see you tomorrow."

Lee had given significant thought to what he was about to ask CJ, but even though they had become close, and he felt he knew her pretty well, he couldn't predict how she would react to it. The last thing he wanted to do was jeopardize their friendship.

He arrived at CJ's house before noon with a bag containing two of Shaneta's jerk chicken sandwiches, chips, and two fudge brownies.

"Ah, a man bearing gifts," she said. "What do you want?"

"Let's not go through that again."

She laughed. "I know better now. C'mon in."

They talked about small stuff over lunch and then retreated to her front porch with glasses of lemonade.

"So what do you want to talk about, Soc?" she asked.

"My current project."

"So you're finally going to tell me what it's all about?"

They spent the next hour talking about Lee's proposal. When they were finished, he asked, "What do you say?"

"I say..." She held him in suspense for several seconds. "Yes. On one condition."

"What's that?"

"My boys are the first to enroll."

He held out his hand.

"Stand up, you big oaf. I think we're close enough for this to be a hug, not a handshake." Holding on to the embrace, she said, "I love you, you big dope. You know that? You have a frickin' good heart."

At that moment, Lee realized CJ would be someone he could always count on, always trust, a kindred spirit of sorts. He would do anything for her, and he had a feeling she would do the same for him. And while there had been times he thought about what it might be like to be in a romantic relationship with her, he knew their being loyal friends was more relevant for them. Not having developed meaningful relationships as a child—not with his parents, his teachers, siblings, or friends—he only now realized their inherent value and was grateful the first meaningful one he did have wasn't encumbered by romance.

"Me too." He pulled away from her and added, "So all this time you were impressed by my heart? It wasn't my stunning good looks and spectacular physique?"

"Get real."

He shot her a sly smile. "I have to get going. Mother will be arriving soon."

"Is she staying overnight again?"

"Mm-hm."

"That's nice. I really mean that."

"I know you do. I look forward to her visits."

"Still no communication with Henry?"

Lee shook his head.

"Probably just as well."

Lee nodded.

Lee thought about his soon-to-be expanded relationship with CJ on the drive home and reveled in the irony that he had lacked someone to look up to his whole life, and now someone was looking up to him.

Then he thought about his mother and what her reaction would be when he gave her the letters she had written to Nelson so long ago that he had held on to all these years.

Shaneta moved out of the guesthouse and into her new residence without fanfare. In fact, Lee wouldn't have known she had moved out of the guesthouse at all if he hadn't found the keys on his kitchen table one morning. Next to them were a four-leaf clover and a handwritten note that read,

> *Thank you for being such a good friend.*
> *Shaneta*

Lee spent the rest of the day preparing the guesthouse for its new occupants.

Three days later, Shaneta invited Lee over to have dinner with her and Dr. Rad...at *their* place. Dr. Rad's living quarters in the back of the lab were modest—besides the bathroom, he had only one room with a twin bed, a five-foot counter with a sink and room for a hotplate, a dorm-size frig under the counter, and a small table where he could eat and work. Lee couldn't imagine how they could entertain in that space. But even more surprising was that "they" were entertaining at all.

Lee drove up to the front door of the lab where Shaneta met him.

"Welcome to my humble home, Mista Lee. Please, come in." She led the way to the back of the lab.

The table had been set for three, but there were only two chairs. Dr. Rad sat in one of them. None of the plates, glasses, or utensils matched. Upon closer inspection, Lee noticed that one of the plates was from his own kitchen.

"Sit down, Lee. Can I get you somethin' to drink?" she asked.

"Sure. What do you have?"

"Water, red clover iced tea, or Jamaican rum."

He was tempted to ask for rum but didn't. "Tea would be fine."

Shaneta went to the frig, pulled out a pitcher of tea, and poured it in three glasses. "Make yourself comfortable while I get the salads," she said as she bustled her way toward the tunnel that connected her residence with the lab.

Lee looked at Dr. Rad.

"Please don't ask," he said to Lee.

"Quite frankly, I don't even know *what* to ask."

"Allow me to change the subject."

"Please do."

"You know I appreciate all you have done for me."

Lee nodded.

"You gave me my life back."

"I may have helped you get back on course, but you had the courage to make it happen. No one could have done that for you."

"Thank you, my friend. In any case, I have been thinking about how I could repay you."

"You don't have to—"

"No, I want to contribute in some way. Please allow me to do that."

"What did you have in mind?"

"I was thinking that if you featured a different plant each month that was particularly good for one thing or another—such as soil erosion, or filtering carbon dioxide, or attracting various wildlife—that would interest your customers."

"I like the idea."

"Good. I can do that for you. One per month. Deal?" He reached out for Lee's hand.

"Deal."

Shaneta, who had been going back and forth between courses via the tunnel, sat down on the bed long enough to ask about Lee's current project.

"So when do the doors open?"

"June 21, the first day of summer."

"Not that far off. Are you ready?"

"I think so. I've taken out ads in all the local papers, and the week before it opens, I'll be doing two radio interviews."

"Does your family know? Will they be comin' openin' day?"

"I know Bennett will be there. And I hope Mother. I'm not sure about the others."

The three of them talked about the project until the two men finished eating, at which time Shaneta got up and disappeared once again into the tunnel. When she returned five minutes later, she was balancing a tray that held three plates of dessert, two cups, and a coffee pot. She put the tray down and looked at Lee.

"Do you know how many steps there are between here and there?"

"Fifteen," said Dr. Rad under his breath.

"Just enough for the coffee to get cold," she said.

"Shaneta, are you trying to—"

"I'm not complainin', mind you. I'm just statin' the facts. Did I tell you I found a job, Lee?"

"No. Where?"

"In Walworth. Workin' for the Seversons."

"Cooking?"

"And cleanin', and shoppin'. Everything. Just the two of them. No children.

Just a big shaggy dog.”

“That’s wonderful. But how are you going to get there?”

“Mrs. Severson will pick me up and bring me home. Except on Wednesdays when Raddie will do the chaufferin’. And every other Friday.”

Dr. Rad forced a weak smile.

“And the day before most holidays.”

“When do you start?”

“Monday.” She turned to Dr. Rad. “I’ll need a ride home. Her bridge club meets that day.”

“Yes, m’am.”

“Don’t you get smart with me, Raddie.”

“I wouldn’t think of it, Shan.”

“I’m going to clear the dishes now and goin’ into my room so you two can chat.”

Lee waited until he heard Shaneta’s door close. “Dr. Rad, I know this is none of my business, but—”

“She means well.”

“I know that, but is this what you want? Or is she pushing herself on you?”

“She may be pushing herself on me, but if I’m being truthful, I don’t mind it. I like the woman. In fact, well...we’re planning to get married.”

“What?”

He smiled. “I think you heard me.”

“What?”

“Is that all you can say, son?”

“No, of course not. Congratulations. I really mean that.”

“Thank you.”

“That changes things, though, doesn’t it? I mean, is this arrangement still going to work? Like I think she was trying to make the point that the table is too small, and the time it takes to bring hot food from her kitchen to your living quarters is too long.”

“I would prefer to keep my work space small and close to the lab where it is. Do you think it would be possible to enlarge her space to accommodate a dining table? That way, we can eat in her space for meals, close to her kitchen, and keep her out of my space.”

“I can talk to Dennis and see what he can come up with. What about a small living room as well? Somewhere for the two of you to watch TV or something.”

“I would like that.”

As Lee recovered from the shock of news of their upcoming marriage, he vowed he would never understand relationships, nor question them again.

“Congratulations, Dr. Rad.”

“Please call me Raddie. I kind of like it.”

L ee stood at the edge of the parking lot to admire the giant helium-filled balloons and GRAND OPENING banner when he saw CJ coming toward him.

"Hey, who's minding the store?"

"Shaneta," CJ responded.

"Oh, dear."

"Don't worry. She's okay. I gave her a five-minute training session on the cash register." She stood next to him and took his arm.

The parking lot that held up to fifty cars was nearing capacity. Some of the townspeople strolled around the display garden Lee had created. Others were inside checking out the displays of indoor planters, lawn ornaments, gardening tools, and planting soil. The greenhouses were packed with people loading up their carts with perennials, annuals, and houseplants. Outside, several landscapers wandered through the groves of hundreds of varieties of trees and bushes. A few families with children headed straight toward the building with the poster in the window that read, THE MOST IMPORTANT CONTROL YOU CAN EVER ACHIEVE IS SELF-CONTROL.

The prominent sign Lenny Vinik had made for him that now hung on the front of his building made him smile.

SOCRATES GARDEN CENTER AND KARATE SCHOOL

"You did it, Soc. You really did it."

"What's that?"

"You turned the tables."

"You never did recite the whole poem for me."

"It's not important. What's important is you overcame being on the outside looking in."

"You did, too."

"Wrong! I was always on the inside."

"Was not."

"Was too."

"Okay. Have it your way."

"By the way," CJ said, "a few people have asked me about the letters you painted on the fence post signs." Lee had painted each of the 109 signs on his fence line so as to cover over his father's *NOS* insignia. Then he stenciled them all with letters or marks of punctuation that, placed in the right order, would spell out Lee's secret declaration to the world.

"Yeah? So what did you tell them?"

"What you told me to tell them—that they're just random letters."

"And did they accept that?"

"Don't know. They probably think you're just crazy."

"Maybe I am."

"Wayne, for one, didn't believe it. He thinks he's cracked some of the code."

"Is that right?"

"He knows there are three sentences based on the three periods. And he knows your first and last names are in there. And maybe the word *I'm*."

"Mm-hm. What else?"

"Of course, he and Travis tried to find letters for all the naughty words they know."

"And?"

"They found three they're admitting to."

"I can tell you there are no naughty words in the message."

"I was pretty sure of that. Can I tell Wayne the word *I'm* is right?"

"Yep."

"And your first and last name?"

"Yep."

"He asked me to ask you for some hints."

Lee pondered the request. "Tell him he has a very wise mother."

"Huh?"

"And I'm thankful to her. That's all you get."

She smiled. "Can I tell you something without you getting all mushy on me?"

It was an interesting question. "You can try."

"You helped me get my life on track—something no one else has ever been able to do." She swiped at a tear on her cheek. "And for that...I thank *you*."

Not giving him a chance to respond, CJ walked toward the garden center entrance and then turned around. "Hey, Soc. The boys want to know if they can build a tree house in that maple tree behind the guesthouse, the one right outside their bedroom window."

"Only if they get someone to help them with it. Not me."

"No shit."

"Watch your mouth. We have respectable customers around here."

"Bite me," she mouthed.

He watched CJ disappear into the garden center, her new place of employment, while her sons played outside in a murky puddle left behind by the previous day's rain. They ran over to Lee.

"Mr. Lee," Wayne said. "Can we keep that black cat that keeps hangin' around our house for our own?"

"I don't see why not. It appears to be a stray."

"All right! We can keep him!" Travis shrieked.

"Thanks!" Wayne said and then turned to walk toward the garden center.

"Hey Travis. How do you know it's a boy?"

"Wayne said so." He lowered his voice to a whisper. "He knows these things."

"I see."

"It better be a boy, 'cause we already named him."

"What did you name him?"

"Mr. T," he said and then skipped to catch up with his brother.

After both boys were out of sight, Lee took a minute to reflect on the rest of his operation—the vast fields of red clover for cancer research and more recently to finding cures for psoriasis and other disfiguring skin diseases; the experimental orchards established in conjunction with two Johns Hopkins consultants; the collaboration with Texas A&M researchers who were close to finding a way to prevent protein from breaking down in red clover; and the grant from AIR that would allow expansion of Dr. Rad's laboratory.

Lee was proud of what he had accomplished and believed his father would have been proud too, not only because of the end result, but also his journey to make it happen.

Thank you, Father, for allowing me to find my own way.

A tall young woman walked toward him with a level of confidence in her gait that he found both inviting and frightening. She held out her hand. "Hi. I'm Violet Jennings. I understand you're the owner here." Her handshake was strong.

She had amazing green eyes. His voice cracked as he spoke the first few words. "Yes, I'm the owner. Lee Winekoop. Nice to meet you, Violet. How may I help you?"

"I have a seven-year-old daughter who wants to take karate classes, but all I see over there are boys. Are girls allowed?"

Lee hadn't given any thought to the issue before now. He had never heard of a girl taking karate classes—he, like everyone else, considered it a boy thing.

"I don't see why not. It may not be conventional, but as you can see by my somewhat odd combination of businesses, I'm not one to be swayed by convention." He caught himself looking down at her left hand. She wasn't wearing a wedding ring.

"Then you've got yourself a new student. Eva will be thrilled. She'll be enrolling under Eva Larson, by the way. Her father and I are divorced. I took back my maiden name—women's lib and all that." Her smile was warm and pleasing.

"There's a sensei in the dojo right now signing kids up."

"I beg your pardon."

"I'm sorry. That's Japanese for an instructor being in the karate school."

"Do you also teach the parents? I can see I have a lot to learn."

He flashed her a wide smile. "I think we can arrange that."

"Look forward to it," she said as she turned toward the dojo.

The light touch on his shoulder startled him. He turned around to face his mother.

"She's very pretty," she said.

"Mother, I'm so glad you came."

Bennett and Francine were right behind her.

"Lookin' good, little brother," Bennett said with a smile.

"There's food inside. Some of Shaneta's specialties."

"Consider us gone," Bennett said as he and Francine walked away.

"Bennett," Lee called to him.

Bennett turned around.

"Thanks for your help with the grant request. It was awarded last week."

Bennett gave him a thumbs-up and proceeded to the garden center, arm-in-arm with Francine.

Lee looked at his mother, who was looking up at the sign. She slipped her arm through his. "I'm proud of you, son. Really proud."

"Thank you, Mother."

"You're making a difference."

"In what way is that?"

She smiled—a natural smile Lee hadn't ever seen on her before, a smile that reached further than anything she could have said. "In your life. In mine. In CJ's, Dr. Rad's, and Shaneta's. Bennett's. Everyone you've touched." She squeezed his arm, still looking up at the sign. "But I have to ask you, where did the name Socrates come from?"

"Socrates. You know. The Greek philosopher."

"Yes, I know that, but why him?"

Lee didn't think his mother would understand the whole "south of center" concept, and if she did, she wouldn't find it amusing. "Oh, I don't know. Just a name that came to me."

"He was an enigmatic figure."

Lee turned toward his mother. "Like me?"

"Yes. Somewhat."

"Henry didn't come with you."

"No, dear. I hope you understand."

"Not really."

"You will someday."

"And Nelson?"

"He had family things to attend to."

He was disappointed but resolved not to let their absence ruin his day.

"C'mon, let's go inside. I'll show you around." He squeezed her arm. "And afterwards, after everyone has gone, would you like to see the research facility?"

"I'd like that very much."

* * *

Basil Stonebugger arrived close to the end of the day. Lee led the way toward the display garden, to the plaque on the wishing well where purple clematis climbed lazily up its sides. The plaque read:

In memory of Loretta Sambourg and Gladys Stonebugger

May the red clover in our lives serve to
Inspire, heal, and bring us closer to being whole

Lee watched the sadness flow through Basil's eyes.

"Thank you for your part in all this," Lee said to him.

They talked for a few minutes, and then Lee excused himself and walked through the display garden toward the garden center where the last few visitors were still lingering. He looked forward to showing his mother the rest of his property and perhaps for the second time in his life hearing her tell him how proud she was of him.

He slowed up when he saw Henry sitting on one of the wrought-iron benches at the edge of the garden. Lee hadn't seen or spoken to him in months, not since he had had that first revelatory conversation with Shaneta. He took a good look at him. Gone was the confident air about him Lee had come to know throughout his childhood.

Henry waved Lee over as soon as he saw him.

"Hello, Henry." As soon as he said it, he realized that was the first time he had ever called him Henry to his face.

The man looked like a complete stranger to him now. It was hard to imagine having lived under the same roof with him, having eaten at his dinner table, enduring his subtle and sometimes not-so-subtle put-downs, internalizing the pain of his hurtful words to the point of physical illness, living life in constant fear of being a failure. It all seemed quite surreal now, even though the effects of it still lingered.

"Do you have a minute?" he asked Lee.

Lee joined him on the bench.

"I've been sitting in my car for the past hour trying to think of the right words to say to you."

"You don't have to say anything to me."

"Yes, I do." He shifted his position to face Lee. "And let me preface it by saying I fully understand that nothing I say will make up for the way I've treated you over the years."

Lee sensed Henry was looking directly at him but couldn't bring himself to look at him. Not yet.

"I know you know the whole story about your mother and Nelson, and the first thing I have to say is that we were wrong to handle it the way we did, by covering it up. It was selfish of us and not fair to you, and for that I'm sorry." His voice was soft yet resolute.

Lee breathed in, and after a long moment, turned to face Henry. He studied the seriousness of his face and then nodded. He believed his sincerity...but wasn't ready to accept his apology. "I'm sorry too."

"I don't think I could have been a worse role model for you if I had tried. Instead of helping you through the tough times, I contributed to them. I'm not going to make any excuses for my behavior. All I can say is you deserved better." He glanced around the property. "This is some place you've got here."

"Thank you."

Henry pulled an envelope out of his breast pocket. "When Nelson and Bennett turned twenty-five, I gave each of them an early inheritance." He handed the envelope to Lee. "I want you to have the same."

"You don't have to do that."

"No, I suppose I don't. But I want to. And last year you told me the University of Wisconsin was planning to build a medical research facility outside of Lake Geneva."

"That's right."

"You asked me for help making contact with the right people, and I didn't do it. I hope this isn't too late. The name of the person you should contact is in the envelope. He's very interested in Dr. Rad's work and is expecting your call."

He stared at Henry for several seconds. "What changed your mind about helping me with that?"

"Your mother."

"How so?"

"She told me it was one thing to treat you like I did when you were young and under the veil of secrecy we were all living, but to continue to do it now made me less than a man." He pursed his lips and closed his eyes, as if trying to prevent his emotions from escaping. "Those words got me to thinking, soul searching I believe they call it, not only about you and your mother...about a lot of things." He touched the top of Lee's hand. "Look, I wouldn't blame you if you never spoke to me again, but if you do find it in your heart to forgive me someday, I hope we can find a way to develop a new relationship, an honest one this time."

After an awkward moment of silence, Henry withdrew his hand and continued. "I suppose you know your mother is leaving me."

His mother hadn't shared that with him. "No, I wasn't aware of that."

"I've been living in the Lake Geneva house for a while."

"Does she know you're here?"

"No."

"Are you going to tell her you're here? She's inside."

"Yes, I know." His eyes focused on the spot where Lee and his mother had talked earlier. "I'm trying to get up enough nerve to ask her to come home with me so we can talk things through."

Lee gazed at Henry's profile—the slight hunch in his posture, the nervous tick in his chin, the soulful look on his face. He sensed the scared little boy that still lingered inside him, giving reality to how self-destructive not facing your fears could be.

"I hope everything works out for you, Henry. I really do."

After Henry left in search of his wife, Lee walked to the edge of the expansive field of red clover, breathing in the sweet powerful fragrance of the blossoms. He stepped into all its splendor, and letting the tops of the flowering plants grace the tips of his fingertips, looked up into the limitless sky and felt blissfully whole.

The End

On The Outside Looking In
By David Harris

The peels of laughter emulate from within
and he stands on the outside forever looking in.
He stands the stranger, which no one wants to know.
Sadness always etched across his brow
with a lonely heart beating inside.

He sees the smiles radiate from within
while he stands alone
always on the outside looking in.
The one who stands apart from any joyous crown
with only tears and a lonely heart.

He is the one who never is invited
to parties at anytime,
but has to watch from outside a window
on the outside always looking in.
He is that someone everyone rejects as a friend.

One day he can only hope and tables will turn.
Until that day arrives
and his loneliness evaporates he will remain
the one who stands
on the outside always looking in.

Reprinted with permission from the author

ARE YOU CURIOUS ABOUT THE FENCE-POST LETTERS?

Below are the letters Lee painted on the 109 fence-post signs. The message Lee wanted to convey made use of all the letters and punctuation marks found on the signs, just not in the same order he painted them.

Hint: The first word is *My*.

The code is fairly easy to crack, but if you must, look on the back for the deciphered message.

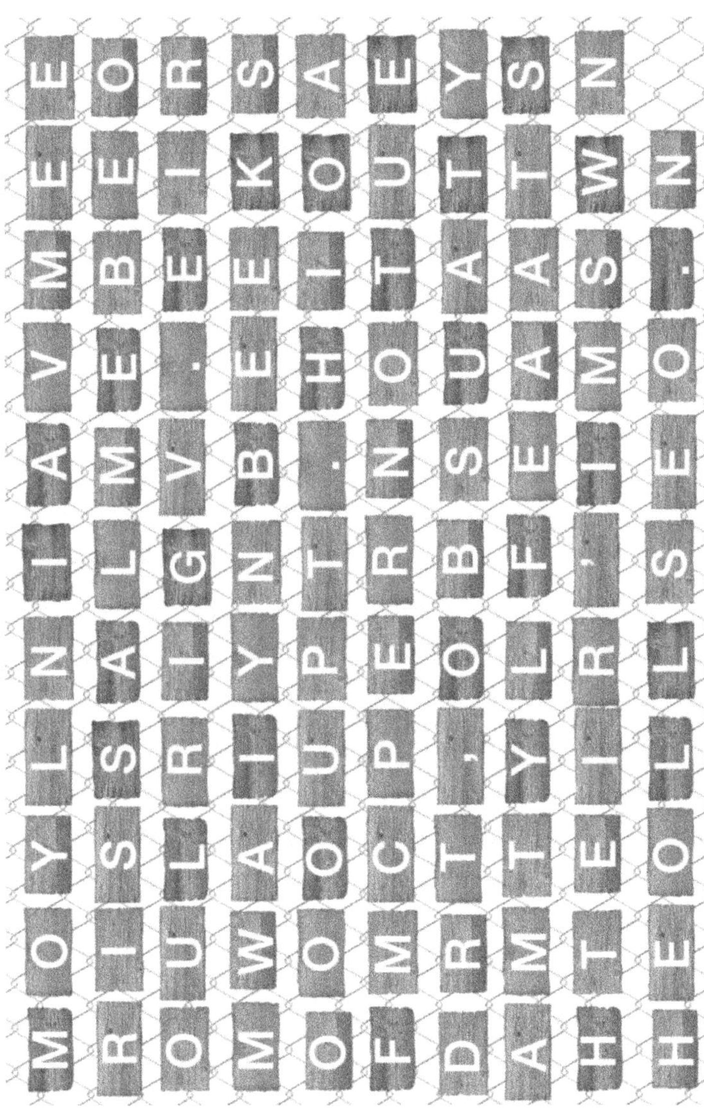

Lee's Message to the World

My name is Lee Oliver Winekoop. I am proud to say my father is Nelson Oliver Sambourg. I may be south of center, but at least I'm whole.

OTHER BOOKS BY FLORENCE OSMUND

The Coach House (2012 B.R.A.G. Medallion honoree)

This book is not only thought evoking but also a genuine pleasure to read.
—BestChickLit

1945 Chicago. Newlyweds Marie Marchetti and her husband, Richard, have the perfect life together. Or at least it seems until Marie discovers cryptic receipts hidden in their basement and a gun in Richard's desk drawer. And when she inadvertently interrupts a meeting between Richard and his so-called business associates in their home, he causes her to fall down the basement steps, compelling Marie to run for her life.

Ending up in Atchison, Kansas, Marie quickly sets up a new life for herself. She meets Karen Franklin, a woman who will become her lifelong best friend, and rents a coach house apartment behind a three-story Victorian home. Ironically, it is the discovery of the identity of her real father and his ethnicity that unexpectedly changes her life more than Richard ever could.

Daughters (sequel to *The Coach House,* 2013 B.R.A.G. Medallion honoree)

Civil rights, gender roles, and political postures are carefully, realistically, and sensitively present in this story. **—Pens and Needles**

Twenty-four-year-old Marie Marchetti has just discovered her father's identity, the father she never knew. Discovering who her father is also means discovering her own ethnicity, and her strong need to understand who she really is and where she belongs drives her to seek peace and truth in her life.

A lot happens as a result of Marie's visit. But the most life-altering consequence of it unexpectedly grows out of an encounter with a twelve-year-old girl named Rachael.

Available at …

Amazon: http://www.amazon.com/author/florenceosmund
Smashwords: http://www.smashwords.com/profile/view/FlorenceOsmund
Author's website: http://florenceosmund.com/buy_the_authors_books
Retail stores: Through distributors Ingram and Baker & Taylor

ABOUT THE AUTHOR

After more than three decades of working in corporate America, Florence Osmund retired to write books. She earned her master's degree from Lake Forest Graduate School of Management and forged an active career in administrative and human resource management. She currently resides in Chicago where she enjoys all the things that great city has to offer and (of course) reading and writing.

If you are a new or aspiring author, Florence invites you to visit her website where she offers considerable writing advice, book promotion and marketing strategies, and many helpful website links.

Contact Information

E-mail: info@florenceosmund.com
Website: www.florenceosmund.com
Facebook: http://www.facebook.com/florenceosmundbooks
LinkedIn: http://www.linkedin.com/in/florenceosmund

www.ingramcontent.com/pod-product-compliance
Lightning Source LLC
Chambersburg PA
CBHW070445120726
47910CB00003B/937